No Mark Upon Her

Deborah Crombie was born and educated in Texas. After living in both England and Scotland, she wrote her first Duncan Kincaid/Gemma James detective novel. She has since been nominated for the Agatha, Macavity and Edgar Awards and is published across the world. Deborah lives with her family in Texas and frequently visits the UK. *No Mark Upon Her* is the fourteenth novel in the Kincaid/James series.

Also by Deborah Crombie

Deborah Crombie

No Mark Upon Her

PAN BOOKS

First published in the United States of America 2011 by William Morrow,
an imprint of HarperCollins Publishers Inc., New York, USA

First published in the UK in 2011 by Macmillan

This edition published 2012 by Pan Books
an imprint of Pan Macmillan, a division of Macmillan Publishers Limited
Pan Macmillan, 20 New Wharf Road, London N1 9RR
Basingstoke and Oxford
Associated companies throughout the world
www.panmacmillan.com

ISBN 978-0-330-53627-1

1 3 5 7 9 8 6 4 2

A CIP catalogue record for this book is available from
the British Library.

Typeset by Ellipsis Digital Limited, Glasgow
Printed and bound by CPI Group (UK) Ltd, Croydon, CR0 4YY

Visit www.panmacmillan.com to read more about all our books
and to buy them. You will also find features, author interviews and
news of any author events, and you can sign up for e-newsletters
so that you're always first to hear about our new releases.

For David Thompson
1971–2010

Who wanted me to finish the book

Chapter One

A glance at the sky made her swear aloud. It was later than she'd thought, darker than she'd realized. Since the clocks had gone back, night seemed to fall like a bludgeon, and there was a heavy wall of cloud moving in from the west, presaging a storm.

Heart thumping, she moved across the cottage's shadowy garden and through the gate that led out onto the Thames path. Tendrils of mist were beginning to rise from the water. The river had a particular smell in the evenings, damp and alive and somehow primeval. The gun-metal surface of the water looked placid as a pond, but she knew that was an illusion. The current, swift here as the river made its way towards the roar of the weir below Hambleden Mill, was a treacherous trap for the unwary or the over-confident.

Breaking into a jog, Becca turned upriver, towards Henley, and saw that Henley Bridge was already lit. Her time was running out. 'Bugger!' she whispered and pumped up her pace.

She was sweating by the time she reached Leander, the most renowned of rowing clubs, tucked into the Remenham side of Henley Bridge. Lights had begun to come on in the dining room upstairs, but the yard was twilit and empty, the boatshed doors closed. The crew would be doing their last training session of the day in the gym, accompanied by the coaches, and that suited Becca just fine.

Opening the small gate into the yard, she went to the boatshed and unlocked the doors. Although her boat was up on an outside rack, she needed access to her blades, which were stored inside. She flicked on the lights, then stood for a moment, gazing at the gleaming yellow Empachers, the German-made boats used by most of the rowing eights. The shells rested one atop another, upside down, long, slender and impossibly graceful. The sight of them pierced her like arrows.

But they were not for her. She'd never been suited to team rowing, even at university when she had rowed in the women's eight. A gawky fresher, she'd been recruited by her college's boat club. All the boat clubs trawled for innocent freshers, but they'd been particularly persistent in their pursuit of her. They had seen something besides her height and long limbs – obvious prerequisites for a rower. Perhaps, even then, they'd spotted the glint of obsession in her eyes.

Now, no team would be daft enough to take her on, no matter how good she had once been.

The thump of weights came from the gym next door, punctuated by the occasional voice. She didn't want to speak to anyone – it would cost her valuable time. Hurrying to the back of the shed, she picked out her own sculls from the rack at the rear. The rectangular tips were painted the same Leander pink as her hat.

'Becca.'

She turned, startled, knocking the blades against the rack. 'Milo. I thought you were in with the crew.'

'I saw the light come on in the shed.' Milo Jachym was small and balding, with a bristle of greying hair still shading the scalp above his ears. He had been a renowned coxswain in his rowing days, and he had also once been Becca's coach. 'You're going out.' It was a statement rather than a question and his tone matched his scowl. 'You can't keep this up, with the clocks going back, Becca. Everyone else has been in for an hour.'

'I like having the water to myself.' She smiled at him. 'I'll be fine, Milo. Help me get the boat down, will you?'

He followed her out, picking up two folding slings from just inside the boatshed doors. Becca took her blades through the gate and laid them carefully beside the launch raft, then walked back into the yard, where Milo had set up the trestles beside one of the free-standing boat racks. Her white and blue Filippi rested above two double sculls, and it took all of Milo's reach to unstrap and lift the bow as she took the stern.

Together they lifted the shell free and lowered it, right-side up, into the waiting cradle. As Becca checked the rigging, she said, 'You told Freddie.'

Milo shrugged. 'Was it a state secret, then, your rowing?'

'I see you haven't lost your talent for sarcasm,' she countered, although for Milo, who used sarcasm the way other coaches might use a battering ram, the comment had been mild enough.

'He was concerned, and I can't say I blame him. You can't keep on this way. Not,' he added before she could draw breath for a heated protest, 'if you want a chance of a place in the semis, much less at winning.'

'What?' Glancing up in surprise, she saw that he was no longer frowning, but regarding her speculatively.

'In spite of what everyone says,' Milo went on, 'I think it's possible that you can win in the trials, maybe even in the Games. You were one of the best rowers I've ever seen, once. It wouldn't be the first time a rower your age has made a comeback. But you can't keep up this half-arsed business. Rowing after work and at weekends, doing weights and the ergo in your cottage – oh, I know about that. Did you think a few beers would buy you silence in a place this incestuous?' He grinned, then sobered. 'You're going to have to make a decision, Becca. If you're going to do this, you'll have to give up everything else. It will be the hardest thing you've ever done, but I think you're just bloody-minded enough to succeed.'

It was the first time anyone had given her the least bit of encouragement, and from Milo it meant more than from anyone else. Her throat tight, she managed to say, 'I'll – I'll think about it.' Then she nodded at the shell, and together they hefted the boat above their heads, manoeuvring it through the narrow gate, and gently set it into the water beside the launch raft.

She slipped off her shoes, tossing them to one side

of the raft. Then she retrieved her blades, and in one fluid movement she balanced them across the centre of the shell while lowering herself into the sliding seat.

The shell rocked precariously as it took her weight. The movement reminded her, as it always did, that she sat facing backwards on a sliver of carbon-fibre narrower than her body, inches above the water, and that only her skill and determination kept her fragile craft from the river's dark grasp.

But fear was good. It made her strong, and careful. She slipped the oars into the locks and tightened the gates. Then, with the bowside blade resting on the raft and the strokeside blade balanced flat on the water, she slipped her feet into the trainers attached to the footboard and closed the Velcro fasteners.

'I'll wait for you,' offered Milo. 'Help you put the boat up.'

Becca shook her head. 'I can manage. I've got my key.' She felt the slight weight of the lanyard against her chest. 'But, Milo . . . ' She hesitated. 'Thanks.'

'Well, remember I'm here if you need me,' he said as she pushed away from the raft. 'Have a good row.'

But she was moving now, letting the current take the shell out into the river's centre, and his words barely registered.

The world seemed to fall away as she settled into a warm-up rhythm, working the kinks out of her shoulders and the stiffness from her thighs. The wind bathed her face as it blew steadily downriver. Between the wind and the current, she would have the advantage – at least until she made the turn round

Temple Island, and then she would have both wind and current against her as she rowed back upriver.

Her strokes grew longer, deeper, as she watched the arched golden lights of Henley Bridge recede in the distance. She was moving backwards, as rowers did, judging the river by instinct, and she might have been moving backwards in time as well. For an instant she *was* the girl who had seen an Olympic gold medal within her reach. The girl who had let it slip away.

Frowning, Becca pulled herself back into the present. She concentrated on her stroke, feeling the sweat beginning to form on the back of her neck, between her breasts. She was *not* that girl. That had been fourteen years ago, in a different world. Today she was a different person, connected to that young Rebecca only by muscle memory and the feel of the blades in her hands. Now she knew the cost of failure.

And she knew Milo was right. She was going to have to make a decision, and soon. Complete commitment to racing would mean taking leave from the job to train full-time. She could quit outright. Or she could take the leave of absence that the Met had offered her.

But that would leave unfinished business.

The thought brought a surge of anger so intense that she instinctively drove the blades into the water, pushing her stroke up to racing rate. The riggers creaked as the boat took the strain. Water flew from the blades on the recovery, splashing droplets across her face.

She was moving now, listening to the whoosh and

thunk as the blades went in, followed by an instant of absolute silence as they came out of the water and the boat plunged forward like a living thing. It was perfect rhythm, this – it was music. The boat was singing, and she was a part of it, lifting from the water like a bird.

Henley receded, a glowing dot in the distance. Now she could really see the sky, rose-gold on the horizon, fading to mauve. Clouds, still visible against the dark dome above, seemed to be flying, matching her stroke for stroke. A few cottages – hers somewhere among them – and clumps of trees on the Berkshire bank flew by in a dark blur.

Ten strokes. Her thighs were burning.

Ten more, focusing on the count, on getting her blades out of the water cleanly.

Ten more, shoulders on fire now.

And one more ten, with all the power she could summon, the boat leaping from the water, her throat searing as she took great gulps of air.

Then, a pale flash on her right, the ornamental folly on Temple Island. This shard of land in mid-river, once a part of Fawley Court, now served as the starting point for the Henley Royal Regatta. Once past the island she'd have to turn back, or she'd lose the last glimmer of light and would truly be rowing blind before she reached Leander again.

She eased up on the stroke, letting her lungs fill, easing her cramping muscles. As she passed the downriver tip of the island, she stabilized the boat, blades resting lightly on the surface of the water.

Suddenly, she realized that her earlier anger had

passed and she was filled with a deep and calm certainty.

She would race. She would not let this last chance pass her by. And if it meant leaving the Met, she would leave, but she would not be fobbed off quietly with a token gold watch and more hollow promises. She would see justice done, whatever the means, for herself and the others like her.

The swift current was carrying her downstream, towards the lock and the weir. A flock of rooks rose with a clatter from the trees on the Oxfordshire bank. As she watched them wheel in a dark ballet, Becca let the boat swing round. When the birds disappeared from her field of view, she was facing downriver. The wind felt fiercer now. It bit at the back of her neck and, when she took her first full stroke, the current's resistance challenged her.

Rowing downriver, she'd stayed near the centre, taking advantage of the swiftness of the current. Now, she eased in towards the Buckinghamshire side, where the current was less brutal, the upriver journey less arduous. Anyone who had ever rowed out of Leander knew every twist and turn and wind shadow along the Bucks bank, and most, like Becca, could row it in their dreams.

But the darkness seemed deeper, facing away from the faint illumination cast by the town, and the temperature was dropping rapidly. In her brief pause the sweat on her body had begun to chill.

Becca slid forward, squaring her blades, then put all the strength of shoulders and legs into the drive. She kept it up, stroke after stroke, counting to herself

– the sculler's litany – judging her progress by occasional quick glances at the shoreline.

She reached the upriver end of Temple Island, saw again the pale wedding-cake shape of the folly, and slowly, slowly, the dim shapes of familiar landmarks moved by. If before she had had the sensation of slipping backwards in time, now she felt suspended, as if only her own efforts could inch the clock forward.

She pulled harder, again and again, lost in the rhythm of the stroke. It was only in the instant of calm following a perfect drive that she heard the floundering splash. The boat creaked as she stopped, as if it were resisting the cessation of forward motion.

The sound had been close, and too loud for a diving bird. A large animal slipping in from the bank, perhaps?

She tasted salt, realized her nose was running from the cold and wind. Shifting her grip on her blades into one hand, she swiped at her lip with her other sleeve. The boat rocked slightly as she twisted to look upriver, and she quickly grasped the blades in both hands again. Then she peered at the bank, but the shadows beneath the trees had deepened to impenetrable ink.

Shrugging, she rotated her blades, putting the sound down to her imagination. But as she slid up to the catch, she heard a cry. The voice was unmistakably human, oddly familiar, and she could have sworn it had called her name.

Chapter Two

Freddie Atterton swiped his member's tag over the scanner at the entrance to the Leander car park, then drummed his fingers on the steering wheel while he waited for the gate bar to rise. The Audi's wipers swished, all but useless – even on high speed – at moving the sheets of water streaming across the windscreen. Peering ahead as the bar lifted, he eased out the clutch and felt the gravel shift under the car's tyres as he inched forward.

'Sodding rain,' he muttered as he pulled into the nearest available space. The car park was fast turning into a bog. He'd be lucky if he could get the car out again. Nor was there any way he was getting from the car to the clubhouse without ruining his hand-stitched Italian leather shoes or keeping his jacket from becoming soaked before he could put his umbrella up.

Killing the engine, he glanced at his watch – five minutes to eight. There wasn't time to wait it out. He didn't want to dash dripping into the club and find his prospective investor there before him. This breakfast meeting was too important to start it off looking like a drowned and harried rat.

And he'd meant to be better informed. Damn

Becca for not ringing him back last night. He'd tried her again this morning, but she still hadn't picked up on either phone.

He'd thought that she might be able to give him some tips on his prospect, who was a recently retired Met officer. Not that one expected run-of-the mill Metropolitan Police officers to be flush enough to sink money into what Freddie admitted was a still slightly sketchy property deal.

But this bloke, Angus Craig, had been a deputy assistant commissioner, and he lived in a nearby village that was definitely on the poncey end of the spectrum. Freddie had run into him over drinks at a local club the previous week and, when they'd got chatting, Craig had said he liked the idea of putting his money into something that he could keep an eye on. Freddie had hoped that Becca could tell him whether or not Craig was a serious player.

And God help Freddie, if not. He'd bought the rundown farm and outbuildings, on the Thames below Remenham, intending to turn the place into upmarket flats – tasteful country living with city luxury and a river view. But then the market had dived, and now he was overextended and he couldn't get the damned thing off the ground.

He pulled his phone from his jacket pocket and checked it once more, just in case he'd missed a call, but there was no message light. His irritation inched over into vague worry. Stubborn Becca might be, but they'd managed to keep up an odd sort of friendship after the divorce, and if nothing else he'd expected her to ring him to tell him to mind his own business.

Maybe he had been out of line, telling her off about the rowing. But he couldn't believe she really meant to put her career in jeopardy for a pipe-dream that any sane person would have given up years ago. He'd felt the siren call of rowing, too, and God knew he'd been competitive, but at some point you realized you had to let it go and get on with real life. As he had.

With a sudden and uncomfortable twinge, he wondered if he'd have let it go so easily if he'd been as good as she was. And just how successful had he been at real life? He pushed that nagging little thought aside. Things would get better; they always did.

Perhaps he should rethink what he'd said to Becca. But first, Mr Craig.

Angus Craig, however, failed to materialize.

Freddie had leapt from the Audi, popping open his umbrella with the speed of a conjuror, then squelched across the car park to the haven of Leander's lobby. Lily, the duty manager, had brought him a towel from the crew quarters, then seated him at his favourite table in the window of the first-floor dining room.

'The crew won't be going out this morning,' he said, looking out at the curtains of rain sweeping across the river. This was rough weather, even for Leander's crew, who prided themselves on their fortitude, although anyone who had rowed in an Oxford or Cambridge Blue Boat could tell them a thing or two about weather – and fortitude.

Freddie's boat had almost been swamped one year

in the Boat Race, in conditions like this. An unpleasant experience, and a dangerous one.

'You've someone joining you?' asked Lily as she poured him coffee.

'Yes.' Freddie glanced at his watch again. 'But he's late.'

'Some of the staff haven't made it in,' said Lily. 'Chef says there's a pile-up on the Marlow Road.'

'That probably explains it.' Freddie summoned a smile for her. She was a pretty girl, neat in her Leander uniform of navy suit and pale-pink shirt, her honey-brown hair pulled back in a knot. A few years earlier he'd have fancied her, but he'd learned from his mistakes since then. Now he was wiser, and wearier. 'Thanks, Lily. I'll give him a bit longer before I order.'

She left him, and he sipped his coffee, idly watching the few other diners. This early in the week and this time of year, he doubted there were many guests in the club's dozen rooms, and the weather had probably discouraged most of the local members who normally came to the club for breakfast. The food was exceptionally good and reasonably priced.

The chef would have his hands full, regardless of the slow custom in the dining room. He was also responsible for feeding the voracious appetites of the young crew, who ate in their own quarters. Rowers were always starving, hunger being as ingrained as breathing.

At half past eight, well into his second cup of coffee and beginning to feel desperate for a smoke, Freddie rang Angus Craig's number and got his voice-mail.

At a quarter to nine he ordered his usual breakfast of scrambled eggs with smoked salmon, but found he'd lost his appetite. Pushing the eggs aside and buttering toast instead, he realized the rain had eased. He could see across the river now, although the watery grey vista of shops and rooftops on the opposite bank might as well have been Venice. But perhaps the traffic was moving again. He'd give Craig another few minutes.

The sound of voices in reception made him look round. It wasn't the big, sandy-haired Craig, however, but Milo Jachym, the women's coach, having a word with Lily. He was dressed in raingear and had a purposeful set to his small, sturdy frame.

'Milo,' Freddie called, standing and crossing the dining room. 'Are you going out?'

'Thinking about it. We might have an hour before the next squall line moves through.' Zipping up his anorak, Milo looked out of the reception doors. Following his gaze, Freddie saw that a few patches of blue were breaking through the grey sky to the west. Milo added, 'I'd like to get them off the ergs and onto the water, even if it's a short workout. Otherwise they'll be moaning for the rest of the day.'

'Can't blame them. Bloody ergs!' All rowers hated the ergometers, the machines that were used to simulate rowing and to measure a rower's strength. Workouts on the ergs were physically gruelling without any of the pleasure that came from moving a boat through the water. The only good thing that could be said for an erg workout was that it was mindless – you could drift into a pain-filled mental freefall without ramming your boat into something and risking life and limb.

Milo grinned. 'Never heard that one before.' He turned back towards the crew quarters. 'I'd better get them out while it lasts.'

Freddie stopped him with a touch on the arm. 'Milo, did you have a chance to speak to Becca? I was hoping you might have been able to talk some sense into her.'

'Well, I talked to her, but not sense.' Frowning, he studied Freddie. 'I think you're fighting a losing battle there. You might as well give in gracefully. And why are you so sure she can't win?'

'You think she can?' Freddie asked, surprised.

'There's no woman in this crew' – he nodded towards the crew quarters – 'or any other I've seen in the last year that could out-row Rebecca at her best.'

'But she's—'

'Thirty-five? So?'

'Yeah, I know, I know. And she'd kill me if she heard me say that.' He imitated Becca at her most pedantic. '*Redgrave was thirty-eight, Pinsent thirty-four, Williams thirty-two . . . And Katherine Grainger won silver at thirty-three . . .* ' Freddie shrugged. 'But they had medals behind them. She doesn't.'

'She has the same capacity for crucifying herself. Which is what it takes. As you very well know.'

'Okay,' Freddie admitted. 'Maybe you're right. In which case, maybe I'd better apologize. But she won't return my calls. When did you talk to her?'

'Yesterday afternoon. About half past four. She was taking a boat out. She said she'd rack it herself when she came in.' Milo frowned. 'But come to think of it, I don't remember seeing it when I went out to check the river conditions this morning. Maybe she took it out at the cottage.'

'Not likely. She'd have to have used the neighbour's raft.' It was possible, though, Freddie thought. But, still, she'd have had to carry the shell through her neighbour's garden to put it in her own, and she had no ready place to store the boat. And why do that when she kept the Filippi racked here?

Unless she felt ill and couldn't make it all the way back to Leander, and that didn't sound like Becca. The uneasiness that had been nagging him ratcheted up a notch. He checked his watch, decided Angus Craig could bugger himself. 'I'm going to check the racks.'

'I'll come with you.' Milo paused, eyeing Freddie's navy jacket and Leander tie. 'You'll get soaked, man. There's a spare anorak by the bar.'

But Freddie was already heading out the doors. The first-floor reception area opened onto an outside balcony with a staircase leading down from either side. Freddie took the left-hand flight, towards the river and the boat yard. The rain had slowed to drizzle, but by the time he reached the boat racks he was impatiently pushing damp hair off his forehead.

The rack where Becca kept her Filippi was empty. 'It's not here,' he said, although Milo could see that as well as he could.

'Maybe she put it in the shed for some reason. She has a key.' Milo pulled up his hood against the rain and turned towards the clubhouse. The boatshed was beneath the first-floor dining room, and on a fair day, with the crews going out, the big doors would stand wide open.

This morning, however, they entered through the smaller door on the right, and Milo flicked on the lights. The space was cavernous, dim in the corners. It smelled of wood and varnish and, faintly, of sweat and mildew. The thump of weights could be heard from the gym next door.

Ordinarily, Freddie found the shed inexplicably comforting, but now his stomach clenched as all he saw were the racks of gleaming, bright-yellow Empachers. These were the fours and eights rowed by the crew. Pink-bladed oars stood up in the racks at the rear of the long room like flags. There was no sign of the white Filippi with its distinctive blue stripe.

'Okay,' Milo said. 'It's not here. We'll see if anyone else has seen her.' He opened the door that led into the gym and called out, 'Johnson!'

The promising young bowman of the coxless four appeared in the doorway in vest and shorts, towelling the sweat from his face. 'We going out, Milo?' He nodded a greeting to Freddie.

'Not just yet,' answered Milo. 'Steve, have you seen Becca Meredith?'

Johnson looked surprised. 'Becca? No. Not since Sunday, on the river. She had a good row. Why?'

'She went out last night, and her boat's not back.'

'Have you tried ringing her?' Johnson asked with a casualness that Freddie found suddenly infuriating.

'Of course I've bloody tried ringing her.' He turned to Milo. 'Look, I'm going to check the cottage.'

'Freddie, I think you're overreacting,' said Milo. 'You know Becca has a mind of her own.'

'No one knows that better than me. But I don't like this, Milo. Call me if you hear anything.'

He went out the way he'd come in, rather than going through the crew quarters in the club. He walked round the lawn to the car park, unmindful now of his shoes or his damp jacket.

Maybe he *was* overreacting, he thought as he climbed back into the Audi. But he rang her mobile once more, and when the call went to voicemail, he clicked off and started the engine. She might chew him up one side and down the other for intruding, but he was going to see for himself.

Although it took a bit of manoeuvring to get the Audi out of the deep, slushy ruts in the gravel, he eventually managed.

A repeated dialogue played in his head. From Becca, *Why can't you get a sensible car for once?*

Because you can't sell expensive property if your prospect thinks you can't afford the best, he always answered, but there were days when he'd kill for four-wheel drive, and this was one of them.

Once out of the car park, he pulled onto the main road and turned immediately left into Remenham Lane. As he drove north, he could see the clouds building again in the western sky.

The red-brick cottage, surrounded by an overgrown garden, was set between the lane and the river. It had been Freddie's job to keep the grounds, which he had done with regularity if not much talent. Becca had simply let things go, until the place had begun to resemble Sleeping Beauty's briar thicket.

Her battered black Nissan 4 x 4 sat in the drive. Becca had no interest in cars, either, except as a means to pull a boat. If the Nissan wasn't mud-spattered, it was only because the rain had washed it off. Her trailer had been pulled up on the patch of lawn beside the drive, and the Filippi was not on it.

Just as Freddie opened the Audi's door, thunder clapped and the sky opened up. He sprinted for the cottage, sliding into the porch as if he'd just made a wicket and shaking the water from his hair.

No lights showed through the stained glass in the door. The bell didn't work – he'd never managed to fix it – so he banged on the wood surround with his fist.

'Becca. Becca! Answer the bloody door.'

When there was no response, he fumbled for his keys and put the heavy door key in the lock.

'Becca, I'm coming in,' he called as he swung the door open.

The cottage was cold, and silent.

Her handbag sat on the bench below the key rack, where she always dropped it when she came in from work. A grey suit jacket had been tossed carelessly beside it, but otherwise the sitting room looked undisturbed. Her yellow rowing fleece was missing from the coat hook, as was her pink Leander hat.

He called out again, glancing quickly into the kitchen and dining room. A stack of unopened mail sat on the dresser, a rinsed cup and plate in the sink, and on the worktop a bag of cat food for the neighbour's cat that she sometimes fed.

The cottage felt, in some way he couldn't explain, profoundly empty of human presence. But he climbed the stairs and looked into the bedroom and the bathroom. The bed was made, the skirt that matched the jacket he'd seen downstairs lay across the chair, along with a white blouse and a tangled pair of tights.

The bath was dry, but the air held the faintest trace of Dolce & Gabbana's Light Blue cologne, one of Becca's few vanities.

He opened the door to the spare room that had once been his office, whistling in surprise when he saw the weights and the ergometer. She was serious about training, then. Really serious.

So what the hell had she gone and done?

Clattering back down the stairs, he grabbed a spare anorak from the coat hook and went out into the garden, ducking his head against the driving rain. Rebecca's neighbour's lawn had the river frontage, but he checked it just in case she'd pulled the boat up there. Seeing nothing but upturned garden furniture, he ran back to the cottage and pulled his phone out with cold and fumbling fingers. Thunder rumbled and shook the cottage.

Becca wouldn't thank him for ringing her boss, but he couldn't think what else to do next. He didn't know Superintendent Peter Gaskill well, as Becca had been assigned to his team a short time before the divorce, but he'd met Gaskill at police functions and the occasional dinner party.

Freddie's call was shunted through by the department's secretary. When Gaskill picked up, Freddie identified himself, then said, 'Look, Peter, sorry to bother you. But I've been trying to reach Rebecca since yesterday, and I'm a bit worried. I wondered if perhaps there'd been an emergency at work . . . ' It sounded unlikely even as he said it. He explained about the boat, adding that Becca didn't seem to have been home since the previous evening, and that her car was still in the drive.

'We had a staff meeting this morning, an important one,' Gaskill said. 'She didn't show, or return my calls, and I've never known her to miss a meeting. You're certain she's not at home?'

'I'm in the cottage now.'

There was silence on the other end of the line, as if Gaskill was deliberating. Then he said, 'So what you're telling me is that Becca went out on the river last night, in the dark, alone in a racing shell, and that neither she nor the boat have been seen since.'

Hearing it stated so baldly, Freddie felt chilled to the bone. Any arguments about her competency died on his lips. 'Yes.'

'You stay there,' Gaskill told him. 'I'm calling in the local force.'

Two families, for the most part strangers to one another, had spent a long weekend cooped up together in the rambling vicarage that anchored the hamlet of Compton Grenville, near Glastonbury in Somerset, while rain rumbled and poured and the water rose around them. The scene, thought Detective

Inspector Gemma James, had had all the makings of an Agatha Christie murder mystery.

'Or maybe a horror film,' she said aloud to her friend and new cousin-in-law, Winnie Montfort, who stood at the old farmhouse sink in the vicarage kitchen, up to her elbows in suds. Winnie, a Church of England vicar, was married to Duncan Kincaid's cousin Jack.

And Gemma was now married to Detective Superintendent Duncan Kincaid, a fact that still caused her a flutter of wonder when she reminded herself of it. Married. Really and truly. And three times, as Duncan still made a point of teasing her. She touched her ring, liking the physical reminder.

They'd begun as professional partners, Gemma a detective sergeant assigned to Duncan's Scotland Yard Major Crimes team. When their relationship had become personal – much against Gemma's better judgement in those early days – Gemma had applied for detective inspector. Her promotion had been a mixed blessing. It had ended their working partnership, but it had allowed them to make their personal relationship public.

Still, Gemma had harboured deep reservations about commitment. They had both failed at first marriages; they both had sons who had been subjected to enough change and loss. And she had resisted, sometimes obstinately, what she saw as a loss of autonomy.

But Duncan had been patient, and with time Gemma had come to see that what they had was worth preserving, at any risk.

So, at last, on a lovely day the past August, they'd had an informal blessing of their partnership in the garden of their home in London's Notting Hill. A few weeks later they'd made it legal in the Chelsea Register Office.

And now, in late October, with the older children on half-term break from school, Winnie and Jack had invited Duncan and Gemma and their respective families to Compton Grenville so that Winnie could give their marriage the formal celebration she felt it deserved.

The ceremony in Winnie's church on Saturday afternoon had been everything Gemma had wanted: simple, personal and heartfelt, and it had sealed their partnership in a way that was somehow different. Third time a charm, as Duncan kept telling her. And perhaps he was right, because now circumstances had brought another child into their lives, little, not quite three-year-old Charlotte Malik.

Winnie turned from the mountain of breakfast dishes, the result of the gargantuan farewell breakfast she'd made for the weekend's guests. 'A horror film? What?' Winnie, having wiped suds on the end of her nose, looked comically quizzical.

The green and tomato-red vicarage kitchen was a comfortable, and comforting, place, and Winnie was a close friend who had seen Gemma through some difficult times.

On this Tuesday morning, with the visit almost over and everyone gone except Duncan's parents, Gemma and Winnie had finally snagged a moment alone for a gossipy post-mortem of the weekend.

Gemma had offered to do the washing up, but Winnie had insisted that Gemma enjoy a last few minutes with Winnie and Jack's baby daughter.

Gemma settled little Constance more comfortably in her lap. 'Well, maybe horror film is a bit steep,' she amended, smiling. But her amusement faded as she thought about the blot on an otherwise perfect weekend. 'Sometimes,' she said, 'my sister is just a bitch.'

Winnie stripped off her washing-up gloves and came to sit at the table beside her, reaching for Constance. 'Here, don't throttle the baby by proxy.'

'Sorry,' Gemma said sheepishly. She kissed Constance's fuzzy head before handing her over. 'It's just that she's infuriating. Cyn, I mean – not Constance.'

'Well, I can understand Cyn feeling a little uncomfortable this weekend. She and your parents were the outsider— '

'Uncomfortable?' Gemma shook her head. 'You're too diplomatic. That's a nice way of saying she behaved like an absolute harpy.' Before Winnie could protest, she went on, 'But it's not just that. She's been horrible since we found out Mum was ill.' Their mother, Vi, had been diagnosed with leukaemia the previous spring. 'I realize that's Cyn's way of dealing with her own worry. I can understand that, even though I want to strangle her. But now, with Charlotte, there's no excuse.'

'What about Charlotte?' Winnie asked, her kind face suddenly creased with concern.

'I think Cyn told her kids not to play with her. Didn't you notice?'

'Well, I did think they seemed a little . . . awk-ward.'

'How could she? They're going to be cousins, for heaven's sake.' The anger in Gemma's voice made Constance screw up her little face in a frown. Gemma took a calming breath, then reached out to stroke the baby's cheek with a finger. 'Sorry, lovey.' Constance had Winnie's English-rose complexion, Jack's bright-blue eyes and the downy beginnings of Jack's blond hair.

But Charlotte, with her caramel curls and light-brown skin, was every bit as beautiful, and the idea that anyone could think differently, or treat her differently, because of her colour made Gemma feel a wave of fury. 'I heard Cyn call Charlotte something unrepeatable,' she admitted. 'I could just kill her.'

'Gemma, you must have been prepared—'

'Oh, we were warned, all right. The social worker was very thorough. "Mixed-race children are some-times not accepted by adoptive parents' extended families,"' she quoted. 'But I suppose I'd seen too many *rainbow children* adverts,' she added with a sigh. If her sister had been rude, her parents had remained stand-offish with the child, which upset Gemma deeply. 'Charlotte's been through enough without this.'

She and Duncan had become foster parents to the little girl in August, after their investigation into the disappearance of her parents.

'How is she doing, really?' Winnie asked, jiggling Constance, who was beginning to fuss. 'This weekend has been so hectic that I've never really had a chance to ask, or to say how lovely she is.'

'Yes,' said Gemma, her voice softening. 'She is, isn't she?' Her arms felt suddenly empty without the baby, and she watched Winnie holding her daughter with an affection tinged only very slightly with envy. 'But . . . ' She hesitated, listening to the happy childish shrieks coming from the back garden. Charlotte's excited shouts rose unmistakably over the boys'. Perhaps, thought Gemma, she *was* overreacting, making too much of normal adjustment issues.

'But?' prompted Winnie, settling Constance over her shoulder.

'She doesn't sleep well,' Gemma confessed. 'She dreams, I think, and sometimes when she wakes, she's inconsolable. She – ' Gemma stopped, making an effort to steady her suddenly wobbly voice. 'She calls out for her mummy and daddy. It makes me feel so – so – ' She shrugged.

'Helpless. Yes, I can imagine. But she's becoming very attached to you. I've seen that.'

'Sometimes a bit too attached, I'm afraid. Downright clingy.'

She and Duncan had agreed that they'd take family leave in turns, until they felt Charlotte was secure enough in her new situation to attend childcare during the day.

Gemma had gladly taken the first stint, but she was due to return to her post as Detective Inspector at Notting Hill Police Station the following week, and she felt a little guilty about how much she was looking forward to work and adult company. She worried whether she was really doing the right thing in planning to go back to work. 'I just hope Duncan will be able to cope on his own.'

'Give the man credit,' Winnie said with a grin, nodding towards the garden, where Duncan and Jack were stomping in puddles with the children. 'He seems to be doing pretty well. He obviously adores Charlotte. And if the two of you are going to make this commitment, she needs to be as bonded to him as she is to you.' She gave Gemma a searching glance. 'You *are* sure about this? There must be other placements that would keep her out of her grandmother's clutches.'

Gemma leaned forward, hugging herself to stop an involuntary shiver. 'I cannot imagine being without her,' she said with complete certainty. 'And I wouldn't trust anyone else to keep her safe, although I don't think it's likely that Charlotte's family is going to have much leverage any time soon.'

Charlotte's grandmother and her uncles had been arrested in August, and it looked as though they would be playing Happy Families in prison for a good while to come.

'We're officially fostering for the time being,' Gemma went on. Hesitating, she added, 'But we intend to apply for permanent custody, and eventually adoption. I just hope my family will come round, and that nothing will happen to muck up Duncan's leave—'

She was interrupted by a loud crash, then the clump of feet in the hall.

'Toby, boots off,' Gemma heard Duncan shout, but it was too late. Her six-year-old son cannoned through the door, his red wellies mud-spattered, his blond hair sticking straight up in damp spikes. He looked, as usual, like an imp from hell.

The door swung open again, this time revealing Charlotte, who had obediently removed her boots. In her striped socks and pink mac, she ran straight to Gemma and climbed into her lap. She wrapped her arms round Gemma's neck in a fierce hug, as she did whenever they had been separated for more than a few minutes. But when she looked up, she was beaming, her face flushed and her eyes sparkling. Gemma thought she had never seen the child look happier.

'I jumped biggest,' Charlotte announced.

'Did not,' said Toby. At his grand age, he considered himself superior in all ways.

Duncan came into the kitchen. Tall, tousled and as red-cheeked from the cold as the children, he looked quite as damp as Toby, if a bit cleaner. Glancing out the window, Gemma saw that the rain was coming down harder than ever.

'You, sport,' Duncan said severely to Toby, 'are incorrigible.' Pointing at the muddy boot prints on the floor, he pulled some towels from the kitchen roll and handed them over. 'Apologize to Auntie Winnie, and mop up. And then' – looking almost as impish as Toby, he grinned at Gemma and abandoned his policeman voice – 'Dad's ordered us all outside, rain or not. He's stage-managing at his most annoyingly coy, and he's roped in Jack and Kit. Knowing Dad, I shudder to think.' He rolled his eyes for emphasis, and Gemma couldn't help but smile. She had adored

Duncan's dad from the moment she'd met him, but Hugh Kincaid was not always the most practical of souls.

'He says he has a surprise for us,' Duncan went on. 'And that we are absolutely, positively, going to love it. I think we had better go and see what he's done.'

The rain came in waves that spattered against the windows of the converted boatshed like buckshot.

Kieran clenched his jaw, trying to ignore the sound, but the rumble of thunder in the distance made him shudder. It was just rain, he told himself, and he would be fine. Just fine, and the shed had withstood worse.

It was one of several such structures scrunched between the summer cottages on the small islands that dotted the Thames between Henley and Marsh Lock. Built of wood siding on a concrete pad, it had not been meant for human habitation, but it suited Kieran Connolly well enough. The single space provided him with a workshop, a camp bed, a wood stove, a primus, a primitive toilet and shower. There was nothing more he needed – although he suspected that if Finn had been given his choice, he'd have preferred somewhere that allowed him a run in the park without having to motor from island to shore in the little skiff that Kieran kept tied up at his small floating dock.

Not that Finn couldn't have swum the distance. A Labrador retriever, he was bred to it, but Kieran had taught him not to go in the water without permission.

Otherwise, Kieran wouldn't have been able to leave him when he rowed, as he did every morning, or he'd be sculling up and down the Thames with a big, black dog paddling in his wake.

Almost every morning, Kieran amended, when the thunder rumbled again. He didn't go out in storms. The boatshed shook in another gust and the windows rattled in concert. He jerked involuntarily, pain searing his hand. Glancing down, he saw a spot of blood on the fine sandpaper he'd been using to smooth a fibreglass patch on the old Aylings double that he had upside down on trestles. He'd sanded his own damned knuckles. Shit! His hands were shaking again.

Finn whined and pushed his blunt snout against Kieran's knee. The thunder cracked again and the shed vibrated like a kettle drum. Or an artillery barrage.

'It's just rain, boy.' Kieran heard the tremor in his voice and grimaced in disgust. Some reassurance he was, sweating and quaking like a leaf. Pathetic! Making an effort to steady his hand, he folded the sandpaper and set it on his worktable.

But even if he could make his hand obey, he had no command over his knees. When they threatened to buckle, he staggered two steps to the wall and slid down with his back against it. He felt as if the very air were a massive weight, pressing him down, squeezing his lungs. Finn nuzzled him and climbed half into his lap, and as he wrapped his arms around the dog, he couldn't tell which of them whimpered. 'Sorry, boy, sorry,' he whispered. 'It'll be okay. We'll be okay. It's just a little rain.'

He repeated to himself the rational explanation for his physical distress. *Damage to middle ear, due to shelling. Swift changes in barometric pressure may affect equilibrium.* It was a familiar mantra.

The army doctors had told him that, as if he hadn't known it himself. They'd also told him that he'd been heavily concussed, and that he'd suffered some loss of hearing. 'Not enough,' he said aloud, and cackled a little wildly at his own humour. Finn licked his chin and Kieran hugged him harder. 'It will pass,' he whispered, meaning to reassure them both.

The room reeled, bringing a wave of nausea so intense he had to swallow against it. That, too, was down to his middle ear, or so they'd told him. An inconvenience. He slid a little further down the wall, and Finn shifted the rest of his eighty-pound weight into his lap.

So inconvenient, along with the shakes and the sweats and the screaming in his sleep, that they'd discharged him. *Bye-bye, Kieran Connolly, Combat Medical Technician, Class 1, and here's your bit of decoration and your nice pension.* He'd used the pension to buy the boatshed.

He'd rowed at Henley in his teens, crewing for the Lea. To a kid from Tottenham, who'd stumbled across the Lea Rowing Club quite by accident, Henley had seemed like paradise.

It was just him and his dad, then. His mum had scarpered when he was a baby, but it was not something his dad ever talked about. They'd lived in a terraced street that had hung on to respectability by a thread, his dad repairing and building furniture in

31

the shop below the flat. Kieran, white and Irish in a part of north London where that made him a minority, had been well on his way to life as a petty thug.

Kieran stroked Finn's warm muzzle and closed his eyes, trying to use the memory to quell the panic, the way the army therapist had taught him.

It had been hot, that long ago Saturday in June, just after his fourteenth birthday. He'd stolen a bike on a dare, ridden it in a wild, heart-hammering escape through the streets of Tottenham to the path that ran alongside the River Lea. And then, with the trail clear behind him, his legs burning and the sun beating down on his head, he'd seen the single sculls on the water.

The sound of the storm faded from his consciousness as the memory drew him in.

He'd stopped, gazing at the water, all thought of pursuit and punishment gone in an instant. The boats were stillness in motion, graceful as dragonflies, skimming the surface of the mercury-gleaming river, and the sight had gripped and squeezed something inside him that he hadn't known existed.

All that afternoon he'd watched, and in the dimness of the evening he'd pedalled slowly back to Tottenham and returned the bike, ignoring the taunts of his mates. The next Saturday he'd gone back to the river, drawn by something he couldn't articulate, a longing that until then had only teased the feathery edges of his imagination.

Another Saturday, and another. He learned that the boat place was called the Lea Rowing Club. He began to name the boats: singles, doubles, pairs, quads, fours and the eights – if the singles had made him think of dragonflies, the eights were giant insects, moving in a rhythm that seemed both alien and familiar, and that made him think of the pictures of Roman galleys he'd seen in school history books.

And they talked to him, the oarsmen, when they noticed him hanging about. He was tall, even then. Awkward, scrawny, black-haired, pale-skinned even at summer's height – all in all, not a very prepossessing specimen. But although he hadn't realized it then, his inches had made him rowing material, and they'd been assessing his potential.

After a bit they'd let him help load the boats onto the trailers or lift them back onto the trestles that waited in the boat yard like cradles. One day a man tossed him a cloth and nodded at a dripping single. 'Wipe it down, if you want,' he'd said. Other days, it was a wrench to adjust the rigging, oil for the seat runners, filler for the dents in the fibreglass.

By that August, he'd become the club dogsbody, his mates forgotten, his dull terraced street subsumed by the river. He learned that the burly-shouldered man who gave him chores was a coach. And when one day the coach had looked him levelly in the eyes and handed him a pair of blades, the world had opened like an oyster and Kieran Connolly had seen that he might be something other than a poor Irish kid with no future.

The Lea – and rowing – had given him that. His coach had encouraged him to join the army. He could row, Coach said, and get an education, too. And so he had done, training as a medic, rowing in eights and fours, and then in the single scull that had been his true love since that very first day on the Lea.

What neither he nor his coach had foreseen in those halcyon days before 9/11 was that the world would change, and Kieran would see four tours of duty in Iraq. On the last, his unit had been taken out by an improvised explosive device and he had been the only survivor.

There'd been nothing left for him in Tottenham when he came home. His dad taken by cancer, the house sold to pay his debts, although Kieran had managed to salvage his father's woodworking tools. After that, he couldn't bear to go back to the Lea, to meet anyone he had known or who – worse still – might offer him sympathy.

So he'd bought an old Land Rover and drifted round the south of England, sleeping in a tent, always drawn by the rivers, but unable to imagine what he might do or where he might fit.

Then, early one May morning, two months after his discharge, he'd stood on Henley Bridge, watching the scullers, feeling as insubstantial as a ghost.

Later he'd walked through town, intending to buy some supplies, when he'd seen the advert for the boatshed in an estate agent's window. It had seemed like a spar held out to a drowning man.

A few weeks later, now the proud owner of the one-room shed, he'd moved in his few possessions, bought a used single shell and begun to row for the first time in years. It was, he thought, like riding a bike – once learned, never forgotten. His body, still healing, had protested, but he'd kept on, and slowly he'd grown stronger.

There was a small fixed dock that allowed him to tie up the little motor skiff he'd bought, and the boatshed's small floating raft gave him a private place from which to launch the shell. He'd had no interest in rowing from a club, or competing again. He rowed for sanity now, not for sport.

But it was impossible to row on the Thames at Henley every day without encountering other rowers, and a few had recognized him from his competition days. A few others remembered that he had a knack for fixing boats, and as the months passed he'd found himself taking on a repair here and there.

The jobs helped fill his days between morning row and evening run, and when he wasn't working on someone else's boat, he'd begun very tentatively to work on a design for a wooden racing single. He was, after all, a furniture-maker's son. To him, wooden boats had a life and grace not found in fibreglass, and the project was in a way a tribute to his father.

But he'd had no one to talk to but himself, and that small voice was little buffer against the memories that thronged inside his head and kept him awake in the night.

And then one day he'd gone to pick up a boat that needed patching, and he'd seen the pen full of puppies in the owner's garden.

He'd come away with the boat, and Finn.

That fat, black, wriggly puppy had, in the two years since then, given Kieran a reason to get up in the morning. Finn was more than a companion, he was Kieran's partner, and that union had given Kieran something he'd thought gone from his life – a useful job.

Not that Tavie didn't deserve credit, too, but if it weren't for Finn he'd never have met Tavie.

Finn, as if aware that he was the subject of Kieran's ruminations, spread his back toes in a luxurious doggy stretch and settled his heavy head a bit more comfortably on Kieran's knee.

Shifting position, Kieran grimaced at the prickle of pins and needles. His legs had gone to sleep. And, he realized, the storm was passing. The rain was pattering now, not ricocheting, the shed was no longer shaking in the wind and his nausea had passed.

'Get off, you great beast,' he said, groaning, but he stroked Finn's ears while he gingerly flexed his legs to get the circulation back.

He felt another tingle, but this time it was his phone, vibrating in his back pocket as it pinged the arrival of a text.

'Shift it, mate,' he said, gently moving the dog before scrabbling for his phone as he stood.

The text was from Tavie – she was the call-out coordinator that morning. MISPER. ADULT FEMALE ROWER. PLS AND LKP LEANDER. REPORT AVAILABILITY FOR SEARCH.

Kieran's translation was now as automatic as breathing: *Missing person. Both the Place Last Seen and Last Known Position, Leander Club.* He felt a jolt of adrenaline, and Finn, up now, whined and danced in anticipation. He recognized the sound of a text, and he loved working almost as much as he loved Kieran.

'Right, boy,' said Kieran. 'We've got a job.' And

thank God the worst of the storm was over and he was steady enough on his feet to report in. But he didn't like the sound of this, not one bit.

In the year and a half he'd been working with Thames Valley Search and Rescue they'd conducted more searches involving the river than he could count. That came with their territory. But they'd never had a call-out for a missing rower.

Chapter Three

Tavie had designated the Leander Club as the team call-out point. As well as being the last place the victim had been seen, it provided a centralized location for the search operations, including access to power and other necessary facilities for the team.

When Kieran turned into the drive, he saw that the other team members had begun to assemble where the lane dead-ended at the meadow. Tavie's shiny, black Toyota 4 x 4, with the distinctive *Thames Valley Search and Rescue* logo emblazoned on its side, was pulled up close to the arched club entrance, flanked by two Thames Valley Police cars.

Tavie stood beside the truck, her cap of blonde hair blazing like a beacon above her black uniform, waving a handheld radio for emphasis as she talked to Rafe Yates and one of the uniformed constables. Sharp, high yips came from the rear of the truck. Tosh, Tavie's German shepherd bitch, was expressing her impatience.

Kieran saw Yates's old estate car and the Bennetts' Subaru, and when he glanced in his rear-view mirror, more sturdy vehicles were pulling in behind him. All the team members drove cars, trucks or vans that could accommodate dog crates.

He found a spot up against the car-park fence, and as soon as he switched off his engine Finn began to bark, to an answering chorus from the other vehicles. 'Steady on, boy,' Kieran told him. Time was of the essence in a missing-persons search, but so was preparation. Kieran had taken time to have a quick wash before changing into his uniform, and had fed Finn some dry dog food and himself a protein bar. It could be a long day and they would need all their energy.

As he checked his gear one last time and climbed out of the truck, he saw a tall, slender man in a sports jacket come through the archway that led to the club entrance and approach Tavie, his hands waving in agitation as he spoke.

At first Kieran thought he might be the club's manager, but as he drew nearer, he could see the distress on the man's fine-boned face, and hear it in the rising inflection of his voice. This was obviously personal.

When he reached the group, Tavie turned to him. 'Kieran, this is Mr Atterton. He's reported his ex-wife missing. She took a boat out from the club yesterday evening and hasn't returned.' Tavie's voice was light, matter-of-fact, the tone she used to reassure relatives.

Kieran studied Atterton more carefully, trying to pin down a nagging sense of familiarity. The man was probably in his mid-thirties, fit, with powerful shoulders that had been disguised from a distance by the elegant cut of his jacket. Where had he seen him? His uneasiness grew.

Atterton turned to him. 'Miss Larssen says you're a rower,' he said, his accent perfect Oxbridge. 'So you'll understand. I know it sounds mad, taking a shell out at dusk. But Becca wouldn't have been careless. She's too experienced.'

Kieran's heart squeezed tight in his chest, as if all the vague dread had crystallized instantly in one spot. 'Becca?'

'Rebecca. Rebecca Meredith. My wife – my ex-wife – kept her maiden name. That's how she was known as a rower. And now she's training again. For the Olympics.'

'Becca,' Kieran said again, through lips suddenly gone numb. A hole had opened in the fabric of the universe, and he felt himself falling through it.

'Kieran, are you all right?' Tavie had waited until they were on their own, and in position, before she asked.

She'd deployed two teams on either side of the river, each team consisting of two handlers and two dogs. On the Buckinghamshire side, she'd put Rafe and Andrea Bennett between Henley and Temple Island, with Scott and Sarah covering Temple Island to Hambleden Lock. On the Berkshire side, she'd given the Leander-to-Temple Island segment to Sophie and Hugo, and the last stretch, Temple Island to Hambleden Lock, to herself and Kieran. Tom Bennett had stayed at Leander as Control.

Once she'd convinced Mr Atterton that he would be more useful staying behind at the club in case his ex-wife rang or returned, she and Kieran had driven separately down Remenham Lane, then over the farm track that gave the closest access to the river path.

They'd stopped at the last fence that lay between them and the Thames meadow. Beyond the meadow she could see the river, bisected by Temple Island, which looked absurdly manicured against the shaggy Buckinghamshire bank on the river's far side. They would take the dogs through the gate into the meadow, boggy from the morning's downpour, and start downriver on foot from there.

Fortunately, the morning's bad weather seemed to have discouraged the usual contingent of dog-walkers, joggers and pram-pushers that used the Thames path, and once the search had been instituted, the police had cordoned off the path between Henley and Hambleden on both sides of the river. This would reduce the number of confusing scents for the dogs.

Opening Tosh's crate, Tavie snapped on her lead. Tosh jumped lightly down and sat, half on Tavie's foot, looking up at her in quivering anticipation. She was ready to go to work.

Tavie glanced back at Kieran, who still hadn't responded. He was pulling his gear out of the back of his old green Land Rover: pack, radio, water bottle, Finn's lead, the squeaky ball that was Finn's reward for a find – all automatic motions – and he didn't look at her.

'Kieran, are you sure you're up to this? I can do this on my own if the storm—'

'I'm fine,' he said, still not meeting her eyes, but

something in his voice made Finn stop whining to get out of his crate. The dog gazed at his master, his lip wrinkled in a puzzled expression that Tavie would have found comical if she hadn't been worried.

She knew Kieran had bad days, and that he was uncomfortable with storms. And although he'd never discussed it, during the time she'd known him she'd begun to put the pieces together.

She remembered the day she'd first seen him, almost two years ago. She'd been running with Tosh in Mill Meadows, and had stopped to watch the tall, dark-haired man doing simple training exercises in the park with a bouncing black Labrador puppy. He'd been obviously inexperienced as a trainer, but she'd liked the way that, rather than losing patience, he'd appeared to stop and think about how to get the puppy to do what he wanted.

She'd been about to move on when a little girl fell from the rope swing in the nearby play area, hitting her head. The man with the puppy had been closer, and as Tavie ran towards the accident, she saw him quickly ask a bystander to hold the dog, then run towards the child himself. He reached the scene before her and took charge with an efficiency she recognized – medic, she thought, or maybe a cop.

By the time she'd arrived and put Tosh into a sit, the child was sitting up, crying for her mum, and looked none the worse for wear.

Disaster averted, the man had stood, brushing playground gravel from his knees while looking round for his dog. And in that unguarded moment Tavie had caught such an expression of loss on his face that it had taken her breath away. But then he'd glanced at her, seen Tosh still sitting calmly, and he'd smiled.

'How did you do that?' he asked, nodding at Tosh as he retrieved his puppy and wrapped his arms around it, to keep it from jumping at Tosh.

'I'll show you, if you like,' she'd offered on impulse, telling herself that it was because he and his puppy might be promising material for the team. But she knew, even then, that what she'd wanted most was to erase some of the sadness from his eyes.

After that, they'd met weekly in the park. She'd learned his name, and Finn's, and that he'd never before owned a dog. And she'd learned that her assumptions had been at least partially correct – he had been a medic, but in the army, and she guessed it was his military training that had made her think he might be a cop.

He'd never said more than that about his past, and as for the present, she knew only that he fixed boats in the little shed on the island above Henley Bridge, and that he rowed.

But in spite of his reticence, they'd become friends. At first he'd resisted her suggestion that he join the group. But as Finn grew and his training progressed, Kieran began to admit that the dog needed a job. Tavie never said that she thought it was really Kieran who needed a reason to get up in the morning, but as he began to ask her to recount the details of searches and finds, she saw a spark come back into his eyes.

Before his first training session with the group,

however, she'd stopped, moved by some impulse to protect him. 'Kieran, you know a good many of our finds are deceased. Will that be a problem for you?'

He'd given her a crooked smile. 'Not as long as they're strangers.'

His answer came back to her now. She touched his arm. 'Kieran, I have to ask. You turned as white as a ghost when you heard this woman's name. She's a rower, you're a rower, and I think it's a pretty small world here in Henley. Do you know her?'

Melody Talbot gazed at the bow-fronted, terraced house, furrowing her brow. 'It's, um . . . it's very . . . suburban.' Then, seeing her companion's crestfallen expression, she amended, 'It's nice, Doug, really it is. It's just not exactly single-guy territory, Putney, is it?' She gave him a calculating glance. 'Unless you have plans that you're not sharing, mate?'

Doug Cullen flushed to the roots of his fair hair. 'No. It's just – I wanted something as different as possible from the Euston flat. It's an easy commute to the Yard. I wanted to be near the river and the rowing clubs. And it was a good deal.' He surveyed the house with obvious pride. 'Just needs a bit of fixing up, that's all.'

Gazing at the peeling paint on the window frames and the door, and the damp stains in the plaster, Melody suspected that might be an understatement. 'You've actually bought it, then?'

'Signed the last papers an hour ago.' Doug fished a set of keys from his pocket and held them up like a trophy.

Melody had been surprised to get a call from him that morning, asking her if she could meet him in Putney for lunch. She knew he'd been flat-hunting. And Gemma had told her that Duncan intended to take a few days' holiday before starting his official family leave, so she'd supposed that Doug, as Duncan's sergeant, might be at a bit of a loose end. She hadn't expected to be told that he'd taken the plunge into home ownership.

'You're full of surprises today. I never thought of you as the DIY type.' She'd never thought of Doug as the athletic type, either, although he'd told her one of the reasons he'd settled on Putney was because he wanted to take up the rowing that he hadn't done since school. When she'd driven across Putney Bridge, she'd seen a lone sculler working his way upriver, and hadn't been able to picture Doug huffing and puffing in sweaty rowing gear. She'd never seen him exert more effort than it took to attack a keyboard.

'I can paint as well as the next bloke,' he said, sounding a little incensed. 'And as for the rest, there are loads of books, and the Internet . . . '

Melody had no doubt that Doug could find out how to fix things – his research skills rivalled her own – but she'd no idea if he had the manual aptitude. Reading about pipe wrenches and actually using one were entirely different propositions, at least in her limited experience. She wasn't exactly the DIY type, either.

'I want to see you in your workman's overall.' She grinned and hooked her arm through his, earning a startled glance. 'Come on, then. Show me the goods.' A snake of wind eddied down the quiet residential road, swirling the brown leaves in the gutters and lifting the hair at Melody's neck. Although the terraced houses blocked any view of the river to the north, they were near enough that she imagined she could smell its dank, earthy scent.

Releasing Doug's arm so that she could turn up her coat collar, she could have sworn she saw a fleeting look of relief cross his face.

She chided herself for teasing him. She knew he wasn't comfortable with physical contact, and she was not usually demonstrative herself. But there was something that seemed to goad her into pushing his boundaries.

They'd developed an odd sort of friendship in these last few months, and she suspected that friendship in general was something neither of them was very good at. She wondered, in fact, if he hadn't been able to think of anyone else with whom he could share his new acquisition.

Melody had always been guarded in her relationships. When she was younger, she'd never been sure if people liked her for herself or if they were just sucking up to her because of her father. Then, after she'd joined the police, she hadn't wanted to let anyone get close because she'd been afraid of being *rejected* because of her dad.

But Gemma had learned the truth, as had Doug Cullen, and then Melody had gone to Duncan. When he'd heard her story, he'd given her an assessing look before nodding once. 'Your family is no one else's business,' he'd said, 'as long as you don't make it so.' That had been that. The revelation had given Melody, for what seemed like the first time, the opportunity to be herself. And it had changed her relationship with Doug Cullen in some indefinable way.

'It's two up and three down, basically,' said Doug, leading the way up the steps to the front door. 'But there's a garden.'

The door, in spite of its dilapidated frame, had some nice Victorian stained glass in pale greens and golds. When they stepped inside and Doug closed the door behind them, the watery sun came through the panes, making Melody think of the light in a spring wood. The original black-and-white tiled floor was intact, and a staircase led up to what Melody assumed were the bedrooms.

Doug motioned her forward with a little theatrical bow, the light from the stained glass glinting off his glasses and giving his blond hair a greenish tint. 'My humble abode.'

To the left behind the stairs Melody saw a cupboard and, tucked next to that, a small toilet. Beyond that a door led into a tiny galley kitchen.

But on the right-hand side of the hall two adjacent doors opened into the two rooms that ran the length of that side of the house. When she walked into the front room she saw that the wall between the two rooms had been partially removed, letting light flood straight through the house and, in the rear, French doors opened onto the garden.

'Oh,' she said, on a breath of involuntary surprise. 'It's lovely. Small, but lovely.'

Doug nodded, flushing again with obvious pleasure at her response. 'There's a full bath upstairs, and
I'll use one room for the bedroom and another for an
office. The kitchen needs new cupboards and worktops.
And in here' – he waved a proprietary hand at the living
areas – 'a new carpet, and a bit of paint, of course.'

'Not going to stick with magnolia, then?' Melody
asked, teasing. The walls were the colour of curdled
cream, with lighter patches where pictures had hung.
Both sitting and dining rooms had fireplace surrounds
that looked original, but the interiors had been
boarded over.

Doug shuddered. 'No. And definitely not grey. I've
had enough grey to last a lifetime.'

'You could use the colours in the stained glass,'
Melody said, considering them. 'With this light, it
would be lovely. And you'll have to put in some gas
fires.' She walked to the back door and looked out.
Steps led down to an oval of broken paving stones.
Beyond that was a weedy patch of lawn, surrounded
on three sides by neglected beds.

Melody, who could live anywhere she chose if she
accepted her father's help, felt a stir of envy. Not that
there was anything wrong with her mansion flat in
Notting Hill, except that it felt nothing like a home.
It was also on the top floor of her building, its only
access to the outdoors a tiny balcony. And lately she
had developed an unexpected urge to get her hands
in the dirt, to smell growing things.

'I could help with the garden, if you like,' she
offered, a bit hesitantly, turning back to him. 'In the
spring.'

'Have you ever in your life worked in a garden?'
There was a hint of mockery in Doug's voice.

'I suspect I know more about gardening than you
do about painting and plumbing,' she said, equably
enough. 'I used to follow my grandparents' gardener
in Bucks around like a shadow. How hard can it be,
compost and bulbs and things?' She studied him.
'What about you? You grew up in St Albans, didn't
you? Suburban Mecca. Surely you must have had a
garden.'

He shrugged. 'I was at school, except for hols,
from the time I was eight. My dad mowed the lawn
with a rotary mower. It was his Sunday relaxation and
he wasn't inclined to share.'

Melody knew that Doug, like her, was an only
child, and that his father was a barrister from a well-
off family that had put Doug down for Eton before he
was born. But although Melody's father could be auto-
cratic, stubborn and infuriating, he and her mother
had always been generous with their time and attention.

She had a sudden vision of Doug as a lonely and
awkward boy, with a father who couldn't bring himself to give his little son the pleasure of learning to
push a lawnmower.

Not wanting him to see compassion in her expression, she studied the fireplace surround, wiping dust
from the mantel with a fingertip. 'You'll have to give
a dinner party, once you're settled,' she said.

'No table. And probably not much else, for a while.
The only things I'm bringing from the Euston flat are
the bed and my audio stuff.'

Several comments sprang to Melody's mind, but none of them seemed appropriate, and all made her feel the colour start to rise in her face. God forbid she should start blushing as badly as Doug. 'Fresh start?' she asked instead, keeping her gaze averted.

'Totally. Only thing is, I've no idea where to begin.' He gazed round the room, looking a little lost, as if just now contemplating the enormity of the undertaking. Then he shoved his wire-framed glasses up on his nose and glared at her, as if daring her to contradict him. 'I've been told I've no sense of style.'

'Hmm.' Taking in his off-the-rack suit and uninspired tie, Melody thought she might be inclined to agree, but wasn't about to say so. There was obviously history here. 'Well, what *do* you like?'

'That's the trouble.' He shrugged. 'I don't know. I hate my flat. It's bare and depressing. And I hate my parents' house. Dark, stuffy and full of my mum's knick-knacks. Nothing was ever meant to be touched.'

'There should be a happy medium somewhere.' Melody turned slowly in a circle as she considered the rooms. She wondered what she would choose for herself if she wiped the slate bare of the hand-me-downs from her mum, the things that just *didn't suit any more* in her parents' Kensington town house. 'I'd start by finding some things you like and not worrying about whether they go together,' she said. 'There's a great auction room in Chelsea, near the power station in Lots Road. You could have a look, see what tickles your fancy.'

Good God, had she really said *tickles your fancy*? What was wrong with her today?

But Doug seemed oblivious to any innuendo. He nodded and said, as if it were a novel idea, 'I suppose I could.'

'It'll come right. You'll see.' Melody felt suddenly claustrophobic, even in the empty rooms. 'I think you've done brilliantly, Doug. I love the flat. But I'd better be getting back to Notting Hill.'

'I promised you lunch,' he said.

'Oh. So you did.' She wondered if she could get through lunch without putting her foot further in her mouth. 'What did you have in mind?'

He grinned. 'Something very appropriate, I think. Now that I know your deep, dark secret. It's called the Jolly Gardeners.'

Shrugging off Tavie's hand, Kieran popped the latch on Finn's crate and hooked the lead to the dog's collar. 'I know who she is,' he said to Tavie, keeping his back turned. He hadn't trusted his face or his voice, not since he'd heard Tavie say her name, dropping it so casually, like a stone tossed in the river.

It had taken a moment for the full weight of it to sink into his mind. Rebecca. Rebecca Meredith. He never thought of her as anything but Becca.

Nor did he automatically connect her with the last name, Meredith, although of course he knew it, as any rower would. But Rebecca Meredith was a stranger to him, a woman who wore suits and went off to London on weekday mornings, worked in an office, left polystyrene coffee cups littered on a desk he'd never seen. A woman who had once been married to this man, Atterton. He knew now why

Atterton's face had seemed familiar. He'd seen a younger version in a few old photos, collecting dust at the back of a bookcase.

Rebecca Meredith was not the woman who rowed as easily as most people breathe, who laughed as she pushed damp hair from her eyes and lifted a boat to her hip, or pulled the sheet up over a bare shoulder gilded by lamplight.

'Becca,' he whispered. *Please let it not be Becca.* But he knew all too well that she took the scull out at dusk, and that the best he could hope was that there was some completely rational explanation for her disappearance. He was letting his mind play games, and that was a dangerous indulgence.

Finn pushed against him and licked his chin. He knew it was time to go to work, didn't understand Kieran's hesitation. 'Good boy,' Kieran said, and stepped back so that Finn could jump down.

The dogs greeted each other with sniffs and wagging tails, but their attention came quickly back to their handlers. Tavie was watching him with an expression of concern that bordered on apprehension, so he forced a smile.

'You look like shit,' Tavie said. The smile hadn't fooled her for a second.

'You're always a one for the compliments.' His stab at their usual banter sounded false, even to him. 'I'm okay, really.' He nodded towards the bag she'd taken from her kit in the truck. 'Let's get on with it. What have you got for the dogs?'

'I raided the laundry basket when we cleared the cottage. Socks or undies for every team. But let's get over the fence first.' Tavie led the way through the gate, with Tosh crabbing sideways and stepping on her boots in eagerness. Finn seemed unusually subdued, and Kieran knew the dog was picking up on his mood.

When they were clear of the fence, with only the muddy expanse of meadow between them and the river path, Tavie stopped. She and Kieran unclipped both dogs' leads and then, slipping on gloves, she opened the bag – bags, really, as a paper bag was nestled inside the plastic one – and pulled out a white scrap of fabric. A woman's stretchy knickers, the utilitarian, moisture-wicking kind that absorbed sweat from a rowing workout. A perfect scent article, and horribly familiar to Kieran.

Tavie held the pants out to the dogs, an inch from their noses. 'Smell it, Tosh. Smell it, Finn,' she encouraged in the high, sing-song voice that made the dogs quiver with excitement.

The dogs sniffed obediently, and Kieran imagined, as he always did, the rush of scent molecules flowing into their noses and triggering the receptors in their brains, a sensation that humans could never duplicate. For the first time the idea made him feel sick rather than envious.

Traffic crackled over the radio as the Henley and Leander teams marked their positions, and Kieran heard the distant drone of a helicopter. Thames Valley Police had got the chopper up. The chopper would search the area simultaneously, using both sight and thermal imaging.

Tucking the pants back into her pack, Tavie said, 'Find her, Tosh, find!'

But before Kieran could echo the command to Finn, both dogs begin to whine and paw at his legs. Finn jumped up, putting his front paws on Kieran's chest, his signal for a find.

'Finn, off.' Kieran pushed the dog down as Tavie stared at him.

'Kieran, what the hell? Did you touch any of my kit?'

He knew she was worried about more than confusing the dogs. She'd have signed off on chain of evidence for all the scent articles and would be responsible if anything had been contaminated.

'Of course not. I haven't been near your pack.' It was only half a lie. He tried to pull himself together. 'Come on, we're losing ground here.' Turning to the dogs, he clapped his hands. 'Finn! Find her!' he managed, but he couldn't bring himself to say her name. He began to trot towards the river, the signal for Finn to begin checking the scent cone. Tavie followed, and the dogs quickly ranged out in front of them, falling into their familiar zigzag pattern.

The wind was blowing upriver, the ideal working condition for the dogs, but he knew the morning's heavy rain would have seriously reduced the dogs' chances of finding an air scent.

Just as they reached the river, they heard the Temple Island-to-Hambleden team on the radio. Scott's voice came through intermittently. 'Dogs . . . alerting . . . can't – '

'They're just opposite us,' said Tavie, then called Tosh to her with the 'Wait' command. 'Look. Can you see them? They should be just there, where Benham's Wood comes down to the water.'

Kieran skidded to a halt behind her, gazing past the end of Temple Island towards the cluster of trees on the far side of the river. Then he saw a flash of liver and white as Bumps, Scott's springer spaniel, broke through the heavy cover at the water's edge, followed an instant later by Meg, Sarah's golden retriever.

The dogs bounced excitedly as Scott and Sarah appeared behind them, but neither dog ran back to its handler to signal a find.

The handlers came to the bank, squatted and reached out. Sarah's voice, a little high, came over the radio just as Kieran made out what they were pulling free of the reeds. 'It's a boat,' she said. 'We've found the boat.'

It floated hull up, the distinctive colours – white with a thin blue stripe – visible from across the water. One slender scull was still fastened in its oarlock.

'It's a Filippi.' Somehow it infuriated Kieran that Sarah didn't know. 'What—'

'No sign of the victim,' Scott chimed in. 'And the dogs aren't alerting strongly on either the water or the bank.'

Kieran keyed his radio again. 'Check the trainers.' He saw Scott look up at him, and even at a distance Kieran could see that he didn't understand. 'Turn the boat over. Check the Velcro straps on the trainers.'

'Kieran,' said Tavie, 'the boat's evidence.'

'Just do it,' he told Scott, ignoring her. Rowers slipped their feet into shoes that were glued to the footboard of the shell. And while it was possible to get one's feet free without unfastening the Velcro closures – the shoes weren't meant to be tight – Kieran felt an illogical hope that if Becca had released the tabs, she might have swum free.

He saw Scott shrug, then lean forward, struggling to right the shell, soaking himself in the process. 'You'll have to release the oar,' Kieran said into the radio. 'Just unscrew the lock.'

Scott fumbled, his mouth moving in a silent swear, handing the pink-bladed scull to Sarah. Then he had the shell right-side up and was peering into the stern. 'They're open, the Velcro things.'

'Okay, don't touch anything else,' broke in Tavie. 'Scott, you and Sarah will have to stay there and secure the scene for the police. I'll have Hugh and Sophie leapfrog you on that side, as the chances are they're not going to find anything upstream. Kieran and I will continue on to Hambleden on this side.'

Scott gave her a wave of acknowledgement, but Kieran was already turning away, sending Finn out with an arm signal and the 'Find' command. Tosh shot out to join Finn, a black and tan streak momentarily merging with Finn's black shape, then she moved away from the Labrador, settling into her own search pattern.

Kieran heard Tavie on the radio, the words unintelligible, fading as they were caught by the wind, then the crunch of her booted feet on the gravel as she jogged to catch up with him.

'If she kicked herself free, she could be caught somewhere, injured,' he said. 'Or unconscious.' He scanned the opposite bank. It would take time to get Hugo and Sophie in place, but he couldn't get there any faster himself. There was no way to cross the river without going back to Henley or on to Hambleden.

'Kieran, if she fell out of the boat, she's been in the water all night. You know how cold it is.' Tavie's fingers brushed his arm, slowing him until he had to look at her. 'You need to leave the search. Now.'

He saw that she wasn't angry at his insubordination, but afraid for him.

Shaking his head, he said, 'I can't. I've got to see – she might be hurt – '

The drone of the chopper grew louder. Looking up, Kieran saw it downriver, moving slowly, inexorably, towards them.

Tavie raised her voice against the increasing noise. 'They're not picking up anything on the thermal imaging.' She was telling him that if Becca was there, she was cold. Too cold.

'She could be hypothermic, under cover somewhere.' But they were passing the manicured grounds of Greenlands college across the river now, and the meadow ran down to the path on their own side. There was no easy cover on either bank.

This time Tavie didn't contradict him, but settled in beside him at a steady trot. The dogs were working fast, but she didn't slow them down, and he knew it was because she didn't believe they would find anything here.

The path turned and the Mill came into view across the river, its perfect mirror image below it in the water, like a painting on glass. Above it, dark clouds were building once more, a bruise against the sky.

On the near side, the water was flowing faster, rushing towards the weir. It flowed between the stanchions of the footbridge in great molten sheets the colour of peat, and poured over the terraced weir in foaming, plunging chaos. A piece of driftwood hung on one of the terraces, a crabbed, dark shape, dividing the water like a body.

A roaring filled Kieran's ears. He couldn't tell if the sound came from within his head or without.

The dogs stayed on the footpath, their pattern tighter now, their tails moving with increased energy. Beyond the weir, the still-turbulent water swirled and eddied into a stand of partially submerged trees and the brush that had collected against them.

Both dogs now homed in on the bank itself. Tosh sniffed the edge, then lowered herself until her muzzle was just level with the water's surface. She looked as if she were lapping the water, delicately, like a dog at a tea party, but Kieran knew she was taking in scent molecules with her tongue. Finn whined and danced beside her.

Tosh backed up and woofed, looking to Tavie for direction. Tavie knelt, a hand on the dog's harness. The current was still strong – she wouldn't want Tosh going in if it wasn't absolutely necessary.

Tavie shielded her eyes from the glare on the water, leaning forward perilously as she peered into the nest of tree trunks and debris. When she stiffened, Kieran dropped to his knees beside her.

Tavie turned to him, pushing him back as if she could keep him from seeing what she had seen. But it was too late.

Beneath the surface, tendrils of dark hair moved like moss, and white fingers, slightly curled, drifted back and forth as if waving, signalling for help.

'No,' said Kieran. 'No!' And the roaring overtook him.

Chapter Four

'An Astra,' said Kit. 'An Astra Estate. And green. What could possibly be worse?'

Duncan Kincaid glanced at his son sitting beside him in the passenger seat, long legs sprawled into the footwell, and bit his tongue on old adages about horses and gifts. He reminded himself that he had hated being patronized when he was Kit's age. He also remembered what it was like to be fourteen, when nothing mattered more than what others thought.

Kit had been unusually quiet as they had driven up through Somerset and Wiltshire, concentrating on his iPod rather than the beautiful autumnal scenery. It was only now, when they had joined the M4 and passed through the unexciting edges of Swindon, that he'd stirred and removed his earphones.

'That's a bit ungracious, don't you think?' Kincaid said, moderately.

'I'm not being seen getting out of it at school.' Kit's expression was mulish. 'And I'm certainly not going to drive it.'

Kincaid was beginning to lose patience. 'You've got a few years before you even need to think about driving, so let's worry about that one when we get to it,' he said, although he was sure his mum and dad had been thinking exactly that when they had offered Duncan and Gemma their old car. The Astra Estate was old, solid, comfortable and supremely safe – all things anathema to a fourteen-year-old boy.

His dad had presented the car with all the glee of a first-time parent playing at Father Christmas. Kincaid suspected that if it hadn't been for the rain, he might actually have wrapped it in ribbon. 'Your mother wants something greener,' he'd said, then chuckled at his own inadvertent humour. 'More ecologically correct, that is. Not that the Astra's bad, mind you. But we thought you could use the extra carrying space, now that you have Charlotte with you.'

Kincaid had to admit he was right. The three kids had been stuffed into the back of Gemma's Escort on the journey down to Somerset, and there had been tears and tantrums aplenty. They did need a bigger car, but he'd been too busy with work and the recent demands of family life to give the matter serious consideration, not to mention that Gemma's recent unpaid leave had seriously cut into their budget – as would his.

He still had his old MG, although he seldom drove it these days. The maintenance on it was a nightmare, but he was reluctant to sell it for the pittance it was worth. He had once rashly promised Kit that he would keep the Midget until he learned to drive, and he hated going back on a promise to his son. Now, however, the thought of Kit actually driving the little car horrified him – only slightly more than contemplating what it would cost to insure him, if he did so.

His dad had given him an easy out. 'I could come up to London and drive the Midget back to Cheshire,' Hugh had offered. 'Keep it in the garage, do some restoration. Get it in tip-top shape.' When Kincaid, who had never seen his dad do more than change a tyre, raised an eyebrow, Hugh had given him a sly wink. 'Never too old,' he'd added.

Gemma had hugged Hugh, then Rosemary, who had come down from her packing to join in the surprise. 'You are dears,' Gemma said. 'But are you sure? How will you get back to Nantwich?'

'Not to worry,' Rosemary assured her. 'Jack will run us to the train. And the new car's ordered – it should be waiting for us when we get home.'

Looking at his parents, it had seemed to Kincaid that his father was a little thinner, and his mother a little greyer, than when he had seen them last. They were unfailingly generous, taking into their lives first Kit, the grandson whose existence they had not even imagined, then Toby, and now Charlotte. He loved them for it, and realized that he told them too seldom.

He'd given his mother a kiss on the cheek, and his father a manly sort of hug-with-handshake. 'Thank you. The car's brilliant. And it means we'll be able to come to visit you more often.'

Toby had begun jumping up and down, shouting, 'The dogs can come now, too, the dogs can come, too,' and was soon joined in the jumping by Charlotte. Jack and Winnie stood on the porch, holding Constance and grinning.

The only one not enthusiastic had been Kit, who stood with arms crossed. Kit had begged to go back to

Cheshire with his cousins for the rest of the half-term break, but as much as Kincaid loved his niece, he hadn't liked the idea of Kit and Lally on their own without his or Gemma's supervision. Not that he and Gemma had kept them from getting into real trouble before, he thought, with the shudder that always accompanied the memory of the previous Christmas.

Now he looked at Kit, fidgeting and scowling beside him, and wondered if there was more bothering him than the car and the end-of-holiday blues.

As they'd had two cars to drive back to London, Gemma had taken Toby and Charlotte in the Escort, and Kincaid had thought taking Kit in the Astra would give them some quality time together. Quality time, he thought now, was relative, and more difficult than he had imagined.

'Maybe we could go to Nantwich over Christmas,' he said, realizing the rashness of the suggestion even as he made it. He felt sure that Gemma would want to be at home – it would be Charlotte's first Christmas as part of their family. 'Or afterwards,' he amended. 'Boxing Day. We might stay a few days between Christmas and New Year'

Kit looked a little mollified, then frowned again. 'What if Lally and Sam have to spend their hols with their dad? He wants them to live with him all the time, you know.' He shot a glance at Kincaid through the hair that was falling into his eyes. 'Now that Aunt Jules is seeing that policeman.'

'What?' Kincaid had to make an effort to concentrate on an overtaking lorry. 'Juliet's seeing a copper? She never said a word.' But now it occurred to him that his sister had seemed happier and more relaxed, and that several times he'd caught her smiling for no apparent reason when she thought no one was looking, and checking her phone for messages. But a copper?

Then the light dawned. 'Surely not Ronnie Babcock, the old fox,' he said aloud, grinning. Ronnie Babcock had been his best mate at school, and was now a senior detective in the Cheshire Constabulary. Ronnie, who had risked his life for them the previous Christmas, was as tough as old boots, and on the surface as different from Juliet as chalk from cheese. But his sister was tough in her own way, and there was no doubt Ronnie was a man she could respect, unlike her ex-husband.

'Lally's dad doesn't like him,' said Kit. 'And he says Aunt Juliet's a . . . ' Kit paused, obviously thinking better of repeating verbatim what he'd been told. 'Uncle Caspar says the ink's barely dry on the divorce papers,' he amended.

Caspar Newcombe, Kincaid's former brother-in-law, had good reason not to like Ronnie Babcock. And it had nothing to do with Juliet or jealousy, which Kit knew as well as anyone. Nor was it likely that Caspar Newcombe, considering his current legal troubles, would have a chance of gaining full custody of the children.

'Your Aunt Jules is free to see anyone she wants, Kit. And you know that Sam and Lally weren't happy when their mum and dad were living together.'

Kit shrugged, unable to deny it, but obviously not willing to agree.

'They'll be fine, Kit. They'll all adjust. You'll see,' Kincaid said, addressing what he suspected was the heart of his son's disquiet. Kit associated change with loss, and he projected himself into other people's situations with a fierce empathy that would be dangerous if he didn't learn to set some emotional boundaries.

Kincaid was beginning to think it was a very good thing that he was going to be spending more time not just with Charlotte, but with Kit and Toby. He'd have to make sure that the boys got their share of attention.

'Let's do something special after school one day next week,' he suggested. 'Maybe we could go to the Natural History Museum.'

Kit glanced at him. 'You're really going to stay at home?' He sounded carefully nonchalant.

'Stay-at-home-dad, that's me.'

'You don't know what Charlotte likes for her tea.'

'I'll find out, won't I? But I'm counting on you to help me out with this.'

Kit nodded, looking gratified, and Kincaid was about to enquire into Charlotte's mysterious preferences when his mobile rang. He glanced at the number, swore under his breath, then switched to hands-free. It was his boss, Chief Superintendent Denis Childs.

'Sir,' he said, then, 'guv, you know I'm taking a few days' holiday this week.'

Childs knew that, of course, and had worked out exactly where he was likely to be at that moment. And, as he listened, Kincaid realized that he might as well give in gracefully. When his guv'nor wanted a personal favour, there was no one more determinedly persuasive. Resistance was futile, and besides, he knew Childs wouldn't ask if he didn't feel it was important.

Nodding, he took in the details, then said, 'Right. I'll get back to you,' and rang off.

He felt Kit's stare even as the connection went dead. 'We've got to make a stop in Henley,' he explained. 'It shouldn't take long.'

Kit looked away, his face expressionless. 'Gemma won't be best pleased,' he said.

Gemma, Kincaid thought, was not the only one who was going to be unhappy.

The Jolly Gardeners was very jolly indeed, thought Doug Cullen. The front beer garden could almost double as a nursery, and as they'd not yet had a hard frost, many of the plants and hanging baskets were still in bloom. But the furniture was wet from the morning's rain, the wind swung the baskets like metronomes, and the only occupants of the patio were diehard smokers huddled at one of the tables nearest the building.

Ushering Melody inside, he saw that the pub's interior was as appealing as the outside – brick walls, wood floors, a long, gleaming bar and simple, but comfortable-looking, mismatched furniture. There was no television in sight, and the pub was pleasantly busy for a weekday lunchtime.

He breathed a quiet sigh of relief, pleased with his choice. When they'd picked a table near the garden windows – Doug carefully avoiding the snogging sofa

– and Melody was examining the menu on the black-board above the fireplace, he studied her. Now that she'd taken off her coat, he tried to work out what seemed different about her since he had last seen her.

She'd abandoned her usual severely tailored suit, for one thing, and wore casual trousers with a cherry-coloured cardigan that set off her dark hair and pale skin. Her hair looked a bit less sleekly tamed as well, but perhaps that was just the wind, or his imagination.

'Very gastropub,' Melody said, but she seemed pleased. 'And I've just realized I'm starving. I think I'll have a burger. And after that, if I've room, the Eton Mess.'

'That's a summer pudding,' he said.

'Nevertheless it's on the menu, and I want it. I thought you were indulging me.'

'So I am.' Unable to concentrate on the menu, Doug opted for a ploughman's. When he'd ordered the meals and half-pints for them both at the bar, he carried the beer back to the table carefully, trying not to slosh it.

'Cheers.' Melody lifted her glass, and he clinked his against it. 'To your new house.'

'And your new job.' He touched his glass to hers once more, then sipped. 'So how *is* the job?'

'I've missed Gemma. But when the posting for Project Sapphire came up, it sounded interesting, and I've loved it.'

Just the idea of interviewing victims of sexual assault made Doug feel uncomfortable. 'Isn't it hard, talking to women about what's happened to them?'

'Not just women,' she corrected. 'Men, too, although it happens less often, and they're more reluctant to file a report.' She paused, sipping a little more of her beer as the barmaid brought their cutlery, then continued, 'And yes, of course it's hard. But just the fact that they've come forward is progress. And besides, I'm mostly working cold cases. I try to find matches between newly reported assaults and unsolved cases. When we get a result, it's brilliant. We may be able to put away a guy who's been preying on women for years.'

Their food came, and as Melody ate bites of her oozing hamburger with surprising delicacy, Doug wished he'd ordered something a bit less crumbly than the ploughman's. The Cheddar and Stilton were delicious, the bread crusty and warm, but every time he took a bite he showered himself with crumbs.

Making a futile attempt to brush off his tie, he looked up and saw a glint of amusement in Melody's eyes. Instead of bristling, he smiled back. 'Can't take me anywhere. Not that I expect to be going anywhere much,' he added, sobering. 'They're sticking me on Superintendent Slater's team in the interim.'

'You don't fancy him?'

'He doesn't fancy Duncan, or me by association. He's a by-the-book kind of guy.'

'And you're not?' Melody looked surprised.

'No, I'm bloody well not,' he said, instantly defensive.

She put down her knife and fork and frowned at him. 'Doug, I've never seen such a stickler for the rules as you. There's nothing wrong with that. It's part of what makes you good at your job.'

'That's easy for you to say.' His tone was accusing, but he couldn't call it back.

'I don't make a habit of breaking rules,' she said sharply. 'And when I have, I've regretted it. You know that.' The camaraderie between them had vanished like smoke. 'And as for Duncan,' she added, 'he may bend little rules now and again, but he doesn't break the big ones.'

'So how do you know where to draw the line?' Doug asked, wanting to re-establish the connection he had so clumsily broken. 'I'm not trying to take the mickey here. I really want to know. Every time I think I've got it right, I seem to screw up.'

Melody sat back, picked up her cutlery again, fiddled with a bit of lettuce on her plate. She met his eyes. 'I don't know,' she said, without her usual assurance. 'Surely it depends on the situation.'

'But you must be able to set some sort of—'

His phone rang. Why the hell hadn't he put it on *silent?* Grimacing, he started to ignore it, then remembered that he was still officially at work.

'You'd better answer it.' Melody pushed her plate away.

When he saw the ID, Doug muttered, 'Bloody hell!'

'Somehow,' said Melody, 'I think you're going to owe me an Eton Mess.'

Gemma had spent the hour since Kincaid's phone call alternately grumbling to herself and trying to jolly the

restless and increasingly cranky children in the
Escort's back seat. When her phone rang, she'd been
a few minutes behind Kincaid on the M4. Toby and
Charlotte had insisted on stopping at the first services on the motorway, although she suspected their
demands had more to do with the siren lure of sweets
than a need for the toilet.

'You simply cannot have let Denis Childs talk you
into taking a case,' she'd said, trying to keep her voice
level when he'd explained his change of plans. 'Not
today. Not this week.'

'I'm not taking a case. I'm simply seeing if there
is a case. Look, Gem, I'm sorry. But it's not far out of
the way. Kit can go home with you, and I'll follow on
as soon as I've got things sorted.' He sounded contrite,
reasonable, and persuasive, all of which irritated her
even more.

However, there had been no choice but to agree
to meet him, as she couldn't very well leave Kit
cooling his heels at a crime scene. Or a potential
crime scene. 'And what would he have done if I hadn't
been so conveniently to hand?' she'd muttered when
she'd hung up. 'Dropped Kit off on the roadside somewhere?'

'Who's going to leave Kit on the road, Mummy?'
said Toby, and she realized there had been a sudden
cessation of the teasing and giggling in the back seat.

'I want Kit,' chimed in Charlotte, sounding apprehensive. 'Where's Kit?'

'And you'll have him soon enough, lovey,' Gemma
reassured her. 'We're just going to pick him up in a
bit and have a nice drive.'

'We're already having a drive.' This from Toby, as always the logician.

'Well, a different drive. You'll see.'

'What about Daddy, then? Is he going to walk?'

Gemma had never insisted that Toby call Duncan *Dad*, but lately he'd been copying Kit and she certainly hadn't discouraged it. Toby's dad had run out on them when Toby was a tiny infant, and Duncan had been a part of their lives as long as Toby could remember, so it seemed only natural for him. It had been harder, she supposed, for Kit, who had not known that Duncan was his father until his mother had died three years ago.

At the moment, however, she could think of other, more appropriate monikers for her newly wedded husband, but she kept them to herself. 'He's going to stay with the new car.'

'I want to ride in the new car,' said Toby, happy to go back to the grievance that had occupied him for the first part of the return journey. 'Why did Kit get to?'

'Because I needed you to be my navigator. And now I need you to watch for the motorway signs. Junction ten.'

Toby was quite proud of his ability to read the numbers on the motorway signs and settled back contentedly enough to watch for their exit, counting to himself in a sing-song voice.

By the time Gemma reached the junction, however, there was no sound from the back at all, and when she glanced round she saw that both children had fallen asleep. Just brilliant, she thought. They'd wake up when she stopped for Kit, then they'd be fractious the rest of the way to London.

And poor Kit. He was bound to be disappointed, not only deprived of time alone with his dad, but having to be collected by the roadside like an inconvenient parcel.

Leaving the motorway, she concentrated on remembering Kincaid's brief directions, but it was easy enough to follow the road signs towards Henley. By the time she reached Wargrave, the dual carriageways had shrunk to a narrow road that dipped and turned through high banks of hedges and avenues of golden trees. A pub flashed by on her left, the St George and the Dragon, and beside it she glimpsed the river and the bright colours of moored narrowboats. As the village vanished behind her, she felt she was sinking inexorably into the heart of the countryside, and she had an uneasy sense of déjà vu.

Before she could pursue the thought she was sweeping down the hill into Henley, and saw police cars clustered down a short lane to her right. Kincaid's instructions had been to go through the town and then take the Marlow road, however, so she resisted the temptation to stop, but her curiosity was aroused.

Crossing the bridge, she only glimpsed the river, the view broken by the railings so that it looked like a juddery old film. Then she was across it, and the town centre flashed by her: the pretty flower-bedecked pub by the bridge, the square of the church tower, a blur of shops and restaurants, the bulk of the town hall sitting astride the top of the square as if asserting its proprietary rights.

She turned right as she left the town behind, and was soon running along another narrow, leafy road cloaked in autumnal colours, her sense of prickly familiarity increasing.

She slowed at the signpost for Hambleden, as Kincaid had directed, then braked sharply as she rounded the next bend. The police cars were clustered on the verges, positioned at odd angles as if they had been scooped willy-nilly from the narrow lane and dropped. Their blue lights strobed like distress signals aimed at the lowering grey sky.

This time she had no doubt she'd reached the crime scene. The green Astra sat among the Thames Valley Police patrol cars, as plain as a female peacock against the bright blue and yellow Battenberg livery of the official vehicles.

Kit was leaning against the Astra, hands in the pockets of his anorak, his downcast face brightening when he saw her.

Gemma lowered her window and showed her identification to the uniformed constable on the scene, then eased her Escort onto the verge as close to the Astra as she could. The children hadn't stirred, so she slipped quietly out of the car, holding her finger to her lips as she walked towards Kit.

'I don't want to wake them if I can help it,' she said. Then, glancing at the Astra, she grinned at Kit. 'It is a bit hideous, isn't it?'

'A bit?' He shook his head in disgust, but his face relaxed into what might almost have been a smile.

'Will you watch the little ones while I find your dad and see what's going on?' she asked.

'He wouldn't let me go with him,' said Kit, but he sounded more resigned than sullen. He pointed towards a narrow passageway that ran between the red-brick houses nearest the formation of police cars. 'It's through there. The river's just the other side, but you can't see it from here.'

Gemma gave his arm a pat. 'I'll be as quick as I can.' She glanced once more at the children, still sleeping soundly. 'Kit, if they wake, make sure to keep them in the car,' she added.

She followed Kit's directions, ducking into the gravelled passageway. After a moment she rounded a bend and saw the Thames spread before her, wide and still except where the water cascaded over the weir.

From the near bank, a metal-railed concrete walkway zigzagged across the water, traversing the river, then the weir, until it reached the lock on the far side, and as Gemma gazed across it, she realized at last why the drive from Henley had seemed so familiar.

She had been here before.

There had been a body in this place, in this lock, a case that had led to secrets in the heart of the Chiltern Hills – a case that had propelled her and Duncan from a comfortable relationship as working partners into something much more complicated, something that had terrified her.

And there had been a woman involved, Julia Swann, an enigmatic artist whose relationship with Duncan had been, Gemma suspected, more than professional.

But that had been a long time ago. And water under the bridge, Gemma told herself, appreciating the irony as she stepped out onto the narrow walkway. She moved quickly, keeping her eyes off the roiling water as she reached the weir. As the walkway twisted, she realized she could see people clustered on the far bank, beyond the lock.

There were uniformed officers on the path on either side of the lock, discouraging the groups of curious bystanders who were beginning to gather. A child pointed, and as Gemma followed his gesture, she saw two dogs in orange SAR vests, a German shepherd and a black Labrador retriever, and their handlers, a man and a woman in black uniforms. She couldn't read the insignia on the handlers' jackets, but assumed they were volunteer search and rescue. The woman stood, the German shepherd sitting beside her, but the man sat with his head in his hands, the Labrador nudging at his arm.

A few yards from them Kincaid was instantly recognizable, hands shoved in the pockets of his jacket in a posture reminiscent of Kit's, his hair ruffled by the gusty wind blowing down the river. Beside him stood a small Asian man in an ill-fitting buff-coloured overcoat that screamed *copper* – he might as well have been wearing uniform.

Two white-suited crime-scene techs worked in the lee of the tangle of trees and brush at the water's edge below the lock, one snapping away with a camera at something on the ground. As Gemma drew nearer, she saw that there was a man kneeling between them, obscuring the object of their interest.

He wore jeans and a scruffy leather jacket, and his blue-black hair was gelled into spikes – all in odd contrast with the medical bag beside him – and she recognized him, too. Rashid Kaleem, the Home Office pathologist they had worked with on the case involving Charlotte's parents.

Looking up, Kincaid caught sight of her. He lifted a hand in greeting, then said something to the overcoated man, who turned and gave her a brief glance. Gemma realized she must look as scruffy as Rashid. She wore jeans as well; her hair was pulled up in a haphazard ponytail and, unprepared for the torrential rain in Glastonbury, she'd borrowed an old Barbour from Winnie. But then she hadn't expected to be making an appearance at a murder inquiry.

When she reached the towpath, both men came to meet her.

'Gemma, this is Inspector Singla,' Kincaid said.

She held out her hand. 'Gemma James.'

Singla touched her fingers as briefly as courtesy would allow, then frowned at Kincaid. 'Superintendent, I'm not sure it is appropriate for a civilian—'

'My *wife*,' Kincaid said with the careful emphasis that Gemma knew meant the man had already begun to try his patience, 'is a detective inspector with the Met. And I would appreciate her professional opinion.'

She looked towards Rashid and the SOCOs. Kincaid had told her nothing except that Denis Childs wanted him to have a look at what might be a suspicious death. 'What's happened here?' she asked, meaning *Why did it need the intervention of a senior officer from the Met*? From DI Singla's expression, he couldn't have agreed more. 'Who's the victim?'

It was Kincaid who answered. 'DCI Rebecca Meredith. West London, Serious Crimes.'

Gemma stared at him. A Met officer. A senior, female Met officer. Not good. Not good at all.

Glancing at the shape on the ground between Rashid and the SOCOs, she caught a glimpse of neon-yellow clothing, a tangle of dark, matted hair. 'They pulled her out of the river? Possible suicide?'

'Not unless she decided to take a dive out of a rowing boat.' Rashid had come to stand beside them, giving Gemma a quick grin, and she saw that the slogan on the black T-shirt beneath his open jacket read *Pathologists Have More Fun*.

'She was a rower?'

'She's wearing rowing gear, and they' – Rashid nodded at the SAR handlers – 'found her shell caught in the bank, about a mile upstream. I'd guess that's where she went out of the boat.'

'Any signs of trauma?' Kincaid asked.

'The head is pretty banged up, but I can't tell you if the wounds are ante or post mortem until I get her on the table.'

'I want to have a closer look *in situ* before you transport her,' Kincaid said, then turned to Gemma. 'Do you—'

'I've got to get back.' She was suddenly very aware of time passing. 'I've left the little ones with Kit, in case you've forgotten?'

'Sorry.' He gave an apologetic grimace. 'I'll ring

you.' He touched her arm, moving her slightly aside. 'Look, love, I'm sure this won't take – '

She shook her head. The SAR handlers had come up to them, and she felt that their domestic discussion was uncomfortably public. 'We'll talk about it later.' The dogs' tails were wagging, so she held out a hand for them to snuffle. The female handler, a small, blonde woman who would have looked elfin if not for the gravity of her expression, gave her a tight smile.

The man was tall and dark-haired, his face drawn and pale. His Labrador watched him anxiously, brow furrowed in doggy concern.

'We've got a team securing the boat,' said the woman. 'I'm Tavie, by the way. Tavie Larssen. Thames Valley Search and Rescue. This is Kieran.' She nodded towards her companion, but he didn't speak.

Kincaid glanced at the sky, and Gemma saw that the clouds were building again, blotting out what remained of the afternoon light. 'I want to see where you found the boat, before it gets too dark,' he said, looking at Singla. 'Inspector, if you could arrange—'

'I'm going with you.' It was the dark-haired handler, Kieran. His voice sounded stretched to breaking. 'I want to see the boat.' As they all turned to stare at him, his dog whined and licked his hand. 'I'm a rower,' he said. 'I can tell you what happened.'

Chapter Five

Gemma heard Charlotte's sobs as she came up the path towards the road. She quickened her steps, her chest tightening with a mother's instinctive reaction to the sound of her child in distress.

When she rounded the corner, she saw Kit standing beside the Escort, holding Charlotte, who was kicking her heels against him as she howled. Toby sat in the car, looking mutinous.

'I'm sorry, Gemma,' called Kit. 'I know you wanted me to keep them in the car, but I couldn't stop her crying.' He bounced Charlotte on his hip, cajoling her. 'See, I told you she'd come back. Gemma's here.'

As Gemma reached them, Charlotte twisted in Kit's grasp and flung herself at Gemma, arms outstretched. Gemma leapt to catch her before she went into freefall.

'Whoa, lovey. Let's not have an aerial ballet,' Gemma said, tucking Charlotte's damp face into her shoulder.

'You went 'way,' came Charlotte's muffled wail.

'Yes, I did. And I came back. See?' She held Charlotte away from her long enough to kiss her cheek, but then the child burrowed her face into Gemma's neck again.

'I don't want to stay in the car,' said Toby from the Escort's half-open window. 'Why does she get to come out and I don't? Maybe I should cry, too.' He scrunched up his face.

'Don't you dare.' Gemma stabbed a finger at him over Charlotte's shoulder. 'And don't you dare get out of that car. We're all going home. Now.'

'Dad, too?' asked Kit.

'No,' she said, hating to be the bearer of bad news. 'He's got to stay here for a bit, but I'm sure he'll come as soon as he can.' Though truthfully, now that she knew what the suspicious death involved, she wasn't sure at all.

She saw that there were now more uniformed officers on the scene. Traffic on the Marlow road had come almost to a standstill as motorists slowed to a crawl, mesmerized by the lure of flashing lights and patrol cars. Bystanders were gathering as well, some coming down the side road that led to the nearby car park and Hambleden village. Uniform was going to have its hands full.

'Does that mean you won't be going back to work?' Kit asked. She glanced at him, unsure if he was pleased or disappointed.

'Let's not worry about that just yet. We'll sort something out, okay?'

And she bloody well hoped she was right about that. Her boss, Mark Lamb, was expecting her back at Notting Hill next Monday. Excuses about childcare

NO MARK UPON HER

difficulties, no matter how valid, would not go down well.

Charlotte had stopped snuffling, but Toby was now hanging halfway out of the car window and looked in immediate danger of falling on his head. 'Toby, back in the car. And buckle up, please.'

She gave a last glance back towards the river, wondering what Duncan and Rashid might find, and feeling a flare of frustration at being excluded. But just now she had to deal with the problems at hand.

'Kit, we need to get out of the way. Can you grab your things from the Astra, and the keys? You can ask one of the officers to keep them for your dad.' Still holding Charlotte, she reached in and popped open the Escort's boot for Kit – she'd learned better than to try putting Charlotte into the car until the last possible moment.

As Kit tossed in his bag, then jogged over to the nearest constable, Gemma saw a flash of bright blue as a small car pulled out of the jam and into the only remaining space on the verge. It was a little Renault, a Clio, but it wasn't until the driver's door swung open that recognition clicked.

'Melody?' she said. 'What are you doing here?'

'Hi, boss.' Melody Talbot grinned. 'I'm just playing chauffeur,' she added as the Clio's passenger door opened and Doug Cullen climbed out.

Gemma's pleasure at seeing Melody, whose company she'd missed since she'd been away from work, quickly vanished.

'Doug,' she said. 'He called you. In fact, he called you first.'

Cullen had the grace to look sheepish. 'It was just in case this turned out to be something more than a false alarm. In on the ground floor, and all that. Sorry if it's buggered your holiday, Gemma.'

She glared at him, then relented with a reluctant sigh. Kincaid had only done what she'd have done in his place, and it certainly wasn't Doug's fault. 'I think you'll find he wants you straight away.' She gestured towards the path. 'I hope you don't have a problem with water.'

'Not unless I'm in it,' Doug answered, sounding relieved.

Gemma thought of the huddled form, pulled from the tangle of flotsam in the river, and shuddered. She must have inadvertently squeezed Charlotte, who said, 'Ow!' and wriggled down from Gemma's arms. 'Want to see Melody,' she added, but stayed leaning against Gemma's leg. Charlotte was very definite about the people she liked, and Melody was one of them, but she still suffered from occasional attacks of shyness.

Melody knelt so that she was on Charlotte's level. 'Hi, sweetheart. Are you having an adventure?'

'I want to see the river,' Charlotte pronounced unexpectedly. 'Kit says there's a river. Is it big?'

Nonplussed, Gemma glanced at Melody, who mouthed, 'Sorry.'

'We can't see the river today, lovey,' Gemma told Charlotte. 'It's getting late, and the dogs must be missing us dreadfully at home.'

Melody stood and gave Charlotte's curls a ruffle. 'You'll have to visit Doug in Putney.' She gave Cullen a sly glance and got a frown in return, making Gemma wonder what she had missed.

'I'd better get down there,' said Doug. 'Thanks for the lift, Melody.' He gave them an awkward little wave and disappeared down the path.

Gemma turned back to Melody. 'What—'

'Where's Doug going?' piped up Charlotte. 'Don't want Doug to go.'

'Mummy,' whined Toby, 'I want to get out. Everyone else is out.'

Gemma rolled her eyes at Melody. 'We really have got to go. Nuclear meltdown approaching.' Suddenly disheartened by the idea of arriving home on her own with three disappointed children, she added, 'Why don't you come to the house when we get back to London, if you're not doing anything? We'll get pizza or something. Have a good natter.'

Melody smiled. 'Deal. I'll bring the wine.'

Kincaid had taken a few moments to fill in Cullen, to have another word with Rashid and to work out a strategic plan.

When the SAR handler, Kieran, had insisted he should go with them to see the rowing shell, his teammate, Tavie, had chimed in that as team leader she was needed on the scene as well. It was her job to tell the team watching the boat to stand down, once the police had the area secured.

But the dog-handlers had left their cars on the Berkshire side of the river, halfway between Leander and the weir. With the daylight fading, there wasn't time for them to walk back, pick up their cars and drive round through Henley to the site on the Bucks bank where the shell had been found.

DI Singla, however, had looked so horrified at the suggestion that the handlers and dogs should ride with him that Kincaid had jumped in. 'Ride with me. I've plenty of room.'

'Thanks,' replied Tavie. 'We'll get Scott and Sarah to give us a lift back round the other side once we're finished.' Leaving Rashid and the SOCOs to deal with the removal of the body to the mortuary van, Kincaid, Cullen, Singla, the SAR handlers and the dogs traversed the walkway back across the river, in single file. Bringing up the rear, Kincaid felt a bit like the tenth Indian, but he was impressed by the dogs' easy nonchalance as they crossed over the rushing water of the weir.

When they reached the verge, Cullen looked askance at the Astra. 'This is yours? Since when?'

'Shut it,' Kincaid said cheerfully. 'It was a gift from my dad. And already useful. You even get to ride in the front.'

Tavie, however, glanced at the car with approval. 'Great. We'll put the dogs in the storage area. This is Tosh, by the way,' she added, reaching down to stroke the German shepherd's head. 'And this is Finn.' She gestured towards the Lab, as Kincaid opened the rear hatch. 'Kieran, can you—'

'Oh, right.' The dark-haired handler led his dog round to the back of the Astra and the Lab jumped in on command, as did Tavie's German shepherd. But the man seemed dazed, and Kincaid had noticed an edge in Tavie's voice when she spoke to him. There was definitely some tension between the two.

'Just as well you won't have doggy-breath down your necks,' Tavie said as she and Kieran got into the rear seat. 'Although it's not far. Do you know the way?'

'Only that it must be back towards Henley.'

'I'll direct you, then, but' – she glanced dubiously at Doug in his suit and light overcoat – 'it's a good walk from where we'll have to leave the car.'

Kincaid suppressed a grin. He'd drawn the lucky straw that day, it seemed, having dressed for sloshing in mud puddles with the children. 'I'm sure we'll manage.'

He motioned for Singla to follow them, then turned left towards Henley when the constable controlling the traffic cleared an opening for them. Fortunately, they were now travelling against the tailback, and the road to Henley was clear.

Kincaid caught intermittent glimpses of the river, then the road moved away from the water as it ran through a cluster of buildings that Tavie identified as the village of Greenlands. After that there were ploughed fields to the right and tree-dotted meadows to the left. Soon Tavie directed him to turn into what looked like a drive leading to a private estate. Two serviceable utility vehicles were parked just beyond the open gate, as was a Thames Valley panda car. All were unoccupied.

'This is the closest access,' Tavie explained. 'That's why Scott and Sarah left their cars here. We'll have to cross the meadows on foot.'

Cullen looked down at his shoes and muttered, 'Bugger!'

Kieran was out of the car before Kincaid had even popped the hatch on the storage area. Within seconds he had his dog on the ground and had started across the field at an oblique angle to the river. He looked back at them impatiently. 'We've got to hurry. The light's going.'

'Can't we stay on the track?' asked Cullen.

'No.' Pointing, Tavie added, 'We've got to cross this field, and the next. You can come in from the other side of Temple Island, but that's even further and wouldn't be any drier.' She snapped the lead on her dog and started after Kieran.

As soon as Kincaid felt the soft, tussocky grass squish beneath his trainers, he felt some sympathy for Cullen – and for DI Singla, who was no better prepared. But Kieran had been right about the light. The hedgerow in the distance, and the treeline beyond that, were becoming grey-green blurs on a grey horizon.

Although the dogs hadn't been given a command to search, they were eager, seeming to sense that they were engaged in work of some kind. Tavie and Kieran kept up with them at a steady trot, while the others straggled out at intervals, this time with Singla bringing up the rear.

What had looked like a hedgerow from a distance turned out to be an inlet snaking in from the river, which they crossed by a single-planked footbridge. By the time they'd crossed the second field, Kincaid's feet were soaked and he was beginning to sweat, despite the chill in the air. Ahead lay the heavy belt of vegetation he had seen from the lane. They'd been following a faint track through the grass, but when the dogs and handlers reached the trees, they veered towards the river and plunged directly into the dense thicket.

Kincaid heard dogs bark, and an answering chorus. Then, as he pushed his way through branches, snagging his anorak, he heard human voices as well. As Cullen and Singla crashed along behind him, he pushed through into a small clearing right on the river's edge.

Tavie stood with two uniformed constables, and a man and a woman who wore the same dark Thames Valley Search and Rescue uniforms as she and Kieran. Tosh, her German shepherd, was nosing greetings with a springer spaniel and a golden retriever, both of which wore the distinctive orange SAR vests.

Kieran, with Finn, had gone straight to the water's edge.

Tavie motioned to Kincaid. 'Superintendent, this is Scott and Sarah. And Bumps and Meg,' she added, giving the spaniel and the retriever affectionate pats. 'They found the boat.'

DI Singla was murmuring to the uniformed officers, but Kincaid looked at Kieran, who had knelt, his body obscuring the object of his attention. Kieran had dropped Finn's lead, but the dog sat beside him, watching his master with what Kincaid could have sworn was a furrowed brow.

Walking over, Kincaid hunkered down, until his shoulder was almost touching Kieran's.

'It's not *a boat*,' said Kieran, his voice trembling. 'I told them before. It's a Filippi. A racing shell.'

Kincaid gazed at the sleek lines of the shell. The Filippi was white, with a fine blue line running its length, and it seemed impossibly long and slender, like a sliver of light. A little water was still pooled beneath the seat and runners. 'Sort of like calling a thoroughbred *a pony*?' he suggested quietly.

Kieran nodded, and some of the tension seemed to go out of his shoulders.

A light nylon rope stretched from one of the shell's riggers to a sturdy sapling near the bank. One oar lay nearby on the bank.

'We had to turn it over,' said Scott, coming to stand beside them. 'The boat. To make sure she wasn't' – he glanced uneasily at Kieran – 'there wasn't anyone trapped underneath. But we didn't want to pull it out of the water until the police had seen it.'

'And the other oar? Was it missing when you found the boat?' Kincaid asked, resisting the temptation to examine the underside of the hull. He'd better leave it for Forensics.

'The blade,' Scott corrected. 'Your partner' – he nodded at Cullen, who had come to join them – 'says it's called a blade. Yeah, it was missing, and I had to unfasten that one in order to flip the bloody thing. Got soaked.'

'How easy is it to flip a single shell like this?'

It was Cullen who answered. 'Happens all the time. You catch a crab—'

'Not to her, it didn't,' Kieran said, his voice fierce. 'Not on a calm evening, not here.' He looked at Kincaid for the first time since they had reached the bank. 'You don't understand. She was an elite rower. Not some amateur out for a Sunday paddle.'

'You knew her,' Kincaid said with sudden realization, and he saw that Tavie had come to stand behind him and was listening, too. She shifted uncomfortably.

'Everyone knew her,' Kieran went on. 'Rowers, I mean. She was – she could have been – one of the best in the world. And she trained on the Reach every day.'

Kincaid gazed out at the Thames, the dark water now as placid as a garden pool. Scattered lights had begun to twinkle in the dusk, but they were distant, and this spot felt as isolated as the moon. He could smell the mist rising from the water like a damp and living thing, ancient as memory.

'So,' he said slowly, 'what if she fell ill? Fainted, even? There'd have been no one to help her.'

'Sudden death.' The reply, unexpectedly, was Cullen's. 'It happens to rowers sometimes. It's called *sudden death.*'

As they trudged back across the meadows, Kincaid realized he'd forgotten how long light lingered in the sky once you were out of the city. But while shreds of violet stained the deep-blue canopy above, the ground beneath their feet was nigh on invisible, and much stumbling and swearing accompanied the progress of all the police officers.

The dog-handlers, however, seemed to be as surefooted as their canine companions, and periodically stopped to wait for the others.

There had been no possibility of getting Forensics to the scene until first light. The uniformed officers had set about trying to get the boat out of the water, when Kieran had motioned them back. Taking off his boots, he'd slipped into the river and lifted the shell onto the bank, as gently as if it were immeasurably fragile. Climbing out, he'd laid the single blade beside the shell and stood for a moment, his expression unfathomable in the gloom.

When the constables had finished cordoning off the small clearing with scene-of-crime tape, they had all gone out the way they'd come in, in single file. DI Singla had another officer waiting at the cars, who on their arrival would be led back to guard the scene overnight.

'I want to talk to the coach at the Leander Club,' Kincaid said quietly to Cullen, when they'd crossed the single-plank bridge into the first meadow and he thought he could see the shapes of the cars in the distance. 'Wasn't he the last person to have seen her?'

'The ex-husband reported her missing,' said Singla, from behind them.

'Him, too. But first the coach, I think. And we'll need somewhere to stay.'

'All in hand.' Cullen sounded pleased with himself. 'I rang the Red Lion on the way down. It's just across the river from Leander.'

Kincaid glanced at him and saw only the glint of his glasses in the darkness. 'How did you get here so quickly anyway? Levitate?'

Cullen's reply came reluctantly. 'Um, Melody gave me a lift.'

'What were you doing with Melody?' Kincaid asked, surprised.

'Buying her lunch. In Putney.' Cullen had begun to sound a bit defensive. 'She came round to have a look at the house.'

'Ah.' Kincaid processed this. He'd been aware of Doug's venture into home ownership, but as far as he knew, Doug and Melody barely tolerated one another. This, however, was not the time or place to enquire further. 'Well, good. It's official then, the house?'

'As of this morning.'

Kincaid patted him on the shoulder, a little clumsily as his right foot twisted in a hollow. 'We'll have a drink on it, later.'

He grimaced as he took another step, but it had less to do with the twinge in his ankle and more with the thought of staying here in Henley, leaving Gemma home alone with the children. This was not what they'd planned for this week.

As if sensing his train of thought, Cullen said very softly as they approached the cars, 'Guv, I know you've got leave coming up. This case – do you think there's anything to it?'

And Kincaid could have sworn there was a note of hope in his voice.

'You've been here before, I take it?' Kincaid asked.

Cullen had directed him over the Henley Bridge and then into the first turning. There was a dark mass of buildings on his left, a gated car park on his right and no obvious place to put the car.

They had left DI Singla to begin setting up an

incident room at Henley Police Station, Cullen murmuring, 'He's a bit taciturn, wouldn't you say?'

'No more than you or I would be under the circumstances, I suspect,' Kincaid had answered. 'Would you want a Met officer dead on your patch?'

Cullen had shaken his head. 'I wouldn't be jumping for joy over the prospect, no.'

Now Cullen said, 'Pull up to the dead end. The field beyond is where they put up the regatta enclosures, but it won't be in use now. The club's on the left.'

When Kincaid had duly parked and climbed out of the Astra, he saw that the building had appeared dark because it was flanked by a high brick wall, a visual moat. Above the wall he saw red-tiled gables atop white-framed panels of pebble-dash, and on the upper floors light glinted from a multitude of windows. There was an arched doorway in the wall that opened onto an inner courtyard.

Kincaid touched his fingers to the brick as they passed through. 'A chastity belt for an Edwardian dowager?' he suggested.

'It's *Leander*,' Doug protested, as if Kincaid had just insulted the holy of holies. 'And it's not dowdy. The building was completely refurbished in the late nineties.'

That didn't make it any more of an architectural gem, Kincaid thought, but he kept his opinion to himself. 'So you rowed here?'

'Oh, no.' Doug sounded shocked. 'I mean, I never rowed *from* Leander, as a member. But I rowed in regattas here in Henley, when I was at school.' The casually mentioned school had been, in Doug's case, Eton – a fact that he rarely admitted in police environs.

'And at university?' Kincaid asked.

'No.' Doug shook his head as they reached glass doors sheltered by a fluted iron canopy. 'Wasn't good enough. Too big for a cox, too small for a really powerful oarsman.'

Kincaid opened the door and they stepped into a lobby that was more elegant than the building's exterior. The decor centred around a glass-topped coffee table with a sculpted bronze hippo as its base.

Lights still burned in a glass-fronted but very businesslike office area on the lobby's right. A young woman sitting at one of the desks saw them, stood and came out, looking at them enquiringly. She wore a pale-pink blouse and a navy skirt, and Kincaid was suddenly aware that he had been tromping across rain-sodden fields in the clothes he'd been wearing since he'd begun the day playing with the children – he certainly didn't look the most reputable of policemen.

'Can I help you?' she said.

He ran his fingers through his hair, pulled his warrant-card case from his pocket and smiled. 'Duncan Kincaid. Detective Superintendent, Scotland Yard. And this is Sergeant Cullen. There was an incident today—'

'Becca?' the young woman said. She lifted her hand, her fingers brushing her collarbone in an instinctive gesture of shock. 'Is she all right? The police were here, and the people with the dogs, but everyone's gone now and no one's told us anything.'

'I'd like to speak to the coach who saw her going out on the river yesterday,' Kincaid said, avoiding the question as gently as he could. Rumours would be flying around, but he wanted to break the news first to the people whom Rebecca Meredith had known best. 'Mr—'

'Jachym. Milo Jachym,' Cullen contributed. He didn't have to consult his notes.

'I – I think he's in the Members' Bar,' the young woman said. 'I'll take you up.' She started towards a flight of stairs that appeared to lead up to a mezzanine, then turned back. 'I'm Lily Meyberg, by the way, the house manager.' She held out a slender hand and, when Kincaid took it, he felt the calluses on her palms and the strength of her grip. A rower, he wondered? And, if so, possibly more than a casual acquaintance of the victim?

He followed her, noticing as he passed a glass-fronted case displaying mugs and teacups decorated with the dancing pink hippos that seemed to be the Leander mascot, along with caps and ties in the infamous Leander cerise.

As he climbed, he saw that the walls of the stairwell were lined with photos: groups of muscular men and women in rowing singlets, sporting gaudy medals.

'Redgrave, Pinsent, Williams, Foster, Cracknell . . . ' Doug's whisper was reverent, and he looked as if he was resisting the temptation to touch the photos as he passed. These, Kincaid knew, were the gold-medal winners, rowing's gods.

At the top of the stairs they reached a reception

area, but the desk and the dining room beyond were empty. Back to the right, however, Kincaid heard the murmur of voices and the clink of china and cutlery.

He peered round the corner into another dining area – a pleasant, casual room with a bar at its end that must overlook the building's front. The few diners at the white-clothed tables looked up at him curiously, implements frozen. As he turned back to reception, he sensed the tension of whispers beginning to build behind him.

'I'll take you in,' Lily was saying. She led them, not through the dining room that he had seen, but along a corridor that ran parallel to it, towards the front of the building.

'It seems there's not much custom tonight,' he said. In spite of the sparseness of diners, delicious odours were wafting from somewhere nearby, and Kincaid realized he was starving. Their breakfast in Glastonbury that morning seemed a world away. They'd meant to have a late lunch once they reached home, so he had missed the meal altogether.

'It's usually quiet on a Tuesday night, unless we have a function on,' said Lily. 'But the chef has the crew to cook for, three meals a day, so it's always busy in the kitchen.'

'That's a job,' said Cullen, sounding impressed.

Lily gave him a quick smile. 'They do eat a good bit.'

As they reached the end of the corridor, two young men carrying kit bags came out of a door marked *Crew*. They made Kincaid, who was a bit over six feet, feel suddenly dwarfed. Like the diners, the young men glanced curiously at the newcomers, giving them the slightest of nods.

'Rowers in training need about six thousand calories a day,' Lily added, glancing back at the oarsmen as they disappeared round the corner. As Kincaid tried to calculate what six thousand calories meant in terms of portions, he saw that they had reached a T-junction of sorts, with the bar he'd seen at the end of the dining room to the left, a small service area straight ahead and, to the right, a smaller, more intimate bar, its walls covered with rowing memorabilia and anchored by a large plasma-screen television.

A petite blonde in the service kitchen was making coffee. She wore the same pale-pink blouse and navy skirt as Lily, which Kincaid surmised must be the Leander staff uniform.

'Milo?' asked Lily, and the pretty blonde nodded towards the small bar.

'He's been ringing the police, but he can't find out any – ' The blonde stopped at Lily's fractional head shake, and her eyes widened as she looked at Kincaid and Cullen.

'I'll take them in,' said Lily, and they followed her into the bar.

A small, balding man sat alone, an empty coffee cup on the table before him. He stood when he saw them, his lined face apprehensive.

'Mr Jachym?' Kincaid asked, before Lily could introduce him. 'If we could have a word. We're from the police.'

Lily left them then, but he was sure that anything they said could be heard from the service kitchen on the other side of the bar. The news would be all over the club in no time.

'I've been trying—'

'I know,' Kincaid interrupted. 'Mr Jachym, I understand you were the last person to see Rebecca Meredith?'

'I – ' Jachym swallowed visibly. 'As far as I know, yes. I told the other policeman, the Asian one.'

'You were Rebecca Meredith's coach?'

'Not officially, no. Although I was once, many years ago. Please, what's happened?'

'Mr Jachym, sit down,' said Kincaid. Milo Jachym, who didn't appear to be a man accustomed to taking orders, sat, albeit with obvious reluctance.

'May we?' Kincaid asked, and at Jachym's nod he and Cullen pulled up the nearest chairs. 'Rebecca Meredith's body was found this afternoon, below Hambleden Weir,' he said, knowing it was best to get it over quickly.

Jachym stared at them. 'You're certain?'

'One of the SAR team identified her. But we'll need an official ID. Do you know who would be her next of kin?'

'Oh, God.' Jachym made a convulsive movement towards his empty coffee cup, but didn't touch it. 'No one's told Freddie? He's been frantic.'

'Freddie?' Kincaid asked, although he remembered the name from the initial missing-persons report.

'Freddie Atterton. Becca's ex-husband.'

'He was the one who reported her missing?'

'I – we – he came to me, this morning. He was

97

worried about her, and I realized I hadn't seen her shell on the rack in the yard. Look, can you tell me what happened?'

Cullen responded. 'The SAR team found her Filippi caught on the Buckinghamshire bank, not far below Temple Island. It was overturned, and one blade was missing.'

'But – if she went in the water there, surely she could have swum to shore. Not that she'd have willingly left the boat . . . ' Milo Jachym shook his head and scrubbed impatiently at the greying stubble on his chin. 'I've been in this sport long enough to know that any rower can have an accident. But I never thought Becca . . . Freddie was right. I should have stopped her.'

'He didn't want her to go out?'

'No. I was the one who told him she was training, and he was furious. He thought it was foolish.'

'And was it?'

'No. At least I didn't think so. She was a gold-medal contender when I first worked with her, after she finished university. But she was reckless. Age seemed to have tempered her a bit. I told her last night, before she went out, that I thought she had a chance if she was serious.'

'A chance?' Kincaid asked. 'A chance at what?'

Jachym looked at him as if he were mentally deficient. 'The Olympics, of course. In the women's single scull.'

Kincaid stared back. Bloody hell, he thought. When Rebecca Meredith had been described as an 'elite rower', he'd assumed she rowed in the occasional local regatta.

But an Olympic contender *and* a senior officer in the Met?

No wonder the brass had wanted their own man on the scene. The press were going to have a feeding frenzy.

And he was not going to get home any time soon.

Chapter Six

'Wait,' Kincaid said. 'Back up a bit. You're telling me that Rebecca Meredith was training for the Olympics? But she wasn't a member of the Leander crew.'

'Didn't have to be,' Milo answered. 'Becca was a member of the club. She could represent Leander in a race. But even that wasn't necessary. Anyone can compete in an Olympic trial.'

Cullen frowned for a moment, then his face cleared. 'Brad Lewis.'

Milo Jachym was already nodding in agreement. Kincaid felt like he was playing table tennis without the ball. 'What are you talking about?'

'Brad Alan Lewis,' Cullen explained. 'He won gold in double sculls at the Los Angeles Olympics in 1984. And he did it from completely outside the system, and with next to no financial backing.'

'And Becca is – was' – Milo's lips tightened in a spasm of distress – 'not dissimilar in character. Stubborn. Obsessive. Determined to do things her way. And, like Lewis, she knew it was her last opportunity.'

'But you said her ex-husband was furious when he found out she was training. Why, if she really did have a chance at something that big?'

'I . . . He was concerned about her safety, I assumed, because she was going out so late. But it was the only way she could row every day.'

'Unless,' Kincaid said thoughtfully, 'she quit the job. And that – '

The phone in his pocket vibrated once, then again: an incoming call. Irritating as the interruption was, he couldn't afford to let it go.

He didn't recognize the number on the display, but he knew DI Singla's voice immediately. 'Superintendent, there's a man at Rebecca Meredith's cottage,' said Singla. 'He's threatening the constable I put on watch there. Do you want me to have him picked up? He says he's her husband.'

'You are an absolute dear.' Gemma stretched her legs out under the kitchen table and raised her glass to Melody in salute. Melody had not only arrived with a very nice bottle of Sauvignon blanc, but had picked up pizza, dripping with olive oil and garlic, from Sugo's, Gemma's favourite Italian bistro at Notting Hill Gate.

'Good thing I left the car at the flat,' Melody said, pouring herself another generous measure. 'And if I come across any vampires on the walk home, they'll take one whiff of me and run the other way.' She blew out a breath, as if testing her theory.

Melody lived in a mansion block on Kensington Park Road, and declared that the half-mile walk between her flat and Duncan and Gemma's house in St John's Gardens provided just the right amount of exercise after an overindulgence of food and drink.

'Do you suppose garlic has a calming effect on children, too?' Gemma asked. 'I think they're probably related to vampires.'

By the time they'd reached home, Toby had been overexcited, and Charlotte more clingy and fretful than usual. While Toby had refused to sit still, dancing around the table with his slice of pizza, teasing the dogs, the cat and Charlotte, Charlotte had only agreed to eat her supper if she was held in Gemma's lap. Kit, unusually unsociable, had grabbed half a pizza and disappeared upstairs, plate in one hand and phone in the other.

'I can do the washing up,' offered Melody. 'Dab hand in the kitchen.'

Gemma considered. 'You know, I've never actually seen you cook. But you get top votes for delivery person.'

'I can cook,' Melody protested, grinning. 'Um, cheese, biscuits, wine . . . ' She furrowed her brow, then shrugged. 'Well, maybe not so much. But I really can wield a mean Fairy Liquid.' She started to stand, but Gemma waved her back into her chair.

'It's only pizza boxes. Easily done when the kids are in bed.' Knowing bedtime would be an ordeal and wanting to enjoy her visit with Melody, Gemma had bribed the little ones with the promise of a video in the sitting room. Once she'd convinced Toby that he really did not need to watch *Peter Pan* for the hundredth time, she'd settled them down with *The Lion King* and breathed a huge sigh of relief.

Now she could hear Toby singing along, tunelessly.

'The West End in his future, for certain,' said Melody, and they both giggled.

'Only if he can swashbuckle,' Gemma said, meditating on Toby's possibly brilliant career. 'But maybe, if I'm lucky, he'll put Charlotte to sleep, and not just future audiences.'

She thought her friend looked unusually relaxed. Melody had changed into jeans, but still wore the cherry-red cardigan she'd had on before, and her cheeks were flushed from taking the dogs for a quick outing while Gemma was settling the kids.

'And that would be a blessing? Putting Charlotte to sleep?'

'Some nights. Most nights,' Gemma admitted. 'And even when she does go to sleep, she wakes up with bad dreams.'

'Does she dream about her parents, then?' Melody asked.

Gemma swirled the wine in her glass. 'Sometimes. Sometimes she calls out for them.' She didn't want to confess, as she had to Winnie, how helpless and inadequate she felt when Charlotte woke up sobbing, 'Mummy! Daddy!' Only recently had she begun calling out for Gemma as well, but Gemma wasn't sure that was an improvement.

Melody glanced towards the sitting room and lowered her voice. 'I'd think that was pretty normal, under the circumstances. I can't imagine what it must be like for a child to lose her parents, her home, everything familiar . . . '

'The odd thing,' Gemma answered slowly, 'is that,

except for the separation anxiety, during the day it seems as if she's adjusting quite well. She does talk about her mum and dad in the present tense, as if they were just away somewhere, but she doesn't ask to go home.'

'Have you taken her back there?'

Gemma shook her head. 'No. We didn't think that was a good idea. But Louise is getting ready to put the house up for sale, and we wanted Charlotte to have some familiar things.'

Louise Phillips had been Charlotte's father's law partner and was now the executor of Naz Malik's and Sandra Gilles's estates.

Although art dealers – including Pippa Nightingale, who had represented Sandra – were begging for the textile collages that remained in Sandra Gilles's studio, Lou Phillips had decided she would store all Sandra's works and her notebooks until Charlotte was of age and could sell or keep them as she saw fit. Her mother's art would be a legacy for Charlotte's future, and the money from the sale of the Fournier Street house, which should be considerable, would go into a fund to pay for her education.

'So I took her to the park one day when the boys were at school,' Gemma went on, 'and asked her to play a game. She had to close her eyes and name her favourite thing from every room in her old house.'

'I can't think of a thing I'd save from my flat even in a fire,' Melody said, sounding wistful. 'It's not like this house.'

Gemma looked round at her cheerful blue and yellow kitchen, with her treasured Clarice Cliff teaset on the shelf above the cooker, then glanced into the dining room where her piano held pride of place.

She'd loved this house from the moment Duncan had shown it to her, when she'd thought their lives held a very different future. And it seemed to her, oddly, that in making Charlotte feel at home, she had grown deeper into the house as well, learning every nook and cranny, every creak and sigh, as if they were etched in her bones.

But the house belonged not to them, but to Denis Childs's sister and her family, and Gemma's love for it was always tinged with the ache of impending loss. One day they would have to give it up.

'What did Charlotte choose?' asked Melody.

Gemma smiled at the recollection. 'From the kitchen, an old eggcup with a chicken-foot base. I imagine her mum picked it up at a street stall. It's hideous, and Charlotte adores it. From the sitting room, she chose the chaise longue.'

Charlotte had called it the 'crazy chase', and it had taken Gemma a moment to work out that she meant the chintz crazy-quilt chaise longue, but she, too, loved the whimsical piece that had seemed such an expression of Sandra Gilles's personality.

When they'd begun officially fostering Charlotte, they'd had to meet the requirements imposed by social services, which included moving Toby back in with Kit so that Charlotte could have a room of her own – the room that had been meant as a nursery for the baby they had lost.

They'd brought Charlotte's bedroom furniture from the house in Fournier Street, and there had been enough space in her new room for the *crazy chase* as well. When Gemma had told her they could paint her room any colour she liked, Charlotte had chosen not a little girl's pink, or blue, or even lilac, but a deep saffron-yellow that picked out the dominant colour in the quilted chaise and glowed like distilled sunlight on the walls. The child had without doubt inherited her artist mother's eye.

'From her parents' bedroom she wanted her mother's petticoats,' Gemma continued, 'although I brought the coloured-glass bud vases that Sandra kept on the chair rail, as well. And from Sandra's studio, Charlotte wanted the duck pencils. When I pointed out that she already had them, she asked for the painting of the red horse that hung over her mother's desk.'

'That's not one of Sandra's?'

'No. In fact, it's signed *LR*, and Duncan said he saw a painting that was almost identical hanging over Lucas Ritchie's desk in the club in Artillery Lane.'

'Ah, so you think it was done by the delectable Mr Ritchie?'

'Maybe. It would be a nice connection for Charlotte to have with her mother's old friend. Someday we'll have to ask him.'

'I'll go with you,' Melody offered, and Gemma laughed.

'I didn't realize you fancied him,' she said. Lucas Ritchie managed a private club in Whitechapel, but had gone to art college with Charlotte's mum, Sandra. He was also tall, blond, wickedly good-looking and apparently quite well off.

'I'm female. I'm not attached. And I'm not blind.' Melody took a big swallow of wine to punctuate her assertions, coughed and wiped her watering eyes.

'I can see that,' Gemma said, still grinning. 'What I don't know is what you were doing with Doug Cullen today.'

'Ah.' Melody was beginning to look slightly owlish. 'He invited me to see his new house. In Putney. It needs some DIY. And I've offered to help him with the garden.'

Raising her eyebrows in surprise, Gemma asked, 'Have you ever done any gardening?' Melody, as far as she knew, had grown up in a town house in Kensington, in a household that lacked for nothing. If it had had a garden, it would have come with gardener attached.

'No. But it should be an adventure.'

Gemma looked at her friend, bemused. She could imagine few things more unlikely than Doug Cullen doing home improvements while Melody mucked about in the garden. 'You must be desperate for excitement.'

'I keep telling you, work hasn't been the same with you gone, boss,' Melody retorted. 'And speaking of the job' – she straightened up rather carefully and set her now-empty glass on the table – 'there's something I've been meaning to tell you. I've put in for my Sergeant's course.'

'Oh.' Gemma felt an unexpected prick of loss. Not that she hadn't nagged Melody to go for promotion. Not that she'd expected Melody to stay at Notting Hill forever. But promotion would undoubtedly mean that

Melody would transfer to another station, if not another division, and Gemma realized how much she'd looked forward to working with her at Notting Hill again.

Seeing the disappointment on Melody's face, she pulled herself together and summoned a smile. 'Oh, congratulations, Melody. I'm so glad for you. You should have done it ages ago. And you know you'll do just fine in the exam.'

'I've liked working with Sapphire,' Melody said, sounding relieved at Gemma's approval. 'I suppose, before you went on leave, I'd been riding on your coat-tails, and the new job gave me a bit of confidence.'

It was always hard for Gemma to imagine that the daughter of one of the biggest newspaper barons in the country could lack confidence. But Melody had gone against her father's wishes even in joining the force, and Gemma knew that this decision would have been difficult for her.

'This business today, in Henley,' Melody said, 'will it interfere with your starting back next week?'

'Oh, I'm sure we can work something out, if it's not sorted by then,' Gemma told her, but in fact she'd been worrying all evening about alternative child-care, if Duncan were to get hung up in this case. They couldn't count on Wesley or Betty Howard for full-time child-minding and, if anything, the events of the day had made her more certain than ever that Charlotte wasn't ready for nursery school.

'What about the girl who used to be her nanny?' Melody suggested. 'Have you kept up with her?'

'Alia?' Gemma frowned, considering a possibility that hadn't occurred to her. 'She's been to visit a couple of times, and Charlotte is always pleased to see her. Maybe I should give her a ring, just in case . . . '

'Maybe they'll find the death in Henley was accidental, and Duncan will be off the hook.'

Remembering Rashid's expression when he was examining the body, Gemma thought she wouldn't hold her breath. Rashid Kaleem was a good pathologist, and she trusted his instincts. And she was still wondering why Denis Childs had been so insistent that Duncan look into the death. There were other detective superintendents – not on holiday – who could certainly have represented the Met. 'Maybe,' she said, trying to muster some conviction.

'The officer whose body they found – did you know her?' Melody asked.

Gemma shook her head. 'No. At least the name didn't ring a bell, and I didn't actually see her face. But Duncan said she worked out of West London.'

'West London?' Looking suddenly sober, Melody straightened in her chair and pushed her wine glass away. 'That's a bit close to home, isn't it?'

'Tell your constable to keep him there. I'm on my way,' Kincaid told Singla, then rang off and repeated what he'd been told to Milo Jachym. 'Did Becca Meredith remarry?'

'No. It must be Freddie. He . . . They were still very close. I don't think Freddie ever really came to terms with the divorce. Look, let me go with you. A friend should break the news.'

Kincaid considered, then shook his head. 'No. I want to speak to him first.'

'But someone should see he's all right – he's got no family nearby.'

'All right. Give me half an hour with him first, then.' He stood, then turned back to Milo with a warning look. 'And please, don't ring him until I've had a chance to talk to him.'

Kincaid drove down Remenham Lane, following the directions Milo had given them to Rebecca Meredith's cottage. The road ran behind Leander, parallel to the river. Although the way was well marked, Kincaid wasn't used to handling a car as big and heavy as the Astra. The curves in the lane swooped upon them with startling suddenness, and a few times he slowed a bit more drastically than necessary.

'Still breaking it in?' Cullen asked, releasing his grip on the dashboard.

Kincaid cast him an evil glance, then looked back at the road. 'And you would do better?'

Cullen had the grace not to reply. In fact, although he didn't own a car, he was a good driver, and usually drove when they had a pool car from the Yard. But Kincaid was not ready to give up the wheel of his new acquisition.

After a cluster of cottages near the main road, their headlamps caught hedgerows and fields, and to the left Kincaid glimpsed the occasional dark void that he knew must be the river. When lights began to appear again, he slowed to a crawl, and soon saw cottages hard against the road to the left.

Two cars were pulled onto the right-hand verge: one bearing the distinctive blue and yellow livery of the Thames Valley Police, the other a new model Audi. On the left, a red-brick gabled cottage stood close behind a fence.

As Kincaid parked and got out of the car, he saw a constable standing inside the gate, and a man sitting on the porch. A faint light shone through the stained glass in the cottage door, but the porch itself was dark.

Kincaid pulled his warrant card from his pocket and raised it to the beam of the constable's torch. 'Scotland Yard. Detective Superintendent Kincaid and Sergeant Cullen.'

'Sir – '

The man on the porch stood, as if suddenly animated, and charged towards them, his words tumbling out. 'Scotland Yard? What are you doing here? Why won't anyone tell me anything? Have you found Becca?'

The accent was posh, the attire odd. From what Kincaid could see in the light shining from the cottage, he seemed to be wearing an old anorak and, beneath that, a suit and tie. The knot on the tie was pulled loose, as if he had yanked at it, but the shirt was still buttoned at the collar.

'Mr Atterton?' Kincaid asked.

The man peered at him. 'How'd you know my name? What's happened? Why can't I go in my wife's house? I have a bloody key – ' He turned for the door and, when the constable reached for him, swung at the officer, managing to smack his arm.

'Now, sir, let's calm down, shall we?' said the constable, in that infuriatingly reasonable tone that was the police constable's first line of defence.

'No, I won't calm down. I want . . . ' He turned towards Kincaid, his expression suddenly pleading. 'I want to see my wife.'

'Mr Atterton.' Hearing himself echoing the constable, Kincaid made an effort not to sound so patronizing. Nor was this the place to give bad news. 'You say you have a key? Why don't we go inside and have a chat?'

Atterton looked suddenly unsure. 'But . . . '

The constable, a small young man who looked as if he might have had a time subduing the six-foot-plus Atterton, broke in. 'Sir, I've been told to keep this scene se—'

Kincaid gave a sharp shake of his head, then glanced at Cullen. 'Doug, if you could.'

'Right.' Doug led the officer a few yards away, speaking softly, and Kincaid took Atterton by the elbow.

'Where's that key then, Mr Atterton?' The anorak, an old Barbour that must have lost its wax, felt damp and slick beneath Kincaid's fingers. 'You've been out in the rain.'

'This morning, when I was looking for Becca. I got soaked and I just never – I never got dry.' Atterton fumbled a key from his pocket. His fingers felt icy as he handed it to Kincaid.

How long had the man been sitting here, wet and in the cold, Kincaid wondered? He turned the key easily in the lock and stepped into the cottage first. A single lamp burned in the tidy sitting room.

'You were in the cottage earlier today?' he asked Atterton, who had come in behind him. The house was cold, and smelled of soap – or perhaps perfume – and coffee. He felt the wall for a switch and two more lamps sprang into life.

'I came in this morning when Becca hadn't answered her phone or turned up for work and I thought – ' Atterton stopped, swallowing. 'I was worried.'

'And when you didn't find her, you rang the police. Did you come back again?'

'To let the search-and-rescue people in. The blonde woman and her dog went through the house. She had a constable with her. I wanted to go with them when they left, but she said I would only slow them down. So I went back to Leander to wait. But no one came, and no one told me anything. And when I came back to the cottage, that plod wouldn't let me in.' Atterton's derogatory reference to the constable was made casually, with the sort of unthinking snobbery that set Kincaid's teeth on edge.

'This morning – did you turn on the lamp?' he asked.

Atterton looked surprised. 'No. It was on when I came in. I never thought . . . '

'Would your ex-wife have left a lamp turned on deliberately during the day?'

'Becca? No, I doubt it. She's very green. Always telling me I'm a drain on the planet. She – ' Atterton's smile faded before it reached his eyes.

In the better light Kincaid could see that Freddie Atterton was a handsome man, fair-skinned, with thick brown hair worn long enough to sweep back from his brow and over the tops of his ears. Now, however, his blue eyes were shadowed, his face creased with worry and fatigue.

'Let's get you out of that anorak,' Kincaid said. When he took the jacket from Atterton, he could see that the suit beneath it was also damp. It looked like a very expensive cut and fabric, and smelled faintly of wet sheep. 'Why don't we sit down?'

But Atterton didn't sit. Instead he said, 'You don't look like a policeman, much less Scotland Yard.'

'I was on holiday with my family. Mr Atterton—'

'Who called you? Was it Peter Gaskill?'

'I don't know Peter Gaskill.'

'He's Becca's boss. Superintendent Gaskill. Why didn't he come himself? Unless – ' Atterton stared at him, his blue eyes going darker. 'You're Homicide, aren't you? That's why they sent you. She's dead.' He nodded once, as if affirming something he had already known. 'Becca's dead.'

Then he swayed, and when Kincaid guided him to a chair, he sat heavily, gracelessly.

'I'm sorry.' Kincaid pulled over an ottoman and sat, as near Atterton as he could. He thought he might have to catch him. Quietly he went on. 'The search team found her body this afternoon, below the weir.'

'Becca. But how . . . ? Was she . . . ? The shell – Becca couldn't have – ' Atterton stopped, shivering. His teeth began to chatter, but he made no move to warm himself.

Satisfied that Atterton wasn't in immediate danger of fainting, Kincaid moved to the brown leather sofa that matched the armchair. The furniture was a bit worn, and reminded him of his parents' old chesterfield.

It was a masculine room, he thought, glancing round. Unadorned, a study in whites and browns. The only splash of colour came from the spines of the books in the simple bookcases, and a few framed photographs. 'The boat was snagged just below Temple Island,' he said. 'We don't yet know what caused Rebecca's death.' He heard the click of the door as Cullen came in. 'Doug,' he called, 'do you think you could rustle up something hot to drink?'

As Cullen disappeared into the kitchen, Freddie Atterton looked up at Kincaid. 'You're sure? You're sure it was Becca? There could be some mistake.'

'One of the searchers is a rower. He recognized her. But we will need you to make a formal identification, when you feel up to it. Unless there's someone else—'

'No, no. Becca's parents are divorced and she was estranged from them both. Her mother's in South Africa, and Becca hadn't had contact with her dad for years. Oh, God, I'll have to tell her mum.'

Cullen came back from the kitchen bearing a glass and a bottle of whisky. 'I've put the kettle on, but in the meantime . . . ' As he uncorked the bottle and poured a neat finger for Atterton, Kincaid saw that it was fifteen-year-old Balvenie, and single-cask at that. Rebecca Meredith had had good taste in Scotch, it seemed, but the bottle had hardly been touched.

Atterton bumped the glass against his teeth as he took a swallow. 'It's my Scotch,' he said and started to laugh. 'Becca hated Scotch. She kept it for me. How appropriate! She'd have thought this was too bloody funny for words.'

Then his face contorted and he gave a gulp of a sob. The glass slipped from his fingers, bouncing soundlessly on the carpet, and the smell of whisky rose in the air like a wave of sorrow.

'Bastard!' said Tavie.

The German shepherd cocked her head and raised a dark enquiring eyebrow.

'Not you, Tosh.' Tavie stopped pacing the confines of her small sitting room and looked down at her dog, smiling in spite of herself. She knelt and rubbed Tosh's head. 'And not your doggy buddy, either. He was a good boy.'

Encouraged by her tone, Tosh got up from her spot before the fire and ran to her toy basket. Pushing her nose into the jumble of toys, she came up with a squeaky tennis ball and pranced back to Tavie with the ball in her mouth, looking inordinately pleased with herself.

'Okay, just the once,' said Tavie, making an effort to sound firm. She tossed the ball into the kitchen and Tosh scrambled after it. Shrill squeaks signalled a successful retrieval. But the dog seemed to sense her mistress's mood, because when she returned with the ball she went back to her place by the fire, squeaking her treasure, but not begging for another throw.

But the play session reminded Tavie that she'd had to reward Finn that afternoon, after they'd made the find, taking his ball from Kieran's pocket and

giving the Lab a good romp and much praise. The first
and foremost rule of search and rescue was that the
handler must reward the dog after a find, and show
just as much enthusiasm for a deceased find as a live
one. The dogs must feel they had done their jobs well,
no matter the outcome.

But Kieran . . . Kieran had stood, white and
speechless, as she radioed Control.

Kieran had not looked after his own dog.

And Kieran had lied. Kieran had known the
victim, and hadn't admitted it to her.

'Bastard!' she said again, but she knew it was just
as much her fault as his. She'd thought he was ready
for anything a search might bring. She'd thought, in
her self-satisfied righteousness, that by training
Kieran and bringing him into the team she'd given
him purpose, and a cure-all for whatever demons
drove him. Worst of all, she'd thought she knew him.
And that she could trust him.

But she could see, now, that he'd lied to her from
the call-out, or at least from the briefing at Leander
when he'd learned the victim's name.

Making another circuit round the room, she
glanced at the reports stacked and carefully restacked
on her small dining table. She'd debriefed the team
and written up the log. There was nothing more she
could do tonight, and she was on early rota at work
tomorrow. She should heat up the single portion of
vegetable curry she'd bought from Cook, the shop
near the police station, and have an early night.

She had every reason to stay in. It was turning
cold, and the sitting room in her higgledy-piggledy

house near the fire station was as welcoming as she could make it. She'd bought the little two-up, two-down terraced house after the divorce. It might have been a comedown from the suburban life she'd led with Beatty, but it was what she'd been able to afford, and it had given her a fresh start. Then, when she'd been assigned to the fast-response car out of Henley Fire Station, which meant she only had to walk across the street to work, she'd begun to think that the house was a charm, and that the rest of her life would fall just as neatly into place.

Looking round the cosy room, with its hand-painted furniture and crewel-worked rugs, the windows curtained in cheery red and white, the mantel and picture rail adorned with carefully placed treasures, she thought of the woman whose house she had searched that day. A woman who, like her, had dealt with trauma on a daily basis. But Rebecca Meredith seemed to have felt no need to insulate herself from the stress of her job by making her home a place of solace.

Rebecca Meredith must have found that solace – if she had found it at all – on the river. Or through something else, Tavie thought. Not food, not alcohol, if she'd been a serious rower. Sex, then?

But that thought made Tavie's face feel hot. The one thing she'd left out of her report was the dogs' response to the panties she'd chosen as a scent article. And Kieran hadn't given her a chance to talk to him about it.

It had been fully dark by the time they'd returned to their cars after looking at Rebecca Meredith's boat.

While Tavie had been speaking to the Scotland Yard detective, Kieran had cadged a ride with Scott and disappeared, leaving Tavie to ask Sarah for a lift back to her own car below Remenham. When she got there, Kieran's old Land Rover had been gone, and he hadn't appeared for the team debriefing in the Leander Club car park.

Although Tavie hadn't wanted to field questions from curious club members, or from the ex-husband, if he was still around, she'd drawn the meeting out, hoping that Kieran might turn up. While the other team members laughed and chatted, stowed gear and played with the dogs, she'd waited, until at last she stood alone in the car park, feeling idiotic.

She'd rung him then, and again when she got home. After the third try she stopped leaving messages.

'Damn him,' she said now, but her anger was becoming steadily more tinged with worry.

The house suddenly felt stuffy, rather than comforting. She took one more turn round the room, then bent and switched off the fire. Tosh sat up, the ball still in her mouth, a bit of dribble hanging from her lower lip. As soon as Tavie turned in the direction of the coat hook, the dog was on her feet, dancing in anticipation and making Tavie trip.

'Okay, okay,' Tavie told her as she reached for her jacket. 'You can come. We'll go for a little walk.'

And if that little walk just happened to take them to Mill Meadows, she'd have her chat with Kieran if she had to shout at him across the Thames.

Chapter Seven

Milo had turned up just as he'd promised, and in Kincaid's view it seemed a timely intervention. Milo moved awkwardly to clasp Freddie's hand, but Freddie seemed too shocked to respond.

'I'm sorry, Freddie. Really sorry,' Milo said. 'I still can't believe it. If only I'd – ' He caught Kincaid's glance and stopped.

'What am I going to do?' Freddie looked up, but his gaze was unfocused. Kincaid wasn't sure he had heard Milo at all.

Cullen had brought a tea towel to mop up the spilled whisky, and then mugs of tea, but he'd been very careful to set Freddie's cup on the side table rather than handing it to him. The smell of the spilled whisky still lingered, but Milo didn't comment on it.

'I'll do anything I can to help, Freddie,' Milo went on. 'You know that. So will everyone at the club. What sort of arrangements will you be making?'

'I – oh, God, I hadn't thought.' Freddie looked ill. 'Becca hated funerals. She said once, after a particularly awful one, that she wanted to be cremated with as little fuss as possible. But,' he stopped and looked at Kincaid, 'you'll be needing to keep her' – his face twisted – 'body.'

'There will be an inquest in a few days,' Kincaid said. 'You'll have to wait to make any funeral arrangements until after the coroner's ruling. It's rout—'

Milo broke in. 'But, surely, there's no question about what happened. Becca's death was an accident.'

Instead of answering, Kincaid turned to Freddie. 'Do you know anyone who might have wanted to harm your ex-wife, Mr Atterton?'

'Hurt Becca?' Freddie stared at him. 'Why would anyone want to hurt her? She may have been hard to get on with sometimes, but to think someone would deliberately . . . That's daft.'

Kincaid glanced round the cottage. The decor might be spare, but it was expensive, and the cottage itself must be worth a pretty penny. 'Let's look at it another way, Mr Atterton. Who stands to gain from your wife's death?'

Freddie Atterton appeared utterly baffled. 'Gain?'

'Did she have a will?'

'When we were married, yes. I've no idea if she changed it.'

'And if she didn't?'

'Then – ' Freddie pushed his hair back with a shaking hand. 'Then I suppose everything comes to me.'

Tavie walked down the steps from her front door into West Street. Tosh, looking most undignified for a German shepherd, bunny-hopped down the stairs beside her. The fire-training tower across the street loomed in the darkness, a hulking shape, but she and Tosh had both climbed it many times in SAR training and it held no fears for either of them.

The dampness that had risen from the river at dusk had dissipated, leaving the air chilly and crisp. She could see stars overhead, and somewhere a fire was burning.

Tavie loved autumn, and as she walked down into Market Place, Tosh trotting easily at her knee, she realized how much she loved this simple thing. When they were working, she and the German shepherd were connected, but they were joined by an invisible line of tension, as if Tosh were the head of an arrow and Tavie the stabilizing end of the shaft.

But when they walked for pleasure, as they did now, swinging along side by side, there was a synchronicity between them quite unlike anything Tavie had ever experienced. She felt herself begin to relax as she took her rhythm from the dog, and her mood began to lift.

Leaving the market square, they crossed Duke Street, and she thought perhaps they would only go as far as the river, after all. Maybe she had overreacted about Kieran, and she should wait and talk to him tomorrow.

Then, up ahead, she saw the dog, tethered to a potted tree outside Magoos, the bar where everyone in Henley seemed eventually to meet and mingle. A black Lab. A black Lab that turned from his vigilant watch over the bar's doorway and began to wag happily when he saw them. Finn.

Tosh strained at her lead and Tavie checked her, the ease of a moment before shattered.

'Hello, boy. What are you doing here?' she said as she reached Finn. Kneeling, she let him give her a slobbery Labrador kiss while she rubbed his ears. What the hell was Kieran thinking, leaving him outside a bar? Tethering a trained dog outside a shop for a moment or two was one thing, but this . . . Finn was a valuable dog. Anyone could have walked off with him.

Anyone could have done what she was doing right now, she thought as she unlooped Kieran's tidy knot. When she'd freed the dog, she tried to peer in the windows of the bar, but the half-shutters blocked her view.

And what the hell was Kieran doing in Magoos, she asked herself? She'd never seen him drink more than a pint, and that was when he'd been more or less coerced by the team. She'd certainly never seen him in a bar on his own.

His lead untied, Finn jerked her into motion, pulling towards the door of the bar and whining. Tavie hesitated a moment, then tightened her hold on both dogs and charged in through the door. Tuesday nights were fairly quiet – no live music, no pub quiz, no DJ – but there was still a good crowd in the long, narrow bar.

Heads turned, and the noise level dropped a fraction. Mike, the bartender, looked up from the glass he was wiping. 'Tavie.' His quick smile faded. 'Hey, you can't bring the dogs . . . ' But Tavie was already shaking her head.

'I'm not staying.' She'd seen Kieran, alone at a

table against the wall. Before him sat an almost empty glass and a large bottle of Strongbow cider. Finn had seen him, too, and strained at his lead, giving a little yelp of excitement.

Tavie stopped, reining in the dogs before she reached the table. 'Kieran.'

He looked up, his long face made suddenly younger by his expression of surprise. But the surprise turned quickly to dismay, then fear. As he started to rise, he bumped the table, sloshing the cider in the glass. 'What . . . ? Tavie, what are you doing with Finn? Is he all—'

'Outside. Now.' Tavie turned and started back towards the door, Tosh at her knee. Finn whimpered in frustration and pulled the other way. But Tavie was strong for her size, and had handled big dogs since her childhood in Yorkshire, where her parents had raised German shepherds and rough-coated collies. Finn came with her.

The buffet of chilly air as she stepped outside did nothing to calm her. She spun to face Kieran as he stumbled out a moment later, but she didn't release his dog. 'You,' she spat at him. 'You don't deserve this dog. Leaving him in the street. What the hell were you doing, Kieran?'

'I – I was only going to be five minutes. I didn't think it would hurt.'

'Like you didn't think it would hurt when you lied to me about knowing that woman today?'

Her anger seemed to sober him. 'Tavie, please.' He reached out, slowly, for Finn's lead, and this time she released it. 'I'm sorry,' he said. 'I didn't tell you because I knew you'd stand me down. And I had to know. I had to know if she was all right . . . if I could—'

'You compromised my search.' Tavie realized that passers-by were giving them a wide berth and made an effort to lower her voice. 'And my chain of evidence,' she hissed at him. 'Those panties: it was you the dogs were alerting on. You . . . you were – ' She couldn't go on. If it was Kieran's scent the dogs had picked up on the victim's underclothes, it could only be because he had touched them, and why would he have done that unless he had slept with her? Her mind skittered away from the picture. She felt sick.

Why had she imagined that he led a celibate life, living alone in his shed, working on his boats, healing, waiting for – waiting for *her*. And all the while, he had been . . .

She had been a fool.

'Don't report for call-out, Kieran,' she said, and even though she knew she'd said enough, she couldn't stop herself from going on. 'You've done enough damage as it is. I'll have to think what to do about my report.'

'It doesn't matter.' He shook his head, his shoulders slumping. 'Nothing matters. I can't keep anyone safe.'

They had ushered Freddie and Milo out of Rebecca Meredith's cottage, leaving the constable on duty until a forensics team could go over the house in the morning.

Once back in Henley, Kincaid had dropped Cullen

– who had come straight from Putney without so much as a toothbrush – at the Boots on Bell Street, while he hunted for the designated hotel parking and then retrieved his overnight bag from the Astra. He'd driven by the hotel while searching for the parking area, so found his way back easily enough on foot to the rambling old inn between the river and the church.

The Red Lion Hotel stood just opposite the Leander Club on the town side of the Thames. The two buildings made Kincaid think of sentinels on either side of Henley Bridge, but of the two, the red-brick, wisteria-covered hotel had the best claim to historical authenticity. Gazing up at it, however, Kincaid thought he preferred the Leander pink hippo to the garish red lion displayed over the hotel's portico.

He'd been tempted to go home – it was less than an hour's drive once the traffic had settled. But when he'd rung Gemma from the car, she'd told him that Melody was there, that they were having a girls' night and that she could manage perfectly well without him. 'I've coped with three children on my own since I've been off work,' she'd said, with a little asperity. 'I think I can handle them one more night. You do what you must to get this business wrapped up.'

Gemma was right, of course. The earlier he got on with things the next morning, the sooner he could get back to London.

He'd need to get in touch with Becca Meredith's solicitor first thing, and he wanted to have another word with Freddie Atterton, and with the staff and crew at Leander. Perhaps by that time he'd have heard something from the forensics crews at the boat and the cottage, and from Rashid.

At the thought of the morning's interviews, he glanced down at his bag. He had clean jeans, a wool sweater and a pair of shoes to replace his mud-stained trainers, but this was not exactly professional attire, especially if he had to deal with the press. Doug at least had been wearing a suit.

Then he realized that he *did* have a suit – he'd got married in it on Saturday. Again.

Cullen, arriving just then with a bulging Boots carrier bag in his hand, said, 'What's so funny?'

Kincaid grinned. 'Nothing.' He gazed up at the hotel. 'I was just thinking that the wisteria would be glorious in the spring. It must be ancient.'

Cullen looked at him quizzically. 'I don't know about that. I'm not very good with plants. But the inn dates back to the sixteenth century and the first-recorded guest of note was Charles I.'

'Not an auspicious omen,' Kincaid said. 'Let's hope we don't end up with our heads on the block. And that the food and the beds have improved over the last five hundred or so years. I'm starving.' It was after seven, and food was beginning to seem a distant memory.

'I always wanted to stay here.' Cullen looked round with obvious delight as they entered the building.

There was a small, cosy bar on the right, and on the left a more formal restaurant, with starched white tablecloths and linen. Ahead, tasteful antique furniture and wooden floors gleamed in the lamplight reception area. Near the desk stood an imposingly hooded cane chair, and Kincaid immediately thought it would make a perfect hiding nook for a child.

'I used to beg my parents to come and stay here whenever I had a race in Henley when I was at school,' Cullen continued, 'but they never did.'

Kincaid looked at his partner in surprise. 'They never came to watch you row?'

'Not that I can remember,' answered Doug, but his tone was a bit too casual, and Kincaid suspected he'd trodden on sensitive territory. 'My dad was busy, and I was never likely to win,' Doug added, shrugging. 'And what I really wanted was to be allowed to have a drink in the bar, and pigs were more likely to fly.'

'Well, the drink in the bar can be remedied, at least,' Kincaid said, dropping his voice as the young woman at the desk looked up and smiled at them in welcome. 'I'm not sure we can do anything about the flying pigs.'

When they had settled into their respective rooms – both with four-posters – they eschewed the formal dining room and met in the aptly named Snug Bar for drinks and dinner. This, tucked behind the small bar they had seen by the entrance, had dark wood-panelled walls and dark leather furniture, relieved by softly lit bookcases and oil portraits of bewigged men. A fire burned cheerily in the grate.

'An Englishman's dream,' Kincaid murmured as they chose a low table near the fire. He realized that the dining room at Leander, with its cane-backed fur-niture, had given him the same teasing impression as this place. There was a hint of the colonial, the cane furniture a reminder of the last vestiges of Empire. And there was a very definite sense that generations of entitlement had stamped their imprint on this rich market town on the Thames. The atmosphere would raise his liberal father's hackles.

But Kincaid was not about to turn up his nose at the steak-and-mushroom pie, an Englishman's dream of a dinner, or at the bottle of Benvulin Single Malt that he'd spied behind the bar.

When they'd ordered and brought back their drinks, he raised his glass to Doug. 'Cheers, mate. To long-delayed pleasures. And to the trials and tribulations of home ownership.'

Looking pleased, Cullen raised his glass, sipped and promptly turned pink. 'Nice whisky,' he said, wiping his watering eyes. 'Bit stout.'

'Sip,' Kincaid suggested. 'But first add the tiniest bit of water. Remember your whisky-tasting lessons.'

He took another sip himself, closing his eyes and savouring the heathery-honey-buttery layers of the Scotch. Was the trip to Scotland that had introduced him to Benvulin really the last time he and Gemma had been away together without the children? And on that trip they'd been involved in a very distressing case, not on holiday.

This definitely needed to be remedied. Having married Gemma three times, he thought that he should at least be able to give her a honeymoon. Maybe he'd bring her back to the Red Lion, once she was settled into her new job and they could make arrangements for the children.

Their food arrived, and both he and Doug tucked in with the silent single-mindedness of the truly ravenous. When the last bites had been scraped off the plates, Kincaid finished the coffee he'd ordered to chase the whiskies and signed the bill to his room.

'You go enjoy your four-poster,' he told Doug. 'Dream of Charles I, but before you do that, see what you can find out about Freddie Atterton for me.' He knew Cullen had come straight to Henley without his laptop, but had confidence in his partner's resourcefulness and his research skills.

He, on the other hand, was regretting a bit too much food as well as the second Scotch he'd had during dinner. Now he felt that what he needed was a walk, and some fresh air.

After parting company with Doug in the lobby, he left the hotel, hesitating for a moment as he took his bearings from what he remembered of his previous visits to Henley. Unlike Doug, whose recollections of the town seemed a schoolboy's idyll, his were uncomfortable, pricked with flashes of things better not done, and roads not taken.

He thought of the woman they had found in the river, and of the neon-yellow jacket that had not kept her safe. Had she liked her life here?

Death had erased all character from Rebecca Meredith's face. He could only form an impression from the glimpses of her that he'd seen in the few photos on the shelves in her cottage – and from the emotion he'd seen on the faces of those who had known her.

What had happened to her last night on the river, this strong and competent woman?

Crossing the street, he walked to the middle of the bridge and gazed downstream. The Thames looked dark, fathomless, and he couldn't imagine going out alone, in the dusk, in a fragile slip of a boat.

On the far side of the bridge, a light blinked off in Leander. What were they feeling at the club, he wondered, with the loss of one of their own? How would they react to this evidence of their own mortality?

Tomorrow, he would talk to them – friends, crewmates, coaches. And he would need to speak to Becca's boss and her colleagues at the Met.

For a moment, he paled at the prospect. He felt stained by others' grief, as if it had steeped into his skin like old tea. He had never, in his more than twenty years of police work, become inured to watching people absorb the shock of death.

He'd hated it as a uniformed plod, as Freddie Atterton had so unflatteringly described the constable. He hated it, perhaps even more, now.

But then his curiosity took hold, as it always did. He wanted to know who this woman had been, who had liked her, loved her, hated her. He wanted to know how she had died. And if someone was responsible for her death, he wanted to see justice done. This was what kept him in the job.

Walking back to the signal, he stood, watching the green crossing light blink. The Angel on the Bridge beckoned on the upstream side of the bridge, but he wasn't tempted by the pub. It was the walk up Thames Side that threatened to seduce him.

Was the gallery still there? Might one of Julia Swann's paintings be displayed in the window? And her flat, a bit further down, where he had once spent a night: did she still live there?

But no. He shook his head. It was better not to know. He was a married – make that much-married – man now, and the past was best left in the past, without regrets.

And it was time to call his boss.

He was turning back towards the hotel when something caught his eye – a glimpse of a man walking down Hart Street and turning the corner by the pub. Then the Angel blocked the figure from view, but the image had registered.

A tall man, his gait a bit unsteady, a black dog at his side. Even in jeans and jacket rather than the dark uniform, he was instantly recognizable as the SAR handler who'd insisted on going with them to the boat. Kieran. Kieran Connolly.

His behaviour had been a bit odd that afternoon, Kincaid thought, and added another interview with Connolly to his mental to-do list.

Shrugging, he returned to the hotel, but he still didn't feel quite ready to go up to his room. He sat on the iron bench under the hotel's portico and rang his Chief Superintendent at home, giving Childs a report on the events of the day.

When he'd related his interview with Atterton, Childs was silent for a moment, as was his usual way. Then he said, 'It would certainly be convenient if it turned out to be the ex-husband.'

'Convenient?'

'Well, you know. Domestic tragedy. Nothing to do with us. Quickly wrapped up.'

Kincaid had to admit he was intrigued by the relationship between Atterton and his ex-wife. It seemed an oddly amicable divorce, and he'd sensed that Freddie Atterton's grief was real, as was Milo Jachym's.

Not that he hadn't known murderers who grieved for their victims, and murderers who could project emotion as convincingly as the most skilled actor. Things were always so much more complicated than they appeared on the surface.

But here . . . there was something else at play, some undercurrent running through this case that he couldn't pinpoint. He would just have to wait and see what developed.

In the meantime, Childs's offhand comment made him feel profoundly uneasy. 'Sir, why would we think it had something to do with us?'

'Duncan, you know as well as I do what happens whenever a police officer of any rank dies under suspicious circumstances.' Childs's tone was unusually impatient. 'You can expect our fevered friends from the media on your doorstep by tomorrow morning. DCI Meredith's life, and her career, will be put under the microscope.' Childs paused, and Kincaid could imagine him steepling his fingers in his familiar Buddha pose. 'Of course,' Childs went on, 'the best result would be that you find Meredith's death an unfortunate accident. Ring me in the morning.' With that, Chief Superintendent Childs hung up.

And without, Kincaid realized, answering his question.

He sat on, under the portico, gazing at the phone in his hand, replaying the conversation in his head. Surely he had misinterpreted what he'd heard. Because he could have sworn that his guv'nor had just suggested that he fix the outcome of an investigation.

Chapter Eight

The persistently ringing phone pricked at Freddie's consciousness. He wanted to swat the sound away, but his brain didn't seem willing to connect with his body. It was only when the noise stopped that he managed to open one eye. He was lying on his back, but what he saw was not his bedroom ceiling.

He squinched his eye shut again, while he tried to place the image. Arched ceiling. White. Black beams. Recognition dawned. His sitting room.

With mounting panic, he opened both eyes and lifted his head. Pain shot through his skull, but before he closed his eyes again, he'd seen that he was lying on his sofa, and that he was still wearing his shirt and trousers, although not his shoes or – he felt his collar – his tie. His phone lay on the coffee table, beside an empty bottle of Balvenie Scotch. There were two glasses. A recollection flickered. Milo. He'd had a few drinks with Milo. But what . . . ?

The phone started to ring again, as if his thoughts had triggered it, and he groaned. 'Just shut it,' he tried to say, but his voice came out in a croak. He grabbed for the phone and the motion brought on a wave of nausea and, with it, memory.

Becca. Oh, God. The pieces clicked together in his fuzzy brain. Milo had brought him home and poured him Scotch after Scotch. They'd stopped at the off-licence on the way back from the cottage, after the Scotland Yard man had told him he couldn't take Becca's bottle of Balvenie. Because it wasn't his. Because it might be evidence. Because Becca was dead.

Freddie lurched to his feet and staggered to the bathroom. He fell to his knees, his forehead resting on the cool seat of the toilet, and vomited until there was nothing left to come up.

When the heaving finally stopped, he lifted his head and sat with his back against the wall, cataloguing what he saw, as if that could block out knowledge. Grey-stained plank floor. Grey walls. Glass shower. White porcelain sink. The free-standing bath, its body wrapped in black riveted metal. And above it all, glimpsed when he painfully raised his eyes, the crystal chandelier.

When he'd bought this flat after the divorce, he'd hired an interior designer from London, hoping, he supposed, that Becca would somehow be impressed with his new lifestyle.

When she'd come to see the flat she'd gazed at the chandelier, then given him the *look*. The look that meant she thought he had utterly lost the plot.

'It's supposed to be eclectic,' he'd said, defending himself.

'Was she pretty?' Becca had replied.

When Freddie's phone started to ring again, he realized he'd left it in the sitting room. He suddenly wondered if it might be someone calling to tell him it was all a mistake, that the body they'd found wasn't Becca after all. Who was this guy who had identified her, anyway? This rower.

He pulled himself up and stumbled back into the sitting room, his heart racing, but by the time he got there the ringing had stopped. He looked at the long list of missed calls – all unfamiliar numbers – and then saw that there was one message. His pulse skipped. What if . . . ?

But when he played it back, a female voice identified herself as a reporter from the *London Chronicle* and wondered if he would be willing to give them a quote about his ex-wife.

Freddie sank onto the sofa, his phone dangling in his hand.

It was true, then. It had to be true. And he realized what he was going to have to do that day.

The phone rang once more, the vibration running through his fingers like a shock. He dropped the phone, made a scoop at it and fumbled it up again. If it was that reporter, he was going to tell her to sod off.

But the name on the caller ID was familiar, and Freddie nearly sobbed with relief as he answered. 'Ross?'

'Oh, shit, mate,' said Ross Abbott. 'Chris heard at work. She wanted me to tell you – I wanted to tell you – we're so sorry. Is there anything I can do?'

Freddie looked at the two dark-blue Oxford oars mounted on the wall in the sitting room. They had rowed together twice, he and Ross Abbott, and they'd been friends since they were spotty boys in the same public school. He clutched at the lifeline of the familiar.

'Ross, I have to . . . I have to go to the morgue today. To identify her. Will you go with me?'

Kincaid had not slept well, in spite of the luxury of his canopy bed. He realized it had been months since he'd spent the night away from Gemma, and he missed the quiet rhythm of her breathing, her warmth as her body touched his in the night. Not that they'd spent many nights in the last two months without Charlotte crawling in between them in the wee hours of the morning, but he found he missed that, too.

Lately Charlotte had taken to snuggling with her back against Gemma and her head on his shoulder, her curly hair tickling his nose. When she drifted off to sleep again, whoever was most awake would pick her up and tuck her back into her own bed, but he always did it with a bit of reluctance. He'd missed that stage with Kit. And Toby, so busy when awake, had always slept as if someone had flipped his 'Off' switch.

When light began to filter through the crack in the heavy bedroom curtains, he got up, showered and dressed in his wedding finery. Not for the first time he was glad he'd worn an ordinary suit for Winnie's blessing, rather than morning get-up. He'd look a right prat trying to conduct an investigation in that.

Eager to get to the incident room at the police station, he rang Cullen and crushed his partner's hopes of the full-monty breakfast in the hotel dining room. 'There's a nice cafe – Maison Blanc, I think – on the way to the station,' Kincaid said. 'We can pick up coffee and pastries, and you can fill me in on your research as we walk.'

A few minutes later they met in the hotel reception area. Stepping outside, they were greeted with watery sunshine and air that felt almost balmy. Kincaid looked up at the clouds creeping across the sky and frowned. 'I don't trust this weather. But, for the time being, it will make things easier for the forensics team at the boat.' He started up Market Place at a good clip. 'So, what did you find on Mr Atterton?' he asked.

Cullen pushed his glasses up on his nose, then clasped his hands behind his back as he walked, settling into lecturing mode. 'Frederick Thomas Atterton, after his father, Thomas, a well-respected banker in the City. Grew up in Sonning-on-Thames, a village just east of Reading. Real Kenneth Grahame country, according to Melody.'

'Melody?'

'There was only so much I could do with just a phone.' Cullen shrugged, a little apologetically. 'Had to enlist some help. Anyway, Atterton went to Bedford School, where he began to show a talent for rowing, then Oriel College, Oxford, where he took an undistinguished degree in biology. He seems to have done better at rowing, however, as he twice made the Blue Boat, bowside, although neither crew won.

'He met Rebecca Meredith at Oxford,' Cullen continued. 'She distinguished herself rowing for her college, St Catherine's, then for the university. She studied criminal justice.'

'She kept her maiden name, then,' Kincaid said. They'd reached Maison Blanc, and as they entered the cafe they were buffeted by the aromas of fresh coffee and baking bread. After perusing the muffins and pastries, they ordered at the counter. Kincaid chose cappuccino and an almond croissant, his usual fare on the mornings when he took the Tube from Holland Park and hadn't time for breakfast at home.

Had he gravitated towards the cafe here because he was homesick, he wondered?

'That's just thoroughly wet,' he said aloud, and both Cullen and the cashier looked at him in surprise. 'Don't take any notice of me,' he told the cashier, giving her his best smile along with the correct change and an extra pound for the tip jar.

'Have a great day,' the girl replied, beaming at him.

'And that's just criminal,' Cullen muttered as they carried their breakfast back into the street.

'You're just jealous.' Kincaid grinned. 'Go on, then. Where were we? Maiden name?'

Doug took a sip of his coffee, winced. 'Oh, right. They married not long after uni, but she was showing serious potential as a rower by then, and I suppose she wanted her name to be recognized. Not that it did her much good, in the end.'

As they turned along Duke Street, Kincaid asked, 'What happened?'

'The year after uni she was the top prospect for British women's single sculls at the next summer's Olympics. But over the Christmas break, against strict orders from her coach, she went on a skiing holiday.

She took a fall and fractured her wrist so badly it took her out of training for months. She was dropped from the squad.'

'And her coach – '

'Was Milo Jachym.' Doug finished his muffin and scoured the bag for crumbs.

Kincaid thought about this as he finished his own pastry and sipped gingerly at his coffee. 'So you might say her relationship with Jachym was conflicted.'

'A bit, yes.'

'And you might think he'd resent her trying to make a comeback when he's got his own women's team that he's grooming for the Olympics now.'

'You might,' Doug agreed.

Having reached their turning for the police station, they paused in natural accord.

'When did she marry Atterton?' Kincaid asked.

'The next year. The same time as she started with the Met.'

'And the divorce?'

'Three years ago. She filed, but there are no details, as he didn't contest. According to the court record, he was quite generous – he not only gave her the cottage, but half his assets. I'd assume he offered the settlement before he realized how badly property investments would be hit.'

'Ah.' Kincaid gazed at the unassuming police station down the street, which faced a kebab house and a taxi service, and was glad not to see lurking reporters. Yet.

He thought about Freddie Atterton. 'That sounds to me like a man who felt guilty. And possibly now regrets his largesse. Is he in financial trouble?'

'Barely keeping his head above water, according to some sources I rang in the City.'

'Then I'd say Rebecca Meredith's solicitor is the first order of the day, as soon as we see what progress the forensics teams have made.' They'd got the solicitor's name and number from Freddie before they left the cottage the previous night.

Cullen looked smug. 'I rang her first thing this morning. She goes into work early. A very obliging lady. She said that unless Rebecca made a new will, everything goes to Freddie, and he's also the executor.'

Kincaid raised an eyebrow. As much as he missed having Gemma on an investigation, he couldn't fault Doug Cullen for efficiency. 'Convenient.'

'Sweet, yes.' Cullen crumpled his muffin bag. 'She also said she believed there were life-insurance policies, and she gave me the name of Becca's insurance broker. I've left a message.'

'Small world, this town,' Kincaid said, but he was thinking that Chief Superintendent Childs would be pleased. It looked as though Freddie Atterton had had plenty of motive for killing his ex-wife.

They found Detective Inspector Singla and two detective constables in the small room assigned for their use at Henley Police Station. Singla had set up a whiteboard for notes and a corkboard for the crime-scene photos, and a conference table had begun accumulating the inevitable piles of paper.

Singla already looked harried, his suit more rumpled than the day before, and the constables – one female, one male – looked anxious, as if they'd been on the receiving end of Singla's ire. The male constable was taking phone calls and, from what Kincaid overheard, it sounded as if he was fielding the press.

'Superintendent,' Singla said, his tone slightly disapproving, as if they were late for class. 'We've a preliminary report from the forensics team at the boat. They've found a streak of pink paint on the underside of the hull. It looks like transfer from the blade of a Leander oar, but there doesn't seem to be any damage to the oar remaining with the boat. There's also some crazing in the hull's fibreglass, which appears to radiate from the paint streak. Possibly point of impact.'

Kincaid glanced at Cullen. 'Could she have done that herself?'

'I can't see how,' Cullen answered, frowning. 'Although, if she tipped, and her blade came loose . . . ' Walking over to the corkboard, he studied the photos, as if the body snagged below the weir might tell him something. 'I suppose if the current was sweeping her away, she could have used the blade to try to capture the shell . . . The first thing rowers are taught is never to leave the boat. A rowing shell floats, unless it's really badly damaged.'

'Any sign of the missing oar?' Kincaid asked.

Singla ran his hand across his scalp, separating the thinning strands of his hair. 'Not yet. It could be anywhere. Forensics is working on a paint match from the remaining oar.'

'Anything else? Any evidence of a struggle along the bank?'

'No.' Singla looked pained, as if he took the failure personally.

Turning to Cullen, Kincaid asked, 'How hard a blow would it take to shatter a fibreglass hull?'

'These days most hulls are reinforced with Kevlar. But still, they're fragile, and brittle, and they do get damaged often enough. I rowed into a bridge abutment once at school. It was an old training shell, but the coach was not happy.'

Kincaid couldn't stifle a grin. 'You rowed into a bridge?'

'You *are* going backwards, in case you hadn't noticed,' Cullen said, sounding offended. 'Some rowers develop a really annoying habit of constantly looking over their shoulder. Slows them down. Others just aim the boat and hope for the best.'

'I take it you belonged to the second group.'

Cullen ignored this quip. 'If you know the course well, which Becca Meredith would have done, you learn to navigate by landmarks.'

'What about the cottage?' Kincaid asked Singla. 'Anything there?'

'Nothing that seems out of the ordinary. I've sent her laptop computer to Forensics. The calls on her home phone seem to correlate with the ex-husband's account. He left a message at approximately the time Milo Jachym saw her take the boat out, as well as several messages later in the evening and the following morning.'

'He could have rung from anywhere,' Kincaid said thoughtfully. 'He could have been checking to see if she'd taken the boat out. What about her mobile? Was it in the house?'

'In her handbag.' Singla nodded towards a polythene bag among the papers on the table. 'I had the duty constable bring her personal effects. But we don't know her voicemail password.'

'Maybe Mr Atterton will be able to enlighten us. But meanwhile . . . ' Kincaid pulled a chair out from the table, sat, opened the bag and took out the phone. It was a sophisticated model, one he'd expect a senior officer to carry. But when he touched the screen, the wallpaper that appeared was a service provider's stock picture.

Intrigued, he checked the phone's photo files and found nothing. 'Odd. She had no pictures stored on her phone.' He tried another application. 'Nor did she use her calendar.'

Quickly he scrolled through her emails and text messages, but they all seemed to be work-related, except for a text message from Freddie Atterton sent at approximately the time she'd gone out in the boat, saying: RING ME!!!! I TALKED TO MILO. The phone also showed two voicemails, but he couldn't retrieve them. There was no visual voicemail.

He checked her contact list – short, which by now didn't surprise him. Going through it would be a job for Doug, but at the moment he was pleased to see that she'd listed her own mobile number. He took out his phone and called it.

The ringtone, like the wallpaper, was standard, a double tone.

He was beginning to form a very curious picture

of Rebecca Meredith. 'She didn't by any chance have another phone?' he asked Singla.

'Not that we found, no.'

Kincaid rifled through the rest of the contents in the bag. 'A pen,' he said, cataloguing the contents aloud. 'Black, fairly expensive, rollerball. No artistic, leaky fountain pens here. A wallet, black leather. And in that we have a driving licence, forty pounds in notes and some change, a debit card, a credit card, a Selfridge's store card.' Going back to the licence, he studied the picture. Although her face was long, Rebecca Meredith's features were good, and in other circumstances she might have been pretty. But in this photo she stared sternly into the camera, as if someone had dared her to smile and she was determined to win the bet.

Closing the wallet, he went on to the next thing. 'Oyster card, standard-issue folder. A packet of tissues.' He unzipped a small make-up kit and dumped out the contents. 'Compact. Lipstick. Lip balm. Tin of aspirin. A packet of tampons.' Moving those items to one side, he shook out the polythene bag, then glanced at Doug. 'And that's it. No crumpled gum or sweet wrappers. No scribbled phone numbers. No pizza-chain loyalty cards. No cologne samples carried for a quick touch-up before a date.'

'Nothing not practical or essential,' agreed Doug. 'And absolutely nothing personal.'

'Sir,' said Singla, 'I really don't see the importance of what this woman did or didn't carry in her handbag. Surely—'

'Think about it for a moment,' Kincaid interrupted. 'Are you married, DI Singla?'

'Well, yes, but . . . '

'Do you know what your wife keeps in her handbag?' Kincaid thought of Gemma, who now carried a tote bag the size of a small suitcase, filled with Charlotte's favourite books and biscuits and, invariably, Bob, the green stuffed elephant that Charlotte refused to leave home without. He wondered how *he* was going to lug all that kit around and still look remotely manly.

Singla shook his head, looking horrified. 'The kitchen sink, if she could fit it in.' He closed his eyes, thinking. 'The kids' school reports, old shopping lists, grocery receipts, sample packets of biscuits. Even teabags, just in case a cafe doesn't have the kind she likes. An umbrella, because you never know when it might rain. And always a book – she's a great reader, my wife. She likes the sort with the book-club questions in the back.'

Nodding, Kincaid asked, 'What sort of biscuits?'

'HobNobs.'

'What colour is her umbrella?'

Singla considered. He'd lost his impatient expression. 'Pink with yellow polka dots. She says if it rains you should carry something cheerful to compensate.'

'What type of tea?'

'Chai. And she always asks for hot milk in a cafe. It's embarrassing to me, but no one else seems to mind.'

'You see?' Kincaid smiled. 'I now know a good bit about your wife.' He didn't add that he liked Singla the better for it. 'I'd wager she's intelligent, perhaps slightly plump and of a cheerful and optimistic disposition. A woman who knows what she likes and usually gets it.'

Singla rolled his eyes. 'You can say that again. And that is a fair description. But what does my wife, or my wife's handbag, have to do with Rebecca Meredith?'

The young female constable, who'd been listening intently, spoke up. 'It's not your wife's handbag that's important, sir. It's Rebecca Meredith's. And I'd say it tells us that she was a woman with something to hide.'

Chapter Nine

The detective constable was tall, with a lanky, coltish grace. She had shoulder-length shiny brown hair and brown eyes, and it occurred to Kincaid that Rebecca Meredith might have had a similar look, ten years ago.

'What's your name?' he asked.

'Imogen, sir. DC Imogen Bell.'

'Are you by any chance a rower?'

'No, sir. But I've gone out with a few. Conceited gits, for the most part. Think just because they can move a boat, they're God's gift to – ' She caught Singla's eye and stopped. 'Um, sorry, sir.'

'No, that's all right. I'm always interested in the inside scoop,' Kincaid said, and saw a flash of a smile before she schooled her face into an expression her guv'nor would approve of.

'Did you know DCI Meredith, Detective Bell?'

'I knew who she was, sir. But not to speak to. I'd passed her in the street a few times. We . . . well, I suppose I looked up to her, as a role model. She seemed as if she'd stand up for herself, you know?' She cast another wary glance at Singla, whom Kincaid suspected wasn't overly fond of uppity professional women who stood up for themselves, but Singla had taken a phone call.

Bell's colleague, a rather podgy young man in an unfortunately snug suit, gave a slight shake of his head and looked away, as if consigning her to her fate.

Kincaid, however, was not concerned with DI Singla's notions of propriety. If these officers were his potential team, he wanted to get a feel for their personalities and for the dynamics between them. 'Do you know Freddie Atterton, her ex-husband?' he asked.

'Again, not to speak to,' answered Bell. 'But he has, um, a certain reputation.'

'And what would that be?'

'A bit of a ladies' man, sir. And he likes to go out to the clubs and bars – you know, the nicer places, like Hotel du Vin and Loch Fyne – although I don't think he's really known as a heavy drinker.'

'You're very well informed.'

Kincaid's remark earned a smirk from the podgy constable. 'That's because she knows all the bartenders,' said the young man. 'And she forgot to mention the strip club.'

Imogen Bell shot him a look of dislike. 'It's a small town. And bartenders make good sources. They always know what's going on, and they usually have a pretty good idea if people are up to something they shouldn't be.'

Kincaid was liking Imogen Bell better and better.

'Henley has a strip club?' asked Cullen, sounding as if that idea was in the flying pigs category.

'It's on the car park.' Bell shrugged dismissively.

'And it's not nearly as bad as it sounds. It's basically a nice nightclub with a few girls who do lap dances. It's where everyone in Henley goes when the pubs close.'

'It's also next door to the senior centre,' said her colleague, 'and has caused no end of upset with the town council.'

Kincaid studied him. 'I'm sorry. I didn't catch your name.'

'It's Bean. Laurence Bean. Sir.'

'Bean and Bell?' He couldn't help grinning, although he knew it wouldn't endear him to DC Bean. 'Or Bell and Bean? Sounds like a music-hall act.'

Bell smiled back. 'I'm the song. He's the dance.'

'Sod off, Bell,' began Bean, but his repartee was interrupted by DI Singla, off the phone and looking thunderous.

'We have an inquiry on, in case you hadn't noticed. And at the moment it seems to be going nowhere. The house-to-house team checking Leander to Remenham has found nothing. Nor has the team I've had querying the narrowboats moored on the Bucks bank between Henley and Greenlands.'

'Not an unexpected result,' Kincaid said. 'But – ' His phone vibrated. When a quick glance at the screen showed the caller as Rashid Kaleem, he excused himself and took the call. 'Rashid? What have you got?'

'Nothing one hundred per cent definitive,' said Kaleem, in the precise Oxbridge accent that always seemed at odds with his rather rakish appearance. The accent, Kincaid thought, was a small but understandable vanity for a man who had grown up on a Bangladeshi council estate in Bethnal Green. 'But,' Kaleem continued, 'I don't like it. Some of the head injuries appear to have been inflicted ante mortem. She was definitely alive when she went into the drink – her lungs were filled with water. And river water, before you ask. No one drowned her in the bath.'

'So, no sudden-death syndrome while rowing?' Kincaid asked, with a look at Cullen.

'No. And most athletes who die from sudden cardiac failure turn out to have an undiagnosed genetic defect. Rebecca Meredith was as fit as anyone I've ever seen.'

Kincaid knew Kaleem well enough to be certain there was more. 'Both the drowning and the head injuries could have been the result of an accidental capsize. What's the catch?'

'Scrapes of pink paint under her fingernails. Her nails were short and very well cared for, so I'd say it's unlikely she was doing a bit of DIY and forgot to scrub up. And there was a bit of bruising on her knuckles, with what might possibly be some flakes of the same paint embedded in the skin. I take it the boat was not a lurid sort of bright peachy-pink, by the way. I've sent samples to the lab to see if they can match it.'

'I think I can guess,' Kincaid said. 'You've just given a very good description of Leander pink.'

Kincaid clicked off and outlined Kaleem's conclusions for the rest of the team. Turning to Cullen he said, 'Doug, you're a rower. She had pink paint under her nails and bruising on her knuckles. Give me a scenario.'

Cullen looked a little pale. 'Well, I suppose someone could have tipped her. If her blade had come loose . . . or if someone took it out of the oarlock, it wouldn't have been that difficult, especially if she was taken by surprise. Then, when she tried to right the boat, they could have held it down with the oar.'

'And when she reached up,' Kincaid continued, 'trying to right herself, she scrabbled at the blade. And then they – whoever this person was – bashed her knuckles with it.'

'Why couldn't she have just kicked her feet out of the shoes and swum out from underneath?' asked Bell.

'If she'd taken a blow to the head, she might have been confused. And she could have breathed in water immediately, from the shock.'

'This hypothetical person who tipped the boat,' broke in Singla, 'this is all conjecture, Superintendent.'

'Conjecture is enough to go on at this point, Inspector.' Kincaid was grim, his levity with Bean and Bell a moment before now forgotten. 'I think we have a murder inquiry on our hands.'

Kincaid rang Denis Childs and apprised him of the developments.

There was a moment's silence on the line, then Kincaid heard a distinct sigh. 'I suppose we have no choice,' said Childs, not sounding particularly happy about it. 'But I want you as SIO. I'll go through channels with Thames Valley. And you'll need more resources. I'll organize some data-entry staff for you. What about the team there in Henley?'

'They'll do for the moment. But, sir—'

'Have you managed to place the ex-husband at the scene?'

'No, sir,' Kincaid said, more formally than was his wont. 'I have not. And I think we should remember that, for the last fourteen years, Rebecca Meredith's life encompassed more than her ex-husband and her rowing. She was a police officer and, to have made DCI, she was clearly a good one. I'm going to pay a call on her station.'

Kincaid concentrated on the merging traffic on the M4 as he drove back into London, but he could feel Cullen's curious glances. 'Out with it,' he said, when he had settled the Astra comfortably into the fast lane.

'What's up with the guv'nor?' asked Cullen. 'You seemed a bit, um, shirty.'

'He's got a bee in his bonnet about Freddie Atterton. I think he's a little premature, that's all.'

'Did he quote the statistics?'

'Not yet. But I suspect it will occur to him.' They all knew that the majority of murders were committed by someone closely related to the victim, and Kincaid was surprised that Childs hadn't already pulled that out of his arsenal, since he seemed so determined to put Freddie Atterton in the frame.

'You have to admit,' Doug said thoughtfully, 'that what we've learned this morning ups the likelihood that the perpetrator was a rower – or at least knew something about boats. And they must have known Meredith's routine. Freddie Atterton fits both parameters.'

'Possibly.' Knowing that Cullen was right on both counts, Kincaid wondered if he was just being stubborn in refusing to put Atterton on the top of his list. Maybe. He didn't like being pushed. But he also knew how dangerous it was to jump to conclusions so early in a case, and he wasn't going to let someone else's agenda drive his investigation.

The CID room at West London Station fell quiet as they walked in. The duty sergeant on the front desk had phoned upstairs to announce them and, as always in police stations, news seemed to travel instantaneously and telepathically. Kincaid had no doubt that every officer on the floor knew who they were and why there were there.

The superintendent's office was at the rear of the room, divided from the general hubbub by a glass partition. Kincaid tapped on the door, and through the half-open blinds saw a man rise from his desk to admit them.

Peter Gaskill shook their hands briskly. 'Superintendent. Sergeant. Have a seat.' A tall man, his fine, neatly barbered brown hair had receded just enough to give him a patrician look. He wore an expensively cut navy blazer that Kincaid thought would have made him look right at home at Leander.

'A bad business,' Gaskill said, returning to his leather executive chair. He seemed even taller sitting down, and Kincaid wondered if he pumped the chair up to its full height for the intimidation factor. 'To lose an officer under any circumstances, but murder . . . ' He shook his head. 'This is dreadful. Are you certain?'

'Chief Superintendent Childs rang you, then?' Kincaid asked, not feeling it necessary to restate what he knew Childs had already told the man.

'Yes, right away. He has every confidence in you, Superintendent.'

Kincaid's hackles rose. First, Peter Gaskill had distanced himself by not using their names, and now he sounded downright patronizing. Who was he to think Kincaid needed a pat on the back?

He ignored the comment and smiled, refusing to give Gaskill the satisfaction of seeing that he'd nettled him. 'I appreciate that, Superintendent.' Gaskill could bloody well hold his breath waiting for the honorific – they were of the same rank. 'And I'd appreciate anything you could tell us about DCI Meredith.'

'DCI Meredith was an exemplary officer. Well respected here in the division.'

'But was she liked?'

'Liked?' For the first time, Gaskill looked nonplussed. 'Is that really relevant, Superintendent? Senior police officers are not in the business of being liked.'

It was Kincaid's turn to be patronizing. 'It's relevant in any murder inquiry, as I'm sure you're aware. I want to know how Rebecca Meredith got on with her colleagues. Were there any inter-departmental feuds or rivalries?'

Gaskill was staring at him now. 'You can't seriously be suggesting that Meredith's death had anything to do with her work here in the division.'

'I don't know.' Kincaid shrugged. 'I don't know anything at this point, except that it appears that someone turned over Rebecca Meredith's rowing shell and held her under until she drowned.'

The only sound in the office was the sharp intake of Gaskill's breath. With his back to the glass partition, Kincaid could only sense the attention of the occupants of the CID room, but he felt as if someone was boring a hole between his shoulder blades.

Cullen pushed his glasses up on his nose, and Gaskill looked away from Kincaid's gaze, breaking the tension of the moment. 'That's terrible, Superintendent,' he said. 'Truly terrible. If you're right, this person must be brought to justice.'

There it was again, Kincaid thought. The properly expressed sentiments, but beneath that, the undertone of contempt. *If you're right*, Gaskill had said.

'Was she working on anything that might have caused someone to harm her?' Cullen asked. Grudge-killings of police officers were not unheard of, and it was a possibility they must consider.

'A string of teenage knifings on an estate,' Gaskill answered, dismissively. 'These kids wouldn't know where Henley was, much less how to get there, or how to turn over a rowing boat.'

Cullen wasn't so easily fobbed off. 'What about her rowing? I understand she'd begun leaving work very early since the clocks went back. Was this causing any difficulties with her performance?'

'Becca assured me that she would continue to manage her caseload.'

Seeing Cullen's quick glance, Kincaid knew his partner had caught it, too. Gaskill had slipped and called Becca by her familiar name.

'And her colleagues here in the unit?' Kincaid asked. 'Were they okay with this, too?'

'You'd have to ask them, Superintendent. I assumed she had come to an understanding with them.'

'Had she, now?' Kincaid settled a little more comfortably in his chair and straightened his trouser crease before he continued. 'Did you know that DCI Meredith was considering training full-time for the Olympics?'

He saw the flash of hesitation on Gaskill's face. It was brief, and quickly mastered, but it had been there. The man had been deciding whether or not to lie. Why?

Gaskill touched the already perfectly aligned stack of papers on his desk. 'She'd talked to me about it, yes, but I didn't think she'd come to a definite decision. She would have had the full support of the force, of course, although we'd have hated to lose her.' Seeming to realize that he'd made an unfortunate choice of words, Gaskill added, 'I mean temporarily, of course.'

He cleared his throat, a deliberate end-of-the-interview signal. 'Now, if you don't mind, Superintendent, I've a luncheon appointment. As for DCI Meredith's team, Sergeant Patterson is out on an interview, but DC Bisik is waiting to speak to you.'

Kincaid decided to accept the dismissal gracefully. He wanted to know more before he pushed
Superintendent Gaskill further. He stood and reached
for Gaskill's hand, giving him no choice but to shake
again. 'Thanks for your time.'

Gaskill stood. 'You will keep me posted?'

'Of course.'

'You'll find DC Bisik at the desk on your right,'
Gaskill said, nodding, then focused his attention on
his papers again. Kincaid would have wagered he
knew the first page by heart.

As they stepped into the CID room and the door
swung to behind them, Cullen whispered, 'Wanker!'

'In spades,' Kincaid murmured back, turning to
look for Becca's constable. But a young man had risen
from a desk to their right and was already coming
towards them.

'I'm Bryan.' He reached out to shake their hands.
'DC Bisik. Is she . . . We've heard – is the guv'nor really
dead?' He was stocky, with buzz-cut dark hair that set
off his pale face, and his apparent distress seemed in
marked contrast to his superior's cool demeanour.

'I'm sorry, yes,' Kincaid said.

'Oh, Christ! I can't believe it. She was just . . . '
Bisik swallowed, then motioned them towards the relative quiet of the corridor. 'What happened?' he
asked, when they had followed him out. 'Can you say?
The rumour mill is going full tilt here.'

'She was reported missing after she went out
rowing on Monday evening and didn't return. Her
body was recovered yesterday. We're treating her
death as a full-scale inquiry.'

'Oh, right. Okay.' Bisik seemed at a loss. 'I can't believe someone would – I mean, she wasn't the easiest boss, but you could count on her to be straight with you.' The flick of his eyes towards the inner office said as plainly as words, *unlike some*.

'Was everything okay at work?' Kincaid asked.

Bisik hesitated. 'Well, there was a bit of feeling, you know, with her leaving early for her training. She was always on at us about our time clocks, and we – Kelly and me – thought Becca was being a right – ' His eyes widened. 'God, I can't believe I said that. I never thought . . . I didn't mean . . . '

'It's all right.' Kincaid came to his rescue. 'It's the shock. You know as well as we do that the dead don't suddenly become saints. And I can't say I blame you for feeling a bit pissed off.' When he saw Bisik visibly relax, he went on, 'What about DCI Meredith's personal life? Do you know if she was having any problems?'

'No way, man.' Bisik shook his head. 'I knew she was divorced a year or two back, but it was more than my life was worth to tread on that territory.'

'She wasn't the chatty type, then?'

'Sphinx doesn't begin to describe it.' Bisik looked suddenly appalled. 'She . . . I've done it again, haven't I?'

Kincaid clapped him on the shoulder. 'Don't worry. It's perfectly natural.' He fished in his pocket. 'Here's my card, if you want to talk, or if you think of anything that might be helpful. And I'm sorry for your loss.' He started to walk away, then casually swung back. 'DCI Meredith – did she get on with her guv'nor?' He nodded towards the inner office.

Bisik's face went blank. 'Not my business to say. Sir.' For a large man, he slipped back into the CID room with surprising speed.

As they came out into Shepherd's Bush Road, Kincaid noticed a woman standing by the railings on the opposite side of the street. She was smoking with rapid little puffs, and she held the cigarette cupped in her hand in a distinctly masculine gesture. When she saw them, she dropped the fag end, grinding it under the ball of her high-heeled shoe, and checked the oncoming traffic before starting towards them.

She was blonde, and thin, but not in the toned way of an athlete like Becca Meredith. The skirt of her grey suit pulled across her stomach, and the jacket hung badly on her narrow shoulders.

As she drew closer, Kincaid saw that her short blonde hair was dark at the roots, and that she was a good bit older than she'd appeared from a distance.

'You're the blokes from the Yard,' she said, and he thought her accent held a trace of Essex. 'I'm Patterson. Kelly Patterson, Becca's sergeant.' Her light-blue eyes were red-rimmed, her nose pink, as if she'd been crying.

'Kincaid,' he agreed, nodding. 'And this is Sergeant Cullen.'

'Bryan says it's official then, about Becca. A murder inquiry.'

'News travels fast.'

She gave him a crooked smile. 'Bry's a wizard with

a text. We call him magic fingers. She – ' Patterson's lips tightened for a moment, then she went on. 'It drove Becca crazy. And she said I was worse. She threatened to bin both our phones.'

'But she didn't.'

'No. Although I'd not have put it past her, if she was annoyed enough. Look.'

Patterson fixed him with a pale-blue stare, then glanced at Cullen as if to make certain he was paying attention.

'I know you're not supposed to speak ill of the dead and all that crap, but I'm going to say it anyway. Becca could be a right bitch. But she was an honest bitch, and if she said something, or told you to do something, there was usually a good reason for it. Look,' she said again, glancing at the door of the station and then up towards the windows before she continued, 'if anyone asks, I never talked to you. I've a four-year-old and a six-year-old at home, and I don't need to be sticking my nose in. But Becca deserved better than this. And if His Highness upstairs didn't tell you about Angus Craig, he's bloody well lying.'

When Kincaid had tried to get more out of Kelly Patterson, she'd shaken her head and, like her partner, had quickly put a closed door between them.

'Angus Craig?' said Doug, when they'd reached the Astra. 'Would that be Deputy Assistant Commissioner Angus Craig?'

Kincaid started the car, but let it idle for a moment while he thought. 'Retired, as of a few months ago, if I remember correctly.'

'Do you know him?'

'Not personally really, although I've met him. He's given talks at some training courses I've been on, and I've spoken to him at a couple of leaving parties. He's one of those hail-fellow-well-met types. A bit too jolly. Edging on pompous.' Frowning, Kincaid checked his mirrors and eased into the traffic. 'But I've no idea what the hell he has to do with Rebecca Meredith.'

Cullen already had his phone out and was tapping in queries. By the time Kincaid had looped round into Holland Park Road, Cullen's hand froze on the phone.

'Bugger!' He looked over at Kincaid, his eyes wide. 'Angus Craig lives in Hambleden.'

Chapter Ten

The face above the carefully arranged white sheet on the mortuary trolley looked nothing like Becca.

Oh, it had her features, all right: the straight nose with the faint dusting of freckles across the bridge, from days spent rowing in the sun; the dark, level brows; the tiny pinprick of a mole near her right ear; the slightly square chin.

But Freddie had never seen Becca's face still or composed. She was always in motion – even in sleep her brow had been creased, as if she were working out a knotty problem, or replaying a training session, and her lips and eyelids had moved in sequence with her dreams.

Someone had taken the trouble to comb her hair, and it fell back in gentle waves that she'd never have tolerated in life. Freddie clenched his hand, resisting the impulse to smooth it, or to touch the fan of dark eyelashes that, under the harsh overhead lighting, cast a shadow on her cheeks.

He nodded to the mortuary attendant. 'That's her. That's Becca.'

'That would be Rebecca Meredith, sir?' the young

man said, and Freddie found himself inordinately distracted by the ring in the man's nose.

He looked away. 'Yes. Yes, that's her.'

'I'm sorry for your loss, sir.' The condolence was rote. 'If you could just sign here?' The attendant handed Freddie a clipboard with all the ceremony of a delivery boy requesting a signature for a parcel.

And that was that.

Freddie walked out into the fresh air of the hospital car park, which felt warm by comparison, to find Ross Abbott waiting. Ross had left the engine idling in his late-model white BMW, a shout-out to the world that he didn't need to worry about the price of petrol. It would have annoyed Becca no end, but Freddie didn't care about his friend's affectations at the moment. He collapsed gratefully into the soft leather seat.

'You all right, man?' said Ross.

Freddie managed another nod. Ross Abbott had picked him up from his flat in the Malthouse just after lunch and driven him to the hospital in Reading. Freddie had asked him to wait outside – he hadn't wanted a witness if he broke down – but in the end he had felt strangely detached, as if the experience was happening to someone else.

'Where do you want to go now?' Ross asked, jerking him back to the present.

'For a drink.'

'Henley? Magoos?'

'No, it's too early for Magoos. They don't open until four.' Nor could Freddie bear the thought of the boisterous atmosphere of the bar on Hart Street. He knew too many of the people who were likely to wander in after work, and the last thing he wanted at the moment were questions or condolences.

'Hotel du Vin?' suggested Ross. 'Not far for you to walk home then,' he added, with what Freddie knew was an attempt at humour.

'Yeah, okay.' The hotel was across the road from Freddie's flat and was, like the Malthouse, part of the old Brakspear Brewery complex. The hotel's bar was quiet, and while locals would filter in later in the evening, in mid-afternoon any custom was likely to be business travellers.

On the drive back to Henley, Ross regaled him with a detailed description of the car's features. It might have been a bit insensitive, but it meant Freddie didn't have to speak, and for that he was grateful.

The hotel's bar was as quiet as Freddie had hoped. A few men wearing polo shirts and sports jackets sat on the leather sofas, conferring over papers, but they didn't look up at the new arrivals. The girl serving was new, which was a blessing. She took their orders with only cursory interest.

'A Hendrick's,' said Ross, giving her the smile Freddie remembered him trying on every girl in Oxford. 'Double. On ice. With a slice of cucumber.'

For a moment, Freddie was tempted to remind Ross that he had to drive, then realized there'd been a time when he'd not have thought twice about driving on a double gin. And it wasn't his business. He shrugged. 'Make that two.'

Ross gave the barmaid his card, but after a

moment she came back and said quietly, 'I'm sorry, sir, but your card's been declined.'

'Bloody bank!' Ross's face flushed with the quick temper that Freddie remembered. 'Stupid buggers couldn't put their bloody socks on straight.'

'Look, let me,' said Freddie, embarrassed for his friend. He reached for his wallet. 'It's the least I can—'

'No, no.' Ross had already pulled out another card. 'No problem. It's just that card. Their computers always seem to be going down, or something.'

The second card seemed fine, as the girl returned with the drinks and a perfunctory smile.

Ross held up his glass. 'Well, *cheers* isn't exactly appropriate, old man.'

'*Salute* then,' said Freddie, and lifted his own. The first swallow of gin went down like fire, and with the smell of cucumber came memories of summer regattas and too many gins and Pimm's drunk in canvas enclosures. He saw Becca, her face flushed with victory after a race, and Ross shaking a bottle of champagne to make it fizz. His head swam. Was he remembering Henley, or Oxford?

He looked at Ross. 'We had some good times, didn't we?'

'Oh, that we did.' Ross downed half his gin and made a face. 'But the no-drinks-in-training thing was a bitch.'

'You never did want to work that hard, did you?' said Freddie. He remembered Ross, always skiving off training with some complaint or other and then, when he'd been put in Isis, the second boat, he'd been furious. But fate had smiled on him when, on the day of the Boat Race, his counterpart in the Blue Boat had come down with a nasty case of stomach flu and Ross had taken his place.

Fate had been fickle, however. Everything had gone against them on race day. The weather was foul, and the crew had lost their synergy. The boat just didn't move, and the harder they tried, the worse it got. They'd been half-swamped, and had lost by humiliating lengths, collapsing in agony at the finish. And afterwards no one had said what everyone had thought. Ross Abbott had not been up to the job.

But Ross hadn't let the disastrous race damage his prospects, and he'd made good use of his Blue. Although Oxford and Cambridge Blues were awarded in other sports, the rowing Blue was still by far the most prestigious. And if you made the Blue Boat, it didn't matter if you won or lost, as long as you didn't sink before the Fulham Bend.

Freddie took another sip of his gin and studied his friend. Ross hadn't been as tall as most of the rowers, so he had tried to make up for the deficiency in height by adding bulk. He'd been good at lifting weights, and it had given him power, if not finesse.

Now, although the shoulders under his light-weight sports coat were still broad, he looked thicker and softer around the middle. A few too many gins, Freddie thought, and raised his own. 'Still working out?' he asked.

Ross looked pleased. 'Got a new gym at home. A new house, in fact, in Barnes.'

'Barnes? That's brilliant. Things must be going well for you.'

'Looking up, yeah,' Ross said, leaning in for a conspiratorial wink. 'I've got a deal in the works' – he shook his head, grinning – 'knock your sodding socks off.'

Like many Blues, regardless of the degrees they'd taken at university, Ross had gone into investment banking, with better results than Freddie had seen in commercial real estate, apparently.

He glanced round at the other men in the bar. Like Ross, they were wearing expensive clothes, drinking expensive drinks, huddled in quiet and self-important conference. Fat cats. They were fat cats. Had he been in danger of becoming one, too? Was that the real reason Becca had left him?

Freddie realized his mind was wandering. The gin was beginning to go to his head. He forced himself to concentrate. Ross had, after all, gone out of his way to be a mate today. 'Listen, Ross. I really appreciate your doing this for me. You're a good friend.'

'Bollocks!' Ross gave him an awkward clap on the shoulder. 'It was the least anyone could do. You let me know whatever else you need. And Chris as well – she'd have come today, if it wasn't for work and the kids.'

'Chris, and the boys? They're doing well?'

Ross lowered his voice again. 'Chris may have a promotion in the works. All hush-hush, but she's made a good job of impressing the right people.'

For an instant, Freddie heard Becca's voice, slightly waspish, murmuring, *And what does that have to do with being a good copper?* He shook his head, wondering if he was going thoroughly bonkers, and tried to focus on what Ross was saying.

' . . . and the boys, well, it's not official yet, but there's a good chance for' – he looked round, and this time spoke in a whisper deserving of a state secret – 'Eton.'

'Eton?' said Freddie, surprised at the rush of resentment he felt. 'Wow! So no old school tie then. Bedford School not good enough for the Abbott offspring?'

'It's not that, man, you know that.' Ross sounded hurt. 'It's just that you've got to do whatever is best for the kids. Help them get on in the world.'

'Right.' Freddie forced a smile. Kids. He had wanted kids. Becca hadn't. And now it would never matter.

Exhaustion swept over him, and suddenly he wanted nothing but to go home and be alone.

Ross tipped up the last of his drink and then, before Freddie could protest, signalled the barmaid and ordered another round for them both. Ross turned to him. 'About today. I really am sorry, mate. Was it bad, at the mortuary? Was she – was she cut up or anything?'

'She was fine,' said Freddie, feeling guilty over his momentary antagonism towards his friend. 'There was nothing that you could see, really. She just looked – ' His throat tightened and he couldn't bring himself to say the word. *Dead*.

'Have the police talked to you? Do they have any idea what happened?'

'They've talked to me, all right. But nobody's told me anything. They called in a superintendent from Major Crimes. Scotland Yard.'

Ross gave a low whistle. 'Big time, buddy. They're bringing in the muscle. So, have they asked you where you were?'

The alcohol from the night before had aggravated Kieran's vertigo, as he'd known it would. After the search he'd managed to avoid the rest of the team. But, once on his own, he'd been unable to shut out the recurring image of Becca's body, trapped in the roots below the weir, the strands of her hair moving like fronds in the current.

So he had gone to the pub, where Tavie had found him. Afterwards he'd stumbled home and fallen onto the camp bed in the boatshed. For a while he'd drifted in a cider-induced doze, in which he'd seen Becca's white face again and again, gazing up at him with open, pleading eyes.

But then the nightmare shifted, and he'd suddenly realized that parts of her body were missing, blown away, and her face became the faces of the men in his unit, and their screams had filled his ears.

Then it was Tavie – Tavie shouting at him, giving him commands he couldn't understand and couldn't follow.

He woke, sweating, and found the reality as bad as the dream. Becca. Becca was dead. And Tavie, his best friend – his only real friend – was lost to him.

At the first hint of dawn, he'd given up on sleep and made coffee as strong as he could bear. Then, with Finn beside him, he'd taken his cup outside and watched the light grow slowly on the river. Grey water melded into grey sky, then the skeletal shapes of trees began to appear on the far bank, and at last, as the mist lifted, the still-green froth of the willows trailing in the water's edge.

The water's edge . . . Kieran frowned in concentration, and then it flickered again, the image that had been teasing him since they'd found the Filippi.

He had seen someone at the water's edge. Not where they'd found the boat, but a good bit further upstream, the other side of Temple Island. A fisherman, or so he had thought, standing there in the shadows when he'd gone for his evening run on Sunday.

And he had been there again, on Monday.

Kieran had made a habit of timing his runs so that he passed Becca rowing her evening workout, but on Monday she'd been late, and he must already have been back on the upstream side of Henley Bridge by the time she'd gone out.

Oh, dear God. If only he'd delayed a few minutes, dawdled on his route, could he have saved her? But she'd been brusque to him over the weekend, and he hadn't wanted to force himself on her.

And the fisherman – what if the fisherman had been waiting for her? She'd have passed right by him after she rounded Temple Island and started back towards Leander, and she'd have been staying close to the Bucks bank, where the wind and the current favoured the upstream stroke.

If she'd capsized there, or been tipped, or been

pulled out of the shell, then the end of Benham's Wood, where they'd found the Filippi, was probably the first place the shell would have snagged as it floated downriver. And Becca – Becca would have gone on with the current, until her body caught in the eddy below the weir.

Kieran stood, determined to examine the place where he'd seen the man, as soon as it was fully light. But then everything reeled and tipped sideways, and the next thing he knew, he was lying on the soft grass at the river's edge.

Groaning, he mumbled, 'God-damned bloody vertigo.' What kind of life was this, when it could fell him like a tree with no warning?

For a long time he watched the whirling, juddering sky grow brighter. At last he drifted into a light sleep. Finn woke him by whimpering and nudging him with his nose.

'Sorry, boy,' he croaked, his mouth dry. 'Fucking useless, aren't I?'

Experimentally, he shifted his head a fraction. So far, so good. The short sleep had helped the dizziness, as it usually did. After a bit he was able to get up and stagger inside, and he managed to pour some food into Finn's bowl before stretching out on the camp bed. He slept again, more soundly, and when he woke in late afternoon he felt stable enough on his feet to venture into Henley.

There was no easy access to the Buckinghamshire side of the Thames path. He could have taken the Land Rover as far as the beginning of the footpath that veered off from the Marlow road, but with the frequency and severity of the vertigo, he hadn't dared drive. So, after taking the skiff the few yards across to the mainland, he walked, occasionally using Finn's sturdy back for support. All the while he half-hoped and half-feared he would see Tavie.

A few of the people he passed, seeing his unsteady gait, threw him the disgusted looks reserved for drunks, but he didn't care. He wanted only to see if he was right, or if the man in the trees had been a delusion.

The sun, partially obscured by the clouds moving in from the west, was low in the sky by the time he passed the entrance to Phyllis Court and turned onto the footpath. Finn watched the meadow by Henley Football Club intently – he knew from previous walks that rabbits played there – but stayed close at Kieran's heel.

The way seemed endless, and Kieran approached the far end of the last meadow with relief. But this was as far as he and Finn had ever ventured, and when he saw what lay ahead his heart sank. Here, an inlet of the Thames snaked into the beginnings of a boggy wood, and a narrow plank footbridge provided the only crossing. There was no way round that Kieran could see, so he held the rails as he crossed, stepping as carefully as a child, and did the same on the next, even narrower footbridge.

As he walked on, brushing at the overhanging branches that caught at his hair, the path grew less defined, twisting and turning deeper into the woods until it threatened to vanish altogether.

And then he came round one more bend and he was there. He knew the place at once.

A small bowl of a clearing lay between the path and the river, hemmed in by trees and trailing brush. A signpost on one of the trees stated: *Fishing Licence Required*. The grass in the clearing looked soft and swampy, and was still vibrantly green, even in late October. In a muddy spot to one side, Kieran thought he could make out a clear footprint.

He didn't dare go closer, for fear of disturbing evidence, but he thought the flotsam at the water's edge had been disturbed. When he looked north, through a gap in the trees, he could just make out the white gleam of the folly on the tip of Temple Island. Was this, then, where Becca had died?

The blood rushed to his head. He crouched, his arm across Finn's shoulders, fighting the dizziness, forcing himself to breathe. Then the skin crawled on the back of his neck.

He knew that feeling. He'd had it in Iraq, when his unit had been observed by hostiles. Someone was watching him. Finn's ears came up, but he didn't growl, and Kieran couldn't tell if the dog had sensed something or was just reading his master's signals.

Finn whined and butted at him, upsetting his balance. 'Okay, okay,' he whispered, steadying himself. Carefully he stood and looked round, checking the path in either direction, then the dense wood behind him.

Nothing. Maybe he had imagined the hidden presence.

He felt a drop of moisture on his cheek, then another. The rain that had been threatening all day was moving in, and the light was fading fast. If he didn't start back, he'd be limping across those foot-bridges and through the meadows in near-zero visibility, and he hadn't brought a torch.

He looked once more at the clearing. He was certain now that he hadn't imagined the man he had seen here. But he was a clapped-out, freaked-out Iraq veteran, who yesterday had destroyed his only fragile claim to credibility. Who would believe him?

When they'd arrived at the Yard, Kincaid found that Chief Superintendent Childs was also out to lunch, and would afterwards be attending a planning meeting in Lambeth.

Kincaid had been tempted to go back to Shepherd's Bush and have another talk with Superintendent Gaskill, but he hadn't wanted to betray Sergeant Patterson's confidence. So after he and Cullen had grabbed a sandwich in the canteen, he shut himself in his office and did his own research on Deputy Assistant Commissioner Angus Craig. He didn't like what he found.

To some degree, all senior officers in the Met rotated from division to division, filling different positions. But it seemed that Craig had moved more than most and after a certain point, although he'd risen in rank, his postings had seemed to carry less and less responsibility.

Kincaid sat back from the computer, frowning, and rang Superintendent Mark Lamb. Lamb was Gemma's guv'nor at Notting Hill, but he was also an old friend of Kincaid's, and someone he trusted to give him a straight opinion.

'Craig?' Lamb said, when they'd dispensed with the pleasantries. 'Well, off the record, he's a bit dodgy, really. I've worked with him on a few committees. He's not a man you want to cross. He likes to use his influence, and not always to the betterment of his fellow officers.'

'Any problems with female officers in particular?' Kincaid asked.

'There were whispers,' Lamb said reluctantly. 'I don't want to tell tales out of school, and I never had anything concrete. But I got the impression that the female officers avoided him whenever possible.'

Kincaid thought of DI Singla in Henley. 'You don't mean just an old-fashioned bias against working with women, I take it?'

'I think it was more than that. Hang on.' Lamb murmured to someone in the background. 'Look, I've got to go. But tell Gemma we're looking forward to having her back next week.'

'Will do,' said Kincaid and rang off.

There was a tap on his office door and Cullen came in. 'I've been on to Henley,' he said, taking the visitor's chair. 'I've assigned a Family Liaison Officer to Freddie Atterton, although Atterton had already made the official identification before I could get the FLO to accompany him.

'I've had a word with the press officer and said the usual: *Deepest regrets, one of our finest officers, putting all our resources towards finding an explanation for DCI Meredith's tragic death, etc., etc.* But they want you in your finest in Henley tomorrow morning for a five-minute stint with the cameras.'

Kincaid nodded. He didn't like doing interviews, but it was a necessary, and sometimes useful, part of an investigation. It was a good thing he would get home tonight for a change of clothes. 'Anything new from the forensics teams, or this afternoon's interviews?'

Shaking his head Cullen said, 'Not yet. What about this Angus Craig business, guv?'

'I don't think we can take that any further until I've had a word with the chief.' He glanced at his watch. It was almost five. His patience with his Chief Superintendent was evaporating, but he wasn't leaving until he'd seen him. 'I'm going to stay on a bit, Doug, but you go home. I expect you have boxes to deal with. When are you out of your flat?'

Cullen grinned. 'This weekend. Good thing I don't have much to pack.'

'You'd best take advantage of a lull then. We'll make an early start for Henley in the morning.'

After Cullen left, Kincaid shuffled papers with one eye on the clock. He was just about to go and knock on the chief's door when Childs's secretary rang and summoned him.

Kincaid entered the Chief Superintendent's office without ceremony, and when Childs gestured towards his usual chair, he shook his head.

'I won't keep you long, sir.'

Childs's usually implacable gaze sharpened. 'What's going on, Duncan? Is there a development?'

Kincaid had worked under Denis Childs for more than six years, and they'd been on first-name terms for much of that time. Not only did he consider Childs a personal friend, but they were also connected through the house in Notting Hill, which Kincaid and Gemma leased from Denis's sister. At the moment, however, he wasn't inclined towards informality.

'Sir, were you aware that there was some sort of connection between Deputy Assistant Commissioner Angus Craig and Rebecca Meredith?'

Childs looked startled. 'Did Peter Gaskill tell you that?'

A heavy man, Childs had made an effort to lose weight in the past year, and now his skin seemed to sag on his body, as if it had belonged to someone a size larger. The resulting fleshy folds around Childs's dark almond-shaped eyes had not made his expression any easier to read, but from his response Kincaid assumed that he had known something.

Avoiding an answer that would implicate Kelly Patterson, he said, 'What I'd like to know is why *you* didn't tell me. If there was some relationship between Rebecca Meredith and DAC Craig, it seems the fact that Craig lives a mile from where Meredith's body was found might be relevant. That's a bit of a coincidence, don't you think?'

'Sarcasm doesn't become you, Duncan. And you're shooting in the dark, aren't you?' Childs looked at him speculatively. 'You don't really know anything.' Then he sighed and folded his pudgy hands together on the pristine surface of his large and shiny desk. 'But I know you well enough to know that you won't leave it alone now.'

'Leave what alone, exactly?'

'Something that I'd hoped would not become an

issue. Something that needs to be handled very delicately. I wouldn't say that DCI Meredith had a *relationship* with Deputy Assistant Commissioner Craig. But she had made certain . . . allegations . . . regarding Craig's behaviour towards her. I'm sure they have nothing to do with her death, but if they became public knowledge it could be very ugly for the Met.'

'Ugly?' Kincaid thought of the sight of Rebecca Meredith's body. 'I can't think of many things uglier than what looks like the murder of one of our senior officers. I think you'd better tell me exactly what's going on here, Denis. What sort of allegations are you talking about?'

Pushing back his chair, Childs said, 'Oh, for heaven's sake, Duncan, sit down. You're giving me a headache looming over me like that.'

Reluctantly Kincaid pulled out the steel-and-leather visitor's chair and sat on the edge.

Childs pursed his lips, as if sampling something unpleasant. 'A year ago DCI Meredith told Peter Gaskill that Angus Craig had offered her a lift after some sort of do – a leaving party, I think. He said her cottage was on his way and, when they arrived, he asked to come in for a moment. And then he – assaulted – her.'

Kincaid had never seen his boss hesitate over a word choice before. 'That's media-speak: *assaulted*. What *exactly* did Rebecca Meredith say?'

'She said' – Childs turned his chair slightly, so that he was facing the window rather than looking directly at Kincaid – 'she said he raped her. And then, at least according to Meredith, he told her that if she made a complaint, she would lose her job. She had a DNA sample taken, then went to Gaskill.'

'And what,' Kincaid asked, 'did Superintendent Gaskill do about it?'

Childs swivelled towards him again, his expression pained. 'Peter Gaskill told her the sensible thing, which was that if her allegations were made public, the whole affair would degenerate into a *he said – she said* slanging match. She had no way to prove that the sex was not consensual and that she hadn't afterwards changed her mind. It would tarnish the reputation of the force, and it would ruin her career. No male officer would want her anywhere near his team. He promised her that Craig would be asked to retire immediately, and quietly, so that no other female officers would be put at risk, and that Craig would receive some sort of censure within the Met.'

Kincaid simply stared at him. 'You're not serious.'

The usually unflappable Childs frowned at him and snapped, 'Could you have come up with a better solution, Duncan? The force has had enough negative publicity the last few years – you know that. Senior officers have made public accusations of racism, sexual intolerance and incompetence against their peers. Rebecca Meredith's story would have been disastrous. And it *would* have ruined her career, without accomplishing anything.'

Kincaid felt as though he couldn't breathe. 'But now she's dead, so there's no need to worry about her career, I take it? And what about other female officers? Or other women, for that matter?'

'You're assuming that Meredith's allegations were true. We have no way of knowing that. Craig denied it, of course.'

'Of course he did.' Kincaid stood, as if movement might contain his rising temper. 'Why would Meredith make up something like that? That would have been suicidal. And Craig didn't take immediate retirement, by the way – I looked it up this afternoon. He only stepped down two weeks ago. He's still listed as a consultant. Oh, and he just happened to receive honours. That's some censure. Becca Meredith must have been livid when she found out. And felt horribly betrayed by her superiors.'

A furrow creased Childs's wide brow. He straightened the Mont Blanc on his leather desk blotter before he met Kincaid's eyes. 'Don't blow this out of proportion, Duncan. There's a bit more to it. Rebecca Meredith made life difficult for herself, and for those around her, as I'm sure you will come to see. And she had her own agenda. She wanted to row, and she wanted to do it on a fully funded leave of absence.'

'I don't believe this,' Kincaid said, looking at Childs in astonishment. 'Are you telling me that Rebecca Meredith was blackmailing the Met?'

'I'm saying that an offer had been made to her, and that she was considering it.'

'An offer.' Had Rebecca Meredith wanted to row that badly? Or had she just been looking for a way to salvage something from the damage Craig had done to her life? 'And if she had turned it down?' he asked.

'Then we would all have dealt with the consequences.' Childs gave a weighty sigh.

Kincaid turned away and walked to the window. Without looking at his boss he said, 'Why, exactly, were you so determined that I should take this case?'

'Because you're my best officer. Because I thought you could get to the bottom of things. And I thought I could count on you to be discreet.'

It was fully dark and rain had begun to fall, blurring the lights of Victoria and Westminster beyond. Kincaid gazed out the window, struggling to find coherent words through the haze of his anger. 'Angus Craig had both the motive and the physical proximity to have murdered Rebecca Meredith. Did you expect me to ignore that?'

'I expected you to do your job professionally and thoroughly. I still do. And I expect you not to make unsubstantiated allegations against another officer. And now,' added Chief Superintendent Childs, levering his still-considerable bulk up from his chair, 'I'm afraid I've got family obligations. Diane's sister has come to stay for a fortnight. Damned nuisance.' He moved towards the door, but turned back as he reached it. 'Oh, and Duncan, I expect you to keep me informed.'

Kincaid had been dismissed.

'"O Mouse, do you know the way out of this pool?"' read Kincaid a few hours later, doing his best to sound like Alice. '"I am very tired of swimming about—"'

'No.' Charlotte slipped her hand under his and turned the pages back. 'Read t'other part again.'

'You mean the part about the little girl who was covered from her toes to her nose?' He had sat at the head of her small white bed, book in his lap, and she had scooted over to make room for him.

Having left the Yard straight after his interview with Denis Childs, he'd come home to find the household in the full chaotic flow of evening routine.

'What are you doing home?' Gemma had asked when he'd finally managed to kiss her, having been boisterously greeted by both the dogs and the younger children. 'I thought you'd be back in Henley for at least another night.'

'Got a date with the milkman again?' he'd quipped.

But Gemma had seen his face. Frowning, she said, 'What's happened? Is—'

He'd shaken his head as Toby broke in. 'Who's the milkman? We don't have a milkman.'

'Never you mind,' Kincaid told him. 'And don't interrupt your mum.'

Toby was undeterred. 'Kit's making a stir-fry. He let me chop. Want to help?'

'Help you chop your fingers off? Of course I do.' And so he had let the current of home life sweep him up, while he tried to sort out his thoughts.

It had been his turn to read to Charlotte while Gemma gave Toby his bath. It was Charlotte who had chosen the book, Kit's old copy, found in the sitting-room bookshelf. Kincaid had raised an eyebrow at Gemma when he saw it. 'Isn't she a bit young for *Alice*?'

Gemma shrugged. 'Not according to her. She won't have anything else at the moment. And I'm rather liking it.'

'You didn't read it as a child?' he'd asked, surprised. But Gemma's family had not been readers, and the children's books were proving a voyage of discovery for her.

Now, Charlotte giggled as he pulled the duvet up to the tip of her nose, but she promptly tugged it down again and tapped the book. 'No. The "Drink Me" part.'

Obediently he found the right page and began. '"What a curious feeling!" said Alice, "I must be shutting up like a telescope." And so it was indeed: she was now only ten inches high, and her face brightened up at the thought that she was now the right size for going through the little door into that lovely garden. First, however, she waited for a few minutes to see if she was going to shrink any further: she felt a little nervous about this, "for it might end, you know," said Alice to herself, "in my going out altogether, like a candle. I wonder what I should be like then?"'

'Poof,' Kincaid interjected, and blew out an imaginary flame.

'You put that in,' said Charlotte. 'That's not fair, making things up.'

'The man who wrote the story, Lewis Carroll, made it all up. The whole thing.'

Charlotte's eyes grew big, then she shook her head. 'Including Alice?'

'Including Alice.'

'No,' Charlotte said with absolute certainty. 'That's silly. It's Alice's story. Do you think Alice liked getting littler?'

Kincaid gave the question consideration. 'I don't know. Would you?'

Charlotte shook her head. 'No. I want to get bigger.'

This gave Kincaid a pang, but he said, 'Then you should close your eyes and go to sleep, because the sooner it's tomorrow, the closer it will be to your birthday.'

'Really?'

'Really.'

'All right.' Charlotte shut her eyes tight, but after a moment they flew open again. 'Will you stay until I'm fast asleep?'

'Yes. I promise.'

'Will you check on me after?'

'Yes. Now snuggle up, and sweet dreams.' He pulled up the duvet again, and this time Charlotte covered his hand with hers and kept it tucked under her chin.

After a moment her eyelids fluttered, then closed, and to his amazement he felt her hand relax and saw that she was drawing the deep, regular breaths of sleep.

Looking down at her hand atop his, he thought he had never seen anything so lovely. Her tiny, pale-brown fingers were loosely curled, her nails like pink pearls. He felt such wonder that this child had come unexpectedly into his life, and that she had begun to love him. And he never wanted to do anything that would make him less than the father she deserved.

Very, very gently he brushed his lips against her cheek and eased his hand free.

Looking up, he saw Gemma standing in the doorway, watching them. She smiled. 'You're a miracle-worker.'

'It was *Alice*.' He stood. 'What about Toby?'

'Reading something a bit less challenging. A *Pirates of the Caribbean* comic.'

'As long as it's not the *Daily Mirror*.'

'Not yet, anyway.' She studied him. 'Come down to the kitchen. I'm just going to put the kettle on, and you're going to tell me what happened today.'

They sat in the kitchen, the dogs settled contentedly under their feet. Gemma's Clarice Cliff teapot held pride of place on the table between them, but they drank out of chipped, mismatched mugs, treasures acquired on Saturday browses through Portobello Market. Kincaid had checked on Toby and Kit, and then, when he'd taken the dogs out, he'd discovered that it was still raining lightly and that the temperature had dropped. The kitchen's dark-blue Aga radiated a comforting heat.

Marshalling his thoughts, he told Gemma everything they'd learned that morning about Rebecca Meredith's death, and then, more slowly, he related the gist of his conversation with Denis Childs. 'I don't want to take this case,' he said when he'd finished.

'You'd resign as SIO?' Gemma looked shocked. 'But you can't.'

'I'm supposed to be going on leave, in case you've forgotten.'

She sighed. 'No, of course not. And I want you finished with this as much as you do. But to walk away

187

from a case like this – you know what it would do to
your career.'

'Would you have me . . . adjust' – his lips twisted
– 'the direction of an investigation to protect a senior
officer in the Met?'

'No, but . . . ' Gemma met his eyes with the honest
gaze he had loved since the moment he'd met her.
'What about Rebecca Meredith? Don't you want to
know who killed her? Doesn't she deserve an answer,
regardless of the consequences?'

'You do realize just how bad the consequences
could be, if it turns out that Craig killed her? And what
we have at stake?' His gesture took in the house, and
the children snug in their rooms upstairs.

Gemma divided the dregs of the pot between their
cups, then added the last of the milk from the little
Clarice Cliff jug. After a moment she said, 'I have
more faith in Denis Childs than that. This senior
officer – what did you say his name was? Craig?'

'Angus Craig. A good Scottish name that I'd be
inclined to like under other circumstances, but – ' He
broke off when he saw Gemma wasn't listening.
'What . . . ?'

'Sandy-haired? Not too tall, a bit burly?' Her voice
had gone up an octave.

'I've only met him a few times, but that would
describe him. Why—'

'Oh, my God.' Gemma's eyes were wide. 'Rebecca
Meredith said he offered her a lift, then asked to come
in to use the loo?'

'Yes. Gemma, what—'

She stopped him, her words coming out in a rush.

'It was after I'd passed my Sergeant's exam, a month or two before I was assigned to you. I went to a party at a pub in Victoria. I don't remember the occasion – it very well may have been a leaving do for someone – but I was encouraged to go by some new mates at the Yard. All in all, a nice enough evening, but by the time things broke up, it was pissing with rain. I hadn't taken my car in because I didn't want to drink and drive, and as the group was breaking up someone said the Central Line to Leyton had been shut down.' Gemma hesitated. 'He offered me a lift.'

'You mean Craig?'

'One and the same, I'm certain of it. He was very – solicitous. Courteous in a sort of paternal way. And a deputy assistant commissioner to boot . . . I suppose I was flattered.' She swallowed and rotated her mug a quarter-turn on the scrubbed pine table. 'So I accepted. We made chit-chat on the drive, about nothing in particular. Films, I think. Then, when we got to Leyton, he asked if he could come in. He'd said he wasn't over the limit, but he'd had a pint or two, and you know, he'd gone a bit out of his way to drive me home. So I said of course, although I was horrified thinking of the state of the house, and I invited him in.'

Kincaid shifted uneasily in his chair, disturbing Geordie, their cocker spaniel, who had been sleeping on his feet. Geordie gave a disgruntled *whumf* and resettled himself. 'Go on,' Kincaid said tightly, not taking his eyes from Gemma's face. He didn't like where this was going at all.

'I hadn't said anything about my personal

situation – why would I, to a senior officer I didn't know? I was uncomfortable enough with being a newly divorced single mother, and I was hoping it wouldn't damage my career prospects.' She glanced at him, then looked away. 'So I suppose he assumed I was alone.'

'But that night my mum had come over to look after Toby, and of course Toby had thrown a total wobbly and had refused to go down. So when Craig walked into the house and saw my mum pacing the sitting room with a red-faced, tear-streaked toddler over her shoulder, he turned round and walked right back out again with barely a goodnight.

'I thought it was odd, but that maybe he was embarrassed at having asked to use the loo, or that maybe he thought he'd step in a dirty nappy if he came any further.' She shrugged. 'And then I forgot about it. I never ran into him after that. But – '

'But what?' said Kincaid, feeling cold. He knew he was constructing the same scenario.

'What if my mum hadn't been there that night? What if . . . What if Angus Craig meant to do to me what he did to Rebecca Meredith?'

By the time Kieran made it back to the boatshed it was well past dark. Soaked through and shivering, he felt light-headed, as if his brain was disconnected from his body. His ears had begun to ring, which was often a sign that the vertigo was about to get worse.

Switching on a light, he rubbed Finn's wet coat with a towel, then poured out some dry dog food. But the thought of making something for himself brought the hovering nausea on again.

When had he last eaten? The protein bar before they'd started yesterday's search? No wonder he was feeling wonky.

He sank down on the camp bed, images stuttering through his mind like frames in a bad film reel. He knew he should get dry, at least, but the steps required to achieve such a simple thing seemed beyond his capabilities.

And he knew he should tell someone what he had seen, but who?

He didn't think Tavie would even talk to him, much less hear him out. The policeman from the Yard? He'd seemed like the sort of man who might listen, but Kieran didn't know how to get in touch, and he couldn't imagine trying to explain himself to an officer at the local nick, even if he could get himself there.

His head swam and he gripped the edge of the bed, bracing for the onset of full-tilt vertigo. When it didn't come, he breathed a sigh of relief. Finn finished the last of his food and came over to lie on the floor at his feet, head on his paws, eyes intent on Kieran's face.

Kieran waited, counting to himself. The seconds passed. He began to think that maybe he was going to be okay – or at least well enough to clean himself up, then get down a sandwich and some coffee. Then maybe he could work out what to do about the man on the bank.

He'd gingerly started to stand when he heard a

soft splash from outside the shed. Finn's ears came up in enquiry. The dog tilted his head and growled low in his throat, the hackles rising on his back.

Then the world exploded.

Chapter Eleven

'Lamb.' Ian waved a paper bag under Tavie's nose. 'Baby sheep. Baa. A veggie's delight.' The bag was filled with kebabs from the takeaway across from the police station. The aroma of roasted lamb wafted through the fire-station break room.

'You'll have the whole lot of them in here, if you're not careful.' She nodded towards the engine bay, where the captain had the crew doing a drill. Ian, her partner on tonight's rota in the Rapid Response Vehicle – or RRV, as it was officially known – loved to tease her about being a vegetarian.

They'd been on a call, dealing with an elderly lady who'd fallen, when the fire-brigade crew had been eating, so Ian had volunteered to go for kebabs.

It gave him an excuse to tease her, since he knew perfectly well that, although a vegetarian by choice since her teens, she'd never been able to stop salivating at the smell of cooked meat.

She thought maybe the response was genetic, coded into the DNA of her long-ago Nordic hunter-gatherer ancestors, when the odour of meat roasting on the fire had meant the difference between survival and death.

'Did you bring me hummus? And falafel?' she asked.

'Of course, madam.' Ian produced another paper bag from behind his back and set it on the break-room table. He pulled out a hard plastic chair and sat, opening his own bag.

'You, Ian, are a prince among men.' Tavie peered into her bag, sniffing. A warm, folded pitta held balls of crunchy falafel, a good dollop of hummus, a squeeze of bright-green coriander/chilli sauce and a sprinkle of lettuce, cucumber and tomato. It was messy, drippy and smelled like heaven. There were some compensations for being a *veggie*.

She started to put the bag on the table, then wrinkled her nose at the brown smears and unidentifiable crumbs spread liberally on the tabletop. 'What did they eat in here? And who cleaned up?'

'Chilli con carne, I think,' said Ian through a mouthful of kebab. 'And the new guy had kitchen duty.'

Tavie grabbed a kitchen towel from the roll near the sink and wiped a square foot of table, clearing just enough space for her bag. 'Well, Bonzo, or Bozo, or whatever his name is, can deal with me when the Captain's finished with him. That's disgusting.'

'It's Brad, Tav.' Ian fished another kebab from the bottom of his bag. 'He seems like a nice enough kid.'

'Yeah. He reminds me of my ex. Nice.' She shot a glare towards the engine bay.

Ian grinned. 'You're vicious.'

'And you're a big softie,' she said, but she smiled as she sat down. She liked working with Ian. He was a good medic, studying hard for more advanced certification, and he didn't give her any grief over the fact that she was more qualified.

On this job they dealt with everything from ill and distressed old-age pensioners to major accidents, heart attacks and strokes, with the occasional nutter in a tin-foil hat thrown in.

Ian was decisive and patient, which made him good at both extremes of the job. He had a wife and two lovely children, and Tavie thought his level-headed competence would make him a good addition to the SAR team.

But then, she reminded herself, she'd thought Kieran would make a good addition to the team, and that hadn't worked out so well.

Her good humour evaporated, along with her appetite. She kept remembering Kieran's face when she'd ranted at him last night. He'd turned away from her, his eyes filled with despair, and she'd have done anything to have called back her words.

She'd spent a sleepless night, worrying about whether she should ring him to see if he was all right, and had gone on call bleary-eyed that morning. There'd been no opportunity to phone him during her busy day, until now – had she been capable of working out what to say.

'Eat up,' urged Ian, eyeing her untouched falafel. 'Or I'll take it away from you. I like it, too, you know.'

'Bugger off,' Tavie said, but without heat. She picked up the bag, then set it down again, fighting a sudden desire to confide in someone, although she couldn't share the details of the search or what had happened afterwards. 'Ian, what if you'd said rotten things to a friend – true, maybe, but still rotten – how would you apologize?'

'I'd buy him a pint.'

She rolled her eyes. 'Yeah, well, probably not the best option, since one of the things I shouted at him for was drinking.'

Ian looked interested. 'Outside Magoos, right? The crazy bloke who fixes boats?'

'What . . . ? How did you – ' Oh, Christ. She should have known every word she'd said had been over-heard, and would have made the rounds of the town within hours. 'He's not crazy,' she protested. 'He was a medic in Iraq.'

'Shit!' Ian's usually jovial expression vanished in an instant. 'PTSD?'

'I think so. And a head injury. But he never talks about it.' She hesitated, then went on uncomfortably. 'I did some, um, research, before asking him to join the SAR team.' Admitting it made her feel ashamed, although she knew she'd had a legitimate reason to snoop. 'He lost his entire unit to an IED.'

'Poor bastard.' Ian shook his head. 'So what did he do that was bad enough to deserve a bollocking from you? I heard you had a search call-out yesterday.'

Of course he had heard, and he probably knew whom they'd found, too, although she hadn't dis-cussed it. 'Look, Ian – I shouldn't have said—'

The fire tone-out drowned her words.

'You should have eaten, that's what you should have done,' said Ian, popping the last bite of kebab into his mouth. 'Falafel won't be any good in the microwave. Wilts the lettuce—'

'Shhh.' Tavie held up her hand. Over the sound of the engine rumbling to life in the bay and the shouts of the crew as they suited up, she'd heard the dispatcher say two words. *Fire* and *island*. Oh, God, surely not . . . Her walkie-talkie crackled with the fast-response car's call sign.

'RRV . . . possible injury,' said the dispatcher. 'Some sort of explosion – structure fire on the island across from Mill Meadows.'

Tavie ran for the car.

She had the Volvo onto the street before the fire engine was out of the bay, gunning the car with a squeal that had Ian, normally the most sanguine of passengers, gripping the dash with one hand as he scrabbled for his seatbelt with the other. They flew down West Street, into Market Place, lights on and siren whooping. Behind them, she heard the engine's siren start. Blue lights flashed in the Volvo's rear-view mirror.

'Hurry, hurry, damn it,' she whispered, exhorting herself as much as the crew on their tail.

'What the hell, Tav?' said Ian through clenched teeth. 'You trying to kill us?'

'I'm afraid . . . ' That was all she could force herself to say. 'Just hang on. The engine will have to go round through the Rowing Museum car park, but this will get us closer.' She went through the light at Thames Side with a turn that nearly put them through the corner of the Angel. At the end of the road she shot the car straight through the gap in the bollards and onto the paved pedestrian path that ran between the river and Mill Meadows. If there was anyone out walking after dark, they had bloody well better be paying attention.

The car's headlamps picked out park benches and rubbish bins on the right as they flashed past, the dark thread of the river steady on the left. There was a rustle and scrape as willow fronds brushed the Volvo's roof. Across the water, a few lights twinkled in the houses and cottages on the island.

Then, as they cleared another willow, she saw it.

Chaos. Utter chaos. Ahead, flames and sparks shot into the sky. It looked as though the river itself was burning.

But it wasn't the river, it was Kieran's boatshed. She had known it in her bones, and now she was certain. She recognized the bend in the river, the cottages on the near side of it.

Dark shapes moved against the orange illumination. When she judged they were directly across the river from the shed, she pulled the car onto the grass and jumped out, her bag in her hand. In the silence as the Volvo's siren died, she could hear shouts across the water, but the wail of the fire engine was still distant.

Ian came round the car to stand beside her. 'Holy shit! How're we going to get over there?' A narrowboat was moored a few feet downstream, but it was dark and apparently unoccupied. 'And they're going to have a hell of a time getting down here from the museum,' Ian added. There was no sign of the engine yet.

One of the dark figures had seen them and begun waving frantically. 'Hey!' he called. 'Can you help us? Where's the fire brigade?'

'Coming. We're medics,' Tavie shouted back. 'Bring the skiff across. There's nothing you can do about the fire until the brigade gets here.' She could see Kieran's little boat, still tied up by the landing raft.

She saw the man hesitate for a moment, then he untied the boat, hopped in and quickly rowed across to them. He handled the skiff's oars easily.

'I don't know what happened,' he said when he reached them and manoeuvred the boat against the bank. 'I live next door. My wife and I were watching telly. There was a boom, then all hell broke loose.'

Boats were not Tavie's forte. She stepped carefully into the skiff, followed more confidently by Ian, and the man pushed off.

'Did you – is Kieran – is anyone hurt?' Tavie asked. She'd been called *ice maiden* because she was usually so calm at a scene, but now her heart felt as if it might pump out of her chest. Suddenly she realized that this was how Kieran had felt while they were searching for Rebecca Meredith, and his worst fears had been realized. Dread settled in the pit of her stomach.

'You know the guy who lives there?' Ian's dismay registered on his face, even in flickering light. 'Don't tell me it's that bloke – '

She didn't answer, focusing on the man rowing. 'Please, what's your name?'

'John.'

'John, is anyone hurt?'

'I don't know. We couldn't get close enough.' There was a crack, and more sparks shot into the air. 'Shit!' John said, pushing the blades harder through the water. The prow of the little skiff lifted from the force.

'My wife – we've got to get people away from there. Where is the fucking fire engine?'

Glancing back, Tavie saw flashing blue lights moving slowly towards the shore. 'They're coming. They've got to go through the park.'

'If they don't get here soon, there'll be nothing left.'

Tavie could feel the heat as they neared the landing raft. As soon as the skiff touched, she scrambled out, nearly missing her step. She could see a woman now, in front of the next-door cottage.

'John!' the woman shouted. 'Are they coming? Everything could go up any—'

'Get away, Janet.' John tied the skiff to a bollard and he and Ian climbed out on Tavie's heels. He motioned the woman towards the open ground to the right of their cottage.

Tavie looked back. The engine was aligned parallel to the river's edge now. They'd be pumping soon.

'Go, both of you,' she ordered. Then she had no more thought for them as she ran towards the flames.

'Tav, are you out of your mind?'

She heard Ian's words, but they seemed to have no connection to her.

She was close now, the heat scorching her face. There were only a few yards between the landing raft and the shed. Then she saw a dark shape and heard the high-pitched keening of a dog over the crackle of the fire.

'Finn! Finn!'

The dog yelped, but didn't come to her. Shielding her face with her arm, she took a few more steps and saw why. He wouldn't leave his master.

Kieran lay face down, legs splayed, arms beneath him, as if he'd fallen without trying to catch himself.

Tavie's training took over. She pulled her torch from her belt and ran the last few steps. Behind her Ian was muttering, 'You're mad, you're utterly mad', but he was right with her.

She knelt, playing the torch over Kieran's supine form. Finn whimpered and tried to lick her face. 'It's all right, boy, it's all right,' she said. 'Easy, now. Sit. Good boy.' The dog sat, but he was trembling with distress. The torch caught the gleam of the whites of his eyes.

Tavie put a hand on Kieran's shoulder and felt a reassuring movement in return. He groaned.

'Kieran, it's me. Can you turn over? Can you move?'

He moaned again and rolled towards her. 'I had to get – I had to get Finn.'

'Don't talk.' She played the light over his face, and for a horrifying moment she thought one side was charred black. Then she felt moisture, saw the sheen of blood on the hand she'd placed on his shoulder.

'My head.' He reached up. 'A beam came down.'

'We've got to move you. Can you stand?' She slipped an arm beneath his shoulder as Ian took his other side.

They got him to his feet, but then he twisted away from them. 'The boat . . . '

'Your boat's fine.'

'No, the *boat*. The shell I was building . . . ' He lurched towards a long, slender shape, made humped by the drape of a tarpaulin. 'Don't let it burn. Her boat.'

Shouts and the chug of the diesel pump carried across the water. Tavie recognized the captain's voice as he yelled, 'Clear the area, clear the area.' The force of the jet from the deck gun could do them serious damage – not to mention what would happen if the shed blew before the fire engine could get the fire under control. With a shudder, she thought of the solvents Kieran used on his boat repairs.

'Come on, Kieran.' She and Ian grabbed him again, half-lifting him off his feet as they pulled him away. They staggered forward, a human caterpillar. Finn ran a few feet ahead of them, looking back and yapping. 'We've got to get Finn out of here, right? You can do this.'

Kieran turned towards her, his face half-obscured by blood, but for the first time there was recognition in his eyes. She felt a rush of relief.

'Tavie?' he said. 'Tavie, somebody threw a petrol bomb through my window.' He sounded more baffled than outraged. 'Some bastard tried to blow me up.'

Gemma sat at the kitchen table, her tea forgotten, her mind spinning with horror at what she'd just learned. Had she imagined the coldness in Angus Craig's eyes that night, when he'd seen Toby and her mum? She didn't think so. How close had she come to something she couldn't imagine?

Across the table, Kincaid's face was tight with anger. 'I'd have killed him. I'd have killed him if he even touched you.'

His tone made her shiver, convulsively. She'd only heard him sound like that, icy and implacable,

a few times. And they had been dealing with murderers.

'You didn't know me, then,' she said.

'That wouldn't have mattered, if I'd found out.'

Would she have told him, she wondered?

And what would she have done at the time, if
Angus Craig *had* raped her, then threatened her with
the loss of her job? She'd had a child to support,
with no help from a deadbeat ex-husband. And she'd
been passionate about her work – had wanted more
than anything to prove herself, to get ahead in the
force.

But everything Peter Gaskill had told Becca
Meredith would have been true for Gemma as well.
She'd been seen leaving the pub with Craig. She
wouldn't have been able to prove that she hadn't
agreed to have sex with him, then changed her mind
afterwards.

And if it had got as far as court, which was highly
unlikely, Craig's defence would have made mince-
meat of her reputation. She'd too often seen what
defence lawyers could do to women who pressed rape
charges. Even bruises and vaginal tearing could be
put down to *liking it rough*. And once the suggestion
had been planted, the truth no longer mattered.

After something like that, even if the Met had
been unable to fire her, she'd have become a pariah.

Rebecca Meredith had more rank and clout, and
even that hadn't helped her.

Kincaid's urgent voice brought her back to the
present. 'Gemma, are you sure he didn't—'

'No, no, he never touched me. But, I wonder . . .

What if Becca's ex knew what happened? Or found out? Would he have felt the same as you?'

'Maybe. He seemed very protective of her.' Kincaid shook his head. 'But then it would have been Craig he killed, not Becca.'

'What if he was jealous?'

'Jealous enough to kill her because she'd been raped?' He grimaced. 'Possible, but twisted. And I don't think Freddie Atterton is twisted.'

'You like him, don't you? Atterton?'

Shrugging, Kincaid said, 'I suppose I do. But more than that, I don't like the idea of him being a convenient scapegoat for the Yard's dirty laundry. Innocent until proven guilty. I'd put my money on Craig, in a heartbeat.'

Gemma stood, gathered their cups and began rinsing them in the sink. Then she closed the tap and turned back to him. 'Craig, yes. I can see that. What I don't understand is why now? Becca Meredith reported the incident to Peter Gaskill a year ago.'

'I'm thinking she found out he'd retired with commendations, and a gong to boot,' Kincaid said, pushing back his chair and reaching down to stroke Geordie's ears. 'She put her faith in her superior officer, and he betrayed it. She must have been furious. I'm surprised she didn't kill Gaskill.'

Hands still dripping, Gemma came back to the table and sat down. 'Yes, but angry as she must have been, she was still just as powerless. Why would Craig kill her?'

Kincaid gave the dog a last pat, then stared past Gemma, his eyes unfocused. 'Unless . . . Unless she had more ammunition, or new ammunition. Unless she'd found some way to prove that what happened to her wasn't consensual. Or . . . Look at the timeline.' He ran his hand through his hair, his habit when he was thinking, making the ends stand up like hedgehog bristles.

'If you were a target four years ago, and Meredith was raped a year ago,' he went on, 'what was Craig doing in the years in between? And even in the years before that?' Kincaid looked at her, his gaze sharp now. 'If this is his pattern, I'd stake my life he's a repeater. You and Becca Meredith can't have been his only targets.' He leaned across the table and gripped her fingers so hard she winced. 'What would you have done, Gem?'

She thought it out, as repugnant as it was. 'I wouldn't have had anyone to turn to – no one I at least *thought* I could trust, the way Becca did Peter Gaskill. And I'd have known, like Becca, that it would end my career if I went public, no matter the outcome. But I'd have wanted – something – something that might one day give me the power to – to damage him.'

She thought of other women, police officers with husbands or children, with careers they'd worked hard to achieve, or just pay cheques that put much-needed food on the table. 'What if some of the others – and I think you're right, we have to assume there are others – what if they filed rape reports, but listed the assailant as unknown? Then there would be a record, and DNA on file, if there was ever a chance to use it against him.'

And if any of the women had done so, had they

lived in silence afterwards, for months? Years? Would the lie have corroded the very fabric of their lives?

Inspiration struck Gemma. 'I could ask Melody,' she said. 'She's working with Project Sapphire. We could check the files. Unsolved cases. There would be a profile, and more than just his targeting of female police officers.' Gemma shifted restlessly in her chair as she thought it through. 'If a woman lied about something like that, she'd put as much truth in the report as possible. It's human nature, the easiest way. So there would be similarities in the reports, if you knew what you were looking for.'

Kincaid nodded. 'You might turn up something. Would Melody be willing to keep this confidential? This is one occasion when I'd just as soon we went outside the usual channels.' His expression told her that his disagreement with Denis Childs was not going to be easily dismissed.

'But we're making one really big assumption here,' he went on, 'which is that Craig only targets police officers. If he operates outside the box, we're talking needle in a haystack.'

'Oh, God.' Gemma thought of other women, more lives tainted, ruined. Then she shook her head. 'No. I don't think so. He has to have leverage. It's the job that gives him that. And he'll look for it.'

She closed her eyes, trying to recall the details of that evening in the pub, four long years ago. Her mates had been teasing her about being newly and officially single. Craig could easily have overheard. And, by asking a few innocent questions, he could have learned that she'd just been promoted and was ambitious about her job. But apparently no one had mentioned Toby.

Something occurred to her. 'He was playing a bit close to home, wasn't he, with Becca Meredith? And I don't mean just geographically. She was a DCI and less likely to be intimidated by his threats. I was only a lowly sergeant when he meant to try it with me, and barely that. Maybe, with Becca, he was getting too comfortable.'

'Or pushing the envelope, more likely,' Kincaid said. 'Needing more risk, more stimulation. And if he was matey with Gaskill, he must have thought he was home fr—' His phone rang. 'Damn!' He fished it from his jeans pocket and checked the caller ID. 'It's Singla, the DI from Henley. I'll have to take it.'

She watched his face as he listened to the tinny voice issuing from the phone speaker. The crease deepened between his brows. He glanced at the kitchen clock, then back at her, nodding although his caller couldn't see. 'Right. I'm on my way,' he said. But when he ended the call, he sat and stared at Gemma, looking puzzled.

'What's happened?' she asked. 'Have they arrested Atterton?'

'No. No, he's fine, as far as I know. But it sounds as though someone's just tried to murder one of the SAR team.'

Chapter Twelve

Tavie and Ian managed to get Kieran as far as the lawn of the next-door cottage before the engine began pumping a jet of water onto the burning shed. But from there he refused to budge. He sank to the ground, his arm round Finn, blood and tears streaming down his face as he watched the flames turn to black smoke.

Tavie looked a question at Ian.

'We're far enough, I think,' he said. Lights were appearing on the river as other residents arrived in boats, and some ferried part of the brigade crew across. 'They'll have it damped down soon.'

John and his wife, a pleasant-looking middle-aged woman, had come back to their own lawn. 'Can we help? Is it safe enough now?' the woman asked Tavie. 'I'm Janet, by the way.' Then she turned to Kieran. 'Kieran, I'm so sorry. Anything we can do . . . '

Kieran made a sound that might have been a whimper.

'How about a towel and some water?' Tavie said briskly. 'And, John, can you direct the boats?' They both went quickly to their tasks.

'Now.' Tavie turned to Kieran. 'I'm going to have a look at your head.'

'Leave it,' Kieran mumbled, but the protest was weak. His gaze was fixed on the fire.

Tavie opened her bag and started pulling out supplies, taking the opportunity to say quietly to Ian, 'Radio the Captain. Tell him what Kieran said about the petrol bomb. They'll need to keep onlookers away from the scene and notify the police as soon as possible.'

When Janet returned with towels and a bowl filled with water, Tavie thanked her and waved her away. Kieran jerked when she began to dab at his face.

'Hold still, damn it.' She shone her torch on the damage, but as she wiped the blood away, she breathed a sigh of relief. The gash ran from his forehead into his scalp – messy, but shallow. The bleeding had already slowed to a seep.

'You need stitches. We'll get you to A&E in no time.'

Kieran started to shake his head, winced. 'Just close it up, Tavie. It's nothing. And I'm not concussed.'

'Oh, yeah? We'll see about that.' Using her small torch, she looked at his pupils and found them normal and reactive, a good sign. But when she saw his eyes move with little repetitive jerks, she sat back, concerned. 'Kieran, you've got nystagmus. Have you been drinking?' She hadn't smelled alcohol on his breath, but checking for involuntary movement of the pupils was a common sobriety test for both medics and law enforcement.

'No. It's vertigo,' he said reluctantly. 'Chronic. There was a bomb, in Iraq . . . '

'Oh, bloody hell, Kieran.' That explained the eye movement, and other things began to add up that hadn't made sense to her before. 'Why the hell didn't you tell me?'

He glanced at her, then back at the diminishing blaze. 'Would you have let me on the team if I had?'

She didn't want to admit he was right. 'And what were you going to do if you fell flat on your face in the field?'

'Tell you I tripped.' He gave a ghost of a smile. 'And it's not always this bad.' A note of pleading entered his voice. 'Really. It's just the storm, and the last few days, and – and the bang on the head . . . '

'You're definitely going to hospital.'

'No. Tavie, please.' He put his hand on her arm, and it occurred to her that he never voluntarily touched her. 'I'll stay here. John can lend me a sleeping bag. I don't want to leave the shed.'

'Don't be daft.'

'I'll sleep in the Land Rover then, by the museum. I've done it often enough.'

'Kieran—'

'I'm conscious. You can't force me.'

Nor could she. And when she thought of what associations hospitals must have for him, after Iraq, she put her mind to coming up with another solution.

'Come to me then,' she said. 'You and Finn. I can put you up until you're sorted. And keep an eye on you.'

A uniformed police officer – a sergeant by his stripes – appeared out of the darkness. 'This the owner of the shed?' he asked, peering at Kieran.

When Kieran nodded, the sergeant went on. 'What's all this about a petrol bomb? Neighbour said you repair boats in there. Sure you didn't get careless and set some solvent alight, mate?'

All Tavie's fear and adrenaline suddenly condensed into a wave of fury, cold and bright. She stood up, her face inches from the sergeant's, and jabbed her finger at his chest. 'Don't you dare take that tone with my patient. Detective Inspector Singla's already been informed about this attack. For your information, this man was on yesterday's SAR team, and he bloody well knows a petrol bomb when he sees one. He could have been killed tonight.'

Finn had been glued to Kieran's side, but now he stood and made a low sound in his throat, a hint of a growl.

The sergeant gave him a wary glance and backed off a step. 'Singla, is it? Don't know him.'

'You will. Thames Valley CID. And he didn't seem the sort to suffer fools gladly.'

'Now, look here. There's no need to—'

Finn growled again, a bit more loudly this time.

The sergeant took another step back and seemed to decide to err on the side of prudence. 'Right. DI Singla. I'll just make certain Control is on it.'

But then, having distanced himself from Tavie and the dog by a few feet, he puffed up with renewed authority. 'Mind you, whether this was arson or an accident, it's a crime scene, and you' – he looked at Kieran – 'are not to go on the property. Or remove anything from it. We'll need a fixed address for you, Mr—'

'Connolly,' said Tavie.

'Mr Connolly, then,' said the sergeant. 'Someone will be along to interview you shortly. And I'd advise you to keep that dog under control.'

'Finn, easy,' said Kieran.

'Mr Connolly is going to stay with me. They both are.' Tavie gave the sergeant her address.

Kieran put his head in his hands.

Tavie looked at Kieran standing in the middle of her sitting room and wondered what on earth she was going to do with him.

He not only towered over her, he dwarfed the small room. And he was swaying slightly, like a large tree about to topple.

'Sit,' she ordered, as if he were one of the dogs, and pointed at the biggest chair.

He sat, if a little unsteadily, and she felt more comfortable now that she could look down on him. She realized she'd spent most of her time with Kieran in unenclosed spaces, where the foot's difference in their heights hadn't seemed so apparent.

And then, as she looked round the sitting room that suddenly felt claustrophobic, it occurred to her that the only men who had ever set foot in her house were her mates from the fire and ambulance brigades who had helped her move.

The little house had been her rebellion against the sort of life she'd led with her ex, Beatty. She'd lived with her parents until she and Beatty married, when she'd moved into the flat Beatty owned in Leeds. A year later they'd both taken jobs in Oxfordshire, and the semi-detached house on the new estate outside Reading seemed to have scooped them up of its own volition.

Eight long years later their marriage had been fractured beyond repair, and that suburban life had paled for them both. Beatty had discovered that what he really wanted was a pliant woman who needed a manly man, and he had no trouble acquiring an obliging red-haired nurse.

And Tavie had found that what *she* really wanted was to make her own choices, thank you very much, and that had included buying a house that hadn't suited anyone's wishes but her own.

Hence the doll's house, and she'd loved it. She loved her single life, her job, her dog and her work with SAR. Still, there were times when the house had begun to seem a bit empty, but sudden occupation by a large, bloody, surly man, and his equally large dog, was not quite the solution she'd had in mind.

The dogs, having finished greeting one another with thorough sniffing and much tail-wagging, sat too.

'Okay,' she said, glancing round the room a little wildly. 'Let's get your feet up.' Spotting the small trunk she used to store extra blankets, she pulled it over and plopped a cushion on top. 'There you are then.'

'I'm not crippled. I've just had a bang on the head.' Kieran glared at her, but the effect was somewhat lessened by the butterfly bandage on his forehead, which pulled the corner of his eyebrow up in an involuntary query.

There'd always been a rakish quality to his looks,

she thought, with his pale skin, deep-blue eyes and dark, tousled hair. Maybe a scar would suit him. At least this one would be visible.

She eyed the length of her small sofa. 'I'll sleep down here,' she said. 'You can take the bed. It's a queen-size, so I don't think your feet will dangle off the end.' The bed was one of the few things she'd kept from the divorce.

Kieran leaned back in the chair and closed his eyes. His face looked gaunt in repose, and when he spoke, his voice was heavy with exhaustion. 'Tavie, I am not going to take your bed. I appreciate everything you're doing for me. I really do.' He touched an exploratory fingertip to the bandage on his forehead, then winced. 'But that's too much. I'll sleep on the floor. And as soon as they'll let me, I'll go back to the shed. I can buy another camp bed if I need to.'

Remembering the flames, and aware of how much damage the pumped water would have caused, Tavie shook her head. 'Kieran, there may not be anything le—'

'I have to see.' He sat up, urgency back in his voice. 'It's all I have. Whatever there is.'

Tavie sank down on the edge of the sofa. Immediately Tosh came over and rested her head on Tavie's knee, looking up at her with her dark German-shepherd brows drawn in a V. She, too, seemed unsettled by the change in their household routine. Tavie stroked the soft spot on the top of her head. 'The boat – the one under the tarp – you said you were building it for her. Did you mean Rebecca Meredith?'

'I'd wanted to build a wooden shell since I first

started rowing, as a kid,' he said, more quietly. 'My father was a furniture-maker, so I knew about wood. It was – she seemed – I thought my boat might take her to the Olympics. It was daft, a stupid daydream.' He shook his head. 'Even if she'd wanted the shell, no Olympic committee would have let her compete in a wooden boat. She'd have had the best carbon-fibre racing single that money could buy.'

'Could she have done it?' Tavie asked. 'The Olympics? Was she – was she that good?'

Kieran rubbed his fingers against the stubble on his jaw and blinked, hard. 'I'd never seen anyone row like that. For her, it was like breathing. Perfection. But winning takes more than that gift. It takes obsession, and she had that, too.'

'And you . . . ' Tavie took a breath. She knew she was treading on forbidden territory, but she had to ask. 'Where did you fit into that obsession?'

Kieran's smile was brief, self-mocking. 'I was . . . convenient.'

'How did you . . . I mean' – Tavie could feel herself blushing – 'I know it's none of my business, but how did the two of you – '

But he seemed almost relieved to talk about it. 'Last summer. I used to see her rowing when I was out on the river in the evenings. Then one day she had trouble with one of her riggers, and I stopped to help. We chatted.'

Finn, having failed in his attempts to get Tosh interested in a rope tug, settled at Kieran's feet. Kieran put his hand on Finn's head, a mirror image of Tavie and Tosh, and for a moment she wondered if they would be whole without their dogs. Who had Kieran been with Rebecca Meredith, without Finn for armour?

He went on, his words slowing as the memory caught him up. 'After that, we seemed to take our boats out at the same time. We'd row pieces, but I couldn't quite beat her, even with the advantage of my height. And we'd talk.'

'Then one evening I didn't go. I was having . . . a bad day. She knew where I lived – we'd rowed upriver past the shed dozens of times. So she came to see if I was all right.'

The silence stretched into awkwardness. 'And after that, you were,' said Tavie lightly, past the tightness in her throat.

Kieran shrugged, gave her the same half-mocking smile as earlier. 'I always knew I was a diversion. I'm just not sure from what.'

'Yesterday . . . ' Tavie thought about how to put it, then continued, hesitantly. 'Yesterday, you said she was too good to have had an accident on a calm evening. And then, tonight – the boatshed. You said it was a petrol bomb. Why? Why would someone do that to you, unless it was to do with . . . ' She suddenly had trouble with the name, although yesterday she had so blithely told the dogs to *Find Rebecca*. Rebecca Meredith had been no more than that to her yesterday. A name. 'To do with her,' she finished.

His face closed, like a shutter coming down. 'I don't know.'

'Kieran – '

Shaking his head at her, he put his hands on the

arms of the chair and struggled to stand. 'I should go, Tavie. It's not . . . I don't want to – whoever threw that bottle tonight could come back.'

So much for getting to spend the night in his own bed, beside Gemma, Kincaid thought. He'd thrown his overnight bag back in the car and driven straight to Henley, without stopping to pick up Cullen.

When he'd rung Cullen from his mobile, Doug had offered to take the train straight away, but Kincaid told him to wait until morning. 'Let me talk to this guy, Kieran, and see what happened. I told Singla I wanted the first interview.'

'Yesterday he seemed a bit off to me, that Kieran bloke.' Doug's voice crackled as the mobile signal faded in and out. 'You'd have thought that boat was the Holy Grail, the way he was fussing over it. Maybe *he* killed Becca Meredith, then tried to blow himself up.'

'I can't see him trying to burn his dog to death,' Kincaid said. He'd dealt with suicides who had shot their dogs, but not something like this. But if the relationship between man and dog was as close as it seemed, he supposed Kieran could have sedated the dog and set the blaze as some sort of ritual funeral pyre.

He thought it much more likely, however, that someone *had* thrown a Molotov cocktail through Kieran Connolly's window. 'Nor do we have any idea why Connolly would have murdered Becca Meredith,' he went on.

'He was a rower,' Doug said. 'He'd have known how to capsize her.'

'True enough.' Kincaid was driving down Remenham Hill, with the lights of Henley ahead. 'But that's means without motive, which doesn't do us much good. I'm almost there. I'll ring you when I know more.' He disconnected and was soon through the town centre. Checking the address Singla had given him, he pulled the car up in West Street, not far from the fire station.

Warm light twinkled through the leaded windows of the little terraced house. As he knocked, the murmur of voices from inside was immediately drowned out by a chorus of barking.

'Tosh, Finn, easy,' a woman commanded, and Kincaid recognized the team leader's voice from the previous day. The barking stopped and the door swung open.

'Superintendent Kincaid, isn't it?' Tavie Larssen looked surprised. 'I thought it would be DI Singla.'

When Kincaid had met her yesterday she'd been wearing a dark SAR uniform. Tonight she was in her paramedic's uniform, which was black as well. The severe, dark clothing suited her, he thought, giving some authority to her small frame and delicate features.

'He sent me. May I come in?'

'Oh, of course.' She stepped back and grabbed a black Labrador retriever by the collar. Connolly's dog – what was his name? 'Sorry, Finn's not used to the house protocol,' said Tavie, answering his unspoken question.

She opened a tin on the table by the door, looked the Lab in the eyes and said, 'Sit.' The dog plopped his rear on the floor immediately and was joined by the German shepherd, which sat as well. They snapped up the two dog biscuits Tavie fished from the tin, with an alacrity that made Kincaid fear for her fingers. 'Good dogs,' she said. 'Go lie down.'

They did.

No longer distracted by the dogs, Kincaid focused on Kieran Connolly, who sat across the room. His forehead was bandaged, his face still smudged with soot and blood, his brown T-shirt and carpenter's trousers splashed with darker brown splotches. He started to rise, but Kincaid waved him back. 'No need to get up.'

'Here.' Tavie gestured Kincaid towards the sofa. 'I'll just make some tea, shall I?' she said, a little uncertainly.

'That would be brilliant.'

'Right.' She smiled at him, then glanced at Connolly with a slight frown before stepping into the adjoining kitchen.

Through the doorway Kincaid could see a cream-coloured enamel range and, on the room's two high, wide ledges, an antique mirror and a few pretty china plates. In the centre of the kitchen a vase of bright autumn foliage and berries stood on a plain wooden table.

Tavie filled an old kettle and set it on the range, then began placing mugs on a tray.

Turning his attention to the sitting room, Kincaid thought that it was just as simple and appealing as the kitchen. There was a wooden chair painted in light blues and greens, adorned with a red throw, a stack of books on the floor beside it. A small table held a globe, and wide ledges like the ones in the kitchen displayed a few unframed portraits in oil. Sisal carpeting covered the floor, and a gas fire burned in an iron fireplace with a tiled surround. Tosh, the German shepherd, had curled up on a floral hooked rug before the fire. Beside her, dog toys spilled from a woven basket.

It was very much a single woman's house, Kincaid thought, and it reminded him of the tiny garage flat that Gemma had lived in before they'd moved into the Notting Hill house together.

Kieran Connolly, squeezed into the small upholstered armchair, looked as awkward as the proverbial bull in the china shop, and just as unhappy. Finn had settled at his owner's feet.

Kincaid sat carefully on the sofa, suddenly aware of his own long legs. 'How are you feeling?' he asked Connolly, who shrugged.

'I'll live.' He reached up as if to touch the wound, then dropped his hand. 'Tavie says I'm going to look like Harry Potter.'

'That might not be a bad thing.' Kincaid smiled, hoping to put him at ease. 'Can you tell me what happened tonight?'

Tavie came back into the room, bearing a tray with a teapot and mugs decorated in an alternating pattern of blue and white hearts and stars. A fanciful touch for a serious woman, Kincaid thought.

'I was – I was having a bit of a rest,' Connolly said. The glance he gave Tavie told Kincaid there was some shared meaning to this. 'On the camp bed in my shed.

I repair boats, and I live in the shop. There's just the one room.'

Kincaid took a cup from Tavie, nodded Yes to milk and shook No to sugar. She poured Kieran's without asking – black, with two spoonfuls – and sat on the edge of the painted chair. 'Go on,' Kincaid prompted Kieran.

'There was a crash. Glass breaking. Then flames shooting up. For a minute I thought . . . ' Kieran wrapped both hands round his mug. The tea sloshed. He was trembling. 'It was like Iraq – ' He held the mug to his lips, sipped, swallowed, and it seemed to steady him. 'But then I saw the bottle burning. What was left of it. It was a wine bottle – I could tell because the label stayed in one piece. So did the neck, with the burning rag stuffed in it. Finn was barking like mad and pushing at me. I knew I had to get him out. We reached the door. Then there was this – this sort of sucking whoosh. I knew what it was – the air goes just before an explosion. I grabbed Finn by the collar and dived for the lawn.'

Kieran closed his eyes for a moment, then drank the rest of his tea as if suddenly very thirsty.

'The next thing I remember is Tavie telling me to get up.'

'Something like that,' she agreed drily, but she looked pale. 'I thought you were bloody dead.' Refilling Kieran's mug, she said, 'Good thing your neighbours didn't dither about calling nine-nine-nine. But still, you must have been out for several minutes. That's quite a blow. You need to get an X-ray – '

He gave her a look that clearly meant this was

one argument she was not going to win. 'I'm fine. Just a little shaky.'

Kincaid held his mug out for a refill as well, although after the pot of tea at home with Gemma, he was about ready to swim in the stuff. 'Kieran, do you have any idea why someone would have done this to you?'

'I – It's crazy. You'll think I'm mad.'

'No, I won't.' Kincaid leaned forward, resting his cup on his knee. 'Why don't you tell me.'

Kieran looked up, met Kincaid's eyes, assessing him. Whatever he saw there seemed to swing the balance in Kincaid's favour. 'I saw something. On Monday evening, before Becca went out on the river. And on Sunday, the same time.'

'What do you mean, you saw something?' asked Tavie. 'You didn't tell me.'

'I didn't have a chance.' He looked back to Kincaid. 'I was running. Since the days have got shorter, I've been rowing in the mornings and running in the evenings. You know where we found the Filippi?'

Kincaid nodded. 'Yes. And you were upset. You said that Becca Meredith wouldn't have capsized on a calm evening. That she was too good a rower.'

'No one believed me.' Kieran's face was set in a scowl.

'We did, actually,' Kincaid reassured him. But he wasn't going to say more until he'd found out what Kieran had to tell them. 'And I believe you now. Is that where you saw something? Where we found the boat?'

'No. But that's not where she went in the water.'

Kincaid sat forward, his pulse quickening. 'How do you know?'

'Because I know where she *did* go in.'

'What?' said Tavie. 'Kieran, what are you—'

The German shepherd, which had been lying quietly by the hearth, raised her head and barked, punctuating her mistress's alarm.

'Okay, okay.' Kincaid held up his hand like a traffic cop. 'Let's all take it easy. Kieran, why don't you back up and start from the beginning.'

Kieran shifted in his chair and shot another uneasy glance at Tavie. 'Look, I know it sounds as if I was some sort of a stalker, but it wasn't like that. When I first met Becca, last summer, I was rowing in the evenings – I told Tavie that. But now I've been taking my shell out at first light. Then, in the evenings, I'd run the river path about the time I knew Becca would be rowing. That made it easy for us to . . . to meet up afterwards.'

Tavie shifted on the edge of her chair. When Kincaid glanced at her, the expression on her delicate face was one of disapproval. And, Kincaid thought, possibly hurt.

'Sometimes I'd go to the cottage, after she'd taken the shell back to Leander.' Kieran threw that out like a challenge, as if her unspoken response had irritated him. Then he sighed. 'But mostly I just liked to watch her row. It was . . . beautiful . . . you can't imagine.'

'I wish I'd seen her,' said Kincaid, and he did.

Kieran nodded, an acknowledgment. 'I was never as good as that, nowhere near, but I could tell when she was doing something wrong, getting into a bad pattern. I suppose I was sort of an unofficial coach. But . . . this last weekend, she was . . . different.' He hesitated, looking uncomfortable again.

'Would you like to speak to me on your own?' Kincaid asked, wondering if the problem lay with Tavie.

Kieran hesitated, then said, 'No. No, I want Tavie to stay. It's just that – how things were with Becca and me – when I try to explain it, it sounds . . . weird. But it didn't *seem* that way. What we did together was something that was just between us.'

'Okay. I get that,' Kincaid reassured him. 'So what was odd about last weekend?'

'I didn't see her on the river on Friday evening. Or on Saturday morning, which was usually her biggest training day. So I went to the cottage. Just to make sure she was all right, you know, not ill or anything. The Nissan wasn't in the drive. I thought she wasn't home, so I was surprised when she came out.' Kieran's frown drew down the corner of his bandage. 'But she was – I don't know – tense. Preoccupied. Not' – his lips tightened – 'pleased to see me. She said she'd taken the train home the night before, and she'd never done that, not once in the time I'd known her.

'And then, when I offered to run her into London to pick up the car, she was . . . short with me. She said she had things to do.'

'Did she say what?'

'No. I just left. What else could I do?' Kieran shrugged. 'I saw her out on Sunday evening, rowing, but she didn't really speak to me. I thought – I thought maybe I'd done something wrong, something to upset her, but I couldn't imagine what. Then, on Monday,

I must have been a bit early for my run, or she was a bit late going out from Leander, because I missed her altogether.'

His face twisted with grief. 'If I'd just been there . . . ' He rubbed a hand across his mouth. 'I might have stopped him.'

'Stopped who, Kieran? You said you saw something. Are you saying you saw *someone*?'

Kieran nodded. 'I thought he was a fisherman. On the Bucks bank, between Temple Island and the last meadow. The woods are heavy there, but there's a little green hollow between the path and the bank. He was there on Sunday when Becca was rowing, then again on Monday evening, the same time. When I thought about it afterwards, I realized he wasn't actually fishing, although he had some gear. It was more like he was . . . waiting. So, this afternoon, I went to look. There was a footprint in the mud, and the edge of the bank looked churned up, as if there'd been a struggle. Becca would have been rowing close to shore there, going upriver, and as late as she was, it would have been almost completely dark . . . She wouldn't have seen someone until she was right on top of them.'

'How deep is the river there?' Kincaid asked.

'Not very. A few feet maybe, that close to the bank.'

'So you think this . . . fisherman . . . could have waded in and capsized her?'

'He'd have to have known how.'

'Ah.' Kincaid sat back in his chair, feeling the weight of what had happened to Becca Meredith.

Kieran's story made sense, put together with what they had already learned. 'I think perhaps he did. You see, we found evidence, both on the body and the shell. It looks as if she was held under the boat with her own oar.'

'Oh, God.' Kieran's face grew almost as white as the gauze on his forehead. 'I thought – I thought I was just being paranoid.' His eyes filled. 'Why? Why would someone do that to her?'

'I was hoping you might tell me.'

Shaking his head, Kieran said, 'I can't imagine. Becca was – she could be sharp with people, you know? She had to be tough, with her job, and rowers in general aren't the most patient sort. But she'd never deliberately hurt someone.'

'What about her competition? Would someone have wanted to put her out of the running that badly?'

'Oh, no.' Kieran sounded horrified. 'Not the girls at Leander. I know them – they're great. I've worked on their boats. And besides, I don't think anyone really knew how serious Becca was, or how good she was. That's one reason she rowed in the evenings, and on Saturdays she stayed downriver, away from the crew's normal training course. She didn't want people clocking her.'

'Milo Jachym knew.'

'You've talked to Milo?' Kieran looked surprised, then nodded, thinking about it. 'Yeah, Milo knew. But he'd coached her, and they were friends. He's a good guy.'

Kincaid reserved judgement. Milo seemed like a nice bloke, and had appeared genuinely grieved about

Becca's death, as well as concerned about Freddie. But how many more chances would Milo have to get one of his own female crew an Olympic slot? Not to mention that Becca would have trusted him, if he'd called to her from the bank – and he would certainly have known how to capsize a rower.

Tavie, who'd been sitting on the edge of her chair, making an obvious effort not to interrupt, stood up and went to her dining table. Shuffling through a stack of papers, she said, 'Kieran, this place – you mean upstream from Temple Island, right?'

'Yeah, it's—'

Tavie held up a sheet of paper. 'I know exactly where it is. The team on that sector – it was Rafe and Andrea – had a minor alert there. It's in the log.'

'What do you mean, a minor alert?' Kincaid asked.

'The dogs showed some interest, but seemed confused and moved on. We log any alert – sometimes they'll form a pattern that will help us locate a victim. But this was isolated.'

Kincaid frowned. 'Could the dogs have picked up Becca's scent there, even though she was never onshore?'

'It's possible. And he – Kieran's fisherman – may have had it on his clothes or gear.'

'They picked up her scent from the Filippi,' Kieran said, 'and it was in the water.'

'Right.' Kincaid thought of the times he'd watched Geordie, their cocker spaniel, run in the park, ears flying, nose to the ground, and he'd envied the rich sensory world that was beyond his perception. 'Can I make copies of your log and your maps? I'll have someone return the originals to you as soon as possible.'

When Tavie nodded, he turned back to Kieran. 'You saw this fisherman from the opposite bank. Would you recognize him?'

'It was almost dark both days, and he wore a hat that shadowed his face. The only thing I'd be willing to swear to was that it was a man.'

'Not a tall woman?'

Kieran thought for a moment. 'No. The body shape was wrong. Too wide in the shoulders. And something about the way he stood . . . with his legs apart.'

'Okay, we'll go with that. But that leaves us with another big question. If we assume that the same person attacked you, how did he know who you were and where you lived? Could he have recognized you, and been afraid you'd recognized him?'

'I – I don't know. I run almost every day, and I suppose people round here know who I am, but – there's something more. This afternoon, when I found the hollow, I could have sworn someone was watching me. Eyes between the shoulder blades. You know the feeling.'

'You think he saw you there?'

'I thought I was imagining things. But I suppose it's possible . . . ' A slight shudder ran through Kieran's body. Finn lifted his head and Kieran reached down to stroke the dog, as if comforting them both.

'Could he have followed you today?' Kincaid asked.

'I think I'd have seen someone crossing the

meadow behind me, even in the dusk.' Kieran paused, thinking it through. 'But he'd have known the foot-path crosses the Marlow road. If he got back to the road by a shorter way and picked up a car, he could have seen me as I came back into Henley . . . '

'You and Finn are not exactly unnoticeable,' Kincaid agreed. 'What about before the fire tonight? Did you hear anything, see anything?'

Eyes wide, Kieran said, 'I'd forgotten. There was a splash. Finn heard it, too, I think. It might have been an oar.'

'So you think your arsonist came by boat?'

'It *is* an island. And if he'd docked further up or down, he'd have walked through my neighbours' gardens to get to my place, then had to go back again. The properties are very small. He'd have taken a huge risk of being seen.' Kieran's face hardened. 'My guess is that he threw the damned bottle from a boat, and hoped for the best. Bastard!'

Kincaid thought of the myriad of boats moored up and down both sides of Henley Bridge and gave an inner groan. Someone could easily have taken a skiff from one of the boat-hire firms. Uniform branch would have their work cut out for them, trying to trace a temporarily missing boat.

He stood. There were many things to set in motion. 'The arson team will get started on your shed at first light, Kieran. We'll see what they turn up. In the meantime I certainly think it best if you stay here. Tavie, I'm going to send a uniformed officer for the map and the log. I want someone guarding that spot until I can get the SOCOs there in the morning.'

Kieran pushed himself up out of the chair, although he wobbled a bit. Both the dogs jumped up as well, panting gently in anticipation of a new activity.

'Thank you,' Kieran said simply.

'I'm the one who should be thanking you. Both of you.' He included Tavie with a brief smile, then turned back to Kieran. 'But there's one thing I don't understand. Why didn't you tell us yesterday, when we found the Filippi, that you had a relationship with Rebecca Meredith?'

'I – I just – I suppose all I could think was to do what she wanted. And she didn't want anyone to know about us.'

'Why? You were both single adults.'

'I used to believe it was because she was ashamed of me.' Kieran looked down at his blood- and soot-spattered clothes. 'Even at the best of times, I'm not exactly the guy you introduce at office parties, or take to your Christmas dinner.'

'Would her ex-husband have minded that she was seeing someone?'

Kieran considered. 'I don't think so. At least, they seemed to be friends. But she said – one time when we'd had as much of a row as you could have with Becca, because she would just shut you out – she said that she couldn't be seen to have a . . . a relationship with anyone.'

From the way Kieran coloured and glanced at Tavie, Kincaid suspected that those weren't the exact words Becca had used. 'Why not?' he asked.

'She said she couldn't risk it being used as ammunition against her.'

Chapter Thirteen

The pain seared through his legs, his arms, his shoulders, his chest. He thought he would do anything to make it stop. Die, even.

But some small part of his brain, hazy from oxygen deprivation, told him he couldn't. Couldn't stop, couldn't die. Not yet.

Water, freezing dirty water from the tidal Thames, lapped over his feet, then began to spill over the sides of the boat. But it might have been treacle, for all the progress the eight was making through it.

The boat felt as though it were made of cement, every stroke of the blades seemed a ponderous effort. Someone had given out, given up, and the rest were pulling a dead weight. Who the hell was it? Anger surged through him, but his lips were too cold to give it voice.

From bow and stroke he heard the hoarse curses of other men too exhausted to shout. Then, 'Move it! Move the fucking boat, you bastards!' screamed the cox, the only one of them with enough energy left to make himself heard. 'Bowside, bowside, watch your oars! We're going to—'

Too late. Their blades clashed and tangled with

the oars of the other boat. There was a crack, a sharp pain in his chest – the handle of his blade hitting him with crushing force – then the oar was torn from his hands.

'No!' he shouted. 'No!' They'd never recover from this. He had to –

But the icy water washed over his mouth, his face. The boat was going down, and he couldn't breathe –

Freddie woke, sweating, thrashing, gasping, his sheets twined around him like ropes.

'Shit. Oh, shit!' He sat up, pushing away the covers. The bloody Boat Race nightmare. He hadn't had that one in years. But this time it had been worse. His subconscious had pieced together what had been a disastrous rough-weather race with – with what must have happened to Becca. Dear God.

But the realization that he'd been dreaming brought little relief, because awake he felt just as helpless and out of control.

Until Ross had brought it up in the bar yesterday afternoon, he hadn't realized that the police actually might believe he'd killed Becca. 'They always think it's the spouse,' Ross had said. 'Or ex-spouse, in your case.'

In the shock of the first hours after Becca's death, Freddie had simply assumed their questions were routine. Now he saw that he had been an idiot, that he had no alibi for the time Becca must have drowned, no way to convince them of his innocence. He was as lost as he had been in the dream.

He lay back against the damp and pummelled pillows. Did it really matter, he wondered? Because nothing that remained to him seemed of any consequence at all.

Kincaid enjoyed the full English breakfast served at the Red Lion – with only the tiniest twinge of guilt for having deprived Doug Cullen of the same delights the previous morning. Then, as he had more than half an hour before he had to meet Doug at the train station, and as it was a gloriously crisp, bright autumnal morning, he left the hotel and walked across the road to Henley Bridge.

Leaning on the parapet, he gazed downriver, where the crews were just going out from Leander. Fours and eights pushed away from the landing raft, the crews taking a few moments to settle themselves and adjust gear or rigging. Then the oars began to dip in unison, and as they rose from the water they cast droplets that sparkled like diamonds in the clear light.

The boats began to slip away downstream, their coaches following along the towpath on their bicycles. Kincaid recognized Milo Jachym, shouting instructions to the women's eight.

He watched until boats and coaches disappeared from view, then left the bridge and walked thoughtfully up Thames Side towards the railway station. When he reached Station Road he checked his watch and, finding that he still had time to spare, continued along the pedestrian path until he reached the River and Rowing Museum. He'd read a brochure about the museum that morning at breakfast and it had given him an idea.

Inside, he bypassed the lure of the museum shop,

filled with potential gifts for Gemma and the children, and resisted the temptation of *The Wind in the Willows* exhibition as well.

Climbing the stairs, he entered the long gallery where the Sydney Coxless Four hung from the ceiling on permanent display. In that boat Steve Redgrave, Matthew Pinsent, Tim Foster and James Cracknell had won a gold medal for Great Britain in the Sydney Olympics. According to the placard, it was a British boat, an Aylings, custom-built for that particular crew and that particular race.

Seen from below, the long white hull seemed almost alien in its proportions, too impossibly long and slender to function. Out of its watery element, it might have been a giant's flying sword.

A video of the race itself played in an endless loop on a large video screen at the room's end. Kincaid had seen the race at the time, of course – the victory of Team GB had dominated every news and sports programme for days – but he'd paid it no more than passing attention.

Now, however, he watched the six minutes of the race intently, mesmerized by the power, the pain and the sheer breathtaking beauty of it. When the loop started over, he turned away reluctantly, the cheers of the crowd still ringing in his ears.

What he'd wanted to better understand was who Rebecca Meredith had been, what had made her tick. And he thought, looking at the boat, watching the film, that rowing at that level must be beyond anything most ordinary people ever experienced – a seductive cycle of pain and exhilaration and inconceivable grace.

But had it meant more to Becca Meredith than anything else in her life? Had it meant so much that she'd been willing to make a deal that would have tarnished her in a way that Angus Craig had not?

'Bugger!' said Doug Cullen. He stood beside Kincaid on the lawn in front of the blackened remains of Kieran Connolly's boatshed.

From the train station they'd walked to the boat hire above Henley Bridge and taken a small motor launch to the island. Kincaid had been happy to turn the boat-driving over to Cullen, who had piloted with finesse, easing the little launch into the landing raft with nary a bump.

Two uniformed arson investigators were moving methodically through the site, photographing, measuring, sampling, and Kincaid guessed that the launch tied up at the next-door neighbour's larger dock belonged to them. The blue-and-white crime-scene tape that had been staked around the shed swayed slightly in the rising breeze.

The photographer came out of the shed and walked across the postage stamp of lawn to meet them.

Kincaid held up his warrant card. 'Superintendent Kincaid, Sergeant Cullen. Scotland Yard.'

'Owen Morris. Oxfordshire Fire Investigation.' Morris transferred the camera to his left hand and shook theirs. 'Been expecting you.' He had grey-blond hair, bristle-cut, and the ruddy complexion of a fair-skinned man who spent too much time in the sun.

The smell of wet ash was strong, even in the cool air, and Kincaid thought that in yesterday's muggy damp the odour would have been sickening.

'This guy was damned lucky,' said Morris, nodding towards the shed, where his partner, a young redhead – who, just for an instant, reminded Kincaid of Gemma – went on taking samples and marking positions on a chart.

Kincaid raised a brow in surprise. 'It looks pretty devastating to me.'

'Messy, yeah, but the structure is still intact. Wall joists, all but one beam, even most of the roof.' Morris shook his head. 'Place was full of solvents. A few more minutes and the whole damned island might have gone up.'

'Is that what started the fire?' Kincaid asked. 'The solvents?'

'No. Have a look.' Morris walked to the shed and they followed. He pointed through what had been a window, now a hole surrounded by a few bits of splintered frame. 'It was a petrol bomb, all right. We found pieces of the bottle and of the rag wick. And you can see the cone of the blaze from the point of impact.'

Peering into the shed, Kincaid could see nothing but soot, rubbish and puddles of water. 'I'll take your word for it. So, if that's the case, did it come through this window?'

'I'd say definitely. Only one tin of solvent exploded, but that might have been what gave your owner the gash on the head.'

Kincaid turned and surveyed the shore, gauging the distance. 'An easy throw from a boat?'

'For someone with a good arm,' agreed Morris. 'Not to be sexist, but most likely a bloke.'

Cullen walked back to the landing raft, gazed upstream and downstream. 'We've been checking with boat hires, thinking maybe someone "borrowed" a little skiff. Why not a rowing single? There's no reason a sculler couldn't have eased in, tossed the bottle, rowed away. Quiet, quick, nearly invisible.'

Thinking it through, Kincaid said, 'We've made the assumption that whoever killed Becca Meredith was a rower. So that would make sense. But where did he get the boat?'

Doug shrugged. 'There are three rowing clubs within easy distance for an experienced sculler. Or . . . ' He gestured towards the single scull resting on trestles a few yards from the boatshed, streaked with soot, but otherwise apparently not badly damaged. 'I'd guess that was Connolly's boat. Who knows how many other boats there are on private property up and down the river?'

'There was a boat in the shed,' offered Morris. 'It looks as if Connolly was repairing it. Some burn damage, but not too bad. And that one' – he pointed towards a canvas-draped shape on the far side of the little lawn – 'I'd call that one a bloody miracle. Not a cinder on it.'

They walked across the grass and Doug lifted the tarp. 'Bloody hell,' he whispered, staring. He pulled the tarp further down, with the slow reverence that a lover might have used in revealing a beautiful, naked woman. When the boat was free, he stepped back and gave a low whistle.

It was a racing single, but it was built of wood, not carbon fibre. The shell was complete, and glistened with new varnish.

It might be a smaller version of the Sydney Four suspended in the museum, Kincaid thought, but the wood gave the boat a sense of richness – it almost hummed with life. He reached out, ran a hand along the grain of the perfectly joined and sanded segments. The wood felt like satin, and it was warm beneath his palm.

'Mahogany, at a guess,' said Morris. 'I do some woodworking, but this' – he shook his head – 'this is beyond anything I've ever seen. Certainly beyond an amateur's talents. It's exquisite.'

'Does anyone still row in wooden shells?' Kincaid asked.

'Some.' Doug stroked the boat, too, as if he couldn't resist. 'Connoisseurs. And a few people race in them, but probably not at championship level. But this – this you would want to own just because it's beautiful.' He walked round the shell, studying it. 'This isn't just engineering. It's art. This is as good a design as I've seen in a high-tech carbon-fibre boat – maybe better, although I'm no expert.'

He looked up, as if suddenly assailed by paranoia. 'You can't leave this boat just sitting out here. Anything could happen to it. And it could be worth a bloody fortune.'

'A fortune?' Kincaid asked. 'That's a relative term.'

'Well, a fortune to someone like me,' Doug admitted. 'But a boat like this would be pricey even for a top-flight sculler. And if the design is unique' – he shrugged – 'who knows?'

Would someone have killed for a boat like this, Kincaid wondered? Was it possible that the attack on Kieran was connected to this boat, and not Becca Meredith? Or were the two things related in a way he didn't see?

'We'll have a word with Kieran about it, as soon as possible,' he said. 'But first, I need to see if Forensics have made any progress at the site Kieran pinpointed. And we need to discover how the guy who did this' – he glanced at the burned shed – 'got here. You're right about the boat, though, Doug,' he added thoughtfully. 'It needs to be kept safe.'

'The neighbour's been very helpful,' said Morris. 'And he's got a little shed. Maybe he could lock it up for Mr Connolly. I'll have a word with him when we finish processing the scene.'

Kincaid nodded. 'Good idea.' He turned to Cullen. 'Doug, I'll organize someone to check with the other rowing clubs, if you can go back to Leander. Talk to Milo Jachym and the rest of the staff. See if anyone took a single scull out last night. And ask if anyone saw Freddie Atterton in the club. You'll fit right in,' he added with a grin. 'In the meantime I'll be at the incident room. I put off the press this morning, but I'll have to—' Cullen's phone rang, cutting him off.

'Sorry, guv,' said Cullen, with a shrug of apology as he pulled the phone from his jacket. He answered, identified himself, shot a glance at Kincaid as he listened. Then, thanking the caller, he hung up.

'You're not going to like this,' he told Kincaid. 'But the chief will. That was Becca Meredith's insurance broker, ringing me back. It seems that Freddie Atterton was still the beneficiary on Becca's life-insurance policy. To the tune of five hundred thousand pounds.'

Gemma had reached the kitchen doorway before she turned back. 'You'll be all right?'

Looking up from the tiny teaset arranged on the kitchen table, Alia gave her a reassuring smile. 'We'll be fine. Don't worry.'

The young Asian woman had been Charlotte's nanny when the child had lived in Fournier Street with her parents. Last night, after Kincaid had left for Henley, Gemma had been unable to get the image of Angus Craig out of her mind. She'd wanted to follow up on her idea of asking Melody to check the Project Sapphire files, so she'd rung Alia to see if she could mind Charlotte this morning.

Alia had been free, and had seemed pleased to be asked. It was an easy journey from the East End on the Tube and, since she'd arrived half an hour ago, she and Charlotte had been having a happy reunion over sips of milk in the teacups. Charlotte had shown no distress over the idea of Gemma going out. Toby was visiting a neighbour, and Kit was closeted in his room with the dogs, working, he'd said, on a project he'd been assigned over the half-term break. The house, for the moment, seemed weirdly calm.

Now, studying Alia, Gemma thought that the girl looked slimmer, her hair shinier, her skin clearer.

'College going well?' she asked. Alia had set her sights on training as a solicitor, although she had little encouragement from her very traditional Bangladeshi family.

'It's good, yeah.' With a delicate brown finger Alia moved Charlotte's teacup away from the edge of the table. Gemma could have sworn she was blushing. 'Rashid's been helping me study.'

'Rashid?' Gemma looked at her in surprise. Surely she didn't mean Rashid Kaleem?

'You know, the pathologist guy,' said Alia, confirming it. 'He says he knows you. He's been helping out at the health clinic, since . . . ' Her voice faded.

Alia had idolized Charlotte's parents, Naz and Sandra, and had volunteered alongside Sandra at the East End health clinic that served neighbourhood Asian women. Gemma realized that she was the one who'd told Rashid about the clinic – how like him to step in without a fuss and lend a hand. And to offer mentoring to this young woman who had lost Naz and Sandra's support.

But Alia was young and impressionable, and one look at Rashid Kaleem was enough to make older and wiser women swoon. She hoped he wouldn't unwittingly break the girl's heart.

'Oh, super. That's great,' she said, realizing that Alia was looking disappointed.

'Lia, I want lorries,' said Charlotte, coming to Gemma's rescue. She rolled one of Toby's toy vans across the table. 'Can lorries have tea?'

Sitting on the kitchen chair beside Alia, she swung her little trainer-clad feet high above the floor. One of the hairslides Gemma had clipped so carefully in her hair that morning had come undone, and there seemed to be a streak of mud – or at least Gemma hoped it was mud – across the front of her T-shirt. So much for her visions of a girly-girl, Gemma thought . . . not that she'd have had much idea what to do with one.

'Lorries drink petrol,' Alia explained, 'but maybe just this once they could have tea.' She shot Gemma a meaningful glance and mouthed, 'Go.'

'Right.' Gemma adjusted the strap of her handbag on her shoulder. 'You have my mobile – '

'Of course I do.' Alia rolled her eyes.

'Okay.' Gemma gave in. 'I'll see you, then.' With an effort, she resisted the urge to give Charlotte one last hug. She was trying to discourage clinginess, she reminded herself, not foster it. Could it be that the separation anxiety was hers as much as Charlotte's?

She took a deep breath and, with a jaunty wave, headed for the door before she could change her mind about going.

Once outside, though, the bright day seemed to welcome her and she suddenly felt bracingly, exhilaratingly independent. She stretched her legs into a welcome adult pace. Turning into Lansdowne Road, she decided to make a quick detour on her way to the station.

Ten minutes later she walked into Notting Hill Police Station, armed with two lattes from the Starbucks on Holland Park Avenue. Melody had brought her coffee often enough – it was time she returned the favour.

'Inspector!' The desk sergeant, a grizzled Scot called Jonnie who had been a fixture at Notting Hill since long before Gemma's time, beamed at her as if she were long-lost kin. 'You're a sight for sore eyes. I thought you weren't due back until Monday.'

'I'm not,' Gemma explained. 'I've just dropped in for a chat with Melody.' She raised the cardboard cups in demonstration.

'How's the new addition to the family?' he asked. 'Have you got a picture?'

'More than one, actually,' Gemma answered with a smile. She set the coffees on the reception counter and took out her phone.

When she pulled up photos of Charlotte, the sergeant scrolled through them with admiring exclamations. 'What a lovely wee lass,' he said, returning her phone. 'I think you'll be missing her when you come back to work.'

'Yes, but I miss this place, too. It will be good to—'

'Boss?' Melody came through the door into the lobby. 'Somebody said you were here.'

'Police station ESP,' said Gemma, grinning. 'I've never understood how that works. The psychic grapevine.' Now she felt truly at home.

'Oh, coffee. Brilliant. Ta very much.' Melody took the hot cup and led the way into the station proper. 'I've commandeered the Sapphire office for a bit. Mike and Ginny are both testifying in court.'

As they walked through the corridor, Gemma felt the station settle around her. The faint odour of chip fat from the canteen, the rise and fall of voices punctuated by the occasional muffled laugh, the click of keyboards and the ringing of phones – all seemed as familiar to her as her own heartbeat. 'What about the Super?' she asked.

'Divisional meeting. He'll be sorry to have missed you – not that you won't see him soon enough. And be back in your own office,' Melody added, sounding pleased.

Gemma hesitated. 'Um, Melody, I'm just as glad he's out, to tell the truth.' She'd always had a good relationship with Superintendent Mark Lamb, her boss, but explaining to him exactly what she was doing would be more than ticklish.

Instantly alert, Melody gave her a searching glance and closed the door of the Project Sapphire office behind them. The small space was cluttered with computers, filing cabinets and the personal belongings of Melody's colleagues. Melody sat at her own desk, which was by far the tidiest of the three. 'So, what's up, boss?'

When Gemma had rung her last night, she'd explained only that she wanted to have a look through the records. Taking one of neighbouring chairs – the absent Ginny's, she guessed, if the hearts-and-flowers mug and the potted plants on the desk were a clue – she said, 'Can we search for any female officer reporting a rape by an unknown perpetrator?'

Melody frowned. 'Female police officers? That's it? Any other parameters?'

Gemma thought back. Rebecca Meredith had reported her rape to Superintendent Gaskill a year ago. Her own mercifully aborted encounter with Craig had been a little less than five years ago. But she suspected that Craig's methods had been long and well practised by the time he'd driven her home to Leyton that night. 'Can we make it ten years?' she asked, with an inner shudder.

Melody's eyes widened. 'You want the moon, too?' She shook her head. 'I'm good, but even I have limits. This may take a while.' Her level gaze met Gemma's. 'So, in the meantime, are you going to tell me exactly what we're doing here?'

Gemma felt a sick clutch of revulsion, her pleasure in the day erased by the thought of what Angus Craig might have done to other women.

And walking into the station, avoiding her own boss, had made her realize just how risky an endeavour this might be. 'Melody, look, I'll understand if you don't want to do this. Duncan's already been warned off by the powers-that-be, and I don't want to ask something of you that could damage your career.'

'Boss. Come on.' Melody's hands hovered over the keyboard. 'You know me better than that. Just tell me what we're looking for. How bad can it be?'

'We're looking for a retired deputy assistant commissioner who's a serial rapist,' said Gemma. 'And I think it could be very bad indeed.'

Chapter Fourteen

Having given his name to one of the women in Leander's front office and asked to speak to Milo Jachym, Doug took advantage of the few minutes' wait in the club's lobby. Hands behind his back, he strolled round the room, trying not to look as if he was gawking at the photos and trophies on display. He'd stopped in front of the gift-shop display cabinet, pondering whether he'd buy a French-cuffed shirt just to wear a set of pink-hippo cufflinks, when a female voice spoke behind him.

'I'd go with the navy baseball cap if I were you.'

Turning with a start, he saw it was Lily Meyberg, the pretty house manager.

'You don't think the pink would work?' he asked, making a valiant effort to appear nonchalant. He nodded at the violently pink cap in the cabinet.

'I think I'd admire such a brave man,' she said, smiling. 'But the colour doesn't suit you. I'd stick with the navy.' Touching his arm lightly, she added, 'Mustn't forget my mission. I'm to take you up to reception. Milo will be along in a few minutes.'

Following her up the staircase, he was torn between watching the way her bum moved in her slim navy skirt and looking at the photos of the Olympic medallists and world champions that lined the stairwell. He'd only glimpsed the photos the other night – he certainly hadn't wanted to stop and gawp in front of Kincaid, but now he was finding the alternative option more tempting.

'We're just setting up for lunch,' Lily said when they reached the reception area at the top of the stairs. 'But the bar's open. Can I get you something?'

'Oh, no thanks. Bit early for me.'

'And no drinking on duty, right?'

Not wanting to sound a complete plod, he shrugged and said, 'Well, an occasional pint at lunch, maybe.'

Slipping his hands in his pockets, he walked to the balcony doors and looked out across the meadows that would house the Regatta enclosures, come June. If he peered to the left he could just see down into the yard where the boats were racked.

Resisting the urge to glance into the dining rooms on either side of the little foyer, he turned back to Lily, but not before he'd glimpsed the oars mounted on the walls. Olympic oars. Dear God! And Rebecca Meredith's blades might one day have joined them.

'Lily, you were here on Tuesday morning, right?' he asked, trying to picture the scene. 'Do you remember who was first worried that Rebecca Meredith might be missing? Was it Freddie Atterton or Milo?'

When she frowned, he noticed she had a sprinkle of freckles across her nose. 'I don't know. Freddie was sitting by the window, there.' She pointed towards the table that directly overlooked the boatshed and the river. 'He got up when he saw Milo in reception. But I had to make more coffee, and when I came back from the kitchen they were both gone. Then Milo came in again from outside and said Freddie was searching for Becca.' Shaking her head, she dropped her voice to a whisper. 'I still can't believe it. We're all just gutted.'

'Were you good friends?' he asked.

Shrugging, Lily looked away and tucked a strand of her honey-brown hair behind her ear. 'Well, I wouldn't exactly say anyone was good friends with Becca. But she was always' – Lily paused, then went on – 'not kind, maybe, but considerate. You'd be surprised how many of the members aren't. She never took advantage of staff, and if you were a rower she treated you with respect. She never made a big deal of who she was.'

He saw her eyes flick over his shoulder. Instantly her posture became more erect, her manner once again managerial. She gave him a professional smile. 'Here's Milo now. I'll leave you two to it then.'

With regret, Doug watched her slender back as she walked into the dining room. He wondered if he might somehow manage to run into her off-duty and ask her for a drink, although he knew he should resist the temptation. It was never a good idea to mix a personal relationship with a case.

Then he turned to shake Milo Jachym's hand. 'Lily said you wanted a word,' said Milo. 'But let's talk somewhere other than the members' areas.' He led Doug along the corridor to the door marked 'Crew'.

As Doug entered behind him, he felt a breathless little bump of anticipation. This was hallowed ground, where the greatest rowers in the country – maybe in the world – had gathered at their leisure.

Reality did not live up to expectation.

For a moment Doug thought he might have been back at his old school dining hall. There was the same utilitarian furniture, the same smell of eggs and chips and bacon frying. And although the handful of rowers scattered at tables – consuming what Doug guessed was their second breakfast of the day – looked freshly showered, the air held the faint but pervasive scent of sweat and mouldering athletic shoes.

'Tea?' asked Milo, gesturing Doug to a seat at one of the tables just inside the dining-room door.

Catching sight of the industrial tea urn near the kitchen, Doug had to force enthusiasm into his reply. 'Yeah, thanks. That would be great.' He wished he'd taken Lily up on the offer of a drink from the bar.

Milo returned a moment later bearing two mugs of milky fluid and a sugar bowl. 'Thanks.' Gingerly Doug sipped. The tea tasted as if it had come from the inside of a cast-iron boiler. He reached for the sugar bowl and shovelled in a coma-inducing amount.

He could feel the covert glances of the rowers, male and female, and at their entrance the room had gone quiet except for the sound of a race video that was playing on the television screen.

Doug loosened his tie. When he'd learned he was going to Leander, he'd been glad he'd worn his best sports jacket and tie that day. It was *Leander*, after all.

But here, with the casually dressed crew, he felt

awkward and overdressed – the odd boy out – while Milo, in his pressed chinos and a navy Leander polo that sported a little pink hippo on the breast, had it just right.

'Baked beans on toast?' offered Milo. 'Chef's special today,' he added with a twinkle. Someone in the room farted, as if on cue, followed by a suppressed snigger. Milo ignored both.

'The rower's best friend.' Doug managed to suppress a snigger himself. 'But no, thanks. I had something at the station this morning, and I'm not fit enough to deserve a second breakfast.'

'You're a rower,' said Milo, eyeing him speculatively. 'The other night – you knew your way around. But not varsity, I think. Not tall enough.'

'School eight.'

'Ah. Bow or stroke?'

'Bowside.'

'What school?'

'Eton,' Doug answered, with less than his usual reluctance. Here, unlike in the force, he would not be teased for having been a public-school boy. He was, however, beginning to feel as if he were the one being interviewed.

Milo nodded. 'Good programme. Do you row now?'

'I've just bought a house in Putney. I thought I'd give the LRC a try.' Doug had rowed out of London Rowing Club at regattas when he was at school, but had not been back as an adult. When he'd been debating whether or not to buy the house, he'd walked down Putney Reach and gazed up at the venerable club. Leander had once been housed there, overlooking the tidal Thames, before its move to Henley, and the two clubs were still closely associated.

Not that the LRC was as exclusive as Leander, but Doug hadn't quite geared himself up to walking in and applying for membership. Most of the members would be more experienced rowers, and he had, as always, the hovering fear of appearing a fool.

'Bought a boat?' asked Milo.

The coach was stalling, Doug thought, perhaps to give the rowers a chance to make a graceful exit. But if he hadn't wanted an audience, why had he picked a common room for their conversation? Surely there were other places in the club where they wouldn't have disturbed the members or the crew.

'No. I thought I'd get my feet wet, so to speak. A club boat should suit me just fine for the moment.' He took another sip of the tea, tried not to grimace. Determined to get things back on track, he said, 'Now, Mr Jachym, if I could just—'

'Becca. Yes, of course.' Milo sighed, as if accepting the inevitable. His burly shoulders sagged a little. 'Terrible business. Everyone is still in shock. And Freddie isn't returning my calls.'

'We'll be speaking to him later this morning. I'm afraid this is now officially a murder investigation.'

Milo's face went still. For an instant Doug had a glimpse of the man beneath the jovial exterior – the man who drove his rowers beyond their endurance and expected even more of them. You didn't coach athletes of Leander's calibre without being tough, and cagey – a strategist of the first order. And Doug had the feeling Milo had been expecting the next move in the game.

The remaining rowers seemed to have read a signal in Milo's body language, or in the change in his voice. They abandoned the remains of their meals and trickled out one by one – not, however, without casting more curious glances in Doug's direction.

When the room was empty Milo nodded, his expression once again inscrutable. 'So. Where do you go from here, Sergeant?'

'You're not surprised by the idea that Becca Meredith was murdered?' asked Doug.

'I'm shocked, yes,' Milo answered. 'But I think I would be even more so if you'd determined that Becca had drowned in a stupid or careless accident.'

'You trained her,' said Doug, taking his measure. 'Stupidity or carelessness would have reflected badly on you.'

'That's part of it.' Milo shrugged, giving Doug a challenging glance. 'Now you seem shocked, Mr Cullen. That's human nature. We always think of ourselves first, and only a liar doesn't admit to it. But that doesn't mean that I don't grieve for Becca,' he went on, his voice suddenly hard. 'And for Freddie, and for what Becca might have done. Or might have become. Or that *I* wouldn't murder whoever did this to her.'

'Perhaps not the best thing to admit to a police officer, Mr Jachym,' suggested Doug mildly.

'Then let's hope you catch your man before I have a chance to lay hands on him.'

Doug gazed at him consideringly. 'Would you still

feel that way if it were your friend who was responsible?'

'My friend?' Milo looked startled, then drew his bushy brows together as realization struck. 'If by that you mean Freddie, you can't be serious. He would never have harmed Becca. He adored her.'

It was Doug's turn to shrug. He wondered if Jachym's disbelief was a bit manufactured. Surely it must have occurred to him that Freddie would be a suspect. 'Human nature, as you said,' he answered. 'Sometimes there's a fine line between love and hate. No one else can be sure how they really got on.'

'I knew them,' said Milo, his jaw set in an obstinate line. 'And I don't believe it.'

Doug conceded for the moment. 'Then have you any idea who *might* have wanted Becca Meredith dead?'

'No.' Milo shook his head. 'I can't imagine. Do you know . . . ? How did she – '

'That's still under investigation. As is last night's attack on one of the members of the search-and-rescue team that found her body.'

'What?' If Milo had not been surprised that they'd determined Becca's death a homicide, he seemed genuinely shocked at this. 'What sort of attack? On whom?'

'His name is Kieran Connolly. He and his partner were the team at the weir. Someone tried to burn down his boatshed last night – with him in it. Do you know him?'

Milo thought for a moment. 'Quiet guy? Repairs boats? I've talked to him a few times. He's done work for some of the crew as well as the members. Does a good job,' he added approvingly. 'Is he all right?'

'I think so, yes. Were you aware that Connolly had a relationship with Becca Meredith?'

'A *relationship*? What do you mean by a *relationship*?' Milo looked disconcerted.

'What people usually mean, Mr Jachym. They were sleeping together.'

Milo frowned, considering. 'I did see them out on the river together often enough, during the summer,' he said slowly. 'But they were both single scullers, and it never occurred to me that there was anything more to it. Are you certain? Did Freddie – ' He stopped, and Doug saw by the sudden wariness in his eyes where the thought had taken him.

'Did Freddie know?' Doug finished for him. 'If he had, would he have been jealous?'

'I – no. I don't know. I don't think so.' Milo looked into his mug as if the sludge at the bottom might yield an answer. 'Becca and Freddie – they were comfortable together. Sometimes they seemed more like siblings. And it was Freddie, after all, who strayed from the marital fold, not Becca.'

'But *she* left *him*?'

'After that, yes. Or maybe I should say, after *them*.'

'Freddie had more than one affair?'

'Freddie can't help being charming,' Milo said, with an indulgence that made Doug wonder if everyone gave Freddie Atterton free passes for bad behaviour. 'And to be fair,' Milo went on, 'with her job, Becca hadn't much time for him.'

'What about the rowing? She must have been very focused on that, as well.'

'Not until this last year. I thought she'd given it up for good, to tell you the truth, although she kept her membership here, for social reasons. Then, in the spring, she bought a boat. But she was secretive about her training. She kept the shell here, but she didn't go out with the crew. Oh, she rowed the occasional piece on the weekend, but I could see she was holding back, coasting. I think, now, that she was just checking out the competition.'

'So when did you decide she was serious?' Doug asked.

'Couple of weeks ago.' Milo looked out at the view over the river, and Doug thought that he was uncomfortable, even a little embarrassed. 'I timed her.'

'Without her knowledge?'

'It's not illegal, Sergeant,' said Milo, with a hint of sharpness. He seemed to have recovered his composure quickly enough. 'It was just a small conspiracy with one of the rowers. This was after one of the boys let slip that she'd bribed a few of them to help her move weights and an erg into the cottage. I was . . . curious. It is my job, after all, to see what my crew is up against.'

'And?'

'She was better.' He met Doug's eyes again.

'Would she have rowed for you?'

'Maybe. But Becca was never exactly a team player. And the other women wouldn't have been happy with her coming in and riding roughshod over their positions.'

'Tricky, then,' Doug said.

'Not really. If Becca had wanted to race on her own, and had the means to do it, she wouldn't have worried about hurting anyone's feelings, including mine.'

'Disappointing for you, after all the work you've put in with your own crew,' suggested Doug, in his best attempt at Kincaid-style casualness.

'What?' Milo gave a bark of laughter. 'You think I might have killed Becca to advance the chances of my own team?' When Doug merely looked blandly non-committal, Milo's amusement turned to irritation. 'That's ludicrous. I have a couple of good possibilities for the single scull. Not top-flight, but we'll see. And if not, there will be others.'

'Then you won't mind telling me where you were on Monday evening,' said Doug.

'Here, of course. I was just doing my evening lock-up when I saw Becca taking out the Filippi. After we spoke, I came back to the gym to oversee evening workout. Then I ate supper with the crew.'

Doug didn't see any conceivable way in which Milo could have spoken to Becca as she left Leander, then made his way to a hiding spot on the far side of the river by the time Becca had rowed round Temple Island and started back upstream. Of course, that was assuming Milo was telling the truth about speaking to Becca, as well as about the time he saw her leave Leander.

But Doug doubted Milo would lie about his movements when his schedule was so easily verifiable. And if Kieran Connolly's story bore out, the man on the other side of the river had been lying in wait for two evenings, just when Milo would have had coaching duties.

He gave the idea up as a bad prospect for the moment and moved on to Kieran. 'Last night, Mr Jachym, do you know if any singles were taken out, or might have been missing, around eight o'clock?'

'A single? Why?'

'Kieran Connolly's boatshed is on the island across from the rowing museum. So unless his attacker just happened to live there, too, I suspect he used a boat. And why not a racing shell?'

'True enough,' Milo agreed. 'Well, if it was a boat, it didn't come from Leander. There are only a few singles racked in the yard, and we've all been keeping a close eye on things here.' The look he gave Doug was pitying. 'But, Sergeant, if you're trying to account for every single scull along this stretch of the Thames, I wish you the best of luck.'

Kincaid stood in New Street, waiting for Cullen in front of the Malthouse, a complex of upscale renovated flats in part of the old Brakspear Brewery. On the other side of the street the Hotel du Vin occupied another of the brewery's buildings, and Kincaid thought he could summon more enthusiasm for a nice lunch in the hotel bar than for the upcoming interview.

The cards were certainly stacking against Freddie Atterton. Kincaid had given a brief and non-committal report to the press gathered at Henley Police Station. Then he'd rung Chief Superintendent

Childs, who'd jumped on the news of Becca
Meredith's life-insurance policy with all the glee of a
terrier after a rat. For Childs, the demonstration of
such enthusiasm consisted of a slight raising of his
voice, accompanied, Kincaid imagined, by a slight but
corresponding rise of the brows.

He was just as glad not to be there to see it.

Ending the conversation on a sour note, he reluctantly assured his guv'nor that he would pull out all
the stops to establish whether or not Freddie Atterton
had an alibi for the time in question.

Then, just as he rang off, DC Imogen Bell had
come in to tell him that the SOCOs had found a
partial footprint at the spot that Kieran had indicated
on the river bank, as well as fibres caught on a
twig and evidence of disturbance at the water's edge.
They were still engaged in a fingertip search of the
area.

So it looked as though Kieran Connolly had been
right about the spot where Becca had been killed, and
Childs would be jubilant if either footprint or fibre
could be tied to Atterton.

But while Kincaid knew his remit was to catch
Becca Meredith's killer, he felt he was being pushed
in Atterton's direction, and by an agenda that had
nothing to do with the serving of justice.

He didn't like it.

Maybe he was just being stubborn, he thought,
like the children when they wanted their own way
and refused to see reason.

Or maybe he was sympathizing too much with
a man who was grieving for a woman he'd loved,

no matter how complicated the relationship. He'd accused Gemma often enough of being too ready to put herself in a suspect's shoes – now perhaps he was guilty of the same sin.

Fidgeting, he watched the passers-by, all of whom seemed to be enjoying the sunshine and the prospect of lunch. The red-brick frontage of the hotel contrasted cheerfully with its white trim, and on the wall of a cottage across the street late pink roses were blooming with a profusion that seemed to shout *last chance*. It felt like a day for last chances.

He was just about to pull out his phone and ring Cullen again when he saw him rounding the corner at the bottom of the street.

Cullen looked jaunty, as if a little of Leander's glamour had rubbed off on him.

'Any luck?' Kincaid asked when Cullen reached him.

'I didn't find a conveniently missing single scull, no,' said Doug. 'Milo Jachym says they've been particularly careful to check the boats at night.'

'Well, that would have been a bit much to hope for. I've got DC Bell going round the other two clubs, just in case. Anything else?'

'I don't think Milo Jachym is a likely suspect. I do think he would protect Freddie Atterton, unless he knew without a doubt that Atterton was guilty. But a funny thing,' Doug added. He pulled off his wire-framed glasses and rubbed the lenses with his tie. 'He seemed quite happy to admit that it was Atterton who broke up the marriage, by cheating. Serial affairs, apparently. Becca was Milo Jachym's rower, and his friend. You'd think he'd have been a bit more incensed on her behalf.'

'Divided loyalties? Or just macho sympathies?' Kincaid speculated. *'Boys will be boys.'*

'It certainly seems as though Atterton felt guilty enough about his behaviour,' said Doug as he slipped his glasses on again. 'We'll see what he has to say for himself.'

The Malthouse flats were protected from the street by an impressive iron gate, but placed discreetly to one side of it was a panel with separate bell pushes for each residence. Kincaid checked the slip of paper he'd tucked in his jacket pocket, then rang the number for Atterton's flat.

Kincaid's first thought was that Freddie Atterton looked like hell.

His second was that Freddie Atterton's flat was enough to make anyone feel like hell. It was black-on-grey, and not even the good lighting and the architectural details preserved by the renovation made much dent in livening the place up.

And that was if you ignored the mess. Rumpled clothes were scattered across the sitting room. An empty bottle of Scotch sat on the coffee table. Beside it, what looked like a cereal bowl held cigarette ends, and an unpleasant whiff of spoiled food drifted from the open-plan kitchen.

'I'm sorry,' said Atterton, and he seemed to be apologizing for more than the state of the flat. He wore only a pair of tracksuit bottoms, and his hair was uncombed and flattened on one side as if he'd just got out of bed. 'I'm . . . Things have got away from me a bit. Let me just find a shirt – ' He looked round as if one might materialize out of thin air, then spotted one hanging on the back of a dining chair. Slipping it on, he buttoned two buttons, both misaligned, then asked, 'Can I make you some coffee?'

Picking up the bowl-ashtray, he looked round, apparently searching for somewhere else to put it. He settled on the mantel, above which hung two dark-blue Oxford oars, the only spot of colour in the room. 'Sorry,' he said again, coming back to the sofa. 'I'd given up the fags, but after . . . It seemed the only thing—'

'Mr Atterton,' Kincaid interrupted, 'we need to talk. Can we sit down?'

Freddie Atterton's already pale face went ashen. He groped for the edge of the sofa, then sank down, unmindful – or unaware – of the suit jacket that had been left on the cushion. 'Oh, God, what's happened?'

Kincaid nodded to Cullen and they both sat, Doug in the armchair, while Kincaid dragged over one of the massively carved grey dining chairs so that he could sit close to Freddie. Who the hell had picked out such hideous furniture, he wondered? The damned stuff might have escaped from the French Reign of Terror.

'Mr Atterton. Freddie. About your ex-wife. We now have reason to believe she was murdered.'

'Murdered.' The dark hollows beneath Atterton's eyes looked soot-smudged. 'Why . . . ? How could she – ' He stopped, swallowed. 'I thought, when they called in the Yard, that it was just because Becca was one of you. Not something like that. Never something like that. Why would someone kill Becca?'

'That's what we're here to find out. And we were called in initially because the circumstances of Becca's disappearance were unexplained,' Kincaid agreed. 'But there have been some . . . developments.'

'You know what happened to her, don't you?' Freddie's voice was a thread. 'You know how she died. Why didn't someone – ' He shook his head, seemed to make an effort to collect himself. 'Okay. I'm sorry. I know you probably can't say.' He took a breath. 'What can I do to help you?'

'I appreciate your cooperation, Mr Atterton. You can start by telling us where you were on Monday evening.'

'Monday?'

Kincaid had the distinct sense that some of Freddie's surprise at the question was feigned. 'The evening your wife died. You can't have forgotten.'

'No. No, of course not. It's just – with everything that's happened, I don't . . . Let me think . . . ' He patted the front pocket of his shirt, seemed to realize it was empty, then dropped his hand back to his lap. The Benson & Hedges packet on the coffee table was crumpled and empty.

'Let's say between four and six,' Kincaid added helpfully.

Freddie blinked, once, twice, lifted his hand towards his pocket again. 'I – I was here.'

'Alone?'

'Yes.'

'Any verification? Neighbour that might have seen you, something like that?'

'No. No, I can't remember seeing anyone. I'd been to the club for lunch. That's when Milo told me about Becca – I mean told me that she was training seriously. I knew she was rowing again, of course, but she'd said she was just trying to get back into shape, relieve some stress from work.'

'But you knew she'd bought a boat, the Filippi,' Kincaid said.

'Yes, well, you wouldn't have expected Becca to row in a club boat.'

'That's an expensive boat,' put in Doug. 'Top-class.'

'She could afford it.'

Had there been just the slightest trace of bitterness in Freddie's reply, wondered Kincaid? Well, he'd get back to that. 'What exactly did Milo tell you that day?'

'That she'd had some lads in the crew help her turn my – her – spare room in the cottage into a training room. She'd moved in weights and an erg. And Milo had clocked her. She was blazing.'

'Timed her without her knowledge,' Doug interjected.

'Well, yeah.' Freddie looked sheepish. 'But she could be bloody secretive, and I can't blame Milo for wanting to know.'

'Because she was better than his own crew?' Kincaid asked.

'No. Because if she'd been willing to row for him, he might have had a champion. And there's nothing the media love more than a comeback story. It would have been good press for the whole team.'

Kincaid thought about this. 'When we first interviewed Milo, he said you were "furious" when you found out about Becca's training. And on the message you left on her home phone, you sounded angry with her. Why, if you thought she had a chance to be that good?'

'I . . . ' Freddie rubbed at the stubble on his cheeks with his palms. 'I suppose I was worried about what would happen if she failed. The last time – she was never really the same afterwards. She never forgave herself.'

'But she broke her arm, didn't she?' Kincaid asked. 'Surely that wasn't her fault.'

'Oh, but it was,' said Freddie. 'And mine, too, because I let her talk me into it. It was the Christmas before the Olympics, and the team was in strict training. Milo didn't want anyone taking the chance of an injury, but Becca wanted a skiing holiday in Switzerland. She thought she was invincible. But she wasn't. She fell on the slopes and broke her wrist, badly.

'Milo was the one who was furious. And afterwards, even though Becca worked really hard at rehab, hoping to get her position back, he didn't believe the break had healed enough to take the strain of serious training.' Freddie sighed. 'They were both stubborn, and they both felt justified in their grudges. Maybe they were, I don't know. But it took them a long time to become friends again.'

'I can see why she might have been a bit reluctant to let him know she was training,' said Doug. 'She had something to prove, and she wanted to be sure of herself.'

'Exactly.' Freddie gave Doug a grateful look.

'So you were worried about her?' Kincaid asked. 'That's all?'

Freddie must have heard the scepticism in his voice, because he coloured. 'What other reason would I have had?'

'Maybe you were worried she would lose her job.' Kincaid stood and began to wander round the room, so that Freddie had to turn his head to follow him. 'Or quit,' he went on. 'Maybe you were worried she would come to you for a handout, and you thought you'd been generous enough already – although rumour has it that she deserved a generous settlement.'

'What – who told you that?'

'Milo Jachym, for one. And Becca's lawyer. And Becca's insurance broker.' Kincaid knew he was stretching it a bit, but he was going for impact.

Freddie had lost the quick flush of a moment before. 'That's not true. I mean, yes, she deserved the settlement. Of course she did. But I never wanted anything back.'

'Rumour also has it that you're in deep financial shit,' said Doug, taking Kincaid's place on the dining chair and leaning in close to Freddie. 'It would only be natural to regret turning over so much to Becca. Even with the recession, the cottage in Remenham must be worth a pretty penny.'

'But Becca appreciated what you'd done for her,

didn't she?' Kincaid ambled round to stand beside Doug, so that they boxed Freddie in. 'That was only fair. And she was fair, wasn't she? Prickly, competitive, not always easy to get on with. But fair.'

'What? What are you talking about?' Freddie pushed against the back of the sofa, as if he'd like to disappear through it.

'She made sure you would be taken care of, if anything happened to her,' said Doug. He gave Kincaid a quick questioning glance and Kincaid nodded affirmation. 'She not only made you the beneficiary and the executor of her estate,' Doug went on, 'but she named you as the recipient of a half-million-pound life-insurance policy.'

In the silence that followed Kincaid heard the sharp rasp of Freddie's breath, then the faint sound of voices from the slightly open window that faced New Street. He watched Atterton's face for the tic that would betray foreknowledge, for the quick involuntary shift of the eyes that signalled deceit.

But Freddie Atterton's face twisted and he put a shaking hand to his mouth. 'Oh, no,' he whispered. 'No, please tell me she didn't.'

'I'm afraid she did.' Kincaid felt a stirring of pity.

'But I can't . . . I don't – ' Freddie shook his head wildly, like a man drowning. 'I can't tell her to take it back.'

And in that moment, Kincaid believed him. If Becca Meredith had ever wanted revenge on her erring ex-husband, she had it now. She had given him a gift that might be beyond bearing.

'Well, it should certainly solve your financial difficulties,' said Doug matter-of-factly, apparently unmoved. 'Unless, of course, you're convicted of murder.'

'No. No. I would have been okay,' protested Freddie. He twisted the tail of his shirt in his hands. 'I've got this project, an upscale development below Remenham. And I had a new investor. That's what I was doing at Leander on Tuesday morning. I was supposed to have breakfast with him, but he didn't show. That's one reason I kept ringing Becca. I wanted to ask her if he was for real.'

'Why would she have known that?' Kincaid asked, wondering if he'd missed a beat.

'Because he's a cop. Or an ex-cop, I should say. His name is Angus Craig.'

Chapter Fifteen

'Angus Craig?' Kincaid stared at Freddie. 'You're having us on, mate, and it's not funny.'

'What? What did I say?' Frowning, Freddie looked from Kincaid to Doug.

'You were meeting Angus Craig, retired Met Deputy Assistant Commissioner, who happens to live in Hambleden. Is that what you're telling us?'

'Why shouldn't I have met him?' Freddie asked, beginning to sound panicked. 'We got chatting one night last week. I told him about the project. He said he was interested, that he might have some money to invest. So we agreed to meet for breakfast on Tuesday morning.'

'Did he know who you were? That Becca was your ex-wife?'

'I don't know. I don't think so.' Freddie frowned, thinking back. 'I never said so.'

Kincaid shoved his hands in his pockets, paced. 'You didn't know him before?'

'No. Like I said, we just got chatting over drinks.'

'Where? Leander?'

'God, no. The place closes down like a tomb by ten o'clock.' When Freddie didn't go on, Kincaid stopped pacing and shot him an impatient glance. 'Okay, okay,' said Freddie. 'It was the strip club, if you must know. But it's not what it sounds.' He ran a hand through his already unruly hair. 'Well, there are girls, but not on a stage or anything. It's just that it's the only place in Henley that stays open after the pubs close, so that's where everyone gravitates. There's music, and a nice bar, and people having a drink sometimes get talking.'

Kincaid remembered Imogen Bell telling him about the place, and her colleague, DC Bean, giving her a hard time. Well, at the moment he wasn't concerned about the city fathers' or DC Bean's definition of moral turpitude. 'Okay, Freddie, if you'd never met Craig, can you remember who started the conversation?'

'I'd seen him in the club before. And at Leander, although he must have been a guest, because I don't think he's a member.' Freddie stopped, licking his lips. 'Could I have some water?'

Doug stood. 'I'll get it.'

Kincaid waited until Doug had filled a glass from the tap and brought it back. When Freddie had drunk half and set the remainder on the coffee table, Kincaid said, 'Go on. So you'd seen him before, although not to speak to. But that means he'd seen you as well.'

'I suppose. But I didn't socialize with Becca at Leander, and she certainly never went to the strip club. I don't understand this. What does Becca have to do with Angus Craig?'

Kincaid debated how to answer. It seemed obvious that Becca hadn't told Freddie she'd been raped, or at least hadn't given him particulars. But considering what Kincaid had begun to learn about Becca Meredith, he doubted she'd said anything at all.

And, as he'd been warned off mentioning her allegations, for the moment he was going to follow suit. 'I don't know. I just think it's odd, that's all, you striking up an acquaintance with a retired Met officer a few days before your ex-wife's murder. And you say he didn't turn up for breakfast with you on Tuesday morning. Did he contact you afterwards, offer an explanation?'

'No,' said Freddie. 'That morning Lily said there was an accident on the Marlow road, so I thought he might have got hung up in traffic. Then – afterwards – I never thought to—'

Kincaid's phone rang. He swore under his breath, but answered when he saw that the caller was DC Bell.

'Sir.'

He'd have recognized her voice, brisk and competent, without the caller ID.

'You wanted me to let you know. The forensics teams are on their way. And I've been to Henley Rowing Club and Upper Thames Rowing Club. No boats reported missing last night, but some of the members keep them racked outside, and no one was keeping a particular watch.'

'Oh, bloody hell,' Kincaid said. He had indeed asked her to let him know when the teams were on their way to take in Freddie's car, and to gather Atterton's shoes and clothes to test against the footprint and fibres found at the river bank.

And he'd meant to time his interview accordingly, asking the pertinent questions and leaving Freddie no time to hide or clean anything before the teams arrived. But nothing in this interview was going according to plan.

'Sir?' Bell sounded nonplussed.

'Not you, Bell, sorry. How long before they get here?'

'Half an hour, maybe.'

'Okay, thanks, Detective Bell. And good work on the clubs. I'll get back to you.' Hanging up, Kincaid shook his head to cut off the question he could see forming on Doug's lips, then sat down facing Freddie.

'Mr Atterton – Freddie – there are some officers coming to examine your car and some of your belongings.' Before Freddie could protest, Kincaid held up a hand. 'This is just routine, okay? They'll try not to inconvenience you any more than necessary.'

'Routine? My car? My things? Why would you . . . ? What things?' Freddie started to push himself up off the sofa, but Kincaid and Doug had him effectively hemmed in.

'Boots or walking shoes, I would think. And outdoor jackets. But before we get to that, we need to ask you some questions about last night,' Kincaid continued. 'Can you tell me what you were doing between seven and nine o'clock?'

'What?' Freddie looked completely befuddled. 'Last night? Why on earth do you want to know about last night?'

'Just answer the question, please.'

'I was here. I'd had drinks with a mate earlier,

271

across the street. He – he took me to the mortuary.'
Freddie stopped and drank the rest of the water in his
glass. 'But then I came home. I was waiting for Becca's
mum to call from South Africa. She's not booking her
plane ticket until we know what we're doing about –
about funeral arrangements.'

'And did she ring you?'

'Yeah.' Freddie grimaced at the recollection. 'Yes,
she did. I guess it was about eight, but I'm not sure.
I wasn't watching the time.'

'Did she ring you here, on a landline, or on your
mobile?' Kincaid asked.

'Landline. Otherwise it would have cost her a fortune, and Marianne is ever mindful of her pennies.'

Kincaid cocked his head, curious about the evident bitterness. 'Do you not get on with Becca's
mother?'

Sighing, Freddie said, 'No one got on with anyone,
to tell you the truth. Becca and her mum never saw
eye-to-eye on anything, including me. Although I suppose you could say Becca came to agree with her
mother's assessment,' he added ruefully, 'but I don't
think that made them any closer. Becca never appreciated *I told you so*. And Marianne – oh, God, when
Marianne finds out Becca left things to me, she's not
going to like that at all.'

It occurred to Kincaid that Freddie Atterton
seemed very much alone. 'What about your family?
Have you been in touch with them? Is there anyone
who could stay with you for a bit?'

'I've rung my mum. I didn't want her to find out
about Becca from the news. She offered to come, but

I think that would be worse than being on my own. My mum can be – a bit much.'

'And your father?'

Freddie's mouth twisted. 'He told Mum to tell me he was sorry.'

'Right.' Obviously there was not much support forthcoming from that quarter. Kincaid wondered what had become of the FLO whom Cullen had assigned to Atterton. 'Freddie, has a Family Liaison Officer from the Met been to see you, or been in touch?'

Freddie shook his head. 'No.'

Had the chief – or whoever was calling the shots at the Yard – conveniently misplaced the FLO? Family Liaison Officers provided support, advocacy and ongoing information on the progress of an investigation to family members of victims. And while they weren't meant to be nannies, the FLO – male or female – often helped the victim's loved ones cope with grieving, deal with arrangements and, in highprofile cases, acted as a buffer between the family and the media.

Freddie Atterton might have been divorced from Rebecca Meredith, but it seemed that he was the one most in need of aid. But he was also – at least according to Chief Superintendent Childs – the most obvious suspect, and while the FLOs' job was to provide support for the family, they were also police officers. They sometimes learned things that implicated the family in a crime, in which case they were duty-bound to report it. It was a difficult job, rife with conflicts of interest for the officer, but in Atterton's case Kincaid thought an FLO might be particularly useful.

For the moment, however, he had other agendas to follow. 'Becca's mother – is it Mrs Meredith?' he asked. When Freddie nodded, Kincaid went on. 'We'll need Mrs Meredith's contact information.' They would also be checking Atterton's phone records, but Kincaid didn't mention that. He wanted to see if there was any collusion between Freddie and his former mother-in-law, before Freddie knew he had no room to wiggle.

'But why?' asked Freddie. 'I don't understand. Why do you care what I was doing last night?'

'Because someone tried to murder one of the search-and-rescue volunteers who found Becca's body.'

'Murder?' Freddie's knuckles turned white as he clutched his empty glass to his chest. 'But – why would someone do that?'

Kincaid leaned forward and met Freddie Atterton's frightened blue eyes. 'It struck us that a jealous ex-husband might have had a very good reason. He was Becca's lover.'

Freddie simply stared at Kincaid, his face wiped blank of all expression. After a moment he glanced at Doug, as if for confirmation, and asked, 'Lover?' His voice shook.

Doug nodded. 'His name is Kieran Connolly. Former army medic. Rower. He fixes boats, and he and his dog, a Labrador retriever, were part of the team at the weir.' He studied Freddie. 'But then maybe you already know all that.'

'No. No, I'd no idea. I saw him. I saw him that morning. A tall, dark-haired guy with a black dog.' Freddie shook his head, as if he couldn't quite take it in. 'Is he – you said someone *tried* to kill him. Is he okay? What happened to him?'

Kincaid thought that if Freddie was really as surprised as he seemed by the idea of Becca having had a lover, his concern was commendable. 'He's all right except for a gash in the head. But his boatshed isn't. Someone tried to burn it down, and made a pretty good job of it.'

'And he and Becca . . . I never imagined she'd . . . ' Freddie laughed. 'That's stupid, I know. She had more than enough reason to have an affair when we were married. And she certainly had every right to – to sleep with whoever she wanted after we were divorced. But I suppose I thought she would have told me . . . '

Looking at Freddie, and thinking about his interview with Kieran last night at Tavie's, Kincaid realized that the two men were physically very similar. Tall, dark-haired, slender, rower's physique . . . Was that why Becca had been attracted to Kieran? And were there other similar qualities that were less evident? He suspected that she'd been the stronger personality in both relationships, and that she'd liked it that way, consciously or not.

'Maybe she didn't want to hurt you,' he suggested. 'Or . . . ' He thought for a moment, then said, 'She told Kieran she didn't want anyone to know about their relationship because it could be used against her. Do you have any idea what she meant?'

'Used against her?' Freddie shook his head. 'No. She certainly didn't mean by me.'

'You wouldn't have asked her to deed the title of the cottage back to you?'

'God, no. And even if I had, I gave it to her in the divorce settlement, free and clear. I wouldn't have had a legal leg to stand on.'

Freddie's certainty made Kincaid wonder if he had considered asking her to give the cottage back and had abandoned it.

In favour of murder?

But Freddie would have had to have known that Becca hadn't changed her will, and given what Kincaid had learned about Becca Meredith, he thought it highly unlikely she'd shared such details with anyone. Unless, of course, Freddie had just gambled on her not wanting to leave her assets to her mother, and had doubted she'd leave a generous bequest to a stray cats' home.

Kincaid considered the man sitting before him – shocked, exhausted, frightened. He'd seen murderers who were all of those things, so it was conceivable that Freddie Atterton had murdered his ex-wife and yet could still display those emotions unfeigned.

But Kincaid couldn't quite bring himself to believe it. There were too many things that didn't add up, and if Freddie had a genuine alibi for last night, it would mean that the attack on Connolly was unrelated to Becca Meredith's murder. And that, he thought, was beggaring belief.

*

When the SOCOs arrived, he'd left Doug to oversee the collection of evidence and the arrangements for towing Freddie's BMW. Excusing himself, he'd found a quiet space in the old brewery courtyard and rung Detective Constable Imogen Bell.

'Sir,' she said, 'is everything all right?'

'Fine. Sorry if I was a bit abrupt earlier. DC Bell, have you had any training in family liaison?'

'Just the basics. Challenging, I thought.'

'Yes, it can be. So . . . how would you fancy a temporary spot of tea-making and hand-holding?'

There was a moment of silence. Then Bell said, with the barest hint of amusement, 'I take it that is not a gender-biased assignment. Sir.'

Kincaid grinned. 'I am firmly of the opinion that a bloke can make tea and hold hands just as well as any woman, if not better. But in this particular case I have to admit I think your gender might be to our advantage.'

He'd remembered that Imogen Bell had reminded him of the photos he'd seen of a younger Becca Meredith. And if Becca Meredith's taste in men had run to type, he thought it worth seeing if the same held true for her ex-husband.

Freddie Atterton had all the symptoms of a man badly in need of a confidant. It was the least Kincaid could do to provide one.

Doug Cullen came out of Freddie Atterton's flat a few minutes after Imogen Bell had gone in. 'Well, she'll soon get him sorted,' he told Kincaid, who had stayed in the courtyard to field phone calls. 'And I wouldn't want to be in her way while she does it. Think he'll tell her anything?'

'It's always possible,' Kincaid answered non-committally.

Doug studied him for a moment. 'You don't think he did it, do you?'

Kincaid gestured at the Hotel du Vin across the street, delaying an answer. 'Let's get some lunch. I'm starving.' The hotel was part of a boutique chain, and the food was reputed to be good.

'Brilliant idea,' Doug agreed. 'I've been starving ever since I watched the rowers at Leander scarfing down plates of eggs and baked beans.' Doug set off towards the hotel with alacrity, and they were soon seated on the leather sofas in the hotel's trendily appointed bar.

They both ordered the day's special, a fish pie made with smoked haddock and vegetables in a creamy Cheddar sauce, and Kincaid chose tea instead of the pint he would have preferred. He needed a clear head.

When the barmaid had brought their drinks, Doug pushed his glasses up on his nose and fixed a steady gaze on Kincaid. 'I take that as a No,' he said, as if their conversation hadn't been interrupted.

Shrugging, Kincaid stirred milk into his tea. 'Freddie Atterton had an obvious motive – financial gain. And maybe a less apparent one: jealousy. He had the expertise, and possibly the opportunity, to have murdered Becca on Monday evening.'

'But if he had a legitimate alibi for the attack on Kieran – '

'Exactly,' Kincaid said. When he'd rung the incident room while waiting for Doug, he'd requested checks on Freddie's phone records, and a confirmation call to Becca's mother. 'It either means the attack on Kieran was random – which I don't for one moment believe – or that it wasn't Freddie that Kieran saw by the river. But that's not the only thing.' He stopped to give the barmaid, a pretty girl in her twenties sporting a bare midriff and pierced navel, a smile of thanks as she brought their cutlery.

Lowering his voice as a couple took a nearby table, he continued, 'None of the scenarios with Freddie as the killer explain what Becca did on Friday night. Why did she leave her car in London and take the train? Why was she short-tempered with Kieran when he came to the cottage on Saturday? Why did she miss training that same morning? What did she have to do in London on Saturday? These were all breaks in her pattern, and I don't like breaks in pattern.'

Kincaid sipped at his tea, grimacing as he found it luke-warm. He hated tepid tea.

'And the thing I like least of all,' he said, returning his cup to the saucer with unnecessary force, 'is Freddie just happening to strike up an acquaintance with Angus Craig days before Becca was murdered.'

'Craig's doing?'

Kincaid arranged his knife and fork precisely on his serviette. 'I think he made a big mistake with Rebecca Meredith. He was poaching on his home territory, and he picked a victim who was tougher than he expected. Maybe he had too much to drink that night and was careless. But whatever the reason, I'll guarantee you he made it his business afterwards to find out everything about her.'

The barmaid brought their food, and Kincaid felt a bit deflated when it was Doug she smiled at, not him.

The small casseroles of fish pie were topped with golden mashed potatoes and smelled delicious. When Kincaid dug in with his fork, steam escaped in a cloud.

Doug lifted a bite and blew on it, something Kincaid felt sure his mother had taught him not to do. 'But if he knew who Freddie was,' Doug said, 'why approach him now?'

'Maybe Becca stirred the pot. We need to know *when* she found out that Craig had been retired with honours, and that Gaskill – and whoever Gaskill reported to – had not kept his promise to her. And we need to know something else.'

Setting down his knife and fork without tasting the dish, Kincaid pulled out his phone and dialled back the number in his caller ID.

'DC Bell? Kincaid here. You're still in the flat?'

'Yes, sir. Making some progress here. The kitchen and Mr Atterton are both tidied up.' She sounded quite pleased with herself. 'I'm about to help Fre – Mr Atterton – make some of the necessary phone calls.'

'SOCOs gone?'

'Yes, sir. I think they got everything they needed, and the lads said to tell you that they'll go over the car as soon as possible.'

'Thanks, Detective. Good work.' Kincaid paused, realizing he needed to be circumspect. 'DC Bell, could you ask Mr Atterton which evening last week he met the gentleman in the bar?'

'Um, right, sir.' There was a muffled murmur of conversation, then Bell came back clearly on the line. 'He says he thinks it was Thursday.' He could hear curiosity in her voice, but he thanked her without further comment and rang off.

'Thursday,' Kincaid repeated in answer to Doug's querying look.

Wincing as he nibbled on a piece of smoked haddock, Doug whistled through his teeth, then said, 'Hotter than blazes.' He took a sip of water. Thoughtfully he added, 'It could have been coincidence, I suppose, Craig running into Freddie.'

'Could have been, yes,' Kincaid agreed. 'And maybe it was just coincidence that Becca Meredith's behaviour altered the next day. But I'd like you to go back to West London Station. Have a word with Becca's colleagues. See if you can find out what was different about Friday.'

'And what are you going to be doing?' Doug asked, giving him a suspicious glance.

'Something I don't want you involved with.' Kincaid contemplated his untouched lunch. He'd suddenly lost his appetite. 'I'm going to have a talk with Angus Craig.'

Doug's eyes widened. His fork hovered halfway to his mouth. 'The guv'nor is not going to like that.'

That was an understatement, Kincaid thought.

He had pushed the envelope often enough in his career, or flown under the radar, knowing that Childs would give him considerable leeway if he solved a case. But he didn't remember ever having gone against the express wishes of his commanding officer.

He'd told Chief Superintendent Childs that he didn't approve of the way Becca Meredith's allegations against Craig had been handled. He'd said he thought Craig was a viable suspect. And he had been warned off.

He drank more of his tea, not caring that it had gone stone-cold. It served to wet his suddenly dry mouth.

If he knew what was good for him, he would walk away from this case now. Let someone else take it over. Let Freddie Atterton, a man he believed to be innocent, be made a convenient scapegoat. And let the whole dirty business of Angus Craig using his authority to prey on women – women like Gemma and Becca Meredith, and God knew how many others – be swept under the rug.

'Well, no, I suspect he's not going to like it,' he said slowly to Doug. 'But I don't intend to tell him just yet.'

Chapter Sixteen

By the time Doug Cullen made his connection in Twyford, and from there the train into Paddington, it was getting on towards mid-afternoon.

He took the Tube to Shepherd's Bush. From there, it was a good walk to West London Station, but Doug didn't mind it. The day was still fine, and after seeing the rowers at Leander that morning, Doug had come to the uncomfortable realization that he had a lot of shaping up to do, if was going to be fit enough to get back in a single scull.

Both the train journey and the walk had given him time to think as well, and he'd worked out a strategy. He certainly wasn't going to attempt to chat up Superintendent Peter Gaskill – in fact, he wanted to avoid Gaskill if at all possible.

Their initial conversation with Sergeant Kelly Patterson had made him think she was unlikely to be any more forthcoming, so that left the DC, Bryan Bisik.

When he reached the station he asked the desk sergeant to ring up for Bisik, and a few minutes later the detective constable came down. Bisik looked worried, and a little the worse for wear. His pale face was pasty, the skin beneath his eyes slightly reddened and puffy, and his gelled dark hair bore flakes of dandruff.

'Sergeant Cullen,' he said. 'Have there been any – any developments?'

'You could say that,' Cullen replied. 'Some of them quite interesting.'

'I'm sorry, but the Super's not in.'

'It's you I wanted to talk to, actually. Is there somewhere we could have a chat?'

Bisik gave a wary glance towards the desk sergeant. 'I don't know what I could tell you that we didn't go over the other day.'

Turning so that his back was to the desk sergeant, Doug lowered his voice. 'If your Super is out, how about I buy you a pint?'

'Well . . . ' Bisik glanced at the reception desk again. The sergeant was now on the phone. He lowered his voice. 'Okay. Look, there's a pub down at Brook Green. Just go back towards the Tube station and you'll see it. I'll meet you there in ten minutes. Wait for me outside. Pint of Foster's.'

Doug remembered the pub, a nice-looking establishment. When he reached the place, it was still early enough that the few pavement tables were unoccupied. He went in and bought two pints, and by the time he'd carried them outside and picked a table, Bisik appeared, walking fast.

'Thanks, mate,' Bisik said, sitting heavily on one of the metal chairs and raising his glass to Doug. After one long draught, he put the beer down and pulled a packet of Silk Cut from his jacket pocket. He shook a cigarette out and lit it with a sigh of relief. 'God, I was gasping.'

Then he frowned, took another drag and ground the cigarette out in the metal ashtray. A plume of blue smoke rose straight up in the still air. He shook his head. 'But the total pisser is that I can't smoke now without feeling guilty. Becca was always on at Kelly and me about it. I think we smoked more just to annoy her. But now . . . Every time I light up, I hear her voice. Kelly, too.'

'Where is Sergeant Patterson today?' Doug asked.

'You don't know?'

Doug shook his head. 'Know what?'

'She got seconded to another division. As of yesterday. No warning.'

'You're having me on.' Doug stared at him, the pint in his hand forgotten.

'I wish I was.' Bisik drank some more beer, shrugged. 'I suspect I shouldn't be talking to you.'

'Did Sergeant Patterson tell you she spoke to us?'

'No. But I saw her, outside the station. Looks like I wasn't the only one who did.'

Doug ran through the possibilities. Had Gaskill seen them? Or had it been the desk sergeant, reporting to Gaskill? Trying to remember who else might have walked by in those brief seconds, he felt suddenly uncomfortably exposed.

When Bisik saw him glance up and down the street, he said, 'Relax. We're a good way from the station. That's why I chose this pub.' He lit another Silk Cut. 'And besides, I don't know anything. I don't know what Kelly told you. If they want to send me to Siberia, at this point I'm not sure I care.'

'So you don't know anything about Angus Craig?'

Bisik squinted at him, then pulled a pair of expensive-looking sunglasses from his pocket and put them on. The sun's rays were dropping lower. 'Who's Angus Craig when he's at home?'

Doug shook his head. 'If you don't know, maybe it's better you don't ask. Where is Superintendent Gaskill this afternoon, by the way?' He wondered if, even now, Gaskill was planning to remove everyone who had been close to Rebecca Meredith.

But that was ridiculous. Paranoid. He was definitely getting paranoid.

'Golfing,' said Bisik. 'Not my cup of tea, but he lives for golfing, our Super. And I suppose it's a good day for it, if you like that sort of thing. Me, I'd rather sit in a beer garden.' He took his sunglasses off again, fiddling with the earpiece. 'The guv'nor – Becca – would have said it was a perfect day for rowing.'

Doug saw his opening. 'Last Friday was fine like this, wasn't it? But she didn't go home to Henley to train. Any idea why?'

'Last Friday?' Frowning, Bisik twirled the sunglasses. Doug found himself hoping they were only Portobello Market knock-offs. 'No. She left at the usual time.'

Disappointed, Doug asked, 'Anything else unusual about that day? She left her car in London and took the train back to Henley, which apparently she didn't normally do.'

Bisik drank some more of his pint with maddening deliberation. 'We were working on that knifing case and getting nowhere,' he said slowly. 'Kids saw their mate get stuck in the gut, but none of them will testify. Can't say I blame them, honestly. They'd just be asking for the same thing to happen to them. But Becca was seriously pissed off. Can't think of – oh, wait.' He beamed at Doug. 'This Vice copper came in from another division. She and Becca were chatting in Becca's office.'

'She?'

'Yeah. Seems like they knew each other. Old girls' palaver.'

'Do you have any idea who this officer was, or why she was in your station?'

'No. I was interviewing stroppy teenagers most of the afternoon.' Bisik gave a little smirk, as if pleased at a recollection. 'Blonde bird, about the guv'nor's age. Not bad-looking. I wouldn't have minded taking *her* out for a drink.' He took a drag on the cigarette, his guilt apparently forgotten for the moment. 'But I wasn't introduced. I just heard enough of the chit-chat in passing to get the impression that they went back a while. You know, "How's your Uncle George, then?" That sort of thing. And Becca was actually smiling. Now that, I would say, was unusual. Maybe *they* went out for drinks,' he added, looking surprised at the idea. 'I suppose the guv did have a social life, although we never saw any evidence of it.'

'So who would know who this woman was?'

'Kelly – Sergeant Patterson – maybe. She was in CID that afternoon. But she's in Dulwich, or

Plumstead, or somewhere. Always confuse those two. And probably the Super, since this bird was on our patch.'

Doug thought it would probably be a very good idea to try other avenues before he asked Superintendent Gaskill for that information. 'Do you have Sergeant Patterson's mobile number?'

'Yeah.' Bisik put out the fag and pulled out his phone, then fished in his jacket pocket until he came up with a crumpled Ladbrokes slip. Helpfully, Doug handed him a pen.

Bisik scrolled down the phone's screen, then scribbled a number on the slip and handed it across. 'Good luck getting her to answer, mate. I've been trying her since yesterday.'

It had taken Kincaid longer to get away from Henley than he'd hoped. When he and Cullen had separated after their rather late lunch, he'd gone back to the incident room. He'd briefed DI Singla and the rest of the team on their interview with Freddie Atterton, leaving out only Atterton's last revelation.

Then he'd made a second statement to the few hardy members of the press – mostly sports writers hoping for a juicy biopic titbit – still camping outside the police station.

He had not called Chief Superintendent Childs, and that was weighing on him.

But passing Hambleden Mill on his drive to the village had brought home the fact that Angus Craig lived within a vigorous walk's distance of the place where Rebecca Meredith's body had been found. And although Craig might not have walked quite so easily to the spot on the Bucks bank where they thought Becca had actually been murdered, he could certainly have got there quickly and easily in a car.

He slowed as he reached the village of Hambleden. The church, the pub, the red-brick, rose-rambled cottages – all were picture-postcard perfect.

And the house, when he found it, just outside the village and set back on a long drive, was imposing enough to make a mere detective superintendent think twice about knocking unannounced at the grand door.

Kincaid might have been tempted to call the place a great pile of brick, if it hadn't blended so gracefully into the landscape. The fact that he couldn't pinpoint the house's architectural origins made him think it had been added on to over the years with more than usual skill.

The sweeping lawns of the grounds were immaculate. The warm brick and red-tiled roof of the house merged into the autumnal blaze of the trees on the hill beyond as if painted against a backdrop.

It was lovely, a place to cherish, and a place meant to impress.

And it was all very grand, even for a deputy assistant commissioner in the Met. Maybe, Kincaid thought charitably, the wife had money.

Stopping the Astra in the drive, he wondered exactly what he was going to say to Angus Craig, then decided it might be better if he didn't think about it too much.

Climbing out of the Astra, he closed the door with

the softest of clicks, straightened his tie and crunched across the gravel drive. He'd just have to make it up as he went along.

The bell was a brass gryphon, and when he pressed it, he heard a clang from deep within the house, then the faint yap of a dog.

He waited, shifting his weight a bit. After the drama of the doorbell, he wouldn't have been surprised to be greeted by a butler in a starched shirt and morning suit, but it was Angus Craig himself who answered the door.

Craig looked as Kincaid remembered, although he might have put a few pounds on an already sturdy frame since Kincaid had last seen him. His thinning, sandy hair was combed back from his broad, florid face, which bore the annoyed scowl of a man interrupted while doing something important. He wore golfing clothes, and was still in studded shoes.

Afraid that the sight of the Astra might make Craig take him for a double-glazing salesman, Kincaid took the initiative. 'Deputy Assistant Commissioner Craig? I'm Superintendent Duncan Kincaid, with the Yard. I doubt you remember me, but I've been on one or two of your command courses at Bramshill.'

The scowl was quickly replaced by a falsely jovial smile, and Kincaid realized that Angus Craig not only knew who he was, but why he was there.

'Superintendent Kincaid, yes, I remember you. I hear you're doing a good job on the Meredith investigation.'

'Thank you, sir. I wondered if I might have a word?'

'Of course,' Craig said, but he looked less than

pleased. 'Come in. We can talk in my study. I was just changing my shoes.'

As Kincaid followed him inside, Craig cast a glance at the Astra before closing the door. 'I should think the Yard could provide an officer of your rank with a better class of vehicle.'

'It's my personal car, sir.' Kincaid felt surprisingly defensive on the Astra's behalf.

Raising a sandy brow, Craig made no apology for the insulting comment. His studded shoes clicked on the wide-planked oak floors as he walked away, and Kincaid wondered how Craig's wife must feel about the man's disregard for the fine fabric of the house. Craig stopped at a bench in the hall, changing his golf shoes for leather slippers while Kincaid waited.

The interior of the house was not as ostentatious as Kincaid had expected. Walls and woodwork were painted a soft white. The furniture and flower arrangements were simple, if expensive-looking, and a tasteful series of charcoal nudes, both male and female, adorned one wall. From somewhere in the back of the house he heard a dog's high-pitched barking.

Craig set the golf shoes to one side of the bench and stood up. 'Damn that dog. The wife's. He does that whenever she's out.' He nodded towards a room across the hall. 'This way, Superintendent.'

Following him through the doorway, Kincaid saw that while the room was as beautifully proportioned as the rest of the house, it was marred by an over-large desk.

Wide windows gave a view of the front lawns,

and, in spite of the unseasonable warmth of the day, a small fire burned in a beautifully curved iron grate.

Two wing-backed leather chairs sat at an angle before the fire, forming an inviting conversation nook. But Craig chose to sit behind his massive desk, leaving Kincaid in the awkward position of having to pull up a small armless chair. It was the same sort of intimidation tactic practised by Peter Gaskill, and would have made Kincaid dislike Craig even if he'd known nothing else about him.

Dark bookcases displayed golfing trophies, interspersed with leather-bound copies of classics that Kincaid suspected had never been read. A console table between the windows held an eighteen-year-old bottle of Glenlivet and two cut-crystal tumblers on a tray, but Craig made no move to offer Kincaid a drink.

Kincaid settled back as comfortably as he could in the small chair, brushed an imaginary speck of lint from his lapel and looked round the room. He wasn't about to give Craig the satisfaction of displaying a reaction to his rudeness, and he wanted to see what line Craig would take about Becca Meredith, if unprompted.

Craig took the bait. 'Tragic, this business with DCI Meredith,' he said. 'But I understand the ex-husband is the likely suspect.' He didn't say who exactly had given him to understand this.

The likely suspect? Kincaid felt as though he'd fallen into an Agatha Christie novel. 'Really, sir?' He kept his tone at mild surprise. 'That's news to me. Mr Atterton is helping us with our enquiries, but we have

no solid evidence that he was involved in Rebecca
Meredith's death.'

Crossing his ankles, Kincaid did his best to keep
his expression bland. A throb of anger had begun
behind his temples. 'But then I understand that you
know Mr Atterton. In fact, you had a breakfast
appointment with him on Tuesday morning. It's too
bad you weren't able to make it. I'm sure someone
with your knowledge and experience could have provided Freddie Atterton with some much-needed
support and advice when he discovered his ex-wife
was missing.'

For just an instant, calculation was visible in
Craig's face, then he arranged his expression into one
of slight disdain. 'I'd met the man, yes, but I'd no idea
at the time that he'd been married to DCI Meredith.
Nor did I know that his investment schemes were just
that – schemes.'

'So you did some checking on Freddie Atterton
after you arranged to meet him at Leander?'

'Of course I did, Superintendent. I was a police
officer for more than thirty years, in case you'd forgotten.'

Kincaid had certainly not forgotten. 'And that's
why you didn't show up on Tuesday morning?' He
gave a little shrug of disapproval. 'You might have
rung to cancel.'

Craig stared at him as if he'd gone utterly daft.
'Superintendent, are you criticizing my *manners*?
Atterton is little better than a con man, and hardly
deserved the courtesy. If you must know, I was put
out with myself for having been taken in, even

briefly.' He put his large hands on the edge of his desk and pushed his chair back, a signal that the interview was over. 'And you, I think, are supposed to be investigating a murder, not wasting my time.'

Kincaid, however, was not going to be dismissed. 'I understand that you knew DCI Meredith rather better than you did her ex-husband.' The pulse in his temples increased to a sledgehammer-like pounding as his heart rate shot up.

He had just crossed his Rubicon, and there would be no going back.

'What are you talking about?' said Craig softly, all pretence of civility gone from his voice.

'I'm talking about the fact that DCI Meredith accused you of rape. And that Peter Gaskill, her superior officer, convinced her not to file charges against you. But her agreement was based on the fact that he promised her that measures would be taken against you within the force.'

The florid colour had drained from Craig's face. 'How dare—'

'But that didn't happen, did it?' Kincaid said, leaning forward, holding Craig's gaze. 'And Becca Meredith only learned the extent to which those promises had been broken a few weeks ago. I wonder what she threatened to do, and what you would have done to keep her quiet.'

Craig's burly chest expanded as he took a breath. 'That woman was certifiably mad. She's lucky she wasn't thrown out of the force for making accusations of that sort. Gaskill and I both showed her a clemency she didn't deserve.'

'Oh, but it's not quite that simple, sir.' Kincaid used the title as a mockery. The room suddenly seemed very warm, and he had to fight the temptation to move away from the fire. 'Because Rebecca Meredith knew the way things worked,' he said. 'So before she went to Gaskill, she had a rape test done. She listed the assailant as unknown, but the DNA sample was kept as evidence. Gaskill knew that. You knew that. The question is whether or not Becca Meredith had decided to risk her career by using that evidence against you.'

Even as Kincaid spoke, he wondered if that chain of evidence had remained intact, or if the damning DNA sample had mysteriously and conveniently disappeared.

But Craig's next words belied that. 'I had sex with the woman, yes. But she was asking for it,' he added viciously, 'and there was no way the bitch was ever going to prove otherwise.'

Kincaid supposed he should have felt vindicated by Craig's admission, but the venom in the man's voice made him feel sick. Were those the things Craig would have said about Gemma, if he'd been successful in his attempt to assault her? And about other women, who had been guilty of no more than trust?

'Peter Gaskill did her a favour by convincing her not to tell the world what a slut she was,' Craig went on. He clasped his right hand round the large glass paperweight on his desk, his fingers clenching and unclenching. 'She'd have ruined her career, and sullied the reputation of the force.'

Kincaid couldn't contain his sarcasm. 'While yours would have remained unblemished?'

'You are impertinent, and I've had just about enough of this.' Craig's colour had come back in full strength. His face was almost purple with fury. The dog's barking, which had been an ongoing counterpoint to their conversation, suddenly escalated, perhaps in response to the menace in its master's tone. Craig scowled and swore. 'Bloody dog. I'm going to kill it one of these days.'

Then, turning his attention back to Kincaid, he said, 'Now, Superintendent, I think you can see yourself out. But don't think I won't be reporting you to your superiors, or that you won't bear the consequences for this intrusion.'

Kincaid stood, slowly. 'You, sir, are not above rules, or the force of the law.' He wondered, God help him, if that was true, but there was no help for it now. 'And just so we are clear, are you telling me you had nothing to do with the murder of Rebecca Meredith?'

'Of course I didn't.' Craig's disdain was scathing. 'I'm warning you, Superintendent. Don't make a bigger fool of yourself than you already have.'

'Then you won't mind telling me where you were on Monday evening, sir,' Kincaid said, ignoring the threat. 'Between, oh, let's say four o'clock and six.'

He saw Craig bite back his first retort, saw the swift calculation again in the pale eyes, as if he was weighing what he had to lose by answering. Then Craig said, 'I was here until five. After that, I had a drink in the pub. That's my usual routine.'

'That would be the Stag and Huntsman?'

Craig gave him a curt nod. 'That's right.'

'And before that, is there anyone who can verify that you were at home?'

'My wife.' Craig bit off the words as if they were shards of glass.

'I'll need to speak to her,' Kincaid said.

'She's not at home. If she were, the damned dog wouldn't be yapping.'

'Then I suppose I'll have to come back. Thank you for your cooperation, sir.' Kincaid turned as if to go, then swung back. 'Oh, one more thing, sir. Last night, about eight o'clock. Where were you?'

He saw the surprise in the widening of Craig's eyes, in the minute relaxation of the muscles around his mouth. He hadn't been expecting the question, and Kincaid stood struck just as dumb, wondering if he had made a dreadful, irretrievable mistake.

'I was at a meeting in London,' said Craig, with a gleam of malice. 'With people you would do well not to cross.'

Chapter Seventeen

'I want a bow,' said Charlotte.

'And you shall have one, lovey,' Gemma told her. They were sitting on the floor in Betty Howard's colourful, crowded flat, picking through Betty's stock of wide grosgrain ribbon.

'Blue.' Charlotte's delicate little face was set in determination. This was serious business. For Gemma, not quite realizing what she was getting herself into, had promised her an *Alice in Wonderland*-themed party for her birthday on Saturday.

Fortunately, Betty had offered to make her a dress – or, more accurately, a costume. Charlotte, entranced with the John Tenniel illustrations in Kit's old edition of *Alice*, had spent hours poring over the colour plates in which Alice wore a yellow dress with a blue pinafore and, atop that, another starched white pinny.

Gemma had shown the book to Betty with some trepidation, but Betty had just laughed and said, 'Sure, I can make that, Gemma. Piece of cake for an old hand like me. You think I didn't whip up things like that for my own girls?'

A seamstress since childhood, Betty had started

in millinery at sixteen, then gone on to sew everything from clothes, to soft furnishings, to costumes
for the Notting Hill Carnival. With her five girls grown
up and only her son, and Gemma's friend, Wesley still
at home, she ran a thriving little business from her
flat in Westbourne Park Road.

This afternoon Gemma had brought Charlotte for
a final fitting. And a good thing it was the last one,
Gemma thought, because unless Charlotte was allowed
to take the dress home, there was no way Gemma was
getting her out of it without a tantrum. If Gemma had
wished Charlotte would take more interest in girly
things, she'd now been repaid in spades.

'What about this one?' Gemma asked, spying a
piece of ribbon in a cornflower blue that exactly
matched the blue pinafore. 'Will that do, Betty?'

Betty eyed the length from her place at the sewing
machine. 'Should be long enough. Did you get a clip?'

Reaching for her handbag, Gemma pulled out
the hairdresser's clip she'd picked up at a chemist's
shop.

As Betty took the clip and the ribbon, she said to
Charlotte, 'You'll have your Alice Bow in no time,
little miss.'

Charlotte, who had picked up the book and was
once more engrossed in studying the illustrations,
looked up at Gemma. 'I want yellow hair.'

'Well, that, lovey, is one thing you cannot have.
And look.' Gemma took the book from her and turned
to another of the Tenniel plates. 'In this one, Alice
has red hair, just like mine. So Alice can have hair
any colour she likes.'

Charlotte nodded in tentative agreement, but her brow was creased in a frown. 'Not curly.'

'Why not curly?' Gemma twined a finger in the mop of Charlotte's curls. 'I'll bet Alice wished she had hair like yours.'

'She did?'

'I'm sure she did.'

From the sewing machine Betty grinned. 'You don't think Alice wished she had hair like mine?' Her kinky dark hair was going grey, and most days she tucked it up in a bright bandanna. Today she wore a scarf in the same yellow as Charlotte's dress.

Charlotte giggled. 'That's silly.'

'Not to me, it isn't,' said Betty with a smile. But when her eyes met Gemma's, Gemma knew they were both thinking of the day when Charlotte might wish her skin was the same colour as Alice's.

Charlotte reached for Gemma's bag and began to root inside. 'I want a clip,' she said.

Gently Gemma took the bag back. She had a surprise buried in its depths that she'd have to be more careful to keep from prying little hands and eyes.

A few weeks ago she'd found an antique brown-glass pharmacy bottle on a stall at Portobello. She'd bought a fancy paper label for it, on which she had hand-lettered the legend *Drink Me*. It was to be the centrepiece of the cake Wes was making for the party.

'There's not another one,' she said. 'You'll have to wait for your bow. And you can't wear that until Saturday, mind you. Don't forget. Why don't you go and help Betty?' she added as a distraction.

Gemma watched Charlotte as she jumped up and

padded over to the sewing machine in her stockinged feet. The idea of being separated from the child in just a few days' time suddenly took her breath away. How was she going to bear it?

And yet, when she'd gone to the station that morning, she'd felt as if she was coming home. She'd realized how much she'd missed the camaraderie, the routine and, most of all, the intellectual challenge. Would there ever be a happy middle ground, she wondered?

Well, she would find out soon enough – if, that is, she got to start back at work on Monday. She'd had a word with Alia about doing a temporary child-minding stint – Plan B, in case Duncan got hung up in this case.

And it was looking increasingly tricky.

Especially after last night. His reaction when she'd told him about her encounter with Angus Craig worried her. Her *husband* – she was still trying that one on – was an even-tempered man, a man whose habit was to think things through before he acted. But the fact that he was slow to anger made the strength of it all the more powerful, and what she'd seen in his face last night had been cold fury.

She couldn't downplay her experience with Craig – she was as certain as she'd ever been of anything that she'd been in real danger that night in Leyton. Nor could she have kept it from Duncan. But now she was very much afraid that he was going to do something rash.

And with no part in the investigation, she felt helpless and frustrated at her lack of control.

Her hopes that she and Melody would come up

with something useful had so far come to naught, although Melody had said she'd keep looking at the files.

Gemma didn't believe she'd been wrong about Craig's pattern. But perhaps it had been overly optimistic to think that other female officers who'd been Craig's victims might have reported the rape without naming the assailant.

'There you are, little missy,' said Betty. While Gemma had been musing, Betty had bunched the ribbon and stitched it into a bow on the machine, then she'd hand-whipped the bow to the clip. Now, she fastened it in the cloud of Charlotte's hair.

Charlotte, her face rapt, touched it with exploratory fingers, then ran to Gemma. 'I wanna see.'

'Oh, my,' said Gemma, turning her in a twirl so that she could admire the full effect. 'I'm not sure if you look more like Alice or a princess. Here, let's have a look, shall we?' She was digging in her handbag for her compact mirror when she saw the message light flashing on her phone. How had she missed a call?

Her heart gave the little skip it always did when she was separated from the children or Duncan. But when she checked the message log, she saw that the call had been from Melody, and it had been followed by a text.

It said: URGENT, BOSS. MUST TALK.

Gemma looked up. 'Betty, would you mind if Charlotte stayed for just a bit? Something's come up.'

Kincaid pulled out of the Craigs' gravel drive into the road that wound back through Hambleden. Dusk had settled over the rooftops, washing the hamlet in rose and gold. Lights were blinking on, making luminous pools of the windows. Smoke spiralled up from the chimneys.

It was such a cliché, Kincaid thought as he gazed at the village, trying to distance himself from the rage that was still causing his hands to shake. A place of perfection, with a monster dwelling at its heart.

Beauty and evil, nested one within the other.

Did the evil go unacknowledged in this place, he wondered? Or were others aware, but powerless?

Reaching the Stag and Huntsman, he made a sudden swerve into the car park. He wasn't going to pass up an opportunity to find out. Besides, if he didn't check Craig's alibi now, before his guv'nor learned of his visit to Craig, he might not have another chance.

He found a space for the Astra and locked it. Then, after a moment's consideration, he turned off his phone and walked into the pub. He might as well gain himself a little time.

The Stag and Huntsman, he saw immediately, was a welcoming establishment, old-fashioned by nature rather than design, the sort of place one would want to go of an evening for a regular drink before dinner.

It was still quiet, and the clientele looked local and at ease. He hoped that, for once, Angus Craig would forgo his evening tipple.

Making his way to the snug, he took a seat at the bar and ordered a pint of Loddon Hoppit. According to the chalkboard behind the bar, it was a local beer, and Kincaid found the name irresistible.

The beer, when the barman brought it, was a shimmering red-amber, and Kincaid could smell the hops before he tasted it.

'That's good ale,' he said to the barman, wiping the foam from his upper lip.

'Brewed just outside Reading,' said the barman. He was a lean man who didn't look as if he over-indulged in his own wares. 'You're not from around here, I take it?' he continued, knowing full well, Kincaid felt sure, that he was not.

Well, it would do as a conversation starter, and the tiny room was empty except for the two of them, a nice advantage. Kincaid decided to stick as close to the truth as possible.

'London.' He drank some more of the Loddon, reminding himself that he had to drive back to Henley, and that the beer was meant as window-dressing. 'Scotland Yard, actually,' he added, lowering his voice to a confidential tone. 'I'm here about the rower who drowned the other day.'

He felt a stab of guilt at referring to Becca Meredith so impersonally. It now seemed to him as if he *had* known her, and her loss felt like the loss of a friend.

'Terrible thing, that.' The barman sounded genuinely sorry. 'My mate's wife is on the search-and-rescue team. They always take it hard. Can't say I blame them.'

'No. Nor can I.' Kincaid thought of Kieran and Tavie, wondered how Kieran was coping.

'Well, it can't be easy for you, either, in your job. I guess you've been to the scene, down at the Mill?'

There was a definite query at the end of the barman's sentence. So the man did like a bit of a gossip – a quality that, in Kincaid's experience, was necessary to a successful publican. 'Hambleden is a bit off the beaten track.'

'I've been to see Deputy Assistant Commissioner Craig, to tell the truth,' Kincaid said. 'A courtesy call. We are working on his home turf, after all.'

'Ah. I'm sure he appreciated that.'

It was a pleasant, non-committal answer. But Kincaid had seen the telltale change of expression, the shifting of the bartender's eyes away from his. This man knew Angus Craig for what he was.

'It was he who recommended you,' Kincaid went on. 'The best beer, he said, and his local.' He took another sip of his pint. 'Lucky man. He comes in most days, I take it?'

The barman wiped an already clean glass. 'Most evenings.' He glanced at the clock above the door. 'Usually about this time.'

Kincaid thought it would be just as well if he didn't linger. He was trying to figure out how he could discreetly check Craig's alibi, when the barman added, 'Missed him last night. He must have been away.'

'I believe he said something about a meeting in London . . . No, no,' Kincaid put on a perplexed frown, 'he said he was away on Monday. That was it.'

'No, he was here. Although he came in a bit late. I remember because we were all talking about it next day – the thought of us all safe in the pub while that poor woman was washing away down the Thames.' The barman shook his head.

'Maybe he'd been fishing,' Kincaid suggested. 'It would have been a fine day for it.'

The barman looked at him curiously. 'Fishing? Whatever gave you that idea? Mr Craig doesn't fish. Hunting's his cup of tea.'

'Ah, well,' said Kincaid, having ventured as far out on a limb as he could go without falling off. 'Then the pub suits him to a T, wouldn't you say?'

Giving him the perfunctory smile the lame comment deserved, the barman nodded. 'He's said the same, himself. Many a time.'

Resigned to the fact that by this time the man must think him a toady, currying favour with Craig, as well as a bit of an idiot, Kincaid said, 'Lovely house. I understand it's been in Mrs Craig's family for a long time. Sorry I didn't get to meet her.'

The barman's face softened. 'Nice lady, Mrs Craig. Her family's been in Hambleden for yonks, and Edie does more for people here than most.' He nodded towards the centre of the village. 'Matter of fact, I think she's at the church, helping with the preparations for a wedding on Saturday.'

'Is that so? Maybe I'll stop and pay my respects.' Kincaid gave an exaggerated glance at his watch. 'Damn! Didn't realize it was so late.' He drank a little more of his pint, then set the glass on the bar, still half-full.

During his brief visit to the Stag and Huntsman he'd presented himself as a nitwit, a stalker, and now a man who couldn't hold his beer.

'Must dash,' he said, and made his less-than-dignified exit.

*

Kincaid left his car in the pub car park and walked through the village centre. A chill wind eddied a drift of brown leaves along the street. He turned up the collar of his jacket, wishing he hadn't left his overcoat in the Astra's boot. The fine day was over.

He'd remembered seeing a signpost for the church as he drove through the village earlier. Like the church in Henley, it was called St Mary the Virgin, but when he reached it he saw that it was much less grand. The long, low building seemed more suited to human comfort than divine glorification.

As he reached the lychgate, a woman stepped out into the church porch, then turned to lock the door behind her. In that moment he'd seen her clearly in the porch light, and he stopped, surprised.

He wondered what he'd expected. It had not been this tall, slender woman, her greying hair cut in a short, stylish bob. She wore a swinging woollen skirt that just brushed the tops of her knee-high leather boots, an anorak and, round her neck, a long green scarf that fell to the hem of her skirt. The scarf was a cheerful colour that made him think of new leaves and green apples.

When she turned round again, the key in her hand, she saw him and stopped. 'Can I help you?' she asked.

There was no fear in her voice, just gentle enquiry.

'Mrs Craig?'

'Yes. I'm sorry, do I know you?'

He stepped forward into the light. 'No. My name's

Duncan Kincaid. Detective Superintendent, Scotland
Yard.'

She walked towards him until she met him under
the gate. 'If you're looking for my husband, I think
you'll find him at home.' She was still gracious, and
perhaps slightly curious.

'No, actually, it's you I wanted a word with,' he
said, with unexpected reluctance. 'Is there somewhere we can talk?'

He saw the caution settle over her like a cloak,
then she moved so that the shadow of the lychgate
fell across her face. 'I'm sure this will suit well
enough, Superintendent.'

'Mrs Craig – ' Kincaid suddenly found himself at
a loss. No subterfuge seemed appropriate with this
woman. He would simply ask what he needed to
ask. 'Do you know where your husband was late on
Monday afternoon, from around four o'clock on?'

A second passed, then another. He heard the wind
move in the trees, saw the light from the church porch
catch the green of her scarf as she reached up to loop
it round her throat. 'He was at home,' she said, 'with
me. Then he went to the pub, as he usually does.'

Had she been relieved at his question, or had he
just imagined it? Perhaps it was just that Angus
Craig's outing to the pub was the best part of her day.

'Mrs Craig. You'll have heard about the police
officer who drowned. Rebecca Meredith.'

'Yes. The rower. The news has been all over the
village.'

'Did your husband mention that he knew her? Did
he tell you—'

'Superintendent.' Her voice might have been a touch on his arm, the only plea she would allow herself. 'Whatever it is that you feel you need to ask, you must remember that he's my *husband*.' There was finality in her words.

She moved, and when the light caught her face, he thought he glimpsed a despair that was beyond his imagining. Then she had stepped past him. 'I must get home. I've left Barney too long.'

'Barney?' he said, confused. Surely there wasn't a child still at home.

'My dog. Angus doesn't care for him in the house. Goodnight, Superintendent.'

'Goodnight, Mrs Craig,' he echoed. And even though they were going the same way, he paid her the courtesy of letting her walk alone, until she had vanished from his sight.

Gemma had rung Melody as soon as she left Betty's flat. She was prepared to go straight to the station, but Melody had hesitated, then said, 'Um, I'm not sure that's a good idea, boss. Why don't we meet for a drink? Say, the Duke of Wellington. I'll be there before you.'

The pub, at the intersection of Portobello Road and Elgin Crescent, was one Gemma knew well, at least from outside. A pair of jazz guitarists – session musicians – busked outside on fine Saturday afternoons and she'd often stopped to listen, smiling with pleasure and dropping a pound or two in the open guitar case.

But, she realized, she'd never actually been inside

the establishment. And for Melody to be there before her, she must have already been nearby.

The building was Victorian, stuccoed in pale pink, and not terribly prepossessing. But when Gemma entered by the Portobello door, she found an air of cheerful bustle. She spied Melody immediately, seated at a small, high table at the very back of the room. Gemma made her way round the bar and joined her, slipping onto the high stool.

Melody handed her a glass. 'I've ordered you a G&T. You're going to need it.'

'What's going on?' asked Gemma. 'And what are you doing here?'

'When you didn't answer your phone, I called the house and talked to Kit. He said you were at Betty's. I was coming to find you.'

Melody looked strained and windblown, her dark hair mussed from the chill breeze that had come up with the dusk. It was unlike her not to have tidied up. She drank from her own glass, which was, Gemma saw, already half-empty.

'Boss, I've found something. First, this.' Melody reached for her bag and handed Gemma a sheet of paper.

Gemma scanned a list of names.

'Six female police officers, in the last ten years,' said Melody. 'There's some variation in the stories, but they all fit the same general pattern. They were either single or their husbands or boyfriends, or in one case a girlfriend, were away. All had been out to a pub or a party, something work-related. All said they were attacked in their homes by unknown intruders. None reported obvious signs of breaking and entering at their place of residence. None could identify their assailant.'

Gemma stared at her, then took a gulp of her drink while she scanned the list again. The gin burned her throat and she coughed. 'Different divisions?' she asked, when she could speak again.

'Yes. And most seem to correlate with Angus Craig's postings at the time. The others were at functions that might have been attended by any senior officer.'

'Bloody hell,' Gemma muttered. 'I was right.'

'Oh, it gets better.' Melody shrugged. 'Or worse, depending on your point of view. That's as far as I'd got when I found this.' This time she handed Gemma a sheaf of papers. 'From six months ago. It was in our records because of the rape.' She glanced round, but the other tables were filled with after-work drinkers absorbed in their own conversations, and the noise level in the pub was rising.

'Her name was Jenny Hart,' said Melody. 'She was a DCI, Tower Hamlets. But she lived in Campden Street, right on the border between Holland Park and Kensington. Not too far from me, actually.'

'You said *was*. And *lived*. Past tense.' Gemma's glass felt cold and damp in her hand.

Melody drank from hers until there were only ice cubes left. 'Jenny Hart was divorced, forty years old and, from the photos in her file, an attractive blonde. She also had a reputation for liking to drink a bit, especially at the Churchill Arms, just down the street from her flat. Ever been there?'

Gemma shook her head. 'I've passed it, though. It's the place with all the flowers.' It looked the epitome of pubs, with its dark wood and mullioned windows, and the profusion of hanging baskets and windowboxes that almost covered the exterior.

'Suffocatingly cosy. Every inch of the place is stuffed with tatty Churchill memorabilia. But the place is bigger than you'd think – it's a conglomeration of small rooms that seem to ramble on forever.'

'As are you,' said Gemma, pointedly. Her mouth felt dry. 'Melody, what happened to Jenny Hart?'

Melody clinked her two remaining ice cubes, then met Gemma's eyes. 'On the first of May, Jenny Hart told some mates that she was going for a drink at the Churchill and that, afterwards, she was going to have an early night. It had been a rough week. They'd had a murdered child on her patch.

'When she didn't show up for work on Monday, her colleagues were concerned. They rang her, but didn't get an answer. By Tuesday, her neighbours complained of the smell.'

Gemma realized the pub had filled with the odour of meat cooking in the kitchen. She swallowed against a sudden queasiness, and the knowledge of what she knew was coming. 'How?' she said simply.

'She was raped. And then she was manually strangled. According to the post-mortem notes, the bruising on her throat was in accordance with thumb and fingerprints. There was considerable damage to her flat. She must have put up quite a fight. But there were no signs of breaking and entering.'

Gemma took a breath. 'And?'

'Our old friend Kate Ling did the post-mortem, by the way. She was, of course, very thorough. There was tissue under Jenny's fingernails. And there was semen in her vagina, and smeared on her torn clothing. Her assailant couldn't be bothered with condoms.

'I cross-checked the profiles. The DNA found on Jenny Hart matches the samples from the other female officers who reported they were raped. The matches had been flagged by Project Sapphire, but there was never a suspect for comparison.'

Like Melody, Gemma finished her gin and tonic in one long gulp. 'There isn't now. Not without corroborating evidence.'

Nodding at the papers in Gemma's hand, Melody said, 'Take a look.'

Gemma flipped through copies of Jenny Hart's post-mortem results, the lab data, statements from her colleagues and neighbours. At the back was something that certainly hadn't been included in the original file – a photo of Angus Craig, one of a group of men in evening dress, some of whom she recognized as other senior police officers.

'Commissioner's Ball,' said Melody, before Gemma could ask. 'Last year. From the very useful files of the *Chronicle*. The thing is, according to the statements, one of the staff at the Churchill thought she remembered seeing Jenny talking to a man that night. But it was packed, and she only had a vague recollection. The closest she could come to a description was "middle-aged". Not very helpful if you had nothing to compare it to.'

Gemma straightened up so fast she bumped her knees against the small table, rocking it precariously. She steadied her glass. 'Did you talk to her?'

'I went to the Churchill. According to the manager, the barmaid's name is Rosamond. She's been on holiday in France for the last few days, but she's on shift tomorrow. Starting at lunch.'

Gemma's head reeled. Could it possibly be that easy, if Angus Craig had been preying on women for years? But sometimes – sometimes if they were very, very lucky – it was. All it took was one sound witness statement, cause enough to request a DNA sample.

It wouldn't matter if the other female officers still refused to testify against him. All they needed was Jenny Hart. And if the samples matched, there was no way in hell Angus Craig could bully his way out of a murder charge.

Chapter Eighteen

When Kincaid reached Henley, he drove down New Street into Thames Side, past the Hotel du Vin and Freddie Atterton's flat. He pulled the Astra into a parking spot facing the river, from where he could see the lights of Henley Bridge and, on the far side, Leander.

It was now fully dark, but he imagined the scene as it would have looked on Monday, a little earlier in the evening – the light fading on the river, the sliver of a boat, ghostly white in the dim light, pushing away from Leander's landing raft.

Rolling down the Astra's window, he listened, imagining the quiet splish of the oars, the rhythmic creak of the shell's seat as it moved up and down on the runners, the thunk of the blades moving against the oarlocks as the boat whispered past. And then, it vanished into the darkness.

Reluctantly, he turned his gaze from the river and switched his phone on, checking for messages. There was nothing from Chief Superintendent Childs, but his relief was short-lived as he thought out the implications.

Did that mean Craig had not complained about

Kincaid's visit and accusations? That Craig was waiting to see if his threats had been enough to warn Kincaid off?

And if that were the case, was that further evidence of his guilt?

Or was it just that Craig was marshalling his support, and the retaliation was yet to come?

No matter, Kincaid thought, whether Craig struck back now or later – he had no more evidence against Craig than he had before he'd spoken to him. In fact, with Craig's possible alibis for both Monday evening and Wednesday night, he had even less.

He gazed out at the river again, putting together the timeline as he'd worked it out. If Becca had left Leander a little after half past four, she'd have rounded Temple Island and started back upriver sometime between five and half past.

Could Craig have murdered Becca at five o'clock, then walked, wet and muddy, back to his car, driven back to Hambleden, got himself cleaned up and strolled blithely into the pub before six?

Certainly not without his wife's knowledge, if she'd been at home, but Kincaid thought he could safely say that they would not get a damning statement from Edie Craig.

It would take physical evidence to tie Craig to the crime – matching hair, fibre or footprints from the scene of Becca's murder to his car or person. But even that would be questionable, as they had no absolute proof that Becca had been killed in the spot Kieran had indicated. In any case, there was nothing concrete enough against Craig to allow Kincaid to float a request for comparison.

And even if he could pin Becca's murder on Craig, it looked as if Craig had a solid alibi for the time of the attack on Kieran's boatshed.

But if Craig hadn't attacked Kieran, who had? Not Freddie Atterton, if the phone records and his former mother-in-law confirmed his alibi.

Kincaid debated staying in Henley. Should he have another word with Freddie? Question Kieran again? He felt boxed in – but he knew there was something on the other side of the wall, if he could only see it. And if he asked the right people the right questions. But who, and what?

The air blowing down the river was cold. He shivered and rolled up his window, having almost made up his mind to put up at the Red Lion, when his phone rang. It startled him so much that he almost dropped it, but when he'd fumbled it right-side up, he saw that it was Doug.

'Guv,' said Doug, as soon as Kincaid answered. 'I'm just back at the Yard. I've—'

'Have you seen the Chief Super?' Kincaid interrupted.

'No, but—'

'Well, make yourself invisible. I've put my foot in a wasps' nest and I don't want you getting stung.'

There was a moment's silence as Doug digested this. Then, he said, 'I'm in your office, and I think the chief has gone for the day.' Carefully he added, 'Um, I take it the visit didn't go well?'

'Depends on your point of view.' Kincaid made an

effort to keep his voice calm. 'I have absolutely no doubt that he raped Rebecca Meredith. He as much as admitted it. But I'm not seeing anything that will let us tie him to her murder.'

'What about Connolly's boatshed?'

Kincaid shifted uncomfortably. 'Craig was surprised when I asked him where he was on Wednesday night. I don't think he knew what had happened. And apparently, at the time, he was in London, meeting with *very important people*, as he put it.'

'Ah. Would one of those important people happen to have been Peter Gaskill?'

'Wouldn't surprise me.'

'That's one of the things I was calling to tell you,' Doug said, with an air of satisfaction. 'I've done some checking. Seems they're very matey, your friend and Gaskill. As in Gaskill owes Craig his promotion.'

'You didn't talk to Gaskill, did you?' Kincaid asked with a jolt of alarm.

'No. I'd have avoided him in any case, but he was out this afternoon. Golfing.'

'Is that so?' Kincaid found he wasn't surprised. 'What a coincidence. Our friend was golfing as well. Who did you talk to?'

'DC Bisik. It seems Sergeant Patterson was right about it not being a good idea to be seen talking to us. She was seconded to another division by the end of the day yesterday.'

'What?' Kincaid's hand tightened on the phone. 'Where?'

'Dulwich. I've checked with the station there. She reported for duty this morning, although the

Inspector seemed rather surprised to find that he needed another detective sergeant.'

Gaskill's doing, no doubt, Kincaid thought. And probably Craig's, setting in motion a chain of commands that had resulted in DS Patterson's quick removal. He wondered how many of the links in the chain were willing participants.

'She'd gone home by the time I rang the station. Bisik gave me her mobile number,' Doug continued, 'but she's not answering.'

'No,' Kincaid said. 'I doubt she would.' He drummed his fingers on the steering wheel. 'I suspect she learned her lesson about talking out of school.'

'Well, we need to speak to her again, regardless. The thing is, Bisik could only think of one thing that was different about Becca's day on Friday. Another female officer came in, a DCI from Vice. Apparently, she was an old mate of Becca's. Bisik wasn't introduced to her, but he had the impression that Kelly Patterson was. He also had the idea that Becca and this copper might have gone out for drinks. Gaskill would know who she was, I'm sure, but I doubt you want me asking him,' Doug added. 'Nor the guv'nor.'

'No.' Kincaid thought about their strategy. 'If Patterson doesn't return your calls tonight, can you be at her station first thing in the morning? Unofficially.'

He couldn't quite get his head round the fact that he couldn't go to his own Chief Superintendent with this. How much did Childs know? Was he privy to all of Craig's and Gaskill's manoeuvring, or was he merely following orders he'd been given?

Kincaid still found it hard to believe that the man

he'd thought he knew, and thought of as his friend as well as his superior, would countenance protecting Craig if he knew the truth about him.

Should he try to . . .

'Hang on,' said Doug. 'Email just came in on your computer. It's the lab results from the SOCOs on Freddie Atterton's car and the things they took from his flat.' There was a moment's pause as Doug read, and Kincaid could imagine him pushing his glasses up on his nose. Then Doug went on, 'You can say *I told you so* to the guv'nor. There were no traces of grass or mud from the river bank, either in the car or on the clothing. No fibre match. And the footprint at the site was a size smaller than Atterton's shoes. And' – there was a spark of excitement in Doug's voice – 'in the debris against the bank they found a chip of paint that matches the Filippi's hull.'

'So she *was* killed there,' Kincaid said slowly. 'And not by Freddie Atterton.' He thought about Freddie and Kieran Connolly, both about the same size and height. 'I'd wager the smaller shoe size rules out Kieran as well.'

'You were thinking Connolly might have made up the whole story about seeing the man on the river bank, then torched his own boatshed for verisimilitude?'

'Watch it, with the big university words,' Kincaid told him, with a trace of returning humour. 'But, yes, I'd considered it, although I didn't think it likely.'

But if they ruled out Freddie, and they ruled out Kieran, that brought them back to Angus Craig, and Kincaid back to square one. How the hell could they—

His phone buzzed with an incoming call. Gemma. 'Hold on. Or let me just ring you back,' he said to Doug, and clicked over.

Gemma didn't give him an opportunity to say more than *hello*. Her words tumbled out on a rising wave of excitement. 'We found something. Or, I should say, Melody did. Going through Sapphire's unsolved rape records. The rape *and* murder of a female senior police officer. Six months ago. It fits his pattern.'

When she came to a breathless halt, his hands had gone cold and he felt queasy. 'Is there any proof?' he asked.

'There might be a witness. The barmaid at the pub where the woman was drinking right before she was killed. We won't be able to contact her until tomorrow.'

'Have you or Melody spoken to anyone else about this?'

'No, I didn't—'

'Well, don't.' He knew his voice was sharp, but he had to make his point. 'Call whoever you talked to at the pub and tell them not to speak to *anyone* about this. No, have Melody do it. I don't want you involved any more than necessary. Where are you now?'

'I'm just about to pick up Charlotte from Betty's.'

'Get Charlotte and go home,' he said, his voice grim. 'Stay there. Don't talk to anyone. Tell Melody not to talk to anyone. I don't want this going any further until we know for certain if the barmaid can give us an ID.'

'You think he's really dangerous, don't you?' Gemma sounded subdued now, the rush of excitement gone.

'Yes. I do.' He thought of the venom, and the over-weening arrogance, that had spewed from Angus Craig, and he wished he had never let Gemma anywhere near this case. 'Just be careful, love. I'll be home in an hour.'

He'd rung Doug as he drove back to London, filling him in on Gemma's news and asking him to keep trying to reach Kelly Patterson.

When he reached Notting Hill at last, he was glad to see their house, with its cheery red front door and the lights shining in the windows. He tried not to think about the fact that they were, at least in some sense, indebted to Denis Childs for it.

Gemma greeted him as he walked in, brushing his lips with hers, then resting her cheek against his just an instant longer than usual. 'Are you hungry?' she asked, stepping back. 'It's pizza again, I'm afraid. I stopped at Sugo's on the way home.' With a little smile she added, 'We're going to turn into pizzas, if we're not careful.'

'Toby would be thrilled with that. What would he choose, do you think? Pepperoni?' Kincaid hung up his overcoat, fished from the boot of the Astra. He bent to stroke Geordie, their cocker spaniel, and Sid, their rather large black cat. Sid had developed a dog-like sense of prescience regarding Kincaid's arrival, and always seemed to have settled down noncha-lantly for a nap on the hall bench just five minutes beforehand.

'You'd be artichoke, then.'

'Shhh. Don't tell the children,' Kincaid said,

making an effort at normality. 'Maybe I'll have to get a bit more inventive on the dinner front when I'm home full-time. I am, after all, going to be a proper house-husband.'

Gemma gave him a quick glance, a question in it, but merely said, 'The children have been fed, and the little ones bathed. Charlotte's waiting for you to say goodnight. Artichoke-and-ham pizza warming in the oven for you, after.'

'Right. Thanks, love.' The house was warm, and as he glanced into the sitting room, he saw that Gemma had lit the gas fire. The room, however, was empty. 'Boys upstairs, then?'

'Supposed to be reading.' Gemma rolled her eyes. 'Heaven knows what Toby's really doing. Kit will be texting.'

'Lally?'

Gemma nodded. 'I suspect we're going to have to rethink the unlimited texting option.'

They'd given Kit a basic mobile phone for his birthday at the end of June, both for safety reasons and because they'd hoped it would help him fit in better at school. However, hours spent texting his cousin Lally every day had not been what they had in mind. And while Kincaid loved his niece, he knew she was both emotionally volatile and needy. He didn't think that much contact with her was healthy for Kit.

'I'll check on them.' He slipped off his suit jacket, hanging it on the coat rack next to his overcoat and the little ones' macs, then climbed the stairs to Charlotte's marigold-yellow bedroom on the first floor.

He peeped through the half-open door. The bedside lamp was switched on low, casting a pool of light on the small huddle beneath the bedclothes. As he came into the room, he saw that Charlotte was fast asleep. The covers were drawn up to her nose, but one small hand was free, stretched towards the bright-blue hair bow on the edge of the bedside table.

He sat on the edge of the bed and smoothed her hair back from her forehead. She didn't stir. Carefully he leaned down and kissed the corner of her eyebrow, conscious of the stubble on his jaw, then tucked her hand beneath the duvet.

He was glad he'd come home.

Tiptoeing out, he checked on both boys, pleased to find that Toby was doing nothing more destructive than building a railway track on his floor.

Kit was, at least ostensibly, reading, but as Kincaid came in he saw the boy slip his phone under his pillow.

Gemma was right, Kincaid realized, but dealing with the combined issues of the phone usage and Kit's relationship with his cousin would have to wait a bit longer. He had other things to settle at the moment.

When he came back downstairs after speaking to the boys, Gemma had put a plate out for him with the pizza slices, and had poured him a glass of red wine. She'd opened the bottle of Bordeaux he'd been saving.

Tess, Kit's terrier, had been upstairs curled on the foot of Kit's bed, but Geordie had stayed in the kitchen with Gemma. Now he settled on the floor, resting his head on Kincaid's foot with a sigh. Sid kept watch on them from the far chair, his eyes on the pizza. The cat was an incorrigible food thief.

Gemma was drinking tea, and had a stack of papers beside her cup. When he started to reach for them, she stopped his hand with hers. 'Eat first.'

Obediently he ate a slice of pizza, his favourite, and drank half a glass of the wine. But he had no appetite, and the wine he'd been anticipating as a special treat left an acrid taste in his mouth.

He thought of the fire burning invitingly in the sitting room. But here they were, in the kitchen, which was where all their important conversations seemed to take place. Was it the same in other families, he wondered? He had an instant's intense longing for his parents' kitchen in Cheshire, where everything momentous in his family had been discussed. And where he and Juliet, as children, had inevitably felt safe.

But he felt no security tonight, even here. He pushed his plate away and reached for the papers, and this time Gemma didn't stop him.

She watched him as he read and, when he looked up, her expression was sombre. 'It was him, wasn't it?'

He nodded. 'I think so.'

'He was escalating, wasn't he? Taking on more powerful women, becoming more violent. He took a big risk with Becca Meredith, and he got away with it. That must have made him feel invincible.' She reached across the table and touched the papers. 'Do you think this woman – Jenny Hart – do you think she told him she wouldn't be blackmailed into silence?'

Picking up the pages again, he glanced at the crime-scene photos. The coffee table in Jenny Hart's sitting room had been overturned. There was broken glass on the floor, as well as scattered magazines and newspapers. 'Not just that,' he said. 'She fought, hard.' He looked up at Gemma. 'The other women – did they report injuries, bruising, any throttling?'

'Bruising, yes,' said Gemma. 'One victim had a shattered cheekbone. And the photos in Becca Meredith's file show contusions about the neck and shoulders.'

Kincaid thought of Angus Craig's powerful arms and shoulders. When he raped, Craig had used surprise, strength and intimidation, probably in that order. But with Jenny Hart, perhaps he'd been past caring about the intimidation part of the equation. Perhaps his need for violence had passed the point of no return.

Kincaid guessed that up until Jenny Hart, Craig's rapes had been crimes of opportunity, although he must have gone to functions and pubs hoping he would find a suitable target.

Had Hart been different? Had he known where she drank, and when she was likely to be there? Had he intended murder when he'd met Jenny Hart in the pub that night?

If so, Becca Meredith's murder seemed a small and rather cautiously executed action. Why had he not surprised her in her home, if he knew she lived alone?

Kincaid answered his own question. Because Craig had known what he was dealing with in Becca Meredith, and he would have known that she wouldn't be taken defenceless again.

But what Kincaid still didn't understand was why Craig had chosen to kill Becca Meredith now, rather than a year ago when she'd first threatened to expose him.

What the hell had triggered it? And hadn't Craig thought Gaskill would be suspicious if Becca died mysteriously? Or was Gaskill so crooked that Craig had felt sure he could depend on him even then . . .

'Earth to Duncan.' Gemma waved a hand in front of his face. 'You're right away with the fairies, love. How about you talk to *me*.'

'I don't like this,' he said, shaking his head. 'I don't like you or Melody being involved with this. Craig has too much power.' The idea of Gemma having even peripheral contact with the man made him see red. 'I'll take over the Jenny Hart inquiry from here on,' he went on. 'Doug and I will interview the barmaid tomorrow – although it might be better if Doug was out of it as well.'

Gemma gave him the look that meant she wasn't having it. 'And if the guv'nor calls you off before you have the chance?' she asked. 'What then? You'll be dead in the water and nobody will be able to touch Craig. Let Melody do the interview. It's a legitimate Project Sapphire follow-up, and she doesn't have to clear it with anyone. If she gets a positive ID, you can take it from there.'

She was right, although he hated to admit it. He

drank a little more of his wine, then said reluctantly, 'All right. But it's Melody's interview, not yours,' he cautioned. 'I don't want you connected with this in any way.'

'Of course not,' said Gemma, but she looked like the Cheshire cat.

He felt his blood pressure shoot up. 'You've got to take this seriously, Gemma. Have you really looked at these photos?' Smacking his palm on the stack of papers for emphasis, he said, 'I don't think you realize just how dangerous this man is. I don't want—'

His phone rang. He'd put it on the table when he sat down to eat, and the vibration made the cutlery rattle against his plate. Geordie lifted his head and growled.

'Bloody hell!' Kincaid muttered as he reached for the offending instrument. 'Now what? I swear I'm going to throw the damned thing in the bog next time it rings.'

The tightening in his jaw made him realize he was still waiting for Angus Craig's axe to fall.

But once again it wasn't the Chief Superintendent ringing to pass along Craig's ire, or to give Kincaid an official reprimand. According to the phone ID, it was Detective Constable Imogen Bell.

'Sir,' she said when he answered, sounding surprisingly diffident. 'It's DC Bell here. Sorry to bother you so late, and you're probably at home – I checked with the Red Lion, but they said you'd gone . . . '

'Never mind where I am, Bell. Out with it.' Meeting Gemma's enquiring glance across the table, he shrugged in consternation.

'Sorry, sir,' said Bell. 'Didn't mean to pry.' She sounded even more uncomfortable. 'It's just that – I, um, I've a little problem here. I seem to . . . well, I seem to have lost Freddie Atterton.'

Chapter Nineteen

'Tell me exactly what happened,' he said.

Bell hesitated. 'Everything?'

'Yes, everything.' He tried to master his impatience. 'You let me decide whether or not it's important, okay?'

'Okay,' Bell repeated, still a little uncertainly. 'Well, after I spoke to you earlier in the afternoon, I put together some lunch with the bits that were in the fridge. I thought he should eat something, you know?'

The question was apparently rhetorical, as she went on. 'Then, well, there didn't seem to be anyone else to do it, so I went with Fred – Mr Atterton – to the undertaker's. I helped him make the basic arrangements. It was – it was . . . grim. I'm glad I don't do that every day.'

'Understandable,' Kincaid said encouragingly. 'I'm sure you were a great help. Then what did you do?'

'We went back to the flat. I helped him with the obituary. It needed to go in *The Times* straight away. And that was – I didn't realize all the things she'd done. She was quite special, wasn't she?' An element of hero worship had crept into Bell's voice.

'She was that,' Kincaid agreed. 'But she was also very human, and I suspect that right now Freddie is not inclined to remember her flaws. But we mustn't forget that she had them.'

As he spoke, Kincaid watched Gemma, who had stood and was quietly putting plates and cups in the sink as she listened to his side of the conversation.

She could be obstinate, he thought, cataloguing her faults. Impulsive. Quick to judge, quick to speak her mind, quick to care passionately about things and people. Slow to make commitments, unless she knew she could keep them.

And he adored her. He wouldn't have her any other way.

He wondered if Rebecca Meredith had wanted to be loved for her flaws as much as her accomplishments – and if she'd realized, too late, that she'd had that and given it up.

'Right,' said Bell, sounding unconvinced. 'When we'd finished, it was getting on for supper, and there was nothing left in the fridge but sour milk and some beer. I said I'd go to the shops. He – Atterton – seemed so . . . lost. He couldn't even put together a shopping list, so I . . . I went to Sainsbury's.' Bell paused again.

And?' Kincaid prompted.

'When I got back, he was gone.'

'Just gone? On foot? By car? You're certain he wasn't in the flat?'

'I knocked and rang, then I tried his mobile and the landline. By that time I was getting seriously worried, so I tracked down the building manager and had him let me in. I was afraid . . . I was afraid of what I might find. But he wasn't there. There was nothing disturbed, no note. His car keys were still on the console table by the door. He seems to have just walked out and not come back.'

'Was he drinking?'

'No. In fact, he poured the remains of a bottle of good Scotch down the sink. Said the smell made him feel ill.'

At least it didn't sound as if Atterton had gone off on a bender, Kincaid thought. To Bell he said, 'Keep trying to reach him. You did the right thing, helping him out this afternoon, and ringing me. But Freddie Atterton's a grown man and we've no right to restrict his movements unless we've charged him with something.'

'We're not going to, are we?' asked Bell. 'Charge him, I mean.'

'The SOCOs found no evidence linking him to the scene of the murder, so at the moment I doubt it.' He sounded more certain than he felt. 'Was there anything else today?' he asked. 'Anything you talked about that was out of the ordinary?'

There was silence while Imogen Bell thought. Then she said, 'He kept asking about the boat, wanting to know when he could have it back. I told him I thought the SOCOs were almost finished with it. I hope that was okay.'

Kincaid frowned. 'I don't see why not – although he won't have any legal right to the boat until the will has been processed.'

When he'd rung off, Gemma sat down across from him again and poured herself a bit of the Bordeaux.

'Becca's ex-husband's gone missing, I take it?' she asked. 'Do you think he's all right?'

'He doesn't strike me as the suicidal type,' Kincaid said. 'And DC Bell, who was looking after him, said he kept asking about the Filippi, Becca's racing shell. Why would he want to know when he could have the boat back, if he was going to kill himself?'

'You don't think – ' Now it was Gemma who hesitated. 'You don't think he's in any danger, do you?'

Kincaid thought of the measures that Craig and Gaskill and their shadowy cronies were willing to take to keep secrets. 'I hope not,' he said.

Kincaid didn't sleep well. He lay, feeling the weight of Gemma's leg against his, inhaling the scent of her lilac bath soap, and worrying about Freddie Atterton – and about Gemma – until well into the wee hours of the morning.

He must have dozed at last, but he woke again when the panes in the bedroom windows began to lighten almost imperceptibly with the coming dawn.

Carefully easing his feet from under Geordie, who slept stretched out across the foot of the bed, Kincaid got up, showered and dressed. When he was ready, he bent and kissed the corner of Gemma's mouth. 'I'm going to Henley,' he whispered.

'What?' She opened sleepy eyes. 'What's happened?'

'Nothing. Shhh. Go back to sleep. I'll ring you.'

He crept down the stairs, trying not to wake the children, and found that he was suddenly aware of the particular early-morning feel of the house. He imagined it as a quietly slumbering beast, waiting for its heart to wake – its exhalations rich with accumulated scents of tea and toast and dogs and the faint mist of children's breath.

He was quite pleased with his fancy, and himself, when he reached the front door undetected. But then he heard the click of toenails on the floor tiles.

Turning, he saw that Geordie had followed him downstairs. The dog looked up at him, his tail wagging, his eyes filled with the soulful reproach that only a cocker spaniel can achieve.

Kincaid squatted and rubbed his ears. 'I can't take you out just now,' he whispered. 'Go back to bed.'

Geordie cocked his head, his tail wagging harder. Kincaid gave his head a last pat. 'Nothing gets past you, does it, sport? Keep an eye on Gemma for me, that's a good – '

He stood, staring at the dog. Why hadn't he thought of that before?

It was fully light by the time Kincaid reached Henley. As he passed over the bridge, he saw the rowing eights going out from Leander, like a many-legged flotilla. The morning was cold, clear and still – perfect rowing weather, he assumed. But it wasn't rowers he wanted to speak to at the moment.

His first stop was the incident room at Henley Police Station.

DI Singla was there, as was the unfortunately named DC Bean, but the industry of the past few days seemed to have dissipated, and the room had a sleepy air. There was little new information for the team to work with, and nothing he could add. Yet.

He was about to ask for DC Bell when she came in, looking rumpled and bleary-eyed.

'Sir.' She nodded at him as she sank into a chair, cradling a plastic cup of coffee in her hands as if she needed its transitory warmth.

'Rough night?' he asked.

Imogen Bell blushed. 'I was concerned about Mr Atterton, sir. I watched the flat.'

Kincaid stared at her. 'All night?'

'Yes, sir. From my car. I parked by the main gate.'

No wonder she looked as though she'd slept in her clothes – she had, or at least had spent the night in them. Kincaid was impressed, although he wasn't sure if she had demonstrated the makings of a very good police officer or a very big crush. Possibly both.

'Commendable,' he said. 'Did he come home?'

'No, sir.' She looked utterly dejected. 'And he's still not answering his mobile.'

DI Singla broke in. 'We've confirmed Atterton's overseas phone call to Mrs Meredith on Wednesday evening, both from the phone records and by speaking to Mrs Meredith. They talked for forty-two minutes. Atterton could not possibly have burned Kieran Connolly's boatshed, unless he has the ability to be in two places at once. Or he and his former mother-in-law are in cahoots,' Singla added thoughtfully. 'I suppose he could have answered her call, then left the phone off the hook – '

'While he walked or drove to the place, where he borrowed or stole a single scull, rowed to the island, tossed the Molotov cocktail, returned the boat and made it back to the flat to hang up the phone, all in forty-two minutes?'

'I'll admit it's unlikely,' agreed Singla. 'And I can't imagine why Rebecca Meredith's mother would have agreed to such a thing, unless she and Atterton knew the disposition of Rebecca's will and planned to share the estate. As far as we've been able to ascertain, however, Mrs Meredith has no need of her daughter's money or property.'

'Not to mention that such a scenario is based on Freddie Atterton having killed Becca, and we know Forensics found no corroborating evidence at the scene.' Kincaid grinned at Singla. 'But then you lost me at *cahoots.*'

It seemed a casual word for such a formal man. DI Singla was proving full of surprises, but just now Kincaid needed Doug Cullen. But he'd asked Doug to stay behind in London, in case Melody – and Gemma – needed backup.

'But what about Mr Atterton,' said Bell. 'Should we report him missing?'

Kincaid considered. 'Let's give it a bit longer. Have you tried Leander?'

'Not since yesterday evening.'

'Why don't you check with them again? I've someone I want to have a word with, then we'll reconvene.' He started to turn away, but something was puzzling him. 'DC Bell, did Freddie give you any reason for being so anxious to get the Filippi back?'

'He said . . . ' She frowned, as if trying to recall the exact words. 'He said it was the only thing he could fix.'

*

Having left Notting Hill without breakfast, Kincaid briefly considered picking up a cup of coffee from the station vending machine. But only briefly. He'd be walking right by Starbucks – not his favourite brew, but a huge improvement over brown slop in a polystyrene cup.

A few minutes later, armed with a paper cup from Starbucks, and having downed a muffin in two bites, he rang Tavie Larssen's bell.

There was a chorus of wild barking, a man's answering shout, then Kieran Connolly swung open the door. His forehead, which had just been beginning to bruise on Wednesday night, was now purple, but he'd removed the dressing and Kincaid saw that he was indeed going to have a rakish Harry Potter scar slanting down to his eyebrow.

But his face brightened when he saw it was Kincaid. 'Have you come about the shed?' he asked, blocking the still-barking German shepherd and Labrador with his body.

'Partly,' Kincaid said. 'Can I come in?'

'Oh, yeah, sure.' Kieran turned to the dogs. 'Finn. Tosh. Quiet. Go lie down.'

The dogs obeyed the first command, but not the second. They had to sniff Kincaid thoroughly as he entered the room, their doggy breath warm against his trouser legs. 'You smell other pups, don't you?' he said, giving them both rubs round the ears. To Kieran, he added, 'You forgot the biscuits.'

'Oh, so I did.' Kieran opened the tin on the table by the door and the dogs sat immediately. 'You have dogs?' Kieran asked, looking at him for the first time as if he might be a person as well as a policeman.

'A cocker spaniel. And our son has a terrier.'

'Good dogs, cockers,' said Kieran. 'Great at drugs and explosives work. Amazing energy, those little guys.'

'Tell me about it.'

Having finished their biscuits, the dogs went to their beds, now side by side in front of the fire. Tavie's sitting room, Kincaid saw, no longer looked as though it belonged in a doll's house. Aside from the two large dogs and one large man, the floor was scattered with dog toys, the tables held empty cups and scattered papers, and several articles of male clothing were draped haphazardly over the sofa and chairs.

Kieran removed a pair of jeans from the sofa back and gestured Kincaid to a seat. 'Sorry about the mess,' he said. 'Tavie's dryer's on the blink. She's borrowed a few things for me from her mates at work, but all my stuff needed washing.'

'Is she here?'

'No. She's on rota today.' Kieran sat on the chair, his large hands clasped on his knees. 'About the shed. Is it . . . ? Can I – I'd like to go home.'

It seemed to Kincaid that, in spite of his assertion, Kieran seemed less anxious about the shed than he had been after the fire on Wednesday night. Understandable, certainly, as he'd been shocked, injured and frightened. But today he also seemed to be moving round Tavie's little house more easily, as if he was beginning to feel comfortable in the space.

'I see you two haven't killed each other yet,' Kincaid said.

'Not yet. Although it's been a near thing.' There was a glint of wry humour in Kieran's eyes. 'But still, I need to see if – if there's anything left – '

'I talked to the arson investigator on the way here. They've cleared your boatshed, as of this morning. They've finished gathering evidence, and they've pronounced the shed messy, but safe.'

'Oh.' Having been granted his wish, Kieran seemed at a loss. 'Great.'

'I went through it yesterday. It's not as bad as you might think, but you'll have a job in store.'

Nodding, Kieran reached up as if to scratch his forehead, then appeared to think better of it and dropped his hand back to his lap. 'Tavie keeps telling me that things are replaceable, that I should be thankful I'm alive. And I suppose I know that, but everything I owned was in that shed. I could – ' He shook his head, as if debating the wisdom of finishing his thought aloud. 'Do you know who did this to me?' he asked instead. 'Or why? Was it the man I saw by the river?'

'We don't know yet. But about that place by the river,' Kincaid said, seeing his opening. 'You were right. There was someone there, and he left physical evidence.' Kincaid sat forward, glancing at the dogs, both now stretched out on their sides and seemingly oblivious to the world. 'It occurred to me . . . is it possible that the dogs could associate scent left in that spot with a particular person?'

Kieran frowned. 'It's been, what, five days? And I've been there, not to mention your forensics team have been over it with a fine-toothed comb. Tavie's the expert, but I'd say it's highly unlikely.'

As if he knew they were talking about him, Finn gave a whuffled groan and raised his head.

'The dogs might react if they had some sort of emotional connection to the scent' – Kieran went on, without meeting Kincaid's eyes – 'like, um, a significant event, or if they recognized a person they already knew.'

Finn stood, yawning, then came over and settled at Kieran's feet. 'But they could just as easily be interested because that person had sausages for breakfast,' Kieran continued. 'You're fickle beasties, aren't you?' he said to Finn, leaning over to stroke the dog's head.

'Okay, thanks,' Kincaid said, disappointed. 'It was a long shot, anyway.'

Kieran met his eyes then, his gaze clear and direct. 'You think you know who did it.'

'I have no evidence,' Kincaid answered.

What he'd hoped was that, if Melody and Gemma got an ID on Craig in the Jenny Hart case, the dogs might provide a strong enough link between Becca Meredith's murder scene and Craig to justify a search warrant for Craig's car and belongings.

He wanted Craig for Jenny Hart, but he wanted him for Becca Meredith even more.

'Look, Kieran,' he said, standing. 'He's still out there, and you're still the only person who might have seen him on the river. Stay here for a while longer. And don't go out on your own at night.' When Kincaid reached the door, he turned back. 'Oh, and by the way, that boat you were building? The one you were worried about? We had your next-door neighbour lock it in his shed.'

He said goodbye, without much assurance that Kieran would take his advice, but he couldn't put everyone who'd been connected to Becca Meredith under lock and key for their own safety.

The day was warming as he walked back into Market Place. He stopped, checking his watch. It was only ten o'clock. It would be at least another two hours before he could expect to hear from Gemma. And he had no doubt that her report would be first-hand. In spite of his cautions, she was just as much a police officer as he was, and she would want to hear the witness statement herself.

In the meantime, he was bloody well going to find Freddie Atterton.

He tried the bar at the Hotel du Vin, even though it was early, just in case Freddie's no-alcohol resolution had been short-lived, but without success.

Then he walked across the bridge to Leander. Not that he didn't trust DC Bell's thoroughness, but it was possible that she and Freddie could have come and gone at cross-purposes. Still no joy, however, although he spoke to the lovely Lily in reception, then checked the dining room, the bars and the crew quarters.

After returning to reception and thanking Lily, an impulse led him to walk out the French doors and onto the small balcony that overlooked the river and the regatta meadows. The fields were empty now, the green sweep of grass marred only by the concrete stanchions that would support the enclosures, come June.

Kincaid had never been to Henley Royal Regatta, but he'd seen photos and videos. He imagined the crowds, the marquees, the sun sparkling on the water, and all the rowers and racing shells going out from the starting rafts, a symphony of colour and motion.

Would Becca have been among next year's rowers, racing to prove she had what it took for the Olympics?

He heard the creak of the door behind him and turned to see Milo Jachym.

'Lily said you were looking for Freddie,' said Milo. 'Is he all right?'

'He walked out of his flat last night and hasn't come back. Do you have any idea where he might be?'

'He rang me last night, but I was in the gym. He didn't leave a message, and he didn't answer when I tried ringing back.' Milo frowned. 'He didn't take his car?'

'No.'

'He won't have gone to his parents, then.' Milo shook his head and, like Kincaid, gazed out across the meadows. 'I'd never have thought he'd take it so hard, Becca's death. Freddie always seemed like one of those blessed few who would slide through life without a hiccup. He had everything: looks, connections, talent. But the charm's grown thinner the last few years. It's as if he's had to make an effort to hold everything together.'

Studying the man beside him, Kincaid wondered if Milo Jachym had been jealous. He had the sense that nothing had come easily to Milo – this man had had to grab opportunities and hang on to them with a coxswain's tenaciousness. And it was certainly possible that his relationship with Becca Meredith had been more complicated than that of coach and crew member. 'You knew Freddie and Becca for a long time,' he said.

'Since they were both still at university. They had such promise, both of them. But there was a worm in it, somewhere.' Milo sounded infinitely sad.

Shrugging, he straightened, the briskness back in full force. 'And I've got a crew to get on the river for a second session. When you find Freddie, tell him to ring me.' He started down the stairs to the boat yard, then turned back to Kincaid. 'Have you tried the cottage? That's the one place Freddie might see as a last refuge.'

Kincaid considered going back for his car, which he'd left in the Grey's Road car park near the police station. But he suspected that if he did, the incident room would suck him in like a magnet, and he still felt that invisibility was the better part of valour until he knew what they had on Craig.

He would walk to Remenham. He'd driven the distance, after all, and it hadn't seemed that far.

He soon discovered that although the lane looked idyllic, the hamlet was considerably further than he'd remembered. By the time he reached Becca Meredith's cottage, he was warm, even in the lightweight leather jacket he'd worn that day, and he'd have given a king's ransom for his trainers.

The cottage looked less tidy by daylight, the lack of routine maintenance more evident. The hedges needed trimming, the lawn needed cutting and the paint around the front porch was beginning to peel.

The front gate was off the latch and, as Kincaid stepped through it, he realized the cottage's front door was standing ajar. A dozen scenarios ran through his head in an instant, none of them pleasant.

He stopped, his heart pounding, examining what he could see of the house and the garden. After lecturing Gemma about being careful, he didn't need to be the one who carelessly walked into a dangerous situation.

There was no sound, no movement. Then he saw the footprints. There had been heavy dew that morning, and the over-long grass in the front garden, which had been shaded by the hedge, was still damp. A distinct single line of footprints led from the front porch, into the grass and around the side of the cottage.

Kincaid followed, cautiously. When he rounded the corner of the house, he saw Freddie Atterton standing at the far end of the garden, looking out over the river. He wore jeans and a faded Oxford-blue T-shirt, and his feet were bare.

'Freddie,' Kincaid said quietly, and Atterton turned.

'Oh. It's you.' The smile Freddie gave Kincaid was tentative, and he seemed a little disoriented.

'Are you all right?' Kincaid asked, going closer. He saw that the Oxford-blue T-shirt really was Oxford Blue – it bore the Oxford University Boat Club emblem on the front. 'You've had us all a bit worried. Especially DC Bell.'

'Imogen. Nice name. Pretty girl.' The smile was a little stronger this time, then Freddie's brow creased in a frown. 'She was looking for me?'

'You haven't checked your messages.'

'No. Turned the bloody phone off. Press.'

'You've been here since last night?'

Freddie nodded.

'What are you doing out here in the garden?' Kincaid asked, as gently as he would have asked one of his children.

'I wanted . . . I just wanted to see – ' Freddie stopped, his teeth chattering. Kincaid saw that the legs of his jeans were soaked halfway to the knees from the damp grass, as were his own trousers. 'You can't quite make it out from here,' Freddie went on. 'Temple Island. But she was so close.'

'Yes,' Kincaid agreed. 'She was.' Just as matter-of-factly he added, 'You seem to have lost your shoes.'

'Oh.' Freddie looked down, and seemed surprised to see that he was barefoot. He touched the front of his shirt. 'I found these. My things from uni. In the wardrobe. She'd saved them.' There were tears in his eyes.

'I think,' Kincaid said reasonably, 'that we should go inside, have a cup of tea and get warm. Then we can talk about it. All right?'

It was obvious from the rumpled duvet on the sofa that Freddie had slept there, and not upstairs in the bedroom. Kincaid couldn't blame him. Sleeping in one's dead ex-wife's bed would be bad enough. Sleeping in the bed you now knew your dead ex-wife had shared with another man would be even worse.

'You should change,' he suggested as he followed Freddie into the room.

'I'll dry. I'm a rower, remember? Or I was, anyway. Wet is a fact of life for rowers.'

The sitting room was cold, in spite of the bright day, as it had been the first time Kincaid had come to the cottage. 'Why don't you light the fire, then? I'm not quite as hardy as you. I'll make us something hot.'

He found teabags in the kitchen – Tetley's. Apparently Becca's taste had run to down-to-earth. A plastic jug in the fridge was half-full of milk that was just skating its use-by date. When he had the kettle on, Kincaid glanced back into the sitting room and asked, 'Milk and sugar?'

Freddie nodded. 'Lots of both. Another old rower's habit. Never let a good calorie pass you by.' Having lit the gas fire, he pushed the duvet aside and sat on the sofa, then began to shuffle what looked liked old photos that were spread out on the small coffee table.

When Kincaid had filled two mugs, skipping the sugar in his, and deciding at the last minute to pass on the milk as well, he carried them into the sitting room and took the chair nearest Freddie. 'What are you looking at?' he asked, handing over Freddie's mug.

'She saved these, too. I'd no idea. I was looking for a pen and I found them stuffed in the drawer of the writing desk.' He began to turn the photos so that they faced Kincaid.

In every one Kincaid saw a much younger Freddie, in Oxford rowing kit. In several, he was at the bow in an eight, his face contorted with a grimace of effort. Several seemed to be at parties, or after races. In one, a much younger Becca was pouring a bottle of champagne over his head, and they were both laughing.

Freddie picked that one up and ran a finger over its surface. 'It was the second year I was in the Blue Boat,' he said. 'We'd just got engaged. No surprise it was Ross who put Becca up to the champagne.'

'Ross?'

'My mate who took me to – ' He faltered, drank a sip of his tea. 'To the mortuary,' he went on. 'We were all at uni together, Becca and me, and Ross and his wife, Chris.'

Freddie nodded at a framed photo of the same Boat Race crew on Becca's bookshelf.

'See, there he is. That one was taken right before the race. Ross was a last-minute substitution from Isis, the second boat.'

Kincaid saw a stocky young man, smiling, as were all the crew, with what looked like a mixture of pride and nerves. 'I thought maybe the champagne was a Boat Race celebration.'

'Not for the losing crew. We were nearly swamped that year. Could have bloody drowned. I think Becca – I don't know. Things were never quite the same after that. Maybe that marked me as a failure in her eyes.'

'It was just a race,' Kincaid said.

Freddie stared at him as if he'd gone utterly daft.

'It was the *Boat Race*. Nothing afterwards ever quite lives up to that, whether you win or lose. But Becca, she wanted me to win, even more than I did.'

'Was she jealous of you, of your opportunity?' Kincaid asked, thinking of everything he'd learned about Becca Meredith. 'That was the one thing she could never do, row in the Boat Race.'

Freddie's eyes widened in surprise. 'Maybe. It never occurred to me. Maybe that was why it mattered so much.'

'Your loss was her loss.'

'She took it hard. Not just angry. Not just disappointed. She was . . . bitter.' He shrugged. 'We went on, got married, as if things were the same. But they weren't. Then – well, you know what happened then.'

'The Olympic trials. Her injury. Her failure.'

Freddie nodded. 'I didn't think we would get through that. But then she went into the job, and for a while things got better. She put all that ferocious energy into work. But there was always a distance between us, a wall, and I could never break through it.'

'And eventually you sought solace.' Kincaid said it without censure.

Freddie's smile twisted. 'I suppose you could call it that. But it never helped. Now I keep wondering if there was anything I could have done that would have made a difference. And I'll never know.'

It was true. There was nothing Kincaid could say that would change it. And now he knew that the things he would have to say at some point would only increase the burden of Freddie's guilt, at least in Freddie's eyes.

If Freddie and Becca had stayed married, Angus Craig might never have had the opportunity to rape Becca. And Becca might not be dead.

Kincaid looked round the cottage, realizing that when he'd been here the first time, on Tuesday evening, he'd had no knowledge of what had happened here.

Now, in his mind's eye, he saw again the crime-scene photos from Jenny Hart's flat, and imagined this room, and Becca, violated. He felt sick.

'What is it?' asked Freddie. 'You look as if you've seen a ghost.'

Kincaid met his eyes, and in that instant he made a decision. Freddie would have to know what had happened to Becca.

But not yet. Because with knowledge would come rage, and if Freddie sought out Angus Craig, Kincaid had no way to protect him from the consequences.

Chapter Twenty

The Churchill Arms was just as cluttered as Melody had described it. It was also packed, suffocatingly warm and reeked of boiled veg and roasted meat.

Gemma was early, so she'd slipped inside to absorb a bit of the atmosphere while she waited for Melody. Patrons were carrying drinks out onto the pavement, so it was easy enough for her to stand to one side of the crush milling about the door. Having dressed casually, in a skirt and boots, she attempted a studied nonchalance and thought it was a good thing she'd never had to work undercover.

It was a beautiful, crisp day, and having asked Betty Howard to watch Charlotte and Toby for a few hours, Gemma had walked the short distance from Notting Hill to the Churchill Arms. She'd glanced down Campden Street, where Jenny Hart had lived, and, like Melody, she'd felt chilled at the thought of the murderer striking so close to home. The initial call-out would have gone to Kensington Station, otherwise it would have come across Gemma's desk. Not that she'd have got any further than the Major Crimes team that had eventually been assigned to the case. They'd done a good job with what they had.

She kept thinking of Melody – young, attractive, single – a perfect target for Angus Craig. Maybe it was a good thing, for Melody's sake, that Craig seemed to have upped his game, going after more senior female officers.

Now, of course, Melody was forewarned, but there were too many other potential victims who were not. They needed to put the bastard out of action altogether, and soon.

Gemma watched the waiting staff, moving busily between bar and kitchen and tables in the pub's crowded rooms, and wondered which of the girls might be their witness.

'Boss,' said Melody in her ear, and Gemma started. 'You still look like a copper,' Melody added, giving her a quick and nervous smile.

'Same to you. And you nearly gave me heart failure. Have you got the photos?'

'Of course.' Melody touched her handbag, which was capacious enough to carry off a good bit of the pub's Churchill memorabilia. 'That's the manager,' she added, nodding at a tall young woman behind the bar. 'Theresa.'

'And the other girl?' Gemma asked.

'Let's find out. And I'm just going to introduce you as my colleague, okay? No names. Just in case – well, let's not go there.'

Gemma stopped her friend with a touch on the arm. 'Melody, are you sure about this? It could mean that you could seriously damage your career by doing this. Or worse.'

'If she doesn't ID him, we've nothing to lose. It

was just a dead-end Sapphire lead. If she does give us a positive, I'll do whatever it takes. Same as you.' Melody's conviction was absolute.

'Right,' said Gemma, and followed her to the bar. She stood back as Melody talked to the manager. The noise level in the pub was so high that she only caught a few words, but when she saw the manager nod towards the girl who was pulling pints at the bar's far end, her heart sank.

The barmaid was plump and freckled, with bleached blonde hair pulled up in a knot on top of her head and a splatter of colourful tattoos down her bare arms. When she came over, at the manager's signal, Gemma saw that the girl was older than she'd first thought, perhaps in her mid-twenties.

'Rosamond,' said the manager. 'These are the ladies from the police.'

Gemma moved in close enough to hear Melody ask, 'Is there somewhere we can talk?'

'There's an empty table back by the kitchen,' the barmaid answered. 'Quieter there.' Turning, she led them through a maze of rooms into – much to Gemma's surprise – a little indoor garden. It was quieter, and cooler, and the three of them squeezed themselves round a small table in the corner.

'The ferny grotto, I call it,' said Rosamond. Her accent, Gemma realized, was educated and middle-class. 'Theresa said you wanted to talk to me about Jenny Hart,' the girl continued, looking at them earnestly. Gemma added forthright and confident as bonuses to the accent, and her hopes rose.

She felt no embarrassment for her bias – she'd

been on the job long enough to know that a middle-class witness was automatically given more credence. And, she thought, studying Rosamond more closely, if you put a long-sleeved blouse on the girl, she might clean up very well.

'So you remember Jenny Hart?' asked Melody.

'Of course I do,' Rosamond said with some asperity. 'She came in two or three nights a week at least, and I served her if I could.' She shook her head, looking stricken. 'I couldn't believe it when I heard what had happened to her.'

'How did you come to know her name?' asked Gemma, forgetting for a moment that she was playing the subordinate role.

Melody gave her a quelling glance and added, 'It's a busy place, and you must serve hundreds of customers in a day.'

'Not that many women come in regularly on their own. And she was friendly, always had a nice word for all the staff.'

'Did you know she was a police officer?' Melody asked.

'Not until one night a few months before she was . . . before she died. There was a bit of aggro: couple of blokes old enough to know better started a row over a football match. Jenny stood up – straight as a die after two Martinis, mind you – pulled out her warrant card and gave them their marching orders.' Rosamond smiled at the recollection. 'They marched, too. She was not going to be messed about, and they could tell it.

'After that, we talked more. I was thinking of going

into criminal justice, and she was nice enough to give me advice.'

'And did you?' asked Melody. 'Go into criminal justice?'

'No. I'm reading law.'

Gemma didn't know whether to be ecstatic or horrified. The fact that this young woman was clever was certainly in their favour; the fact that she would understand what she was getting into might not be.

Melody opened her bag and Gemma's heart sped up. Even though they'd moved away from the rooms with open fires, she suddenly felt much too warm.

'Rosamond,' said Melody. 'You told the police that Jenny was here the night she was killed. And that you thought you saw her talking to a man. Can you tell me about that?'

Rosamond nodded. 'It was a Saturday – well, you know that. Place was packed to the gills. I served Jenny a couple of Martinis at the bar. Vodka with just a whisper of vermouth, and a twist – just the way she liked them. I remember she looked tired.'

Rosamond shifted in her chair and crossed her tattooed forearms across her chest.

'People were shoving to get served, so after the second drink she moved back a bit. Then I saw her talking to a bloke.' Rosamond frowned. 'I got the impression that she knew him – I'm not sure why. When you work in a bar and you watch people all the time, you just get a feel for the body language. This was different from a stranger pick-up.' She shrugged. 'Anyway, I think this guy bought her a drink, but I'm not sure. I didn't serve him. Then I lost sight of them. That's all,' Rosamond added, sounding as if she was terribly disappointed in herself. 'When the police came to talk to us after they'd found her body, I couldn't believe it. If I'd only paid more attention—'

'Stop,' said Melody. 'Right now. You mustn't even begin to think that way. Nothing that happened was your fault. But you *can* help us now.' She leaned forwards, her elbows on the table. 'You weren't able to give the police much of a description, even with the help of the sketch artist.'

Rosamond shook her head in obvious frustration. 'He was just . . . ordinary. And I wasn't trying to remember.' She thought for a moment. 'I know he was older – he reminded me of my Uncle John. Fair-skinned, hair receding a bit. Slightly stocky build. Not tall. But when the police artist put together features, nothing gelled.'

'Had you seen him before?'

'No, I don't think so.'

'Would you recognize him if you saw him again? It's been six months.'

Rosamond looked at Melody, then Gemma, her expression anxious now. 'I don't know. But I think so. It's not the sort of thing you forget.'

'Okay,' said Melody. 'Not to worry. I'm going to show you a photo of a group of men. You tell us if any of them look familiar. It's that easy.'

From her bag she took the photo of Angus Craig in a group of other senior officers, all in evening dress. There was nothing about him, Gemma thought, that stood out. Unless you knew.

She realized she was holding her breath.

Taking the photo carefully, Rosamond studied it, her eyes flicking from one side of the picture to the other. Then she stared straight at it and gave a little gasp.

'Oh, my God. I can't believe it. That's him.' She touched a black-lacquered fingertip to the man who stood dead centre in the group. Angus Craig.

Kincaid had returned to the incident room, courtesy of a ride from DC Bell, when he got Gemma's call.

'We've got him,' she said, her voice vibrating with suppressed excitement.

He closed his eyes. It was too good to be true. 'In writing?'

'Signed and sworn. Melody took the girl into Notting Hill Station to make her statement. She's a law student, so she knows what she's doing. Her name is Rosamond Koestler. We explained . . . Melody explained' – Gemma corrected quickly – 'that making a formal identification might cause personal . . . difficulties . . . for her. We suggested that she stay with friends for at least a few days, and not give out her whereabouts. She still insisted on making a statement.'

'Do you think she could pick him out of an identity line-up?'

'Without a doubt. Melody showed her the photo of him in a group at the Commissioner's Ball. She picked him out without any hesitation. Melody's sent the statement to Doug at the Yard.'

'Right. Good.' Kincaid struggled to collect himself.

He realized he'd believed it was pie-in-the-sky, the idea that a witness could reliably tie Craig to Jenny Hart on the night of her murder.

Of course, the Crown Prosecution Service wouldn't consider this girl's statement sufficient for a murder charge, but a judge should deem it merited a warrant for a DNA test, and that was all they needed.

If they were right. God help them if they were wrong.

'Still there, love?' asked Gemma.

'Oh, yes. Miles away. Sorry.' DC Bell, DC Bean and DI Singla were all watching him curiously. 'I think it's time to have a word with the guv'nor,' he said to Gemma. 'Face-to-face.'

Imogen Bell caught him up as he was leaving the station for the car.

He'd merely told the assembled team that he had an urgent lead on another case in London, and that he'd be back with them as soon as possible.

'Can I walk with you?' asked DC Bell. She'd been unable to conceal her relief when he'd rung from Remenham with the news that Freddie Atterton was all right.

When she'd picked them up, however, she'd been decidedly frosty with Atterton until he'd apologized nicely for worrying her, and promised to keep his phone turned on in future.

'Of course,' Kincaid said.

She fell into step beside him, and with her long legs she had no trouble keeping up. The wind blowing down Grey's Road scattered strands of her light-brown hair across her face, which she pushed away impatiently. 'This case in London – is it connected to this one?'

He considered prevaricating, but a glance at her intent face made him decide against it. 'I don't know. It's possible. But I can't say anything about it until I know more.'

'It's a murder, isn't it? And you have a witness.'

He looked at her more sharply. 'Have you ever considered a career in journalism, DC Bell?'

'Sorry.' She didn't sound at all contrite. 'It's just that – does this case affect Mr Atterton? If it's on my watch, I think I should know.'

She was right, Kincaid had to admit. But he couldn't afford for this lovely young woman to come to Craig's attention. She had just the sort of confident personality that Craig seemed increasingly driven to crush.

And he certainly couldn't afford for Craig to get even an inkling that they actually had something on him.

'Yes, you should know,' he said. 'But it's complicated. And there may be – repercussions. I promise I'll tell you as much as I can, as soon as I can.'

They'd reached the car park. He stopped, turning to her. 'Look, Imogen. I really do have to go. But in the meantime just keep a reasonable eye on Freddie. I think he'll be more cooperative now. And don't tell anyone we have a witness in a connected case. Got that?' He jabbed a finger at her for emphasis. '*Anyone.*'

*

Although Kieran had badgered all and sundry – especially Tavie, who had no control whatsoever in the matter – about getting back into his boatshed, now that he'd been given permission, he found himself delaying.

After Superintendent Kincaid had left, Kieran tidied the flat, finished the washing and made himself a cheese-and-pickle sandwich for lunch, although he still felt guilty about eating Tavie's provisions. Perhaps he'd pick up some things for dinner on his way back . . .

On his way back from the shed.

Sitting at Tavie's small table, holding his half-finished sandwich, he saw that his hands were shaking, and realized that he didn't want to go home. Not to stay. Not yet.

He was afraid. Afraid of what he might find, of who he would be, if he'd lost everything that had begun to make him feel like a whole person again.

And he was afraid, full stop. Noise and smoke and flames and panic – they were all still much too close.

But if he didn't go back now, when would it be any easier?

The dogs were sitting at his feet, gazing up at him expectantly. 'All right, you greedy buggers.' Kieran broke the remaining half of the sandwich into two pieces. 'Down,' he said, and both dogs dropped like felled marionettes, then inhaled the offered treats in matching gulps.

'Okay. Good dogs. All gone,' he told them, rubbing his slobbery fingers on his jeans as he looked at their eager faces. He had backup, after all, he thought, right in front of him, ready and willing.

And he could make a small deal with himself. That was one of the things he'd learned in these last two years, and he couldn't afford to forget it. You didn't have to tackle things all at once. Small steps led to bigger steps.

He would go, but he would take the Detective Superintendent's advice, and come back to Tavie's house, at least for tonight. There was no shame in that.

By the time Kieran reached Mill Meadows, both he and the dogs were panting. Having made up his mind to go, he'd jogged, not giving himself a chance to waver, and he'd been grateful that the clear, dry day seemed to be holding his vertigo at bay.

He slowed when he realized there was a man standing on the pedestrian path just across the water from the boatshed, gazing at it.

The man wore jeans and a long-sleeved dark-blue T-shirt, but no jacket, in spite of the cool breeze. And even though he appeared slightly dishevelled, there was something indefinably elegant about him. When he turned, Kieran recognized him instantly.

It was Freddie Atterton, Becca's ex-husband.

'I know you,' said Atterton, his glance going from Kieran to the dogs. 'I saw you that day, on the search team.'

Kieran felt the hair on his arms stand up. He nodded, cautiously. 'That's right.'

'I don't know how to thank you,' said Atterton. 'And the dogs,' he added. 'They're brilliant.'

Finn and Tosh, who always seemed to know when

they were being talked about, wagged appreciatively and sat. No alarm there.

'Yeah, they're great.' Kieran stroked Finn's head and Tosh nosed him, and then Atterton, seeking her share of attention, and Atterton gave a good rub to both dogs.

What the hell did you say, Kieran wondered as the silence stretched, to the man whose ex-wife had been your lover?

Freddie Atterton smiled, as if he'd read his mind. 'I know about you and Becca,' he said. 'Superintendent Kincaid told me. That's not why I'm here.'

'Okay.' Kieran waited, feeling stranger and stranger, and trying to keep his eyes from straying to what remained of his home.

'Well, I have to admit to a bit of curiosity,' said Atterton. 'Wouldn't be human, otherwise, I suppose. But mostly I came to see if you could repair Becca's boat.'

'The Filippi?' It was the last thing Kieran had expected.

'Apparently it has a crack in the hull. I haven't seen it yet. But I don't like to think . . . She'd have wanted – ' Atterton stopped, his voice unsteady, and Kieran realized suddenly that this was a man teetering on the edge of emotional collapse. He knew, because he had stared into the precipice himself, and even now might stumble into it.

Kieran steeled himself to look across the water. 'I would, of course. But I don't know if I can. My workshop—'

'Superintendent Kincaid told me what happened,'

said Freddie. 'It doesn't look too bad from here. How do you get across?'

'I've got a skiff.' Kieran gestured towards his little rowing boat, tied up a few yards nearer the museum.

'Can we go over? All of us?' Freddie's nod included the dogs.

Kieran was still feeling befuddled by the whole exchange, but found he was glad enough of an excuse not to go alone, however odd his companion. 'Yeah, okay.' He dropped Finn's lead. 'Finn, go get the boat.'

Finn bounded down to the skiff and, taking the rope in his mouth, pulled the boat up against the bank.

As soon as Kieran reached the boat and grabbed the rope, Finn leapt in, grinning at them in Labrador glee.

'He'd rather swim, I'll wager,' said Freddie, laughing.

Tosh jumped in only after Kieran and Freddie had joined Finn in the skiff, her dark eyebrows furrowed in a look that said she didn't like this particular adventure, but would make the best of it.

Kieran rowed across to the island, where Freddie tied them up with quick expertise.

'You row, don't you?' Kieran asked as they climbed ashore.

'Did,' said Freddie. 'But that was a long time ago. Water under the bridge.' He shrugged, then nodded towards the shed. 'Let's take a look at the damage, shall we? Are you game?'

Kieran put the dogs in a stay, swallowed hard and followed him.

*

It wasn't as bad as he'd feared. Broken glass, water-sludged ash, scorched beams – but his tools and the structure itself seemed to be intact. His clothes, camp bed and personal belongings were undoubtedly smoke- and water-damaged, but those were things that could be replaced, or done without.

The boat he'd been repairing, however, was buggered. Its carbon-fibre hull was blistered and crazed, the scorch marks clearly visible.

'Oh, God,' said Kieran, staring at it. He felt a wave of dizziness. 'This – I don't have insurance to cover this. Bloody hell!'

Freddie joined him in his examination. 'Can it be fixed?'

'Well, maybe, but it'll be a hard job, and can't be done without clearing up this mess and repairing the damage to the shed.' Kieran shook his head, overwhelmed.

'Look,' said Freddie slowly. 'I know it sounds weird, but if it's hard labour you need, I'll help. I can sand and scrub and sweep, or whatever.'

Perplexed, Kieran looked at the man he'd first seen standing outside Leander in a perfectly tailored suit, looking as if he'd never dirtied a finger. But Freddie Atterton was an Oxford Blue – God knew Becca had told him that often enough – so he had to be tougher than he looked. 'I don't understand,' Kieran said. Why should you—'

'Look at this place,' Freddie interrupted, his gesture taking in the undamaged tins of solvent, the paint, the polishing rags. 'I'm not much for miracles, but the fact that there's anything left of this place, or of you, is bloody astounding. You can't just give up. It would be – it would mean that whoever did this to you and to Becca had won. Do you see?'

'I don't—'

Outside, Finn gave the distinctive little yap he used to greet people he knew, and liked.

'Hi, Kieran,' came a shout.

'It's John, my neighbour,' said Kieran. He suddenly felt he couldn't stand the stink of wet ash another second. 'Let's go out.'

When they emerged onto the patch of lawn, John greeted Kieran with a handshake and a pat on the back. 'That's quite a bruise,' he said, 'but I'm just glad to see you in one piece. You gave us a fright the other night.'

Freddie held out a hand and introduced himself. If John wondered what connection Freddie had with Kieran, he was too polite to ask.

'I've got something for you.' John held out a key to Kieran. 'Your single's in my shed. Keep it there as long as you need.' With a wave, he walked back towards his house.

'Your single?' asked Freddie. He glanced at Kieran's old shell, up on trestles near the landing raft. 'I thought – '

Wordlessly Kieran walked to John's shed and unlocked it. He pulled the double doors wide, so that the afternoon light flooded in, then drew the tarp off the single. Becca's single. It was unblemished, and even though he had made it, his heart leapt at the beauty of it.

Freddie stared, first at the boat, then at him. 'You built this? A wooden shell?'

'I know most people don't race in them any more, but I thought if I made some design adjustments . . . '

'You made this,' said Freddie, his voice little more than a whisper. He went closer, ran his hand over the silky wood of the hull, then touched the moulded seat and moved it slightly on the runners. 'For her.'

Kieran nodded.

'Did she know?'

'No. I thought, when it was finished, I'd tell her . . . But I'm not sure I'd ever have shown it to her, to tell the truth. She might have laughed. Or, worse, felt obligated to row in it.'

For the first time Freddie seemed at a loss. Shaking his head, he walked away. When he reached the lawn's edge, he stood gazing at the river for a moment, then sank to the grass and wrapped his arms round his knees, like a child seeking comfort. Kieran saw a shudder run through his shoulders.

Reluctantly Kieran followed and hunkered down beside him, pushing away the dogs when they butted him.

'I never made anything for her,' whispered Freddie. He lifted his head and rubbed the back of his fist across his wet cheeks. 'I envy you that,' he added, and Kieran heard the bitterness.

'I lied, you know, when I said I didn't mind about the two of you,' Freddie went on. 'Not that I had any right – but still, there it is.' He looked at Kieran. 'Did you love her?'

Slowly Kieran nodded.

'Did she love you?'

There was nothing left for Kieran but to face it. After a long moment, he said, 'No. I don't think she did. But we had something that worked for a while . . . maybe because I didn't ask anything of her. Because I knew she had nothing to give.'

Kincaid had asked Doug to send the witness statement and the request for a DNA comparison to a magistrate with whom he had often worked, a man he liked personally and one whom he thought would not be influenced by Angus Craig's threats.

As he drove into London, he stopped at home and changed into his Paul Smith grey suit, a white shirt and a dark-blue tie. It was the best he could do for armour.

Gemma and all the children – according to the latest family update texted from Kit – were at their friend Erika Rosenthal's, making German brown-sugar cookies for Charlotte's party tomorrow.

Kincaid had no excuse to tarry, and he knew he had to catch Chief Superintendent Childs before he left for the weekend.

He drove to the Yard, gathered the file on Jenny Hart and a copy of Rosamond Koestler's statement from Doug, and took the lift up to Chief Superintendent Childs's office.

Childs's secretary sent him straight in.

The surface of his guv'nor's desk was clear as usual and, as always, Childs didn't seem to be doing anything. As Denis Childs was the most efficient superior officer he knew, Kincaid had sometimes wondered if the man simply had a computer wired to his brain.

'Sir.' He gave Childs a nod in greeting.

'Oh, dear,' said Childs, steepling his fingers. 'How very formal of you.' He looked Kincaid up and down. 'And the suit. Very nice, the conservative touch, but I suspect this means you've come to tell me something you think I won't like. Do sit down, Duncan' – he waved at a chair – 'and don't pace about in my office again. It makes my neck hurt. What have you got, there?' Childs's eyes went to the papers in Kincaid's hand.

Sitting down, Kincaid handed over the file and statement. Then he crossed his ankles and folded his hands in his lap. It was a Childs pose, used by his boss to convey a complete lack of nerves, and Kincaid hoped he did it half as well.

Childs went through the Jenny Hart case quickly, but with a slight frown, and Kincaid had the feeling he'd seen the material before. When he came to the end, he gave Kincaid a quick glance that might have been surprise.

Then he turned to Rosamond Koestler's statement. As he read, he went very still. When he'd finished, he looked up at Kincaid.

'Is this credible?'

'According to Melody Talbot. And I have complete confidence in her judgement.'

Childs settled back in his chair. 'I sense Gemma's hand in this. And yours. Why else would Project Sapphire suddenly follow up on what seemed a dead-end case?'

'Project Sapphire was looking for cases that matched the pattern of the rape alleged by DCI Rebecca Meredith,' Kincaid admitted. 'At my request. But DC Talbot certainly did not expect to find *this*.' Kincaid gestured at the Hart file.

'Were there other cases that fit the pattern as well?' Childs asked.

'Yes, several. But only one murder.'

Childs considered Kincaid with his slow, inscrutable gaze. Then something flickered deep in his brown eyes, and Kincaid recognized it.

It was rage.

'An unexpected result,' said Childs, quietly. 'Jenny Hart was a good officer. And a friend. She served under me when she was a detective constable.' He tapped his fingers on his desk. 'You've requested a warrant for DNA comparison? And not from one of that lot, I hope.' He cast a scathing glance at the photo of Craig amongst the senior officers in evening dress.

'Yes, sir.' Kincaid tried to contain his surprise, both at Childs's revelation about DCI Hart and at his comment about Craig and his cronies. 'It should be coming through any moment.'

'You realize this doesn't get you any closer to Rebecca Meredith,' said Childs. 'Or the attack on the boat-builder. What was his name? Connolly.'

This, Kincaid thought, was the reason there were never any papers on Childs's desk. Childs remembered everything that came across it.

Kincaid had also begun to suspect that Denis Childs knew about his visit to Craig – that, in fact, Childs knew everything he had done since the beginning of the investigation. 'I realize that,' he answered. 'But if this' – he gestured towards the Hart file – 'pulls Craig's fangs, then perhaps his alibis for Meredith and Connolly won't look quite so tidy. All I need is a crack, enough to get a warrant to search his car and belongings.'

He leaned nearer the polished expanse of Childs's desk. 'Craig thought he was untouchable. And I think that will have made him careless.' Kincaid studied his boss. 'You were on to this from the beginning, weren't you? You knew about Becca Meredith's accusations and, when she was found dead a mile from Craig's door, you suspected him. Why didn't you tell me?'

'I always have the utmost confidence in your abilities, Duncan,' Childs said. 'You know that.'

Kincaid felt a surge of anger, adrenaline-fuelled. 'You let me take the heat for going after Craig.'

'I counted on you to take action where I couldn't, and not to be intimidated by Angus Craig.'

If that was a compliment, Kincaid wasn't in the mood to take it that way. 'Why push me towards Freddie Atterton, if you thought it was Craig all along?'

Shrugging, Childs said, 'There are always those who would prefer the obvious solution. I obliged them. I thought it would make you stubborn.'

Kincaid realized he was clenching his teeth so hard that his jaw ached. 'Begging your pardon, sir, but I don't like being used.'

Childs frowned, and when he spoke, his voice held a rare flash of temper. 'Would you rather I'd assigned the case to some dunderhead who would have arrested Freddie Atterton? And do you not see what would have happened if I'd directed you towards Craig? I think it very likely someone would have stopped you, one way or another. Then, if you *had* managed to pin Meredith's murder on Craig, my involvement would have been obvious. And it would have been used in Craig's favour by his defence. As it is, you did your job, and we have an unexpected' – Childs touched Jenny Hart's file – 'conclusion.' His eyes gleamed.

Kincaid's phone beeped with a text. 'Sorry,' he said. 'But that should be Cullen.' He slipped the phone from his jacket pocket and read the message, then looked back at Childs. 'We've got the warrant.' He couldn't keep the jubilation from his voice. 'I'm going to serve the bastard tonight.'

'No,' said Childs. 'You're not.'

'What?' Kincaid stared at him, thinking he'd misheard.

'You are not going to serve the warrant. Not yet.'

'I don't believe this.' Kincaid shook his head in astonishment. After everything Childs had said about Craig, was he suddenly changing his mind? 'Why the bloody hell not?'

Ignoring the insubordination, Denis Childs pulled up the knot on his tie. Then he heaved his bulk from his chair. With Childs looming over him, Kincaid suddenly felt he might be felled by a mountain.

'Because,' answered Childs, looking down at him, '*I* am going to pay a call on retired Deputy Assistant Commissioner Craig.'

He sighed, pinching his lips together in an expression of distaste. 'I suppose I shall be obliged to take Superintendent Gaskill with me, although he won't like it. But, that way, Peter Gaskill – the little worm – will know he's gone far enough.'

'*You're* going to serve Angus Craig? An officer of your rank?'

'No.' Childs sounded infinitely patient. 'As one senior officer to another, I'm going to give Angus Craig the opportunity to come into the Yard and provide a DNA sample. Voluntarily. Just to clear this inconvenient little matter up.'

He reached for the Burberry hanging neatly on the coat rack behind his desk. 'It's a necessary courtesy, Duncan. I'd be pilloried if I didn't make the gesture. And . . . ' Childs paused, and Kincaid saw once again a flash of emotion that moved beneath his Chief Superintendent's implacable facade, like a shark's fin just breaking the surface.

'And,' Childs went on, sounding profoundly unperturbed, 'I want to see his face.'

Chapter Twenty-One

By noon on Saturday, Charlotte's birthday party was in full swing.

Gemma thought the weather gods must be hovering somewhere nearby, because the day had once more dawned fine and clear. The air seemed to hold the anticipation of bonfires, and pumpkins appeared to have sprouted overnight on steps and in front of shops in Notting Hill.

No ghoulies and goblins were attending the festivities at their house, however, as the guests who'd bothered with fancy dress were straight out of Lewis Carroll.

Gemma's friend and former landlady Hazel Cavendish had dressed her daughter Holly, who was Toby's age, in a white bunny costume. It was meant for Halloween, but did well enough for the White Rabbit.

Wesley Howard had found, somewhere in the bowels of Portobello Market, an old morning coat with tails and a battered top hat. He'd decorated both hat and coat with coloured ribbons, and with his dreadlocks springing up around the hat's brim, he made a lovely Mad Hatter.

Betty Howard had made Gemma a Queen of Hearts pinny as a surprise, and Toby had, of course, dressed himself as a pirate. When Gemma had gently informed him that there weren't any pirates in *Alice*, Toby had replied, 'It's a silly book, then.' Toby, Gemma suspected, was always going to march to his own drummer.

Kit had reached the age where he thought himself too grown-up to wear fancy dress, but he was quite pleased with himself over having found a Mock Turtle T-shirt.

And Charlotte, in her dress and hair bow, had gone so quiet and wide-eyed with excitement that Gemma feared she might be sick. She was like Kit in that way, and Kit seemed to understand. He'd taken her aside and asked her to help him in the kitchen, and after a few minutes with him she'd joined in playing with Toby and Holly, although she was still unusually subdued.

It was a very adult party for a three-year-old, thought Gemma as she surveyed the gathering from the kitchen doorway. But Charlotte was in many ways more comfortable with adults than with other children, and Gemma now thought it just as well they'd kept the gathering to close friends and family.

Gemma's sister Cyn had begged off, saying that Brendon and Tiffani had a Halloween party they'd be devastated to miss. Gemma supposed she should feel offended that Charlotte's birthday so obviously took second place, but in truth she was just relieved.

But her parents had made the journey from Leyton. Gemma knew it had taken an enormous effort of persuasion on her mother's part to convince her father to let hired help take over the bakery, especially on a Saturday, so she'd been fussing over them, trying to let them know she appreciated their presence.

She'd settled them in the dining room with plates of finger sandwiches – cut carefully into hearts and spades by Kit – and cups of tea. When Erika Rosenthal joined them, she heard her father mutter something about being glad there wasn't any of that 'funny food' – referring, Gemma knew, to the Caribbean stew Betty had made for their wedding party in August.

Sighing, she let it go. Perhaps it was time she stopped trying to broaden her father's horizons. She was happy enough that her parents were chatting comfortably with Erika, and that her mother looked brighter than she had the previous weekend in Glastonbury.

Had it really only been a week, she thought, since they'd repeated their vows in Winnie's church?

Kincaid came through from the sitting room, where he'd been chatting with Tim Cavendish, and put a hand on her shoulder. 'I've put the dogs in the study for a bit of quiet time.' With Toby and Holly running and shrieking, the dogs had gone into play overdrive, barking to join in the game. 'I could see your dad's blood pressure starting to rise,' he said more softly. Nodding at her parents, he added, 'Seems to be going well.'

'I only gave them the sandwiches with white bread. That's the secret.'

He smiled, and she realized this was the first time

she'd seen his face relax since he'd come home from the Yard the night before.

While they were doing the washing up after dinner, he'd given her a terse account of his interview with Denis Childs. The simmering anger was coming off him in waves, like steam.

'Well, you couldn't really expect them to go in full force and drag him off to the nick, a deputy assistant commissioner,' she'd said, feeling her way. 'I mean, what if we're wrong? There would be hell to pay. It could cost Denis his job.'

'And what if we're right?' Kincaid had asked, dunking a plate into the soapy water with such force that Gemma had winced.

'I think Craig will be retaining the best defence lawyer he can find,' she said. 'He'll claim the sex was consensual, of course, and that he has no idea what happened to Jenny Hart afterwards. But the skin and blood under her nails might cause him a bit of a problem. Not to mention the hair, fibre and prints found in her flat.'

'What if the lab evidence goes missing?'

Frowning, she'd glanced at him, seen the strain in his face. 'Now you're being paranoid,' she said quietly.

He'd shaken his head. 'I don't like it, Gemma. I have a really bad feeling about this.'

Toby had come in then, asking about Charlotte's birthday cake for the hundredth time, and they'd dropped the subject of Angus Craig.

But for the remainder of the evening Gemma had watched Kincaid check his phone every few minutes for missed calls, his scowl growing deeper as the hours passed and there was no word from Chief Superintendent Childs.

Nor had there been a call that morning.

Now he said, 'We're missing Doug and Melody.'

'Melody rang. They're coming together in her car. She ferried a load of things from Doug's flat to the new house.'

Kincaid glanced at her in surprise. 'That's an interesting détente.'

'Don't you dare tease him,' Gemma warned. 'I'm glad to see them a bit less prickly with each other. But if you take the mickey, he'll go all sensitive about it. You know what he's like.' From the speculative gleam in Kincaid's eye, Gemma suspected she was wasting her breath.

But now that he was a little less taciturn there was something she needed to say. 'Alia rang as well, begging off. Family commitments.'

Or at least that was what Alia had told her, but Gemma guessed that Alia's father had dissuaded her from visiting on a strictly social occasion. Mr Hakim was a very conservative Bangladeshi, and he didn't approve of their rather odd blended family, or of Charlotte's mixed-race heritage. He and her dad would probably get on like a house on fire, Gemma thought ruefully.

'But I need to ring her back about Monday,' she said, touching Kincaid's arm to make sure she had his full attention. She looked up at him, trying to read his expression. 'Duncan, I need to let Alia know if she has to look after Charlotte.'

He stood quietly for a moment, looking round the house as though taking stock. Gemma followed his gaze. In the kitchen, Kit and Betty were conspiring over the punch bowl. In the dining room, Erika was still chatting with her mum while her dad looked on, his teacup resting on his knee. Beyond them, in the sitting room, Hazel and Tim were directing the little ones in some kind of indecipherable game, and Charlotte was looking overly warm and flushed.

'I think we're going to have a birthday-girl meltdown soon, if we're not careful,' Kincaid said. 'Has Wes gone for the cake?' They hadn't trusted the children not to find the cake in the house, so Wesley had left it at Otto's cafe.

Gemma nodded, puzzled, not sure he had heard or understood her question.

Then he turned to her, meeting her eyes. 'It's my watch now, running this show.'

'What about the case?' she asked.

He shrugged. 'There's nothing more I can do about Angus Craig. It's out of my hands. I have no evidence that will link him directly to Becca Meredith's murder. I've no other viable suspects.' There was a slight tic of a frown, quickly erased, as he went on, 'I've been warned off the Hart case, and I'm obviously out of the loop as far as any developments there.'

He paused, watching the children, and she felt him trying to master his frustration.

'But no matter what's happened with either of those cases, I am unavailable as of Monday. Because' – he met her eyes again and smiled, the broad grin that lit his face and that she loved so – 'I have promises to keep. To you, and to a certain little Alice.'

Before she could reply, the bell rang.

'Speak of the devil,' Kincaid said, glancing out the side-lights in the hall. 'Or devils.'

It was Melody and Doug, both in jeans and sweaters, looking oddly unprofessional, and both red-cheeked and bright-eyed.

'Have we missed the cake?' asked Doug as they came in. 'Do say we haven't.'

'I need some reward for lifting boxes like a navvy,' Melody said.

'It was only a few CDs,' protested Doug.

'Right. Just a few CDs.' Melody looked at Gemma and rolled her eyes. 'Ha. I necd refreshment. I seriously *deserve* refreshment. We left the car back at my flat so I wouldn't get done for drink-driving.'

'It's a children's birthday party, for heaven's sake,' said Doug, but the scold seemed mock.

'It may be a children's party, but the grown-ups are provided for. There's mulled wine on the Aga.' Kincaid waved them towards the kitchen.

Gemma heard the beep of a horn. That was Wesley's signal. Looking out, she saw the cafe's white van manoeuvring into a parking spot.

'The cake's here,' she whispered. 'Positions, everyone.'

It was everything Wesley had promised. The round layers of lemon cake – Charlotte's favourite – were swathed in intricately scalloped white icing. And, in icing sugar on the top, a perfect rendition of Alice in a blue dress, but this Alice had pale-brown skin and a mass of light-brown curls. Just within her reach, nestled at an angle, was the little pharmacy bottle Gemma had found at the market.

'Oh, my God,' Gemma had whispered, when Wesley centred the cake on the dining-room table. 'It's perfect. Wes, how did you – '

'I made the cake. It was Otto who did the decorating. You know he trained as a pastry chef.'

'Where am I going to put the candles?' asked Gemma, feeling suddenly frantic. 'I can't ruin it. It's a work of art.'

'We're going to eat it, remember,' said Wes, laughing. He'd taken the three swirly candles she'd bought and placed them strategically round the edge. 'Hurry. I've got the camera. You light the candles. Here she comes.'

Hazel and Tim brought the children trooping in from the garden, along with the dogs, which had been allowed out of confinement, and the room was soon filled with a pandemonium of barking and a more than slightly off-key rendition of 'Happy Birthday'.

Gemma thought she would never forget the expression of wonder on Charlotte's face when she saw the cake.

Then, with encouragement from Kit, and some unsolicited help from Toby, Charlotte blew out her three candles and promptly burst into tears.

Before Gemma could go to comfort her, Duncan scooped her up and whispered something in her ear. With her head against his chest, Charlotte nodded in answer and peeked at the cake again.

Duncan reached down and lifted out the little brown bottle. Wiping the icing from the bottom, he licked his finger clean with an exaggerated 'Yum' and handed Charlotte the vial.

'What does it say?' he asked, pointing at Gemma's little home-made label.

'Drink me,' she whispered, her fingers closing tight round it.

'See what a big girl you are, now that you're three? You can even read!' He set her down with a hug. 'Let's have some cake.'

Wesley and Kit were already slicing and serving, while Betty and Hazel poured tea and punch and mulled wine, and the room was soon abuzz with laughter and conversation.

Charlotte, however, refused to eat cake, and instead carried her little bottle round the room for everyone to examine.

Gemma wondered if she remembered her last birthday, if her parents had made her a cake and sung to her. There was no way of knowing, unless Sandra Gilles had recorded it in her journals or photos, and those were locked away as an inheritance for Charlotte when she was old enough to appreciate them.

But Charlotte had a new family now, Gemma told herself, and they had their own memories to make.

Hazel appeared beside her and gave her a quick hug. 'Great party.' Leaning closer, she turned Gemma slightly to one side and whispered in her ear, 'Tell me if I'm seeing things.'

Gemma looked where Hazel directed and saw Charlotte leaning on her dad's knee. He was holding out his teacup as Charlotte added a few imaginary drops from her brown bottle. Then he mimed drinking a sip, and Charlotte giggled. He scrunched down in his chair, as if shrinking, and this time Charlotte gave a peal of laughter.

'Well, I never,' murmured Gemma, closing her mouth from a gape. Her dad had never played with her or Cyn like that, at least that she could remember, or with Toby, or Cyn's kids. 'Will wonders never cease!'

She looked round for Duncan, wanting to share the moment with him, but he had migrated into the kitchen with Doug and Melody.

Wandering in, she caught a fragment of conversation.

' . . . nothing,' Doug was saying. 'If a DNA sample was submitted, it hadn't come through the system last time I checked this morning.'

They were talking about Angus Craig.

Gemma hesitated at the edge of the room. For one jealous moment she wanted to shut out any thought of Angus Craig and the things he had done. She wanted to keep her family encased in the safe, bright bubble of the last hour and pretend that it was impenetrable.

But she knew better.

'Oh,' said Doug. 'I did find out what Becca Meredith did on that last Friday afternoon. I finally tracked down Kelly Patterson this morning, at Dulwich Station. She didn't want to talk to me – can't say I blame her. But when I asked, she decided she didn't see any harm in telling me that the Vice cop who came into West London Station that day was called Chris Abbott. Becca introduced her as an old mate from uni. I didn't have a chance to—' He stopped as Kincaid pulled his phone from the pocket of his jeans.

'Sorry,' Kincaid said. 'I've got to – ' Then he had the phone to his ear and he turned away, covering his other ear to cut down on the ambient noise.

Gemma saw him nod, and she assumed he made some reply before ringing off. Then he stood for a moment, his back to them.

When he turned, his face had drained of colour.

'That was Denis,' he said. His eyes sought Gemma's. 'Angus Craig's house burned to the ground in the early hours of the morning. Both he and his wife are presumed to have been in it.'

Chapter Twenty-Two

Kincaid could smell the fire as they came into Hambleden, even with the car windows closed.

He and Cullen had driven from London in grim silence, Doug looking slightly green in the passenger seat, Kincaid unwilling even to speculate until he knew exactly what had happened.

'I could have done without the mulled wine,' Doug said now.

Kincaid nodded agreement, suspecting that he would regret even the slice of birthday cake and the cup of punch he'd finished before Childs's phone call. He kept thinking of Edie Craig, who had been kind and gracious to him when it hadn't been necessary.

He'd known they should have had Craig brought in, but this – he hadn't expected this.

The narrow village streets were chock-a-block with cars, the pub car park filled to overflowing – certainly more than the usual Saturday crowd. Tragedy always made for good business.

There were even a few bystanders in the road itself. Kincaid had to beep the horn and motion them aside as he reached the drive to the Craigs' house.

Rolling down the window, he flashed his warrant

card to the uniformed constable blocking the drive's entrance. As he drove through and pulled the car onto the grass, the stench hit them like a wave. Was he only imagining the distinct signature of charred flesh beneath the acrid tang of smoke?

Then he looked up and saw the house.

'God!' whispered Doug beside him.

The lovely, rosy brick was blackened, the windows shattered, the roof caving in in places. It was clear that the blaze had raged out of control before the fire brigade arrived.

Two of the fire engines still stood in the drive, like red sentinels, hoses snaking into the house. A group of men in plain clothes stood aside from the firefighters and uniformed officers, and it was impossible to mistake Chief Superintendent Denis Childs's bulk. As Kincaid and Cullen climbed out of the Astra and walked over, he separated himself and came to meet them.

'What happened?' Kincaid asked, not trusting himself to say more.

'The alarm came in at two a.m., but the entire structure was fully alight by the time the brigade got here. They've only managed to get a team inside half an hour ago.' Childs wore his Burberry coat over corduroys and an old jumper, and his usually immaculate dark hair was uncombed and ruffled by the wind.

The oddness of seeing his chief so dishevelled added to Kincaid's sense of unreality. 'Is it true? Both of them dead?'

Nodding, Childs looked away.

Kincaid swallowed. 'How?'

'According to the investigator' – Childs gestured towards a man coming out of the house, and Kincaid recognized the arson specialist from the scene at Kieran Connolly's boatshed – 'it looks like murder-suicide. The first assessment is that Mrs Craig was shot at close range. Then it appears that Craig started the fire, before shooting himself.'

Kincaid shook his head. 'I want to see it.' As he started towards the house, Childs clasped his arm in a firm grip. 'You can't go in, Duncan. It's too hot. It will be hours yet, and then the scene has to be processed. You know that.'

Shaking him off, Kincaid turned back. 'What I know is that it didn't have to happen this way. We should have used the warrant, taken him in. Craig would be in a cell waiting for his solicitor, and Edie Craig would be alive. I want to know exactly what you said to him.'

'Guv – ' Doug was looking at him in horror.

Kincaid ignored him. He seemed to have lost control of his tongue. 'Did you tell him to fall on his own gun? Did it not occur to you that he might take his wife with him?'

Denis Childs looked at him impassively, and only someone who knew him very well would have seen the narrowing of his dark eyes. 'Superintendent. You are out of line. I did no such thing. I merely—'

'Extended the courtesy due a senior police officer.' Kincaid didn't try to keep the disgust from his voice. 'And now we have another victim, Edie Craig, and no doubt any forensic evidence linking Craig to Rebecca

Meredith's death is gone. Did Edie Craig not count? Did Becca Meredith not count? And what about the other women whose lives he damaged – or took? Did they not deserve some sort of justice?' Kincaid stopped just long enough for a breath. 'But this is all much tidier for the Met, isn't it? *Respected former officer killed in tragic fire.*'

Denis Childs shot Cullen a look that said he'd wish he was dead if he ever repeated a word of this conversation.

Then, to Kincaid, he said in the level tones that made officers under his command tremble, 'Justice? Don't talk to me about justice, Duncan. Do you really think things would be better for these women, for their families, for their careers, if what happened to them was made public? If it had been Gemma, would you want that? Would she want that?'

'I—'

'As for Jenny Hart' – Childs jabbed a finger the size of a sausage at him – 'I will guarantee you that those DNA comparisons will be processed, and that the results of those tests will be made public, regardless of damage to the reputation of the Met. And if you can find me anything concrete that ties Craig to Rebecca Meredith, I'll do my best to see that his involvement in her death is made public as well.'

'Off the record, is that it?'

'If that's the best means.' Childs gave Kincaid a considering glance. 'These things can be arranged. I believe you are on close terms with an officer who has a connection to a major newspaper?'

Kincaid gaped. He'd never repeated to anyone

Melody Talbot's confession that her father was *the* Ivan Talbot, owner of the *London Chronicle*. And although she'd told him that both Doug and Gemma knew, he couldn't imagine either of them had spread that information around.

Having dropped his bombshell, Childs straightened the lapels of his overcoat, just as if he was wearing a City suit rather than a moth-eaten jumper. 'And now,' he continued, 'I suggest that you let these officers do their jobs, and go home. As will I.'

'Clever bastard,' Doug said quietly, when Childs had driven away. 'Did you know that he knew about Melody?'

Kincaid shook his head. 'No. And I wonder what else he knows that he's not telling us.'

'You're not going to do what he said, are you?'

'No.' He should, Kincaid knew. If he had any sense, he'd go back to his little girl's birthday party and consider that all was well that ended well, at least as far as the Met was concerned.

But it wasn't Monday yet. He was not officially off the job for another thirty-six hours, and his case was not closed. 'I'm going to have a word with the fire-brigade investigator. Nice chap, wasn't he?'

Doug grinned and adjusted his glasses. 'I thought you'd say that.'

When Gemma had seen Kincaid hesitate after the phone call, she'd whispered to him, 'Go. Just go.'

'But what about Charlotte . . . the party—'

'She'll be fine. I'll explain to the kids. Ring me when you know something.'

He and Doug had made quick apologies and slipped out, fortunately before he'd seen Charlotte start to cry.

Gemma had scooped her up and comforted her, then distracted her by asking for a drink from her little bottle.

Charlotte gave her a pretend sip, then tucked the bottle against her chest and relaxed in Gemma's arms with only an intermittent sniffle.

Would she become accustomed to disappointment, Gemma wondered as she swayed a bit and patted Charlotte's small back? Were the boys any the worse for always having one or both parents haring off after some case or other?

Of the two, Toby coped best. He'd been too young to remember being abandoned by his father and, since then, he'd accrued layers of security in his life, like a little pearl in an oyster – although no one, she thought with a smile, was likely to refer to Toby as a pearl.

Kit, like Charlotte, had suffered loss, but also betrayal – by the man he'd thought was his father, and by his grandmother. And yet he seemed to be mending, although there was no way to tell if he would ever be entirely whole.

At the moment, however, he was teasing his brother by playing keep-away with Toby's pirate sword. He looked like any other mischievous fourteen-year-old. And that was good.

Charlotte, over her tantrum and tiring of being

held, began to squirm. 'I want down, Mummy,' she said.

'What?' Gemma was so startled she loosed her hold and let Charlotte slide the last foot to the floor with a thump.

'I wanna play with Holly,' said Charlotte, more firmly. And then she was gone, skipping across the room in her blue dress, unaware that she had uttered anything significant, or momentous.

Gemma stood, knuckles pressed to her suddenly trembling lips. It was nothing, she told herself. Charlotte heard Toby call her 'Mummy' all the time, and even Kit used it teasingly. It was only natural that Charlotte should start to parrot what she heard. But still . . .

'You okay, boss?' asked Melody, coming up beside her. 'You look a bit . . . gobsmacked.'

'Oh.' Gemma made an effort to collect herself. 'I'm fine. Too much cake, I think.'

Melody gave her a sceptical look, perhaps having seen Gemma take a bite, then put her plate aside to tend to someone else. But instead of challenging Gemma's evasion, she shifted and said a little hesitantly, 'Boss, I know Charlotte's party has been disrupted enough already, but . . . that woman, the Vice copper that Doug said Becca Meredith saw on her last day at work. Chris Abbott.'

'What about her?' asked Gemma. She felt an odd little twist in her stomach, as if her body had fore-knowledge.

'I've just realized why her name seemed familiar,' said Melody. 'It was in the Sapphire files.'

*

'Superintendent Kincaid,' said Owen Morris, the fire-brigade investigator. 'And Sergeant Cullen. Sorry I can't shake.' He raised his gloved hands in an explanatory shrug. 'We seem to keep meeting this way.'

Morris, still in full protective gear, had just come from the house, and Kincaid had glimpsed his red-haired assistant going back in.

'Can we go in, if we suit up?' Kincaid asked.

'No, sorry. It's still too hot, and the structure's not safe. The pathologist and the SOCOs will have to wait as well.'

Frustrated, Kincaid glanced at the open front door. 'Give us a description then.'

'Not pretty, this one,' said Morris, shaking his head, and Kincaid wondered if there were such a thing as a pretty fire scene. 'But the victims were on the ground floor, and as the fire moved upwards, the bodies are still fairly intact.

'The wife – we'll assume it was Mrs Craig, for the time being – was in the kitchen. It looks as though she was shot in the back of the head.'

Edie, Kincaid thought. Not just Mrs Craig. Not just *the wife. Edie.*

'The Deputy Assistant Commissioner was in what looked to be his study.'

'You're certain it was him?'

'I'd met him a few times,' Morris said with a grimace. 'What remained of the face was recognizable. The study was the fire's point of origin. There was a petrol can near the body. He still had the gun gripped in his hand, but the weapon was pretty badly damaged. Some sort of small-calibre handgun, but big enough to do the job. I'm sure the SOCOs will be able to tell you the make.'

'Can you tell what happened?' Kincaid asked, although his mind was playing it out, whether he liked it or not.

'It looks like he shot his wife, then doused a good bit of the ground floor with petrol, backing into his study as he poured. Then he tossed something – a lighter or a match – into the petrol trail. After that, my guess is he'd have waited until he was sure he had a good burn. Then he shot himself in the side of the head.'

They all stared at the house, as if mesmerized, and Kincaid wondered how anyone could possibly do what Angus Craig had done.

A horn beeped. Turning, Kincaid saw a little lime-green Ford pull through the gate. Imogen Bell got out and walked over to them, looking considerably tidier and more rested than she had the previous morning. Apparently she hadn't felt it necessary to spend last night doing surveillance on Freddie Atterton's flat from her car.

'Sir,' she said to Kincaid, including Cullen and Owen Morris in a nod of greeting. 'DI Singla sent me to coordinate with you. He wanted me to tell you that the SOCOs and the Home Office pathologist are on their way. And we've got extra officers coming to cordon off the property. It won't be long before the press show up in force.' She glanced at the house, shaking her head. 'It's really true? Deputy Assistant Commissioner Craig?'

'The pathologist will have to make the formal ID,

but it looks that way. Did you know him?' he asked, with a lurch of concern.

'I'd seen him round Henley. He spoke to me once or twice. He seemed like a nice man.'

Kincaid closed his eyes in a little prayer of thanks that Imogen Bell hadn't got to know Angus Craig better.

'Oh, sir,' said Bell. 'There was a man at the gate just now, wanting to speak to someone in charge. A neighbour. He says he has Mrs Craig's dog, and he wants to know what he should do with it.'

'No matter what Angus Craig's done now,' said Gemma, 'we still don't know why he would have killed Becca Meredith when he did. And I can't believe it's coincidence that Becca talked to another of Craig's possible victims on the day she began behaving oddly. Especially if this woman really was an old friend.' She chewed her lip as she thought. 'We need to talk to her.'

'Now?' Melody glanced round at the other guests. It looked as though the party was beginning to wind down. 'What about the kids?'

'I'll ask Betty or Hazel if they can look after the little ones for a bit,' said Gemma. The bubble of domestic perfection had popped even sooner than she'd thought. But although she hated deserting the children and her guests, she couldn't leave such a loose end dangling. 'We don't know yet exactly what happened at the Craigs',' she added slowly. 'If we've missed something – something important – Duncan and Doug need to know as soon as possible.'

'She lives in Barnes, this Chris Abbott. I remember that from the file. I can check the address.'

'Do it, then. There's something not right here.' Suddenly uneasy about Duncan and Doug in Henley, Gemma felt too edgy to stand still. But before anything else, she had to speak to her parents.

While Melody pulled out her phone, Gemma went into the dining room and knelt by her mum and dad. She was pleased to see that her mum was still looking bright.

'Mum, Dad. I'm so sorry, but something's come up. Melody and I have to go.'

'Something always comes up with you,' said her dad.

Her mother gave him a quelling glance. 'Is it that business of Duncan's?'

'I think it might be connected, yes.' Seeing the beginning of Vi's worried frown, Gemma hastened to reassure her. 'It's just an interview, Mum. But it needs to be done now.'

Her mother's gaze went to the sitting room, where the three small children had subsided into playing a game on the floor with Toby's cars. 'What about Charlotte? It's her birthday and all.'

'I know, Mum. But I won't be gone that long. I'll ask Hazel or Betty to look—'

'We can stay,' said her dad. 'Can't we, Vi?'

Gemma stared at her father as if he'd just spoken in a foreign tongue.

Her mum looked just as surprised, but recovered quicker. 'Well, that we could, Ern. That's a good idea. If it's all right with Gemma, of course.'

'There's nothing I'd like better.' She gave her mum, then her dad, a kiss on the cheek, and she could have sworn she saw her father's lips twitch in a smile. 'You're sure you'll be all right? You know Toby can be—'

'Stop fussing,' said Vi. 'We're his grandparents, in case you've forgotten. We've looked after him since he was a tot. Just mind you take—'

'Boss.' Melody stood in the hall, her phone still clasped in her hand. 'Sorry to interrupt, but I think you should see this.'

When Gemma joined her, Melody showed her the photo she'd pulled up on the phone's screen. A young blonde woman in rowing gear smiled into the camera. The caption read, 'Christine Hunt; St Catherine's College.'

'I should have done my research,' said Melody. 'Chris Abbott, née Hunt. I should have seen the rowing connection.'

Gemma frowned. 'Why would you have looked for it?'

'Because,' said Melody, 'that's my job. I should have checked for any previous link between Becca Meredith and any of the women who showed up in the Sapphire files. I let myself get distracted by the Hart case. I thought we'd hit eureka.'

'We all did. And we don't know that this Chris Abbott has anything to do with Becca Meredith's death.'

'So,' Melody lowered her voice, 'are you going to let Duncan know we're going to see her?'

Gemma debated only for a moment. 'No. He'd tell us not to go.'

*

Kieran had spent the afternoon at the boatshed, armed with plywood to cover the broken windows, a broom and industrial-size rubbish bags.

After his talk with Freddie Atterton the day before, he'd felt oddly heartened. He could at least make a stab at clearing up. Then he could assess the extent of the damage. Maybe, just maybe, he could put himself, and his business, back together again.

In the meantime he feared he was becoming frighteningly domestic. Tavie had ended up working a double rota last night, filling in for a crewmate who'd called in sick at the last minute. She'd come home early in the morning, exhausted and reeking of smoke. She said she'd been called to a fire scene in Hambleden – a retired police commissioner's house, no less – but the fire had been too far advanced for the medics to get in.

'I'm so glad you were here, Kieran,' she'd said, collapsing into one of the dining chairs while Tosh tried to lick her soot-stained face. I'd have been calling in every favour I had to get someone to see to Tosh.'

He knew she had an arrangement with a neighbouring teenager who came in to look after the dog during the day, but she had no backup for a short-notice night rota.

'And besides,' she added, smiling at him, 'it's nice to see a friendly face. No recriminations.'

He looked at her, puzzled. 'Why should there be?'

'There. You see?' She shook her head. 'You've no idea what I'm talking about. You don't seem to think a woman should know her place.'

'Tavie, if it weren't for you, I'd be—'

'Oh, shut up.' She waved away his gratitude. 'You can cook, can't you? Eggs and toast? And tea?'

Nodding, he said, 'Yeah, although no one ever said it was gourmet.'

'I don't care. Make me some. That's a proper repayment. I'm going to get in the bath.'

He'd set to it as she trudged up the stairs. He even whistled a little, tunelessly, pleased that he'd already worked out where things were in the tidy kitchen, and that he'd picked up essentials at the shops that afternoon.

When he'd served two plates and filled the teapot, he glanced at the dogs, lying side by side in the kitchen doorway, watching him intently. 'Don't even think about it, mates,' he said, and then, erring on the side of caution, he stuck the plates in the warming oven. Tosh, he trusted. Finn, he wasn't so sure about.

Going to the bottom of the stairs, he called Tavie. When she didn't answer, he trotted up, thinking she hadn't heard him over the sound of the taps or maybe the hairdryer.

Just as he reached the top landing Tavie walked out of the bathroom, naked except for a towel wrapped loosely round her waist. Her fair hair was dark from the damp and stood up in spikes where she'd towelled it.

'I just – ' He swallowed. 'Sorry. I didn't – breakfast is ready.'

'Right. I'm just coming.'

'Okay. Good.' He turned and nearly slid back down the stairs, but not before he'd seen the blush travel down her throat to her chest and then to the swell of her small breasts.

She came down a moment later, clad in a sweat-shirt and baggy tracksuit bottoms. They ate, and if Tavie felt awkward she didn't show it. Kieran mostly kept his eyes on his plate, and tried not to think about the slender body beneath the concealing clothes.

'I'll take the dogs for a good run, why don't I?' he'd said when they were finished. Tavie, who had cleaned her plate with astonishing speed, was nodding over her second cup of tea.

'Good idea.'

'You go to bed. I mean, get some rest.' He could have slapped himself for sounding like an idiot. 'After-wards I'm going to see what I can do at the shed. I'll take them with me.'

Tavie opened sleepy blue eyes. 'Don't stay after dark. Remember what the Superintendent said.'

'Yes, ma'am,' he said, cheekily.

'Oh, shut up,' she'd told him again and staggered upstairs to bed, but he'd seen a hint of a smile.

The picture of Tavie in her towel had stayed with him as he swept and hammered through the after-noon. He'd felt guilty for being aroused, as if he were betraying Becca, and weird about thinking of Tavie in that way. But Tavie hadn't seemed to mind – in fact, it occurred to him that she could easily have put on a dressing gown if she'd been worried about her mod-esty. Surely, she hadn't meant for him to . . . No. He scolded himself for being stupid.

And as for Becca – he couldn't let himself go there, not yet. He couldn't separate the memories of lying with her, touching her, from the image of her face below the weir. When he tried, it made him feel sick and disoriented.

Shaking his head, he tipped the last scoop of rubbish from the dustpan into the big bin that he kept in his work area. The bin was, miraculously, undamaged. He'd cleared up a good deal of the mess, but ferrying the bags across to the mainland and disposing of them would be a job for another day. At least he'd got the windows covered, and could shut up the shop and his tools. But it was getting late, and he didn't want Tavie to worry.

Locking up, he greeted the dogs, which had lain in a warm hollow in the grass, waiting patiently for him while they watched the comings and goings on the river.

As he looked round, he realized why it had seemed as though the afternoon was fading unexpectedly fast. The clouds had come in, heavy in the west, bringing an early dusk. Kieran shuddered, dreading the onset of bad weather.

But to his relief he realized that his head felt clear. Maybe this one was not going to be bad.

He rowed across with the dogs and tied up the skiff, then walked along the path, turning up his collar against the wind. The dogs frisked beside him, rambunctious with the cold, so when he reached Mill Meadows he pulled a couple of tennis balls from the pocket of his anorak and let the dogs off-lead for a few minutes of happy ball-chasing.

He hadn't dared ask Tavie if she'd changed her mind about taking him off the SAR team, and only now did he realize how much he would miss it. And Finn – Finn, like Tosh, was born to work, and it would be cruel to deprive him. That, thought Kieran, was an argument that might sway Tavie in his favour.

Clipping the dogs on their leads again, he walked faster, wondering if Tavie was up, eager now to get back to the little crooked house.

As he reached the narrower confines of Thames Side, a few pedestrians crossed to the other side of the street to avoid the dogs. It amused Kieran a little – for all their size, Finn and Tosh were big softies – but he might have done the same himself, before he'd had Finn.

He had crossed the Henley end of the bridge and turned up Market Place, when he saw Freddie Atterton come out of the Red Lion. He picked up his pace, meaning to speak to Atterton, to tell him he'd made some progress with the shed, when he realized Freddie wasn't alone.

Another man had come out of the hotel with him, and they appeared to be, if not arguing, at least having a heated discussion.

Maybe it was just as well if he didn't interrupt, Kieran decided, although he was going to pass right by them. But something drew his eyes back. What was—

Then all thought fled Kieran's mind as Finn leapt forward, nearly tearing the lead from his hand, barking and lunging like a mad thing.

Chapter Twenty-Three

'So, what else do you know about Chris Abbott?' Gemma asked Melody as they crossed the Thames at Hammersmith Bridge.

It had taken them more than half an hour to make a graceful exit from the house. Gemma had insisted that everyone else stay as long as they liked, but even as she gave her parents over-elaborate instructions, she'd felt increasingly worried about Melody's news.

While Gemma was dealing with the domestic front, Melody had made phone calls and done some research online. Gemma had learned better than to ask her sources.

Now, as they drove towards Barnes in Gemma's Escort, heavy cloud had darkened what had begun as a beautiful day, and the Thames looked grey as slate. She beeped her horn impatiently when the driver ahead slowed and almost made her miss the green light at the bridge end.

Melody gave her a startled glance, but said, 'Chris Abbott, DCI, Vice. Works out of West End Central. A career officer out of university, like Becca Meredith, both of them high-flyers with their Oxford educations.

Married, husband works in investment banking. Two kids, both boys, and both down for Eton.'

Gemma whistled. 'On a cop's salary? Let's hope the husband has a better income. When did she report the rape?'

'A little more than five years ago. She was a sergeant then, so she's had two promotions in a very short time. Rewards, do you think, for keeping her mouth shut?'

Gemma had been a sergeant five years ago as well. Would her life have taken the same path as Chris Abbott's, if she'd been less lucky the night Angus Craig had driven her home? No matter how often she went over it, she couldn't be sure what she'd have done. Would she have risked her career and the security of her child, in an attempt to see Craig prosecuted?

'Were there particulars in the rape report?' she asked. If Abbott had had a husband and children at home, it seemed likely that Craig's usual method of courteously offering his victim a lift would have failed with her, as it had with Gemma.

'There was a dinner at a hotel in the West End, after a staffing conference,' Melody continued. 'Abbott said she was walking to the Tube when she was pulled into an alley and assaulted.'

Gemma frowned. 'Then my guess would be that Craig had a room in the hotel. And convinced her to come up for a friendly nightcap, after the conference, when everyone had had a few post-meeting drinks. I wonder, though, about the promotions . . . ' Gemma negotiated a roundabout as they entered the outskirts of the very comfortable suburb of Barnes. 'Were they a reward, or could Abbott have decided to make the best of a bad deal and indulge in a spot of blackmail? A two-way street.'

'If Craig and Abbott had reached a stalemate,' Melody continued thoughtfully, 'maybe he took out his frustration with her by choosing more and more powerful female officers as victims. Substitutes, if you will. A dangerous game.'

'Fatal, in the end,' agreed Gemma. 'Although I doubt that was how he thought it would play out.'

They were running along the river now, passing Barnes railway bridge. It was, Gemma realized, the last major landmark on the Boat Race course. Had Abbott been drawn to this village because she was a rower?

'It's White Hart Lane,' Melody directed. 'On your left, then the address is down near the far end.'

The street was narrow, lined with a mixture of expensive-looking shops and boutiques, and charming terraced houses. And cars, which all seemed to be monstrously large 4 x 4s. 'Yummy-mummy territory, all right,' Gemma muttered as she looked for a parking space. She'd passed the address Melody had given her by a good distance when she saw a car pull out. She put on her signal and manoeuvred the Escort into the spot.

'Top marks on the parallel parking,' teased Melody as Gemma killed the engine, but even as she spoke, she was tucking her dark hair behind one ear and checking the contents of her handbag, signs that she was keyed up. 'Do we know what we're going to say?' she asked.

'We'll wing it,' said Gemma. 'It's your show.'

A moment after Gemma rang the bell there was a twitch at the wooden blinds of the neat terraced house. Then a thin blonde woman opened the door. She wore tight designer jeans and an expensive-looking top, but the polished effect was marred by her harried frown and unfriendly gaze.

'Can I help you?' she snapped.

'DCI Abbott?' asked Melody. She showed her warrant card. 'DC Talbot, Notting Hill. And this is DI James. If we could just have a quick word?'

No amount of neatly applied make-up could conceal the terror that washed over Chris Abbott's face at the sight of their warrant cards. 'What's happened? My boys . . . Are they all right? My husband – oh, God, Ross—'

'Your sons are fine,' Melody hastened to reassure her. 'And your husband. But we do need to speak to you. If we could come in?'

Abbott slumped and touched one hand to the door jamb for an instant's support, as if relief had hit her almost as hard as the panic.

Then she dropped her hand and stared at them suspiciously, the copper in her taking over as she seemed to notice their casual clothes and obvious lack of official presence. And she was, Gemma guessed, taking into account the fact that she outranked them.

The curious glance from a neighbour jogging by

seemed to decide Abbott. She shrugged and said, 'All right. I can give you five minutes. I have to pick up my sons. That's why I was worried. They're at a friend's, and you never know what could happen.'

It was just a bit more explanation than necessary – a sign of nerves, Gemma thought. And, she thought, a detective chief inspector should certainly have known better.

They stepped inside at Abbott's grudging gesture and Gemma looked round with interest.

The house would fetch a high price, even post-recession, because of the area and the amenities. But it was still small, and the sitting room seemed over-stuffed with large leather furniture and a coffee table the size of a boulder. A media centre, anchored by a flat-panel television that rivalled the sofa in scale, took up an entire wall.

And although the shelving on the media centre was packed with DVDs, there were no books in sight. Nor was there any of the childish detritus that littered Gemma and Duncan's house, although at a second glance she realized that one of the cubby holes in the entertainment centre held a toy basket.

Still, the place seemed sterile somehow, as if it never saw the ordinary flow of family life.

But the wall opposite the media centre held evidence of the children – framed family photos. Mum, dad and the two small boys, all looking unnaturally neat, all with the kind of frozen smiles that made one's jaws ache.

In most of them Chris Abbott looked tense, and she held the boys' shoulders in what looked like a restraining grip. Abbott's husband, a tall man with thinning hair and a heavy face that fell just short of handsome, rested his arm on his wife's shoulders in a gesture that seemed to Gemma more possessive than protective.

As for the two children, the older boy was dark-haired and resembled his father, while the smaller son was gingery-fair.

The dark-blue Oxford oar mounted above the photos seemed disproportionately large, as if it was intended to dwarf the family.

Melody, who was not easily intimidated by rank, money or pretentious furniture, smiled and gestured at the photos. 'Nice family. And I see your husband was an Oxford Blue,' she added, nodding at the oar. 'You must be very proud. Do you mind if we sit?'

'I do, actually. I told you I didn't have much time. Why don't you tell me exactly what it is that you want?' Abbott gave a quick glance at the front door.

'I take it your husband's not at home?' asked Melody.

'No. He had to go out.' Abbott frowned at them. 'Not that it's any of your business. Aren't you a bit off your patch, detectives? And on a Saturday afternoon?' She'd taken the lead – another error, thought Gemma, that spoke of nerves.

'This couldn't wait,' said Melody.

Abbott cast another anxious glance towards the door, and Gemma wondered if she was expecting her husband – and if that was worrying her as much as their presence.

Abbott switched her gaze to Gemma. 'Are you the silent partner then, DI . . . it was James, wasn't it?'

Gemma had no doubt that Abbott remembered her name. She was fishing, wondering what a DI was doing at her door. Mistake number three, in Gemma's book.

Melody answered her. 'I'm with the Sapphire unit, Detective Abbott. Your name has come up in the course of our inquiries. DI James is pursuing a linked matter.'

'Sapphire? Linked?' It was a moment before Abbott controlled the panic on her face. 'I'm not working on anything related to a Sapphire investigation.'

Melody gave Gemma the slightest nod, but it was signal enough.

'DCI Abbott,' said Gemma, 'I believe you were an old friend of Rebecca Meredith's?'

'Becca? Oh, yes. We were friends at uni, and we were at police college together. I still can't believe she's gone.' The regret sounded rehearsed, as if she had been prepared for the question, but she didn't say the most obvious thing – that she had seen Becca Meredith just a few days before she died.

Putting on her most sympathetic expression, Gemma said, 'Then it must have been a great comfort that you saw her so recently.'

Abbott's eyes widened with an involuntary ripple of shock, making it clear she hadn't expected them to know that particular bit of information. 'I – yes,' she said, then went on in a rush. 'Yes, yes, it was. Last Friday. Becca rang and asked me to come to her station. She said she'd run across some information she thought might be helpful to a Vice investigation.'

'But that was just a pretext, wasn't it?' asked Melody. She pulled some papers from her bag – papers Gemma suspected had nothing to do with the investigation – but it was an effective tactic. 'DCI Abbott,' Melody continued, scanning a page as if her memory needed refreshing, 'five years ago you filed a sexual-assault report after a police function in the West End. And although you said you couldn't name your assailant, you had a rape test done, and the results of that test went on file. A year ago the same thing happened to Becca Meredith. When it occurred to her that other female police officers might have been victims as well, she started searching through the records. She found several officers who had reported rapes by unknown assailants. But only one of them happened to be a woman she knew, and an old friend. You.'

Melody paused for a beat, to let it sink in. Then she said, 'And she knew that you knew who your assailant was, as did she.'

Abbott was shaking her head before Melody finished. 'That's absolute bollocks. I've no idea what you're talking about. I think it's time you—'

'DCI Abbott. Please don't take us for fools.' Gemma's words stopped Abbott in mid-protest. When Gemma had her full attention, she went on. 'It was Angus Craig. You and Becca Meredith were both raped by Deputy Assistant Commissioner Craig, who then threatened you in order to procure your silence. Don't waste our time by denying it.'

Abbott's prominent collarbones rose sharply with

the intake of her breath. 'You can't prove that. And he's dead. I heard he was dead.'

Abbott hadn't denied it. Masking the rush of exhilaration that came with knowing she and Melody had been right, Gemma said levelly, 'That hasn't yet been confirmed. But what matters to me is that we have his DNA, and that it will match your semen sample, and Becca Meredith's sample. And it will match DCI Jenny Hart's.'

She was stretching the truth a bit, but they would have Craig's DNA soon enough, and she wanted answers from Abbott now.

'Jenny?' Abbott's voice was a whisper. 'What are you talking about? Jenny was murdered – oh, God. You don't mean he *killed* Jenny?'

'Becca didn't know about Craig's connection to Jenny Hart, did she?' asked Gemma. 'She missed that one, because the case was in the database as an unsolved murder, not as an unsolved rape. If she'd known about Jenny Hart, she wouldn't have needed you. And that was what she wanted from you, wasn't it, Chris?' Gemma leaned forward, intent and trying to make a connection with this woman, who seemed to have built a fortress around any emotion other than fear. 'She wanted you to file a rape charge against Angus Craig.'

Abbott shook her head, as if she meant to deny it, but when she saw their faces, her shoulders sagged. 'Okay, okay,' she said. 'That lead Becca said she had – when I got to the station, it was useless. But then she wanted to go for drinks. Becca wanting to do the jolly old-girl thing was odd enough, but Becca the

Abstentious wanting to go out for a tipple – that was a real red flag. I went because I wanted to know what she was up to. She suggested a pub on Holland Park Avenue. Not too far away, but out of her station's orbit. She waited until we'd both had a few drinks before she told me what she really wanted.'

Abbott raised a finger to her mouth and nibbled at the quick. Her nails were bitten as well. 'Bitch!' she said. 'I told her to bugger off. I told her that all happened five years ago, and I've moved on. I've worked hard to get where I am now.' The words spilled out as if she couldn't stop them. 'We've got two kids in school, and I'm up for another promotion. Why should I have risked everything so that Angus Craig would get a slap on the wrist – if even that. Look at you, both of you. You know how the system works. You know it would all have been for nothing.'

Suddenly her anger seemed to drain away. Shivering, she rubbed at her bare arms and sank down on the arm of the sofa. 'But I didn't – I didn't know about Jenny.'

'Did you know her well?' asked Melody.

'We were on a command course together at Bramshill a few years ago. I liked her. We met up for a drink every now and then. She was funny, and sharp, and never condescending. And she liked being single.' With a strangled laugh Chris added, 'Sometimes I used to wish I had her life.'

'And you never told Jenny what Angus Craig did to you?'

Chris shook her head, vehemently. 'God, no. I never told anyone. I only made the report that night because one of the constables in my division found me crying and bleeding outside the hotel, and I had to say something. It was the best I could do under the circumstances. Oh – ' She caught her breath as realization struck. 'Oh, God. If I'd told Jenny, she'd never have gone with him – is that what happened? I know she was killed in her flat. Did she – did she invite him up for a drink?'

'What about Becca, Chris?' said Gemma. 'You'd been friends since university. Did she not count? If you'd told her, she'd never have accepted a lift home from Craig the night he raped her. And now she's dead, too.'

'Why should I have told Becca? She wasn't exactly the shoulder you'd pick to cry on. And besides, I'd never have dreamed she'd be as stupid as I was. Always in control of everything, Becca.'

Gemma wondered what lay at the root of Abbott's bitterness, a bitterness so corrosive she couldn't find a kind word to say about her murdered friend. 'So, last Friday night,' she said, 'what did Becca do when you told her you wouldn't cooperate?'

'She was livid. But then Becca always expected that what *she* wanted should come first.'

Gemma had a sudden hunch. She threw it out like bread on the water, to see what it might fetch. 'Is that why she came back on Saturday? To try again to convince you?'

Abbott's face closed like a shutter. 'I don't know what you're talking about.'

'Oh, come on, Chris.' Gemma knew now that she'd

been right, and she wasn't going to be fobbed off. 'Do you want us to ask the neighbours? This is a small street, and I've no doubt that everyone knows everyone else's business.

'Becca left her car in the city on Friday night after she met you. When she came back into London to pick it up on Saturday afternoon, she drove here, didn't she?' Gemma glanced at the window, as if assessing the neighbours. 'How many people do you think will remember her car? And Becca? She wasn't exactly a woman you'd easily overlook. Did you argue at the door?'

After a long moment, Abbott gave a shrug that was meant to be nonchalant, and Gemma was certain she'd decided it wasn't worth risking a house-to-house and being shown to be a liar. 'So what if she did? She tried to bully us, if you want to know. Ross told her to sod off. She was always a bitch to him, so I'd say it was no better than she deserved.'

As if she realized how venomous she'd sounded, Abbott rubbed a hand across her face and said, 'Look. I don't mean I'm not sorry Becca's dead. I was devastated when I heard. We both were. But it's nothing to do with us, and I can't see why you've come to me with this, in the first place.' She stood. 'With Craig dead, none of it matters any more. And I've had enough.'

As if the assertion of Craig's death had given her courage, she said, 'I told you, I've got to pick up my kids. Your time's up.'

Gemma's glance at Melody told her they'd had the

same thought. 'DCI Abbott,' she said, 'how did you know Angus Craig was dead?'

'Mrs Craig's dog?' said Kincaid, staring at Imogen Bell. 'Bloody hell. I'd forgotten all about the dog. It must have got out somehow during the fire.'

DC Bell looked confused. 'During the fire? The neighbour says he found the dog – it's a little whippet – running loose around midnight. He was going to return it to Mrs Craig, but when he walked over, he said he found the house was dark, and he didn't like to ring the bell. He thought he'd just keep the dog until morning and ring Mrs Craig first thing. But then the smoke and the fire brigade woke him in the night and he was frantic about the Craigs. He's been trying to speak to someone ever since—'

'Barney,' interrupted Kincaid. 'The dog. The dog is a he, and his name is Barney.' He didn't know why he felt so relieved that Edie Craig's dog had survived. But why had the dog been out two hours before the fire? 'Midnight? The neighbour said midnight?'

'Yes, sir. I'm sure of it,' answered Bell.

Kincaid turned to the fire investigator. 'Owen, if Craig set the fire before midnight, could it have taken until two to fully take hold?'

Owen Morris shook his head. 'I'd say very unlikely. There was a flash at the point of origin, and from the amount of accelerant poured round the house, I'd think the surrounding rooms went up pretty quickly. Fire's a funny thing, though. It can play tricks on you. It's possible it smouldered for a bit. We'll know more when things cool off.'

'Still . . . ' Kincaid let the sentence trail off, not sure he wanted to verbalize the unwelcome scenario that had come to him.

What if Edie Craig had suspected violence was brewing? Angus Craig had made no bones about hating the dog – perhaps she'd feared Barney would be a target. But surely if she'd realized just how bad it was, she'd have got out herself . . . Or would she?

She was a woman, Kincaid suspected, who'd spent the better part of her married life trying to limit the damage her husband caused. But had she known, before Denis Childs's visit last night, just how much havoc Craig had wreaked, how many lives he'd destroyed? And, if not, could she now have lived with the truth?

She had been a gentle woman and possessed of unexpected grace. He hoped she had not guessed what was coming.

'Sir,' said Bell, 'the neighbour. He's still waiting at the gate. Should I—'

Kincaid shook himself back to the present. 'Get his name and address. Ask him if he wouldn't mind keeping the dog until we track down any friends or relatives of Mrs Craig. And, DC Bell, when the SOCOs get here, I want them to check Craig's car for any trace evidence that matches the scene of Becca Meredith's murder. If there's any outerwear left undamaged in the house, I want that checked, too.'

Bell gaped at him. 'You don't think . . . ' she began, then she collected herself and nodded. 'Yes, sir. I'll just speak to Mr Wilson – that's the neighbour.' She

413

left them and walked towards the gate, but not without an uncertain backwards glance.

The timing of the fire wasn't the only thing bothering Kincaid. Turning to Owen Morris, he said, 'Can you tell if the same accelerant was used here as in Kieran Connolly's boatshed?'

'It seems to have been common petrol in both cases.' Morris gave Kincaid a speculative frown. 'And even if Forensics can narrow it down to the refiner, it may not get you anywhere. You think Craig had something to do with Rebecca Meredith's murder *and* with the boatshed?' The question was rhetorical, as Morris looked back at the smouldering house and added, 'That would explain why he decided to go out with a bang.'

Except, Kincaid thought, that it didn't. Because they still had no proof that Craig had been connected with Becca Meredith's murder, or with the attack on Kieran. 'We don't—' he began, when his phone rang.

When Kieran had managed to wrestle both dogs up Market Place and back into Tavie's house, he found her gone. She'd left him a note on the little chalkboard in the kitchen, saying she'd gone out to the shops and would pick up something for their dinner.

'Go lie down, both of you,' Kieran told the dogs. Looking chastened, they did as they were bid. But Finn was still panting and trembling, and Kieran's heart was still racing from the shock of seeing his friendly, easy-going dog become suddenly unhinged. When he pulled out his phone to ring Superintendent

Kincaid, he realized his hands were shaking, the way they had in Iraq when his unit had seen action.

Closing his eyes, he took a breath and, when Kincaid answered, he made an effort to give him a clear description of what had happened. 'It wasn't Freddie,' he said. 'Both dogs spent a couple of hours with him yesterday, and they were fine. It was the other guy. I've never seen Finn do anything like that. I thought he'd take the guy's head off.'

'You're sure you didn't recognize this man?' Kincaid had asked.

'No. Never seen him before,' Kieran had said. But now, his mind was beginning to play little tricks on him, little fragments of memory flaring like ghosts, just on the edge of perception.

He shook his head, but that made him dizzy.

Tea. Tea would help, he thought. But when he went to put the kettle on, he found himself getting dog biscuits instead. Fighting the spinning in his head, he took the biscuits into the sitting room and knelt by the dogs, praising them as he gave them their treats. He'd shouted at Finn, and Finn had only been trying to –

Kieran sat back so hard it made the room rock. Protect him. Finn had been trying to protect him.

But why would Finn . . . Wait. Kieran reached out and touched the dog's black coat, now warm from the fire, as if the contact could give him an answer.

Something familiar. There had been something familiar . . . The image tickled the edge of his subconscious, then suddenly the fuzzy outline became clearer. The man on the river bank, in the dusk – was that where Kieran had seen Freddie's friend? But Finn wouldn't have recognized someone seen at a distance as a threat . . .

'Oh, Jesus!' Kieran whispered as realization hit him.

It hadn't been sight, it had been smell that Finn recognized. That was what had terrified him.

When Kieran and Finn had found the spot where Becca was killed, *he* had been there, close enough for Finn to scent him.

And then, when *he* had rowed right up to the shed with his petrol bomb, Kieran remembered, Finn had lifted his head, nostrils flaring, a moment before the bottle crashed through the window. Both the window and the door of the shed had been open, to clear any solvent fumes.

It hadn't been the sound of voices that had alerted Finn that night. The wind had been blowing down-river. Finn had caught the bastard's scent.

And tonight – tonight Finn had associated that scent with Kieran's fear on the river bank, and with the terror of the fire.

His hand still unsteady, Kieran lifted his phone again.

Then he stopped, his fingers going lax on the keypad. There was something more.

He closed his eyes and tried to bring back the man's face, first glimpsed in that instant when he'd walked out of the Red Lion after Freddie.

But what Kieran saw against the blackness of his eyelids was not the scene outside the Red Lion, but a photograph. And in that photograph he saw a younger version of that likeness amid a group of faces, all in a frame on a shelf in Becca's cottage . . . a photo of a Boat Race crew.

'He's a bit bonkers, don't you think?' said Cullen, when Kincaid had told him about Kieran's call.

'Maybe not as much as you'd think.' Kincaid was already dialling Freddie Atterton's number. After a few rings, the call went to voicemail. Kincaid swore, but didn't leave a message. Disconnecting, he turned to Cullen. 'We'll try the flat.'

After a brief word with Owen Morris and DC Bell, they were on their way back to Henley.

'So, is this a case of what the dog did in the night, or what the dog didn't do in the night?' asked Cullen, as they turned onto the Marlow road at Hambleden Mill.

Kincaid was not in the mood for flippancy. 'We may never know why Edie Craig's dog was loose two hours before the fire. But if Kieran Connolly says his dog was panicked, I believe him. I also believe someone tried to kill Connolly, and I'm not convinced it was Angus Craig.'

'If Peter Gaskill and his cronies were Craig's alibi for the attack on Connolly, I'm not sure I'd give the alibi too much credence,' argued Doug. 'And it seems rather obvious that Craig liked to burn things up.'

'Does it?' Kincaid braked hard behind a car with hire-car plates going miles below the limit. 'Anybody can buy a tin of petrol. And I'd swear Craig didn't know about the attack on Kieran. The bastard was too self-obsessed to be that good an actor.'

'What about Becca Meredith?'

'I'm still not certain we can fit him for it. The bartender at the pub in Hambleden had no reason to lie about the time Craig came in. And Craig's motive is still questionable, unless Becca found out about Jenny Hart, and I don't think she did.'

'Then . . . '

'Damned if I know. But I'd feel a whole lot better if I had Freddie Atterton in my sight.'

When Freddie buzzed them into the Malthouse and opened the door of his flat, Kincaid's relief swiftly turned to anger. 'Where the hell were you?' he said, pushing past Freddie without giving him a chance to invite them in. 'Why the hell didn't you answer your phone?'

'I just didn't pick up,' said Freddie, looking puzzled. 'I was on long-distance with Becca's mother, making arrangements to meet her at the airport – '

Kincaid waved him into silence. 'Okay. But before that. You were at the Red Lion with another man: who was he?'

'What? How did you – '

'Kieran Connolly rang me.'

'Oh, yeah, Kieran.' Freddie frowned. 'I saw Kieran, all right. What was up with that? His dog, the lovely black Lab – he went absolutely bonkers. I thought he was going to take Ross down in the street. And then the other one, the Alsatian, went just as mad. I thought they were trained search dogs, not attack dogs.'

'They are search dogs, and they're very well socialized,' Kincaid said, frowning. 'Which makes it even odder that Finn would go after your mate like that. Your friend – Ross. Tell me about him.'

'I did. Remember? He's my mate who took me to the mortuary. We're old friends from Oxford.'

That was right. Kincaid remembered Freddie saying something about a university friend who had taken him to make the formal identification of Becca's body. 'Kieran said you and your friend seemed to be arguing when he first saw you. Why?'

'Ross kept asking me what I knew about Angus Craig. I told him the guy stood me up for a meeting, and I thought he was a right prick. But Ross had had more than a few drinks, and he gets . . . stroppy. He said he couldn't believe Becca never told me about Craig. He said' – Freddie stopped, colour flushing his face – 'he said he'd never realized I was blind *and* stupid. He was always a bit of a shit, Ross, and to tell the truth I never thought he deserved to be in the bloody boat. But to say something like that – he can't have been suggesting Becca had an *affair* with Craig. I don't believe it.'

'What did you tell him?' asked Kincaid, his mind racing.

'Nothing. Kieran showed up with the dogs just then and all hell broke loose. And after that, Ross took off like the hounds of hell were after him. Can't say I blame him, but—'

'Why was your friend so interested in Angus Craig?' Kincaid broke in.

'I've no idea. I didn't even know that he knew him. But I suppose it would make sense that Chris did.'

'Chris?'

'Ross's wife. She's a DCI with the Met, like Becca, though they worked in different divisions.'

'Chris?' said Doug, his voice rising. 'What's her last name?'

Freddie took a startled step back. 'Abbott. It's Abbott. What of it?'

Waving his hands in agitation, Doug turned to Kincaid. 'That's who Becca saw, that last day. Remember, at Charlotte's party, I said I'd got her name from Sergeant Patterson? The old friend who came into the station – it was Chris Abbott.'

Kincaid stared at him. A female police officer, a female police officer who knew Angus Craig; and hadn't Freddie also told him, after he'd been to the mortuary, that his friend's wife was a cop?

Bloody hell. He'd been so focused on Angus Craig – and on proving Denis Childs wrong about Freddie – that he'd walked right over a bloody landmine and hadn't seen it. He was the one who'd been blind and stupid.

'Christ!' he said. 'She – this Chris Abbott – has to have been one of the victims. But did Becca find out that day, or did she already know? Something happ—'

'Victims?' Freddie broke in. 'What the hell are you talking about? Victims of what?' He looked from Kincaid to Cullen, but it was Kincaid who answered.

There was no longer any need to protect Freddie from Craig, or vice versa. Freddie would have to know the truth and it might as well be now. 'Look,' Kincaid said. 'Why don't we sit down.'

'I'm tired of being told to sit,' Freddie retorted. He was less fragile tonight, edgy, rocking on the balls of his feet, and the look he gave them was challenging. 'Say whatever it is you've got to say.'

'Okay, then,' Kincaid agreed, although he was still reluctant. 'A year ago Becca reported a sexual assault. She didn't identify her assailant. She did, however, tell her superior officer, Peter Gaskill, what had happened. Deputy Assistant Commissioner Craig had offered her a lift home after a Met function in London. He asked to come in to use the toilet. He then assaulted her. Afterwards, he threatened her. He told her he'd make sure she lost her job, and her credibility, if she told anyone what had happened.'

Any doubts that Kincaid might have harboured about Freddie's knowledge disappeared in that moment. Shock made Freddie's features sharp, as if the skin had fallen away from his bones. Then the rage flooded in, suffusing his face, and Kincaid remembered that this was a man who had been strong enough – and bloody-minded enough – to earn the oars mounted on the sitting-room wall.

As had his friend, Kincaid realized, with dawning horror. Becca's killer had known how to drown a rower, and had been strong enough to do it. Kieran's attacker had rowed near enough to the boatshed to throw a bomb through the window, then disappeared, a feat that had required speed and accuracy in a boat. Had it—

'I'll kill him,' said Freddie. 'That bastard Craig. She

wouldn't have stood for it, Becca wouldn't. He killed her, didn't he, to shut her up? And you' – he turned on Kincaid, his hands balled into fists – 'you knew all along, didn't you? You've been protecting him. You're just as bad as—'

'Freddie, shut up and listen to me.' Kincaid had to restrain himself from shaking him. 'I haven't been protecting Craig. I've been trying to find proof that he killed Becca and attacked Kieran Connolly, but I don't think he did. And now he's dead. He killed himself, and his wife, last night.'

'What?' Freddie stood, his hands still raised, looking like a boxer reeling from a knockout blow. 'But why . . . ? What – '

'We found out something else about Craig,' Kincaid said. 'Something that had nothing to do with Becca. Something he knew he couldn't cover up.'

'Then, if it wasn't Craig, who killed Becca?' Freddie's handsome face contorted as he bit back a sob. 'Why would someone else kill her?'

Kincaid thought of the man Kieran had seen on the river bank, and of big, friendly Finn, suddenly frightened into frenzy by the sight of a man in the street. And he went back to Freddie's friend Ross Abbott, the rower, the Oxford Blue – a rower whose wife had known Becca and Angus Craig. But why, if Craig had raped Chris Abbott, would her husband kill Becca, and not Craig himself? And why was Ross Abbott so frantic now to learn what Freddie knew about Craig?

Kincaid shook his head. He didn't have all the pieces, but he felt the violence building, the hair on the back of his neck rising in atavistic anticipation. This wasn't over.

And if Ross Abbott was their killer, he'd targeted Kieran once. After that afternoon's encounter with Kieran and Finn, he would be even more certain that Kieran posed a threat.

'Freddie,' he said. 'Your friend Ross Abbott – where is he now?'

Chapter Twenty-Four

'She's lying,' said Gemma, as she and Melody got back into the Escort. They'd run to escape a pattering of rain, but now that they were protected, the shower seemed to have stopped.

'Yes, but about which part?' Melody responded. 'How she left things with Becca? How she found out about Craig's suicide?'

'I suppose she *could* have heard about Craig from someone at work.' That had been Abbott's curt response to Gemma's last question. Then she'd come close to shoving them out the door, and they'd had had no recourse but to leave as gracefully as they could manage. 'It's been more than twelve hours since the first reports began to come in about Craig,' Gemma went on, making no move to start the car, 'and you know rumours are flying like wildfire. So . . . that I might believe. But Abbott was ready to be asked about Becca, and to me she seems close to panic. I think she's involved in Becca Meredith's death.'

Had Chris Abbott been so convinced that the truth would ruin her career and her reputation that she'd been willing to kill to protect her past, Gemma wondered?

'I suppose Becca could have told her about her training routine, but she'd still have needed time off work to watch Becca, to find a good ambush spot, and she'd have had to juggle the time away from her kids as well,' mused Melody. 'But she was a rower, so she'd have known how to tip the boat and hold Becca under.'

'Her kids,' said Gemma as realization hit her. 'Christ! Melody, did you get the ages of her kids from her personnel file?'

Frowning, Melody pulled the pages from her bag. It seemed they had not been strictly window-dressing. She flipped through them, then stopped, her finger holding her place. 'The older boy, Landon, is nine. The younger one, Logan, is four.'

'Four?' Gemma's stomach plummeted. 'Shit!' She looked at her partner. 'Four, Melody. He's four. And we're blinking idiots.'

'Oh, God.' Melody eyes went wide. 'The little one. He's Craig's baby, isn't he? You don't usually happen to have protection when you're being raped. But why didn't she just abort – '

'Maybe she doesn't believe in it. Maybe she really wanted another child and she wasn't sure whose he was.'

'Or maybe she didn't want to tell her husband what had happened – or at least not the whole truth,' put in Melody. 'Maybe she stuck to the story in the police report, rather than admitting that she'd gone up to Craig's hotel room. Even if her intentions were innocent, it was questionable behaviour, especially if her husband's jealous.'

Gemma thought about the photos again, of the

possessive drape of Ross Abbott's arm across his wife's shoulders. She didn't think this was a man who would want to admit that his little son was another man's child, no matter the circumstances of the boy's conception. Or particularly in the circumstances of the child's conception.

'Whatever Ross Abbott might have known before,' she said, 'after Becca's visit on Saturday, he will have had the whole truth. And whatever Chris Abbott knew about Becca's training routine, she will have told—'

A movement in the rear-view mirror caught Gemma's eye.

Chris Abbott had come out of her house and was running towards the street, fumbling in her handbag. When she reached a white Mercedes SUV, she yanked some keys from the bag and flung the car door open. When Abbott's headlamps flashed on, Gemma realized how dark it had become.

'Boss?' said Melody.

'What's she up to?' said Gemma. 'Something's happened.' She started the Escort, throwing it into gear as she watched Abbott in the mirror.

'Boss – ' said Melody again, but as Abbott pulled out and barrelled down the street towards them, Gemma backed up, then jerked the Escort's wheels hard and stepped on the pedal. The car shot into the street, barely missing the Lexus parked in front and screeched to a stop directly in Abbott's path.

Abbott slammed the Mercedes to a halt, an inch from the Escort's side panel. She was out of the Merc while it was still rocking from the sudden braking.

'What the fuck do you thing you're doing?' she shouted. 'Move your damned car, you bloody – ' Then she saw Gemma get out of the driver's side and stopped dead. 'You,' she said, but it came out a croak.

'Where are you going, Chris?' asked Gemma. She reached Melody, who'd climbed out of the Escort's passenger side, but she didn't take her eyes off Abbott.

'None of your business. I told you. Get out of my way.' Abbott's mouth was pinched in a tight, white line.

'I'm not going anywhere. And neither are you, unless you reverse out of here, and I don't think that's going to happen any time soon.' Another car was coming down the lane behind Abbott, and Gemma suspected they'd have an irate motorist added to the mix at any moment. 'Get us backup,' she mouthed to Melody.

Abbott looked over her shoulder, saw the on-coming car, then turned back to Gemma. 'You move your car, or your job won't be worth the paper your warrant card's printed on.'

'That's not going to work with me,' said Gemma, keeping her voice level. 'You're a cop, Chris. Whatever you've done, you know the only thing that will help you now is to talk to us.'

'Done?' Abbott shrieked at her. 'I haven't done anything. You don't know what you're talking about. And if you don't let me out of here, God help us, you're going to be the one regretting it. I won't be responsible.'

'Responsible for what, Chris?'

'Backup's coming,' whispered Melody, moving the phone cupped in her hand down to her side.

'I don't know.' Chris's anger seemed to collapse, and her voice rose in a wail of despair. 'But my gun's gone.'

'Your gun?' Gemma felt her own jolt of panic as she thought about Duncan. Where was he now? Why the hell hadn't she called him and told him what she suspected?

'Don't look so surprised. I work bloody Vice, for God's sake. You know people who know where to get things. After that bastard Craig, I said I'd never let anything like that happen to me again. You'd have done the same.'

Gemma nodded. 'Yeah, I would. Especially if I thought I might need to protect my kids.' She saw a little of the tightness leave Abbott's body as she heard the sympathy in Gemma's voice. It didn't matter that Abbott would have used the same technique herself hundreds of times – her body had responded to Gemma's tone with a will of its own.

'Where's your gun, Chris?' Gemma asked, as gently as if she was talking to an old friend. 'Think about your kids. They need you, and that means you need to do the right thing now.'

The car behind Abbott flashed its headlights, then beeped its horn. Gemma cursed the driver under her breath. The last thing she needed right now was a confrontation.

A bearded man leaned out the window. 'Move your damned show, ladies,' he called. 'This isn't the freaking Globe.'

A siren whooped faintly in the distance. Abbott looked back again, then forwards, her head whipping round. There was no way out.

Then suddenly she sagged, her body curved in despair, fear etching lines like crevasses in her thin face.

'I keep it on the top shelf of the bedroom cupboard, where the kids can't reach it,' she said. 'It's gone. My gun's gone. Ross has it.'

'I've no idea where Ross went,' said Freddie. 'I told you, he just took off.'

'Does he live in Henley?' Kincaid asked, trying to master a sense of urgency so strong that his palms were beginning to sweat. He knew he had to keep Freddie calm, steer him away from the thought of what Craig had done to Becca, if he was going to get anything helpful from him. The large space of Freddie Atterton's flat suddenly seemed breathlessly stuffy. The humidity must be rising.

'No, he lives in Barnes.' Freddie sounded confused. 'But he rows out of Henley Rowing Club. Why do you want to know?'

'Why not row out of Leander?' asked Doug. 'Especially as he was a Blue?'

Freddie fidgeted and moved away from them for the first time, going to the far end of the dining table, where he pulled out a chair, but didn't sit. 'To tell the truth, some of the members don't like him. He's a bit of a braggart, Ross, and he tends to make too much of his connections and possessions. Not that he's the only one, but you know the sort of thing. And to hear him tell it,' he added with a bitter little laugh and a glance at the Oxford oar, 'you'd think we won the Boat Race. Anyway, his membership was . . . discouraged.'

Kincaid raised an eyebrow. 'But you're still friends?'

'We keep in touch. He keeps in touch, really. Although I hadn't heard from him for some time before Becca . . . ' Freddie swallowed. 'I was surprised when he called, actually. I'd heard rumours that some of the investments he'd made for his firm had gone belly-up. But that day, when he took me to the mortuary, he said he was doing well. Brilliantly. I remember thinking it was just like Ross to be going on about his new car when – when – '

Kincaid hurried to redirect him. 'What else did he say to you that day?'

'That Chris had heard about Becca at work. That he and Chris were . . . sorry. But – ' Pressing his knuckles to his lips, Freddie gazed somewhere between Kincaid and Doug, his eyes unfocused. 'But – but then, when we were having drinks, he kept asking me what the police knew about Becca's death. And he made me realize I could be a suspect. It hadn't even occurred to me until then that someone might think I killed her.'

Kincaid saw Doug's quick glance and knew they were on the same page. Ross Abbott had been fishing and, in the process, he'd tried to frighten Freddie, perhaps in the hope that he would do something that would make him appear guilty. It smacked of premeditation. And viciousness.

'But why are you asking about Ross?' said Freddie. 'And why did Kieran's dog go off on him like that?'

Why indeed, Kincaid thought? Could Finn have recognized Ross's scent from the scene of Becca's murder? Why the fear, though, unless he'd associated the scent with Kieran's unease by the river bank. But surely that wasn't enough to –

Realization struck. Fire was enough. Fire in the boatshed, the dog's terror, and the man's. If Finn had recognized Ross Abbott's scent from the attack on the boatshed, then he'd have had a bloody good reason to go bonkers.

And by now Kieran would have realized that as well.

Kincaid followed Freddie to the end of the dining table. There was something that still didn't make sense to him. 'You said you'd seen Kieran yesterday. Where?'

Freddie looked reluctant. More than reluctant. Embarrassed. He stood with the chair back between them, as if he needed armour. 'It wasn't anything.'

'Out with it, Freddie. It's important. Where?'

'I went to see the boatshed. I wanted to see where he lived. Where he and Becca – it was stupid.' He shook his head. 'But while I was standing there staring at the place like a sodding idiot, Kieran showed up with the dogs. I could tell he thought I was a bit weird, but I explained that I'd come to thank him. I went across to the shed with him. We looked at the damage. We talked. And it was – okay.' Freddie sounded as if that still surprised him. 'He seems like a good bloke. Bloody shame about the workshop, but maybe he can put it right. And' – he met Kincaid's eyes at last – 'I

431

saw the boat, the boat he was building for Becca. It's . . . ' Description failed him.

'Did you see Ross anywhere near Kieran's shed?'

'Ross? No. He rang me after I got back to the flat and said he wanted to meet at the Red Lion. And when I got there, he started asking about Craig.'

'At the Red Lion, did you say anything to Ross about Kieran? About where he was staying?'

'No.' Freddie sounded incensed. 'I told you, Ross took off right after we saw Kieran. And besides, Kieran didn't tell me where he was staying. But why would Ross care?'

Kincaid didn't answer. He was visualizing the town centre in the fading light, Kieran struggling to control the dogs as he walked up Market Place towards Tavie's. Had he looked back?

And Ross – he'd have seen which direction Kieran took. When he left Freddie, he could have ducked into a doorway until he was sure Freddie wasn't watching, then followed Kieran. Even if he'd been too far behind to see Kieran going into Tavie's house, he'd have known the direction that Kieran had taken. And he could have waited, hoping for another glimpse.

Ross Abbott was good at waiting.

Kincaid's dread grew. Taking out his phone, he found Kieran's number and dialled.

Two rings, three, then a woman's voice said a tentative *Hello.*

'Sorry,' Kincaid said. 'I was trying to reach Kieran. Is this his—'

'Superintendent? It's Tavie. He left his phone in

my kitchen.' She sounded perplexed. 'I can't imagine why he'd—'

'Do you know where he went?'

'He left a note on my chalkboard. Something about "going to the cottage". Did he mean . . . her cottage? Becca Meredith's? Why would he do that now?' There was a hint of hurt in Tavie's voice.

'He didn't say?'

'No. But . . . '

'How long ago?'

'He hadn't come home when I left for the shops an hour ago, so I know it's been less than that.'

It suddenly seemed very important to Kincaid that Kieran wasn't alone. 'Did he take Finn?'

'Yes, but he left Tosh here. Superintendent, what's—'

'Just stay there, Tavie. I can't explain right now. And if Kieran comes back, tell him to call me. Right away. Don't let him go anywhere else, and don't let anyone into the house.'

He hung up before she could ask anything more.

Freddie was watching him as if he'd gone suddenly daft, but Doug had had no trouble following the one-sided conversation. 'Where?' he asked.

'Becca's cottage. Freddie, do you have—'

His phone rang, startling him. Thinking it was Kieran, he picked up with a rush of relief. 'Thank God. What were—'

'Duncan?'

'Gemma?' he said, surprised. 'Look, love, sorry, but I can't talk—'

'There's something you should know,' she broke

in. 'I should have rung you sooner. There's this guy,
Ross Abbott. His wife—'

'I know who Ross Abbott is.' Kincaid's gut
clenched. 'How do you – never mind. What's happened?'

'I think he may have had a pretty good reason to
kill Becca Meredith. And now he's got a gun. I don't
know what he means to—'

'I do,' said Kincaid.

The rumble of thunder came with a gust of rain and
a spatter of wind, just as Kieran dug the key from
beneath the flowerpot at the corner of the cottage.

It was dark enough now that Kieran couldn't see
the storm, but he didn't need to – he could sense it.
His head felt full, as if it might explode. Beside him,
Finn whined. He knew the signs as well as Kieran.

Kieran flinched as thunder cracked, nearer, but he
rose unsteadily to his feet and said, 'I'm going to be
okay, boy.' He wasn't going to let the damned weather
keep him from doing what he'd come here for.

The porch was dark, and he fumbled at the lock,
wishing he'd brought his torch from the Land Rover.
It had seemed odd to park on the verge in front of the
cottage. Always before he'd parked up by the church,
so as, according to Becca, not to give the neighbours
food for gossip. Now he wondered if she'd been protecting Freddie as much as herself.

The lock clicked open and he stepped inside, Finn
at his knee, and switched on the lights.

As the lamps illuminated the familiar sitting room
in a warm glow, Kieran's heart contracted with the

buffet of memories. He'd been so focused on his task that he hadn't realized how the cottage would feel, with Becca gone.

'Not just gone. Dead,' he said aloud, and steeled himself. The photo was on the shelf in the bookcase, just where he remembered. Crossing the room, he took it down and sat carefully on the sofa beside the lamp, Finn settling at his feet.

Kieran held the photo between his hands, examining it, and the frozen faces captured in the photo stared back at him. He picked out Freddie, looking impossibly young, gazing into the camera with hungry defiance.

Then, beside Freddie, the man he'd seen at the Red Lion. Younger, leaner, less heavy in the jaw, but unmistakably the same.

And he remembered the story Becca had told him, the night she'd taken the photo down and held it under this very lamp. It was late summer, after dark, and they'd made love half on the sofa, half on the floor. Then, lazily curled up beneath a throw, they'd begun – of course – to talk about rowing. It was all they'd ever talked about, really.

'Do you know how easy it is to nobble a rower before a race?' she'd asked.

'I've heard of it being done,' he'd said. 'I've never seen it happen. At least not that I know of.'

'I have.' Slipping from beneath the blanket, she'd padded, naked, to the bookcase, and he'd admired the long, muscled line of her back. She took the photo down and came back to the sofa, snuggling under the blanket again, her bare shoulder resting against his.

She'd touched the now-familiar face in the photo, and he remembered how he'd always thought her hands remarkably delicate for a tall woman – that is, if you didn't notice the calluses from the oar grips on her palms. 'This guy – he was bowside – barely made the second boat. But he always thought he deserved better than he got, and he was convinced he should have been in the Blue Boat. He bitched and moaned for weeks, until Freddie told him to shut up and get on with his job. He kept quiet after that, and I didn't think any more of it, until it was too late.'

'What happened?' Kieran had sat up, interested.

'They usually keep the crew pretty sequestered before the race, but some of the wives and girlfriends were invited to a press party the day before. The guys weren't supposed to be drinking – it was all squash and lemonade, and everyone on the very proper sportsmanlike up-and-up, with some fancy canapés to make up for the lack of alcohol. But other people were being served drinks, and when I saw him' – she tapped the photo – 'switch his glass with that of the guy rowing the same position in the Blue Boat, I thought it was just a prank, maybe a bit of vodka in the lemonade or something.'

She'd looked up at Kieran then, her hazel eyes flashing with an anger that hadn't faded. 'Until the next day, when the Blue Boat went out with *him* in it. I couldn't believe it. I'd got a place on one of the following launches, cold and rough as it was that day. Not very pleasant, but I wanted to see Freddie win. It meant so much to him, to all the crew. They'd worked so hard, and they were all my friends.'

'What happened to the guy who was supposed to be in the Blue Boat?' Kieran asked.

'Ill, the rumours were. Maybe food poisoning, oysters on the canapés at the press party the day before. Later I found out he was so dehydrated that they had to send him to hospital. But,' Becca added, her voice dripping sarcasm, 'what unexpected good fortune for his replacement! Except that his replacement couldn't bloody do the job. He wasn't fit enough, he wasn't good enough, and by the halfway mark you could see him weighing down the boat like a lead anchor. Oxford never had a chance. But *he* got his sodding Blue.'

'What happened afterwards? You reported it?'

She'd shaken her head. 'No. And I've never forgiven myself. But his fiancée was one of my best friends. We rowed together, we were going into the police together after uni. When I told her what I'd seen, she said I had to be mistaken. She begged me not to say anything, for her sake, and after all I had no proof. Not that I'd have needed any. Hearsay would have been enough to damn him forever in the sacred community of Old Blues.' The note of derision was unmistakable.

'So you didn't tell? Not even your boyfriend?'

'No. Not after I'd promised my friend.' Becca had shivered and drawn the blanket up to her chin. The anger drained from her face. 'But it didn't matter that I didn't tell. It ruined our friendship anyway – the secret ate away at it like a cancer. Obligation made her hate me more in the end than outright betrayal would have. Betrayal, maybe, we could have got past.'

'Why tell me, now?' Kieran had asked, brushing a stray strand of hair from her face.

'Because . . . ' She'd shrugged, her brow furrowed. 'Because you don't know them. You don't belong in that world. That' – she'd smiled, touching his cheek – 'is a good thing.' Then she'd trailed her fingers along his bare arm, making him shiver in turn, but her eyes had still been far away. 'And because,' she'd added slowly, 'I needed to remind myself that secrets only fester.'

The image of Becca, for a few moments so vivid, faded, and Kieran sat alone in the cold cottage, holding nothing but a photo.

A photo of a man who had killed Becca, and tried to kill him, he was certain now. But if this man had been willing to murder Becca to keep his secret, why had he waited all these years? What had changed?

Thunder cracked, and the wind blew a fusillade of rain against the old cottage windows. Kieran jerked and the photo slid from his hands, bouncing on the faded carpet that covered the floorboards in front of the sofa.

But there'd been another sound, beneath the drumming of the rain – or had there? He couldn't pinpoint it. His ears were ringing now, his head pounding, his palms sweating, the storm bringing the onslaught of adrenaline that he'd tried so hard to learn to control.

Finn raised his head, listening. Maybe, thought Kieran, his mouth dry, maybe he wasn't crazy. Maybe Finn had heard something, too.

He held his breath, but the only sound that came

to him was his heart beating in his ears. It must have been a car door that he'd heard, or some other ordinary noise, a neighbour coming home, someone calling their cat in from the rain. Not shelling, not here.

All he had to do was calm down, he told himself, and remember that his mind could control his body. He would be all right, if he just—

Finn stood, the motion so fast it knocked Kieran's knees sideways. The fur rose along the dog's neck and back like a stiff-bristled brush.

And then he growled.

As hard as Tavie had worked to make a new life for herself, and as much as she'd come to enjoy being on her own, she found her house without Kieran's large – and sometimes awkward – presence weirdly and uncomfortably empty.

Why had he gone to Becca Meredith's cottage? Was it because he was grieving? But this had been sudden, hence the dashed note on the chalkboard. And he'd been in a panic, or he'd never have forgotten his phone.

Then, when she'd talked to Superintendent Kincaid, he'd been short with her. Not rude, but abrupt in the way she recognized – a commanding officer working out strategies in an emergency. But he hadn't said where he was, or how long it would take him to get to Kieran.

The thought of Kieran, alone at the Remenham cottage, facing some unknown danger, made up her mind in an instant. She pocketed his phone, in case the Superintendent called back, then ran through the sitting room, grabbing her jacket off the hook by the door.

Tosh's yap stopped her. The German shepherd danced eagerly at her feet, then nipped at the lead hanging on its own hook. 'I know you want to go,' said Tavie.

She was torn. Knowingly, she risked the dog's safety every time they went out on a search, because that was their job, Tosh's job, and Tavie knew the rules and the risks. But this – she had no idea what she might be walking into. No, she decided. Fearing for Kieran was bad enough; she couldn't put Tosh in a situation where she was blind to the danger.

Kneeling, she cupped her dog's muzzle in her hand. 'Not this time, girl. You stay here.' She gave a last glance at her safe haven, absently tucking the lead in her pocket as she ruffled Tosh's coat. 'Guard the house, girl.'

They'd taken the Astra, against Freddie's protests that he knew the road better and his BMW was faster. But taking Freddie had been against Kincaid's better judgement – he was not going to compound it by letting a civilian drive.

He'd only been convinced to let Freddie come with them because Freddie knew the cottage and, more importantly, because Freddie knew Ross Abbott. Maybe, as a friend, Freddie could convince Abbott to be sensible.

If they weren't too late.

The rain was coming down in sheets now,

rendering the Astra's windscreen wipers virtually useless, and Kincaid was struggling to follow the lane. He'd no idea how close he was to Remenham.

'Here,' said Freddie. 'Cut the lights.'

'I can't bloody see, as it is,' Kincaid replied, but he slowed and switched off the headlights. The world changed, as drastically as a photo seen in negative, the landscape now visible as a vista in blacks and silvery greys.

'Now the engine. Coast into the verge. We're close.'

Kincaid wondered if Freddie had entertained secret fantasies of tactical ops, but he trusted his judgement on their position.

As the Astra came to a stop, wipers down, the rain closed in on them like a curtain and roared against the roof.

Then the downpour lessened for a moment, and Kincaid made out the dim shape of a car parked ahead of them on the verge.

'It's Ross's,' said Freddie flatly, and Kincaid knew that their worst fears were confirmed.

Doug had called for backup, asking them to come in quietly, but Kincaid had no idea how long it would take. Beside him, Doug clicked off his seatbelt. 'Guv, you sure you don't want me to call again?' His voice was a little high.

'No time. We've got to get in there.' Was it the right decision, he asked himself? But he couldn't sit and wait, knowing Kieran's life was in danger.

'Water rats it is then,' said Doug, with forced nonchalance. None of them had weather gear, so any entrance they made was likely to resemble spectres from the deep.

Kincaid turned to Freddie in the back seat. 'Your keys.' When Freddie handed them over, Kincaid added, 'You stay back unless I tell you otherwise. Agreed?'

He had to assume Freddie's nod was the best answer he was going to get. 'Quietly then.'

As soon as he stepped out into the rain, he realized that no one was likely to hear the soft closing of car doors. He was instantly soaked, water plastering his hair, running in rivulets down his face. From the corner of his eye he saw Doug take off his glasses and slip them into his inside pocket, and he wondered if Cullen would be more blind with the water-fogged glasses or without them. A fine trio they made.

And after all his admonishments, it was Freddie who had to lead the way. They passed Kieran's Land Rover, parked hard by the garden gate, and then they could see, through a gap in the sitting-room curtains, light inside the cottage.

Oriented now, Kincaid motioned Doug and Freddie back. He'd seen something else – a crack of light seeping from the cottage's front door. Someone had failed to shut it all the way.

He sidled up to the door, feeling, for a moment, ridiculously like a cop in an American TV show. In his career there had been few moments when he'd wished he carried a gun, but this was one of them. He thought he heard a low growling sound.

Peering in, he saw Kieran sitting on the floor with his back against the sofa, his arms wrapped in a bear hug round a struggling, snarling Finn. All the dog's attention was focused on the man who stood between Kincaid and Kieran, his back to the door.

Ross Abbott, Kincaid assumed.

The widening of Kieran's eyes as he glanced towards the door gave Kincaid away.

Abbott spun round, and Kincaid saw that he held a small-calibre handgun. It looked like a toy in Abbott's large hands, but it was certainly big enough to do someone fatal damage. The gun bobbed and waved as Abbott moved back a step, trying to keep Kieran and Kincaid in his sight at the same time. He was obviously not used to handling a gun. Kincaid wasn't sure if that frightened him more or less.

'Get back,' said Abbott.

Kincaid raised both hands, palms open, and stepped into the room. 'It's Ross, isn't it? Why don't you put the gun down. I'm sure this is all a misunderstanding. I'm Duncan, by the way,' he added, taking another step forwards.

'You're a bloody cop. Don't take me for a fool. Do you think I don't know a cop when I see one?' Abbott sounded close to hysteria, but he'd instinctively moved further from the door, leaving Kincaid more room to advance.

'Your wife is worried about you,' Kincaid said, not bothering to deny his identity. Gemma had told him everything she'd learned from Chris Abbott, but now he had to decide how much he should reveal to Ross.

'You've been talking to my wife? You bastard.' The gun steadied on Kincaid.

The low rumble of Finn's growl rose into a snarl

again. From the corner of his eye, Kincaid saw Kieran grip him tighter.

'Your wife talked to some of my colleagues, Ross,' he said. 'We know what Angus Craig did to her. We know you have good reason to be upset. But Craig's dead, and there's no reason to keep secrets any more.' He wasn't going to tell Abbott they knew that he'd murdered Becca, not when he had a gun in his hand.

'Right.' Abbott flicked his eyes from Kincaid to Kieran and back, but there was no way he could easily keep them both in view. 'And I'm Father Christmas. He' – he gestured with the gun towards Kieran – 'saw me. At the river. He's not walking out of here. And, now, neither are you.'

Freddie's voice came from behind Kincaid. 'What about me, Ross? Going to shoot your old friend, too?'

A glance showed Kincaid that Doug had come in behind Freddie, his glasses back in place. Kincaid swore under his breath. They were into damage limitation now. How many of them could Abbott take down before someone got the gun away from him?

Kincaid tried to keep his voice calm. There was obviously no point in further subterfuge, but maybe he could talk Abbott down. 'Don't be a complete idiot, man. Your wife knows everything, and so do we. Harming anyone else will only make things worse for you and your family.'

Ross ignored him, his attention now focused on Freddie. 'You're a shit, Freddie Atterton. You were always a prick with your supercilious *It's all about the crew* crap. That was fine for you, because *you* were better than the rest of us. Did you think I didn't know you were sneering at me?' Ross bared his teeth in a smile. 'I've wanted to hurt you for fifteen years, and now I'll be more than happy to shoot you, too.'

The gun steadied, levelled at Freddie.

Kincaid tensed, calculating how fast he could reach Ross, praying Freddie would keep him focused for a moment longer.

But it was Kieran who spoke. 'Why are you talking about Craig and this bastard's wife? He killed Becca because she knew the truth about him.'

Ross swung back towards Kieran, but Kieran seemed oblivious to the gun. 'He cheated in the Boat Race,' he said. 'Becca told me. He sabotaged another rower to get his position, and he lost Oxford the race. But his wife was Becca's friend, and Becca promised her she wouldn't tell.'

'That bitch,' Ross shouted. The gun swung wobbled, then steadied again, this time aimed at Kieran. 'That's a lie, you—'

But Freddie moved towards him, his voice cold with disgust. 'So that's what it was, Ross. Did you slip him laxatives? I always suspected, you know. It was just too convenient, that food poisoning, but I couldn't just come out and accuse a crewmate, could I? It wouldn't have been sporting, and we couldn't have that. But Becca – so Becca knew all along.' Freddie didn't hide his satisfaction. 'Becca used it against you in the end, didn't she? When Chris refused to help her bring down Craig, she threatened to tell.

'And that was the one thing you knew would ruin you utterly, wasn't it, Ross, old buddy? You betrayed your boat, your crewmates. No one would touch you if they knew. You'd have been blackballed for life. You've been trading on that Blue for fifteen years, with all your deals and sucking up to anyone it impressed, and she was going to take it all away from you. So you killed her, you snivelling little coward.'

'Shut up.' Ross looked round wildly, then turned back to Freddie. 'Just shut the fuck—'

But Freddie came closer. 'And you needed that next deal desperately, didn't you, Ross? Everything was crumbling. Your credit card wasn't declined by mistake in the bar, was it? You were the one drowning.'

One look at Ross Abbott's expression told Kincaid that if Freddie had meant to make Ross give up, the strategy had gone horribly wrong. Behind Freddie he saw Doug's white, frightened face, and he knew he had to stop this, whatever the cost.

'Ross, we can work this—' he began, but Freddie seemed determined to throw petrol on the fire.

'You don't seriously think you're going to kill all of us and walk away?' Freddie taunted him. 'After what you've done?'

'Just watch me,' said Ross, and pointed the gun at Freddie's chest.

There was a flurry of motion as Finn managed to free himself from Kieran's grasp. A black blur, the dog launched himself at Ross.

Ross spun and fired, more from surprise than intent, it seemed to Kincaid, in a fraction of disjointed thought.

The dog went down with a squeal of pain. Ross

staggered back towards the door, as if shocked by the gun's recoil, and Kieran sprang to his feet with a scream of rage and horror.

Kincaid dived towards Ross, aiming for his gun arm, just as another figure hurtled through the front door, swinging a long stick.

He . . . no – his brain registered, *she* – Tavie, it was Tavie, and it wasn't a stick, it was an oar. The oar made a thwacking sound as it connected with Ross's shoulder. The gun flew out of his hand, skittering across the floor and under a table.

Kincaid ploughed into Ross. He heard the grunt of pain and the whoosh of exhaled breath as Ross hit the floor beneath him. Then Kincaid had him pinned and Freddie and Doug were piling onto him, grabbing for Ross's thrashing arms and legs. Freddie got Ross by his thinning hair and smacked his head against the floor.

'Stop! Both of you, stop! Just hold him,' Kincaid shouted, but Freddie, his face tight with fury, got in another good thump.

Tavie stood over them like a small ninja, the oar raised to strike again, but the cracks on the head seemed to have stunned Ross momentarily.

'Hold him,' grunted Kincaid, reaching for his belt. Ross had gone down on his stomach, and Kincaid meant to keep him that way. Handcuffs, he thought. Why did he never have bloody handcuffs?

Then Tavie lowered the oar and reached in her pocket. 'Here,' she said, sounding surprised. 'It's Tosh's lead. I brought it by accident.' She handed him the supple length of leather.

As Kincaid wrapped the lead round Ross's wrists and yanked hard, Freddie said, wonderingly, 'That's Becca's old Oxford oar. Where did you—'

'It was in a bin at the side of the porch. The first thing that came to – ' Tavie stopped with a gasp as she glanced past him, then her voice rose in a wail of distress. 'Oh, God! Finn!'

It was then that Kincaid realized Kieran wasn't with them. When he looked up, he saw Kieran on the floor in the middle of the room, cradling Finn in his lap.

Kincaid couldn't see any blood, but the dog was panting, the whites of his eyes showing. As Tavie knelt beside them, Kieran lifted a hand from the dog's dark coat and it came away bright red.

'No,' whispered Kieran, looking up at Tavie imploringly. 'Please, no. I can't – I can't tell how bad it is.'

While Tavie ran her small, deft hands over the dog, talking quietly, Kincaid levered himself off Ross. Freddie held Ross's shoulders down. Doug sat on Ross's feet, his phone out, shouting for backup to hurry the hell up, for an ambulance, and *for God's sake a vet*.

Ross spat a stream of curses at them all, and Freddie steadily and repeatedly told him to shut up or he'd bloody thump him again.

They were all, Kincaid thought with a delayed sense of astonishment, okay.

Except the dog.

Finn, who had identified Becca's killer. Finn, who had tried his best to protect them. Kincaid couldn't bear the thought of Kieran, who had lost so much, losing him too.

Crossing the room, Kincaid scooped the gun from under the table. Then, keeping an eye on Ross and his captors, he knelt by Tavie and Kieran.

She was using Kieran's sweater as a compress, and the oatmeal-coloured wool was soaked with blood. But it was the dog's shoulder she was treating, not his head or chest.

'Is he . . . ?'

Looking up, Tavie brushed her hair back from her forehead with her free hand, leaving a red smear. 'It's messy, and I'm more used to treating people, but I think it's just a flesh wound. I can see entry and exit through the shoulder, and the bullet seems to have missed bone and organs.'

'Good boy,' whispered Kieran, and Finn's tail thumped. Kieran's voice was still shaky, but his hands were not, and he was assisting Tavie with steady confidence.

'It's all right,' said Kieran, more strongly, as if reassuring himself. But it was Tavie's eyes he met. 'Everything is going to be all right.'

Chapter Twenty-Five

Sunday lunchtime found Kincaid still finishing up reports in his office at the Yard. He'd sent Doug Cullen home mid-morning, a little sharply. Doug had been lingering, inventing tasks, looking more anxious and morose by the minute.

'Go,' Kincaid had finally said. 'Get on with your house-moving.'

'You'll need me to proof that for you,' Doug protested, nodding at the computer screen.

'I'm perfectly capable of writing a proper report on my own, thank you.' Kincaid knew exactly what Doug was feeling, but drawing it out was not going to make it better. We'll have a pint next weekend,' he said. 'And as soon as you're settled, we'll come for dinner, if you're brave enough to have us, that is.'

'Right,' said Doug. He stuck his hands in his pockets, fidgeting with his keys. 'I'll investigate the takeaway options in Putney.'

'That will keep you busy, if your new guv'nor doesn't give you enough to do.'

Doug gave the joke the weak smile it deserved.

The moment stretched into the sort of awkward

silence faced by men who could not find a graceful way to say goodbye.

'I'll be back,' Kincaid said at last. And then, 'You'll be all right.'

'Right.' Doug nodded and pushed his glasses up on his nose. 'Thanks. See you, then.' He ducked his head and slipped out the door.

Cullen's departure brought the reality home to Kincaid. He would not be back for two months, unless they decided that Charlotte was ready to go into child-care before then. His life was about to change in ways he couldn't yet imagine, and he wasn't sure how he felt about it.

He lingered, gazing at the familiar walls of his office, thinking how many years this job had defined him, and wondering who he would be without it. And thinking about what had happened the previous after-noon, and how near any one of them might have come to tragedy.

He'd spent the better part of Saturday evening interviewing Ross Abbott at Thames Valley head-quarters.

Once subdued and hauled off to the Thames Valley nick, Abbott had gone quiet and had refused to say another word without representation.

Studying Abbott in the custody suite, Kincaid had seen the mask come down, the man's desperation and viciousness wiped away by the cool, plausible and highly affronted City banker. But there was no hiding the calculation in Abbott's eyes, and his story, when his slightly befuddled solicitor had finally arrived, had been a masterful work of invention.

He had, he said, been deeply worried about his grieving friend, after Freddie's irrational behaviour earlier that afternoon at the Red Lion. Having not found Freddie at home, he'd gone to the cottage looking for him.

Then, seeing a strange car out front and the cottage door standing slightly ajar, he'd suspected a burglar and had felt obliged to go in. He'd then been threatened by Kieran and his mad dog, and had tried to defend himself.

As for the gun, he said he'd grabbed it from the drawer in Rebecca Meredith's sideboard, when he'd been searching for something to defend himself against the lunatic with the dog.

'And then you and your mate' – he gave a pointed look at Kincaid and Doug – 'came barging in and failed to identify yourselves as police officers. I thought you were part of the gang.'

'Gang?' Kincaid said. He'd looked down at his now definitely worse-for-wear Saturday clothes – muddy chinos, soggy button-down shirt and pullover – and thought wistfully of his soaked leather jacket, hanging up to dry in an anteroom. And Doug, with one earpiece of his glasses bent from the scuffle to subdue Abbott, his now-dry fair hair sticking up like a schoolboy who had just got out of bed, looked even more unlikely. 'Gang?' Kincaid repeated, brows elevated as high as they would go. If Abbott could dramatize, he could do him one better. Not even Abbott's solicitor could repress a smile.

'I think perhaps you need your eyes examined, Mr Abbott,' Kincaid continued. They had not actually identified themselves as police, so he stepped carefully over that one for the moment. 'As for the gun, your wife has already told police that it was her illegally obtained firearm, and that you took it from the house without her knowledge. That, in my book, goes down as intent to harm.'

He'd then reiterated, for the tape, what they knew about Becca Meredith's visit to the Abbotts' the previous Saturday, and why Abbott had then put in motion a plan to murder her.

'Bollocks,' said Abbott. 'Absolute bollocks! And you can't prove a bit of it.'

'Oh, I think we can. We've impounded your car, and a forensics team has taken your clothes from your house. I know you think you're clever, Mr Abbott, but there will be traces you missed, and you will have left fibre at the scene. Not to mention the fact that Kieran Connolly will identify you as the man he saw lying in wait in the spot where Rebecca Meredith was murdered. As for what happened at the Remenham cottage, you have four very credible witnesses who will be happy to testify as to your actions and intent.'

He spoke, however, with more conviction than he felt. A good defence barrister could get round trace evidence unless it was DNA – juries loved DNA – and he'd heard from Gemma that Chris Abbott was already denying everything she'd told Gemma and Melody, including possession of the gun.

It would be a long and painstaking business to put together a case against Abbott that would stick, but at least the man would do no further damage.

The medics who had arrived at the cottage along with the police had been surprised to find they had a canine rather than human patient, but they were Tavie's colleagues and had willingly loaded Finn, Tavie and Kieran into the ambulance. Tavie had arranged for the vet who worked with the SAR team to meet them at her clinic.

DC Imogen Bell had arrived with the local coppers and offered quite solicitously to give Freddie a lift home, although it had seemed to Kincaid that Freddie was suddenly much less in need of looking after.

They had all been high on adrenaline for the first few hours after Ross Abbott's arrest. But now Kincaid felt more shaken than he liked to admit, and he kept wondering if he should have handled things differently. Had he let his anger over the Craigs' deaths affect his judgement? He'd endangered his partner and three civilians. And yet, if he'd waited for tactical backup, he felt very sure that both Kieran Connolly and Finn would be dead.

So why was the decision weighing on him so heavily?

Maybe, he thought, maybe it was time he had a break.

A shadow fell across his office. He looked up, startled, to find Chief Superintendent Childs standing in his doorway. Childs, for such a big man, always seemed to move soundlessly.

Unlike yesterday at the Craigs', Childs was perfectly turned out in his usual bespoke dark suit, his Remembrance Day poppy bright as a spot of blood in his lapel.

'Sir,' said Kincaid, starting to stand.

'No, stay as you are.' Childs waved Kincaid back into his chair. 'But I won't sit, if you don't mind.' Kincaid's visitors' chairs were not made to fit Denis Childs.

'Sir, what are you doing in, on a Sunday?'

'A meeting with the Commissioner.' He studied Kincaid for a moment. 'I suppose all's well that ends well with the Meredith case. A good result.'

Kincaid was not about to be patted on the back. 'Ross Abbott would have had no motive to kill Becca Meredith, if not for Angus Craig.'

'I told the Commissioner you'd say that.' Childs sighed. 'He feels, however, that making public the ordeals of the female officers involved would only do them more harm. That is, if any of the women would agree to it, and I think it unlikely.'

Kincaid stared at him. 'You can't mean to sweep Jenny Hart's murder under the carpet as well.'

'The DNA from the crime scene will be compared with Craig's,' Childs said obliquely, and Kincaid took that to mean that the results of the comparison might conveniently fail to be released.

'What about a DNA test on Chris Abbott's youngest son?'

Childs shook his head. 'I doubt very much that his mother would agree to that. Or that a magistrate would grant a warrant against her wishes. And what exactly do you feel that would accomplish? Even if DCI Abbott is found not to have been aware of her husband's actions, or of his intentions, do you not think her life will be difficult enough, without having the legitimacy of her child brought into question?' Childs went on. 'Not to mention the damage done to the child. Let it go, Duncan. Spend some time with your family, and when you come back this will all seem much less complicated.'

Meaning, Kincaid thought, that *he* had better be less difficult. It was a dismissal, and for an instant he wondered if he would have an office to come back to.

He stood, so that he met Childs's eyes directly. 'Sir.'

'Good man.' Childs brushed his lapel. 'I must dash. Diane's kept Sunday lunch waiting.' He started towards the door, then turned back, casually. 'Oh, by the way, I heard this morning that the DCI heading one of the murder teams in Lambeth had a massive coronary yesterday. Poor chap. It's touch and go at the moment, I think. But someone will have to fill his post for the time being, and Gemma's name has been put forward as acting DCI. Would she be interested, do you think?'

Temporary promotion? Heading a murder team?

It smacked of a bribe, Kincaid thought. And yet Gemma was both capable and deserving. He couldn't take the opportunity away from her, and certainly he could never tell her he thought the offer was a convenient sweetener designed to keep him quiet.

'Sir,' he said. 'That would be entirely up to her.'

Doug Cullen stood in the middle of the sitting room of his new house in Putney, disconsolately surveying the boxes that he and Melody had ferried over from the old flat the day before. He hadn't thought he had much in the way of possessions, but the things seemed to have found a way of multiplying, and now he'd no idea what to do with them.

He'd scheduled a half-day off work tomorrow to oversee the removal van bringing the rest of his bits and bobs. Not that that was likely to win him any points with his new guv'nor, but his lease on the old flat was up as of today and he'd had no choice.

Perhaps having the bigger pieces of furniture would help, he thought, although really, there wasn't much point in doing more than making a place to eat and sleep until he'd tackled the painting and decorating.

He sat down on one of the sturdier boxes, his chin in his hand, wondering if he'd made a dreadful mistake with the whole house idea, when there was a rap on the door. Guiltily he jumped up, as if he'd been caught slacking, then chided himself as he went to the door. He wasn't expecting anyone; besides, it was his house and he could sit on a bloody box if he liked.

But when he opened the door he felt a flush of surprise and pleasure. It was Melody, carrier bag in hand.

'You'll have to fix the bell, you know,' she said. 'It doesn't work.'

'Do come in, why don't you?' he snapped back, instantly irritated. 'I'll add it to the list.'

Unperturbed, Melody followed him into the sitting room and surveyed his lack of progress. 'Feeling a bit overwhelmed, I take it? I thought maybe you could use some help.'

'Sorry,' said Doug, abashed. 'You're right. I can't quite figure out where to start.'

'This should help.' Melody opened the carrier bag and pulled out a bottle of champagne. It was, Doug saw, already chilled. And expensive. 'And I thought you might not have glasses here yet,' she added as she removed two champagne flutes carefully wrapped in a tea towel.

Yet, thought Doug. Trust Melody to unthinkingly bring champagne that he could never afford, but to try and be tactful about the fact that she knew he wouldn't own champagne glasses.

'I thought we could toast to new beginnings,' she said, a little more tentatively. 'New house, new boss.'

'Brilliant! Thanks.' Doug wasn't sure how he felt about either of those things at the moment, but at least, thanks to his former girlfriend, he knew how to open a bottle of champagne properly. Taking bottle and glasses into the kitchen, he peeled back the foil, then used the tea towel to cover the cork as he eased it out.

There was a soft pop of escaping gas as the cork came free, then he tilted the pale-gold liquid deftly into the glasses.

'You've missed your calling,' teased Melody as she accepted hers.

'Head waiter? That's a thought,' he said as he lifted his own glass. 'Probably better pay and easier hours.'

'Cheers.' Melody clinked the lip of her glass against his. 'And I hear you were a bit of a hero yesterday, so we should drink to that, too.'

'Me?'

'With the arrest and everything. I wish I'd been there,' Melody added on a wistful note.

'No, you don't,' said Doug, more harshly than he intended. He couldn't tell her how ashamed he felt, remembering how he'd stood there, frozen as a dummy, while Ross Abbott waved his gun at them. He should have been the one to tackle Abbott, and instead he'd let his guv'nor risk his life.

It didn't bear thinking about.

'Sorry,' he said, again. 'Cheers.' He tipped back half his glass, then sputtered as the bubbles went up his nose.

'Easy with that stuff.' Melody smiled, but he detected a hint of concern beneath it. 'I'll tell you what. The boxes can wait. Let's have a look at the garden. Then I believe you owe me an uninterrupted lunch, Sergeant Cullen, with an Eton Mess for afters. We can make sock monkeys together.'

'Sock monkeys?' he looked at her as if she'd gone completely round the twist. Was this some sort of weird proposition?

'At the Jolly Gardeners,' Melody explained. 'I saw the notice when we were there before. You can make sock puppets while you're having Sunday lunch. They even provide the socks.' She finished her glass, her cheeks going slightly pink. 'Where's your sense of adventure, Dougie?'

Where was it indeed? Doug thought his life had suddenly taken an unexpectedly surreal turn. But, then, what did he have to lose?

'Okay,' he said. 'The boxes can wait. Sock monkeys. Why ever not?'

*

Freddie had mopped the mud and blood off the cottage floor. Yesterday's storms having blown through and left the day washed sparkling clean, he'd opened the windows to air the place out, and turned on the central heating to take away the chilly damp that seemed to have settled into the bones of the cottage since Becca's death.

He swept and tidied, and when he found the photo lying face down on the carpet, he looked at it for a long moment, then put it away in a drawer. He didn't want to think about Ross Abbott again, at least not until the trial.

He'd taken his revenge last night. It had been swift and sweet, and he felt no remorse.

He'd rung every one of the crew of their year's Blue Boat and told them what Ross had done in the Boat Race. That would be enough. While Ross's career might survive a murder trial, the power of the rowing grapevine would send his reputation up in flames.

A token, against Becca's life, but fitting that Ross Abbott should lose the thing that mattered to him most.

Freddie, however, wasn't at all sure what mattered to him any more. It came to him, as he looked round the cottage, that he loved this place, and felt at home here in a way he never had in the Malthouse flat. Once the legal criteria had been met, he could sell the flat and move back into the cottage. Maybe he could make a Guy Fawkes bonfire of the Malthouse furnishings, he thought wryly.

Would he mind sharing this house with Becca's ghost, he wondered? As he stood, quietly, he realized he'd come to see that, in spite of their flaws and their mistakes, they had loved one another. And in some odd, bittersweet way, it helped salve his grief. He would be all right here.

But although Becca's generosity would leave him once more financially stable, he found he'd lost all interest in developing property, or in moving in the circles where nothing one had was ever quite good enough.

What, then? Convincing people to invest money in one scheme or another was all he'd ever done. He had no real or useful skills.

Through the open window he heard the sound of tyres on tarmac. When he looked out, a battered Land Rover was stopping on the verge by the cottage.

It was Kieran's car – he recognized it from yesterday – and tied on the roofrack was the canvas-covered but unmistakable slender shape of a single shell.

Freddie went out and met Kieran at the garden gate.

'I thought you might be here,' said Kieran, looking pleased, and Freddie realized it was the first time he'd seen him smile. It transformed his thin face, and Freddie knew he'd glimpsed the man Becca had known.

'Are you all right?' he asked. 'How's Finn?'

'Stitched, bandaged and a bit groggy from the pain meds. But the vet says he'll be okay. We just have to keep him from overdoing things until he heals. Tavie's home, keeping an eagle eye on him.'

The last was said with such easiness that Freddie

461

thought Kieran might not be needing the boatshed as a place to live any time soon. He felt glad for him, and a little envious.

'I've been cleaning up the shed,' Kieran went on, 'seeing what's salvageable. And I thought' – he nodded towards the roofrack – 'as it survived by a miracle, it was time someone gave the boat a trial run.'

He walked round the Land Rover and pulled the canvas free. The rich mahogany hull of Becca's boat shone in the sun, and Freddie felt his breath catch in his throat.

'Will you help me get her down?' asked Kieran. 'I don't think Becca's neighbours will mind if we launch from their raft.'

Kieran pulled a pair of oars from the back of the Land Rover, then together they lifted the shell and carried it down to the water. The shell seemed weightless to Freddie, the wood warm as a woman's skin.

'I've made some adjustments to the rigging,' Kieran said as they turned the boat over and set it gently in the water beside the small floating raft. Kieran placed an oar across the shell's midsection to hold it steady, then looked up at Freddie. 'You'd better take your shoes off. I've attached a pair of my trainers to the footboard. They should fit you well enough.'

Freddie stared at him. 'You want *me* to take her out? But—'

'Who better?' said Kieran. 'And I'd like your opinion. I need to know if this whole idea was utterly daft.'

'But I haven't rowed in . . . '

'Don't worry. You won't have forgotten how.'

Freddie looked at the shell, then at the Thames, gleaming back at him, still as a pond.

Wordlessly he pulled off his shoes and stepped into the boat. Sliding his feet into the trainers, he found that they did indeed fit. He took the second oar from Kieran and fastened both in their gates, then moved the seat backwards and forwards a few inches, testing the action of the rollers.

Then Kieran gave him a push and he was out into the current and moving downstream. His hands fitted the oar grips as if moulded to them, and as the blades bit into the water at the catch, he felt the boat lift.

Muscle memory took over. Drive, release, drive, release, and he was at one with the boat, and the boat was singing over the water.

Droplets slung from the rising blades spattered his face, the water a cold benediction. A bubble of joy rose in his chest, and he realized that not since he was a child had he rowed just for the pleasure of it.

And then he saw that there was one place his skills might be of use. He had the old farm, right on the river, a place that could be put to better use than luxury flats. It would, in fact, make a perfect boat-builder's workshop.

He'd spent years talking investors into buying property. Why couldn't he convince rowing enthusiasts to invest money in something much more useful: beautiful, one-of-a-kind boats. And in the builder who made them.

If Kieran would have him as a partner.

*

By early Sunday evening the Notting Hill household was a beehive of activity, not all of it productive.

The boys were wound up over tomorrow's return to school after half-term. Toby expressed this by imitating a human ping-pong ball, zooming round the house and sometimes literally bouncing off the walls.

Kit, who had hardly spoken a word to anyone since their return from Glastonbury, was suddenly voluble, rattling on about a biology project he hadn't finished and spreading books and papers all over the kitchen table, although Kincaid couldn't detect any actual work being done.

As for Gemma, ever since Kincaid had returned from the Yard, she'd been rushing round the house like a dervish, tidying, organizing and making reams of complicated lists, which she then tacked up on every available surface.

Charlotte, unsettled by the activity, clung to Gemma whenever possible and periodically burst into tears. They had told her about the coming change in routine as casually as possible, just saying that she and Duncan would have some special time together for a few hours every day while Gemma went into the police station and the boys were at school.

'You will remember that she doesn't like Marmite?' said Gemma, sticking yet another list to the fridge door with a Quidditch-broom magnet. Aware that she was being talked about, Charlotte wrapped her arms round Gemma's leg and whimpered. 'Just butter on her toast in the morning,' Gemma went on, 'and no marms in her orange juice.'

'Marms?' Duncan shook his head over that one.

Then, exasperated, he said, 'For heaven's sake, Gemma, you're not going on the *QE2*. And none of this is rocket science. I'm sure we'll manage perfectly well.'

Gemma gave him a surprised glance, then suddenly looked so appalled that he was sure someone, somewhere, had made a critical mistake.

'Dinner,' she said. 'With everything else, I completely forgot. We've nothing for dinner.'

'Pizza!' shouted Toby, and everyone else, including Kit, groaned.

'Not again,' said Kit. 'I don't think I can face another pizza.'

Kincaid grinned. 'Never thought I'd hear that. The earth just rocked on its axis.' And, he thought, it was time that he started as he meant to go on. Opening the kitchen cupboard, he peered in. 'There's spaghetti, and a jar of pasta sauce. Kit, the dogs need a run, if you can tear yourself away from your project. While you're out, you can go to Tesco Express and pick up a salad and some Italian sausage.'

Kit rolled his eyes at the project comment, but said, 'Okay. No prob.'

'Spag bol,' Toby chanted. 'Spag bol, spag bol – '

'That sounds disgusting,' Gemma scolded him, although she looked relieved at having had the dinner issue taken out of her hands. 'Say it properly. *Spaghetti bolognese.*' She gave it an exaggerated Italian emphasis.

'Sounds like eyeballs,' said Kit wickedly. 'Eyeballs and worms, just in time for Halloween. Yum!'

Charlotte began to wail. 'Don't want eyeballs.'

But the boys were poking each other and dancing round the kitchen making scary noises, and that in turn made the dogs begin to bark.

'Enough!' said Kincaid, his level of tolerance breached. He hadn't quite shouted, but for a moment, at least, the pandemonium stopped.

'Okay. Sorry, Dad.' Kit held out his hand. 'But you have to *gimme the cash, mon.*'

This time it was Kincaid who rolled his eyes, but he pulled a note from his wallet and handed it over.

'I want sweeties,' chimed in Toby. 'I want to go.'

'No. And no.' Kincaid was not going to hear any argument. 'You get your books in your backpack for school in the morning.'

Kit called the dogs, and when Kincaid heard the sound of their nails clicking on the bare floor, he suddenly realized he'd forgotten all about Edie Craig's dog. Barney.

Going into the hall, he fished in his jacket pocket until he found the crumpled piece of paper with the neighbour's name on it. The files hadn't revealed any close kin for either of the Craigs, but something would have to be done about the dog.

He'd take Charlotte to Hambleden, he decided, one day when the boys were at school. He'd talk to the barman at the pub again, and perhaps the vicar. And if no one in the village wanted Barney, perhaps Tavie would know someone who did.

It seemed the least he could do for Edie Craig, and he felt, once again, how badly he had failed her.

'Dad?' said Kit, softly. He'd clipped on the dogs'

leads, but had stopped at the door, watching him. 'You okay?'

'I'm fine.' Kincaid smiled and tucked the paper back in his pocket, but this time he folded it neatly. 'You'd better hurry or there'll be riots below decks.'

He watched Kit and the dogs out the door, then went back into the kitchen, trying to remember where he'd seen an onion and some garlic for the spaghetti sauce. He would get the hang of this, he thought, with a little practice.

'The yellow bowl to the right of the sink,' said Gemma, and grinned at him.

'How did you—'

But before he got any further, her phone rang. He knew, even before she answered, what the call was.

While she retrieved the mobile from beneath Kit's schoolwork, Kincaid shooed Toby from the room. 'Go put your jammies out on the bed,' he said. 'You can have the skull ones, for Halloween.'

Then he detached Charlotte from Gemma's leg, hefting her onto his hip. 'If you're really, really good,' he whispered in her ear, 'we'll play aeroplanes after dinner. Or maybe before,' he amended, thinking perhaps that flying a child upside down after spag bol was not the best idea.

'Before,' said Charlotte firmly, for entirely different reasons.

'Oh, hi, Mark, how are you?' Gemma was saying. She sounded pleased, but a little uncertain.

Mark Lamb, Kincaid thought. Gemma's boss, and his old police-college mate. They'd made Lamb emissary.

Gemma was listening, nodding, but her face had gone very still.

'I'll read you a story after dinner then,' Kincaid murmured to Charlotte.

'*Alice?*'

'*Alice* always.' He wondered how soon he would know the entire book by heart. 'Always *Alice.*'

Charlotte giggled and buried her face against his shoulder.

'Right,' said Gemma into the phone. She was looking at him now, her brows lifted in surprise. 'That's too bad,' she responded to the faint voice issuing from the mobile's speaker. 'But of course I'll be glad to help out. Right. Lambeth. Tomorrow morning. First thing. Thanks, sir. I'll see you then.'

Gemma clicked off, then stood with the phone still in her hand, staring at it with a stunned expression.

Then she looked up at Kincaid, and the smile lit her face like a sunrise.

'I've got a new job,' she said.

Acknowledgements

Books are a little like children – it takes a village to make one, and my village spans the Atlantic.

Many thanks to all who have provided help, support and encouragement on both sides of the Pond, but especially to: the staff, crew and members of the Leander Club, Henley-on-Thames, particularly Kerry Smith, Mariam Lewis, Nick Aitchinson, Paul Budd and Graham Hall, all of whom were unfailingly generous with their time, hospitality and advice.

A very special thanks to Steve Williams, OBE, two-time Olympic gold medallist and former Captain of Leander, who not only gave me insight into the life and mind of an elite rower, but risked life and limb by taking me out on the Thames in a rowing shell. It was an experience I will never forget, and the book was much the better for it.

For assistance with K9 Search and Rescue, I owe much to Susannah Charleson for her patience in answering my questions in the early stages of the book. Daryl and Niki Toogood of Berkshire Search and Rescue (with treats and wags to Guinness and Scrumpy) gave invaluable help and advice – as well as letting me practise being a victim and handling a search dog. Hugs to you both.

Ian Richardson is responsible for introducing me to Leander; Rosalie Stevens for touring me around Barnes – a huge thanks to you both.

Then there are the first-line readers and brain-storming crew, all deserving of medals: Kate Charles, Marcia Talley, Julie Gerber, Diane Hale, Tracy Rick-etts, Barb Jungr, Steve Ullathorne and especially Gigi Norwood, who should get a gold star for her patience, support and encouragement. You all made the book possible.

And I am, as always, grateful for the support and encouragement of my agent, Nancy Yost; my editor at HarperCollins, US, Carrie Feron; and my editor at Pan Macmillan, UK, Trisha Jackson, all of whom keep me writing.

Last but not least, love and thanks to my husband, Rick, and my daughter, Kayti, for being there.

All the characters and events portrayed in this book are entirely fictional, and any mistakes are entirely my own.

extracts reading groups
competitions books new
books discounts extracts extracts events
competitions reading groups discounts
books new extracts events
events books reading groups
new extracts events
reading groups books new titles reading groups
interviews events new
reading groups events extracts extracts books
books discounts interviews
new books events events new books extracts
discounts events new interviews new books
discounts extracts discounts books
www.panmacmillan.com
extracts events reading groups books
competitions books extracts new